Band of Brothers
The Complete Campaigns

RICHARD FOREMAN

© Richard Foreman 2016

Richard Foreman has asserted his rights under the Copyright, Design and Patents Act, 1988, to be identified as the author of this work.

First published 2016 by Endeavour Press Ltd.

Published in 2018 by Sharpe Books.

ISBN: 9781717888174

CONTENTS

Quote	i
The Game's Afoot	1 - 118
Epilogue	119
Harfleur	127 - 246
Epilogue	247
Agincourt	248 - 356
Epilogue	357
End Note	359

"The strawberry grows underneath the nettle,
And wholesome berries thrive and ripen best
Neighboured by fruit of baser quality."
Henry V, William Shakespeare

"Faith is to believe what you do not see."
St Augustine

THE GAME'S AFOOT

1

The archer felt incomplete, vulnerable, without his bow. His hand tightened around the handle of his short sword in readiness and compensation. Robert Cooper was the tallest and broadest of the three men who stood in the market square on Bankside, just outside the entrance to *The Golden Anchor*. Despite the volume and variety of thoughts running through his mind – as the archer prepared himself for a possible fight – his expression remained remarkably unmoved. His flat, wide face resembled the stern of a ship. His light-brown hair was not much longer than his stubble. Cooper's features projected a sense of strength (but not brutality).

"Well, time and tide wait for no man," Thomas Chaucer remarked, quoting his late father. The small, slim, middle-aged man was well-dressed and well-spoken. The agent to the King dabbed himself with scent again in order to help ward off the oppressive stench of ordure from the nearby gutters. Chaucer was a long way from home, inhabiting the murky bowels of Southwark, but like his father – or rather because of his father – he was as familiar with an English tavern as he was with the great state dining rooms of foreign princes. Flecks of grey had started to line his hair and neatly trimmed forked beard. His narrow, dark eyes flitted about and took in the scene. Streaks of silver-tinged clouds marbled the night sky. Above the lop-sided roofs of the surrounding buildings the silhouette of the spire of St Paul's vaunted upwards towards heaven, back-lit by a full moon. The painted sign, advertising the tavern, gently swung in the breeze. Lamps glowed, like fist-sized fire-flies, in a number of windows. The sound of a couple of carousing drunks emanated from an alley just off the square. The sound of a curse – and a threat to pour a bucket of piss over the pair of off-key singers – rang out too.

"Are you sure de Lacy is here?" Edward Fordham asked. His eyebrow expressed scepticism. "Does he come here for the girls?"

"Don't be absurd. Edmund de Lacy is a respected young nobleman from Cambridge. He comes here for the boys of course," the agent replied, raising the corner of his mouth slightly in a smile.

Fordham smiled too. There was the light of amusement in the soldier's eye. Edward Fordham was looking forward to a possible fight. It would help ward off the oppressive sense of boredom the sometime poet regularly suffered from.

The archer and man-at-arms had been summoned by Thomas Chaucer earlier in the evening. Their task was to help the agent escort de Lacy to the Tower, so Chaucer could have "a friendly discussion" with him. The soldiers knew their paymaster well enough not to ask too many questions about his means and ends.

The door creaked as the three men entered. The cobweb-strewn oak beams running across the ceiling bowed, almost to the point of breaking. Sawdust, spit, grime and crumbs of stale bread covered the floor. A smell of roasted pork, second-rate ale and sweat congealed together and festered in the air. Fordham noticed a long-tailed rat scuttle along a wall, heading towards the kitchen. Either he was looking for something to eat or he would be eaten himself; the cook would doubtless add him to the stew being advertised, the man-at-arms thought.

A red-eyed, jowly patron sat across the table from a buxom whore and licked his lips at the dish of the woman, and the plate of eels, in front of him. A couple of gnarled-faced regulars eyed the strangers with suspicion. Thomas Chaucer met their grimaces with a polite smile. A trio of sailors played dice in the corner and told such jokes that would cause a prioress to pray for them – or damn them. Cups of ale were lifted up to mouths and placed down upon tables but few patrons released their grip from their lovingly clasped tankards. The talk was of the impending campaign against

France, the scandalous behaviour of Members of Parliament (and the lack of justice they faced), the rising price of white bread and the violence that had broken out during recent football matches. Countenances varied from the lusty-eyed to the world weary. Some peered into their ale hoping to find answers. Perhaps the problem was that some found too many answers there. The agent's sage father had repeatedly told his son how "the tavern rather than the church houses the true soul of England". One could find virtue and vice in equal measure in a tavern – and appreciate them both. When he was no older than ten Chaucer's father had taken him for his first drink at their local inn and proclaimed, as they each held up a cup of ale, "Your life now begins in earnest my son". As the agent glanced towards the far corner however – and the dozen armed men surrounding de Lacy – Thomas Chaucer ironically considered how his life might now end in a dimly lit tavern.

"Good evening, Thomas," de Lacy exclaimed, his voice betraying a slight sibilance. "I cannot imagine that this is your usual watering hole in London. But do not worry, I have no intention of telling your lovely wife. I'm very good at keeping secrets."

Edmund de Lacy was neither surprised nor fearful at seeing Chaucer. He had half expected to encounter the agent whom he had met on numerous occasions at court. He smiled as he spoke, although his sharp features barely softened. The nobleman smoothed back his pomaded hair. He wore a fine scarlet coat, trimmed with fur and embroidered with silk. His chin jutted out in defiance and arrogance. In one hand de Lacy held a cup of wine and in the other he twiddled a horsewhip between his ringed fingers. The horsewhip was spotted with blood, from de Lacy having used it on the young boy that the owner of the tavern had procured for him for the night.

A few of de Lacy's men-at-arms sniggered at his comment. The long-haired, fearsome looking Welsh mercenaries carried an assortment of weapons: swords, hand-axes, daggers, maces. Drink emboldened their spirits. Some offered Cooper and Fordham goading looks, confident in the quality and quantity of their force to easily best the spy's brace of soldiers.

"Gentlemen, I should tell you that you are in distinguished company. This is Thomas Chaucer, our sometime Speaker of the House and Chief Butler of England. He married Matilda Berghersh. Some say he married for love – having become enamoured with the sizeable dowry his wife came with. As respected and powerful as you may consider him to be however, he still lives in the shadow of his father. Geoffrey Chaucer spoke great truths, whilst his son has dedicated his life to lies and propaganda. Cut him and, rather than blood, poison will gush out. Thomas here has the ear of the King. You should use it to inform the usurper that he will soon lose his life or crown. The political winds will soon be blowing in a different direction. Revolution will spread, like wildfire, across the country," de Lacy stated with fanaticism and triumph glowing in his aspect.

"Then the King's archers will make it rain and put the fire out," Robert Cooper calmly, but firmly, stated. Every man present had witnessed the sight of a mass of Henry's bowmen unleashing a shower of arrows against the crown's enemies.

"You should choose your words carefully. You should also choose the right side to be on. This is Robert Cooper, my friends. His father was the legendary Matthew Cooper, who fought under the Black Prince's banner at Crécy and Poitiers. Robert here was considered the best archer in his county by the age of twenty. Many now consider him to possess the best bow arm in the entire army. He served alongside the King at Shrewsbury. And he probably now desires to serve the Henrying on his imminent campaign in France, in order to make his fortune. But if it is wealth you crave, Robert, then you should fight under a different banner. I will pay you double what Thomas and the Henry are offering. Given that the campaign is akin to a suicide mission your length of service will be over twice the duration too," de Lacy said, as he used his horsewhip to scrape a piece of mud off the side of his calf-skin boot.

"He talks a lot. He may well indeed be suited to a career in politics," Edward Fordham remarked to his two companions.

The smile briefly fell from de Lacy's face as he screwed his countenance up in disdain at the man-at-arms.

"And finally, gentlemen, we have Edward Fordham. He is no stranger to entering a tavern at this time of night. As well as a drunk he's a poet, would you believe? And the son of one of the wealthiest landowners in Norfolk. People are not quite sure which he will piss away first, his life or his fortune. He also served alongside the King at Shrewsbury and cut down your countrymen. As many men as he's killed on the battlefield though I dare say that he's cuckolded even more. I hope you haven't introduced Fordham to your wife, Thomas."

"I'm more worried about introducing you to my stable boy," Chaucer drily replied.

Edmund de Lacy's mouth twitched in shame and resentment. His face crimsoned. The vain and vicious young aristocrat would not allow anyone to slight him in front his men.

"I suspect that you are here, Thomas, so as to ask me to confirm or deny your intelligence reports. Your intelligence reports must be lacking though, else you would have brought more men. As such I think that the shoe is on the other foot – and I will interrogate you. It is only natural for someone who lurks in the shadows to disappear off into the night. We shall see how good you are at keeping secrets."

Edmund de Lacy felt a swell of pride and glory. Reynard would be impressed with him for capturing one of the King's agents.

I will extract information from the spy but deliver him, still breathing, for Reynard to scoop out from his body any final piece of intelligence that could prove useful to our cause.

He nodded his head towards the two mercenaries sitting closest to Chaucer and his men. Both unsheathed swords, mottled with blood and rust. One was battle-scarred. He looked the fine-boned man-at-arms up and down and snorted at him, derisorily. The other, equal in size to the archer, grinned at Cooper, revealing a solitary tooth in his mouth. He had lost half his teeth to scurvy, the other half to the battlefield and tavern brawls.

A few of the other patrons in the tavern moved forwards to get a better view of the unfolding drama whilst a few others moved backwards. The perspiring landlord was tempted to interject and ask for any disagreements to be taken outside but he thought better of it. At best they would have ignored his words, at worst they may have turned their antagonism towards him. He looked at Hugh Bull, the heavy-set old soldier he employed to police the drunks and any trouble that broke out at the tavern, but Bull merely shrugged his shoulders, intimating that he couldn't do anything even if he wanted to.

In an act of compromise, not wanting to throw oil on the fire, Fordham drew his dagger rather than his sword. Robert Cooper inwardly sighed, rueing the lack of his bow, and also drew his weapon.

"This is your last chance Thomas. You may still be able to save yourself and the lives of your friends. Will you yield?"

"This is *your* last chance Edmund. You may still be able to save yourself and the lives of your friends. Will *you* yield?" the agent replied, with a sly smile playing on his lips.

The nobleman sneered, shook his head at the folly of his opponent's defiance and then gave a nod to his two mercenaries, who were awaiting their orders. The battle-scarred soldier attacked first, thrusting his sword forward. Fordham anticipated the attack and deftly shifted his body to the side whilst jabbing the point of his dagger into his opponent's hand. The Welshman dropped his weapon and let out a yell, which was quickly curtailed by the man-at-arms plunging his knife into the mercenary's neck. The sawdust on the floor soaked up a fresh splash of blood. The man-at-arms offered up a curse for having stained the sleeve of his new coat.

The mercenary facing Robert Cooper let out a wide-mouthed roar as he swung his heavy sword at the archer's head. Cooper raised his arm to defend the blow and, instead of cutting through his leather jerkin to strike his forearm the sword hit a piece of thick plate armour, concealed beneath the bowman's jacket. For a moment the assailant was taken aback, confounded. Cooper lost no time however. The brawny archer punched his sword upwards. The blade entered just under the man's chin, knocked out his enemy's remaining tooth and lodged itself in his brain.

Welsh jaws dropped. Curses coloured the air. Blades scraped free from their scabbards. A sense of shock was quickly succeeded by a desire for vengeance. Everything happened quickly and yet slowly. Cooper and Fordham were not accustomed to retreating, but the veteran soldiers hadn't survived for so long without knowing when prudence should sometimes get the better of valour. Outnumbered, by more than three to one, Chaucer and his men took their leave. The conspirator's men clambered over each other to pursue their enemies. They would kill rather than capture now. Their blood boiled rather than simmered. Edmund de Lacy's shrill instructions, to bring Chaucer back alive, were drowned out by the sounds of falling tables and war cries.

The lank-haired mercenaries scrambled out of the door to the tavern, like hounds who had picked up the scent of their quarry. There was now a biting chill to the night air. They heard fleeing footsteps and observed the ghostly outlines of their enemies running across the market square. Some of the Welshmen grinned, relishing the hunt and the kill. They would exact their revenge, both for their comrades who had died at Shrewsbury and also for the deaths of their two friends in the tavern.

They spilled out into the night like spectres from the underworld – but they would soon be forced back to hell. An arrow struck the first man who made it out the door. The steel bodkin sliced through his thick leather coat as if it were made of gossamer. The second arrow felled the man next to him. The hunt had turned into a trap.

A proficient archer could fire eight arrows a minute. Robert Cooper's chosen men, John Walworth and Stephen Hall, were able to fire ten to twelve in that time. The two men seemed like ten men. Their goose feather flights, ash shafts and steel tipped arrowheads were of the highest quality. Their eyes were accustomed to the dark. Their black cloaks helped conceal their location. The deadly missiles appeared from out of nowhere. Every shot hit its mark. A sense of confusion and fear gripped the mercenaries.

Every time the Londoner, John Walworth, let loose a shaft he, as was his habit, let out a curse beneath his breath.

"Bastard ... piss pot ... Welsh twat ..."

Walworth stood even broader and taller than his friend Robert Cooper. His chest was as wide as a cannon's mouth. His bull neck, shaven head and craggy features projected an air of strength – and brutality. Walworth was a former butcher's apprentice who was now skilled in a different kind of butchery. The veteran thought he was currently engaged in a slaughter rather than a fight, but his pay for the night didn't distinguish between the two. Nor did his conscience. The arrowheads continued to thud into the chests of the enemy, often knocking them off their feet. From such short range the professional bowmen couldn't miss.

"Cocksucker ... sheep shagger ..."

Stephen Hall, standing a dozen or so paces to the side of his colleague, was young but accomplished. Unlike the veteran he had been nervous before the fight – and concentrated more during it. He neither wished to let himself down nor Robert Cooper. Thomas Chaucer had first spotted the talented youth at an archery tournament near his village, but it had been Cooper who had spoken to his parents, taken the boy under his wing and forged him into a professional bowman. With each month that passed he could draw the string back a little bit further on the powerful war bow, and with each month that passed he purchased a new shirt as his arms, shoulders and chest expanded. Hall was fresh-faced with a shy disposition. Before the mercenaries had swarmed out of the tavern he had clutched a small wooden cross, which his mother had given him before leaving to serve in Thomas Chaucer's company, and devoutly prayed that his companions would survive.

Whether it was due to bloodlust or their dull wits the mercenaries still charged forwards rather than seeking cover. By this time though Robert Cooper had retrieved his weapon, which lay beside Walworth. He quickly put on his linen arrow bag and placed one of the ash shafts on his bow. He drew back the hemp string, controlled his breathing, picked his target and fired an arrow into the sternum of his enemy. Cooper permitted himself a smile. He no longer felt incomplete or vulnerable.

Chaucer and Fordham also turned to face their opponents as the sound of arrows zipped through the air. They drew their swords. Geoffrey Chaucer had been conscientious enough to provide his son with a scholarly education – and a fencing tutor – when he was growing up. The snarling Welshman who rushed towards him, clasping a much-used mace, was stronger than the agent, but not as agile. The mercenary swung his weapon ferociously through the air whilst Chaucer thrust forward in one movement, extending both his body and sword reach at the same time, and plunged the tip of his blade into his opponent's neck.

Fordham's combatant shouted out an insult as he engaged the man-at-arms, but his bark was worse than his bite, and the soldier parried two predictable attacks before punching the mercenary in the face to unbalance him, sheathing his sword into his stomach.

Arrows sprouted up out of torsos like flowers. Blood dribbled out of the mouths of the fallen. Some of the wounded drew their last, rasping breaths. Some of the corpses twitched. The five companions briefly looked around at each other to make sure no one was injured. They nodded, smiled and breathed a collective sigh of relief. But de Lacy was missing from the scene and still needed to be apprehended.

Without a word Cooper raced back into the tavern, leaping over a couple of dead Welshmen as he did so. The conspirator had escaped through the back of the establishment during the fighting outside but the archer knew he could catch-up with de Lacy – and all he needed was one good shot to bring him down. But the bowman would only be able to wing his prey. The soldier knew that his paymaster would have no desire to interrogate a corpse.

The archer pursued the distant sound of footsteps and found himself running down a long narrow alleyway. Buildings lurched towards each other above him, to the point where those that lived on the top floors could reach out and shake the hand of their neighbour each morning should they wish to. He continued to close the distance between them. He hoped that, as his arrow bag slapped against his thigh, the flights wouldn't be damaged.

But I only need one good shot.

Cooper offered up a short prayer to St Crispin, the patron saint of cobblers, that his old boots would grip rather than fall apart as he pounded along the grimy cobblestones.

Sweat glazed de Lacy's forehead. His chest and thighs burned. He panted, almost yelped, as he ran. He could hear the sound of someone pursuing him but he dared not slacken his pace and look behind him. If he could just reach the end of the alley he could lose his enemy in the maze of small streets which ran parallel to the river. And if he could survive the night all would be well. The different parts of the plan – and different factions – could come together and Henry's days would be numbered. He would be given a baronetcy as a reward for his service in ousting the King. He could marry into one of the great noble families of France. He could have it all. But should de Lacy be captured tonight then he would have nothing. He might not even live to see the morning. Chaucer's veneer of culture and charm masked a ruthless heart. As his heart pounded and his breathing became more laboured, de Lacy cursed everyone under his breath – the tavern owner, his company of mercenaries, Chaucer and his lackey soldiers. Indeed the perverted nobleman blamed his fate on everyone but himself.

Cooper nocked his arrow. A sign hung above the soldier's head with a picture of a bandaged arm upon it. The archer fleetingly thought how Chaucer wouldn't be afraid to wake the surgeon up in the middle of the night if he injured de Lacy too seriously. The agent would either bribe or threaten the physician to save the life of his prisoner, so that he could torture him to death afterwards. From a lifetime of felling animals – and men – the bowman judged the pull and arc he would need to hit his target. As Cooper pulled back the bowstring the muscles in his arms tightened and bulged. The veins became pronounced, like rivers marked out across a map.

The arrow flew from the bow, shimmering slightly in the inky darkness. The sound was barely louder than a whisper. The conspirator was nearly at the end of the street. Salvation. His hopes were at their highest when the bolt cut him down. Edmund de Lacy cursed and then whimpered, clawing the cobblestones as he tried to crawl forward and escape the archer.

The shaft protruded from his right buttock. Chaucer smirked to himself as he walked towards his prostrate quarry.

"Nice shot," the agent remarked to the bowman, who was placing his bowstring back in his pocket.

"Well you did mention earlier how much he likes to take things in the arse," Cooper said.

Edmund de Lacy groaned.

"I am afraid I'm going to need you to be more articulate than that when I ask you questions later. We can judge how good you really are at keeping secrets then, eh?" the agent cheerfully said, thinking how he would use the minnow to try and catch a bigger fish.

2

"The King's mad enough to think that he's got God on his side," Edward Fordham remarked, downing another cup of the establishment's most expensive Bordeaux.

"But not so mad to brave it on his own. He's taking five thousand archers and two thousand men-at-arms over to France," Robert Cooper countered to his friend as they both sat, accompanied by Walworth and Hall, in *The Parfit Knight*. The inn was one of the finest – and most expensive – lodgings in the capital, but Thomas Chaucer was keen to reward his men.

A log fire crackled in the background. The floor was strewn with rose petals, rushes and herbs to temper the smell of the tallow candles burning in the private dining room. Various dishes, on pewter plates, lay before them on a large oak table: white bread, honey-glazed pork, leeks, cheese, boiled cabbage, game pie and fresh-ish fruit. The entertainment for the evening had been provided by two minstrels. The first Fordham paid to play on, the second he paid to stop. The stout, obliging proprietor mentioned he could send in an acrobat to keep his patrons amused but Fordham replied that, after a few more drinks, they would be able to fall about on their own.

John Walworth whistled on hearing the numbers that Henry was planning to take on campaign to France.

"It seems that every boy and greybeard able enough to carry a bow or sword will be sailing across the channel soon. What about if we get invaded ourselves? The Scots may cross the border, if only to escape their dour weather and wives," the hulking bowmen said whilst carving off another sizeable chunk of meat from the joint he had strategically placed close by to him.

"God save us but Henry has persuaded the clergy to take up arms and defend the country if the need arises. The King has more faith in them than I do, I must confess. They'll need to fire off more than a *Te Deum* at the old enemy should the Scots invade. I suppose that we need only tell them that our opponents will be carrying gold in their pockets. They'll soon cut them open then. I've known priests that would whore their own mothers out for the promise of a penny," Fordham (half) joked, winking at a serving girl to indicate his cup needed refilling. The winsome wench smiled back, indicating that more could be on offer than just wine for the evening.

Walworth laughed and raised his cup in a toast to agree with his friend. Despite the class and cultural divide between Fordham and the archers he had earned their trust and admiration over the past few years. He would watch their backs (and often pay for the drinks) and similarly he could rely on the bowmen to watch his back in a fight. Fordham particularly respected Robert Cooper. The archer was a far nobler and finer soldier than any man-at-arms or knight he had encountered. It had been Cooper's idea that evening, after peering through the window of the tavern and realising how much they were outnumbered, to set a trap for their enemies and draw them into the market square – "the killing ground". Thomas Chaucer trusted and admired the archer too. Both Cooper and Fordham had travelled with the diplomat on recent missions to Brittany and Holland. The purpose of their diplomatic visits had been to secure truces and lessen any chance of invasion and piracy on their shared sea lines. Even with God on his side Henry couldn't fight everyone.

"And your mother wanted you to join the clergy, did she not?" Walworth said, after one final hearty guffaw.

"Neither God nor I answered her prayers, thank God," Fordham drily replied and spared a thought for his parents whilst doing so. His merchant father had wanted him to become a banker. Perhaps he had hoped that his son would be motivated by the pursuit of money, as he had been at a similar age. But, for better or worse, poetry, women and drink inspired him. His ambition had been to become a writer, though Fordham freely conceded that even with God on your side it would be difficult to make a living that way.

His mother experienced pity, shame and condemnation – not necessarily in that order – when her only son descended into a life of debt and debauchery. But all was not lost. Seeing something in him Thomas Chaucer gave the young man a second chance. The agent paid his gambling debts, when his father refused to do so, in return for Fordham becoming a man-at-arms in his company.

"I should warn you, you might well be selling your soul to the devil," Chaucer had said, when Fordham signed the contract.

"You should keep a receipt. My soul may prove so worthless that you'll want to sell it back to me."

Although the would-be Horace could still devote himself to wine, women and song, Fordham had turned himself into an accomplished soldier. He hadn't just proven his worth on the battlefield though. Chaucer used the handsome and cultured man-at-arms to sleep with the wives of his enemies and gather intelligence. God and Thomas Chaucer worked in mysterious ways. Tonight was not the first time Fordham had bloodied his sword on English soil for his paymaster.

After securing their prisoner that evening Chaucer dealt with the beadle and constables who arrived on the scene.

"If anyone asks, tonight was a quiet night for you," the agent instructed. Coins glinted briefly in the moonlight, before being pocketed. Thomas Chaucer was used to purchasing both information and silence. "Feed them to the pigs or cremate them. Either way make sure they disappear into the night," he added, making reference to the corpses still lying in the square.

Cooper and Fordham didn't always approve of their employer's methods but they were content to remain in his service, despite being offered greater sums of money to serve with other companies.

Better the devil you know.

As Chaucer and the manacled de Lacy were swallowed up by the darkness Fordham had felt a shard of sympathy for the misguided conspirator. As much as the soldiers might stay up late into the evening the prisoner's night would be even longer

– and morning might never come. The sound of the screams emanating from the Tower would be even more unpleasant than the sound of the second minstrel singing, Fordham mused as he eyed the serving girl again to refill his cup.

After taking a swig from his freshly filled cup Fordham looked at his friend, who appeared somewhat dislocated from the group. Robert Cooper gazed into the fire, his features and heart seemingly as hard as slate. The dancing flames entranced him as much as dancing girls, his companion fancied. Was he wistfully staring into the fire, envisioning the imminent campaign? Was he dreaming of the glory – and fortune – of capturing and ransoming a French nobleman? Or was he imagining the horror of being captured himself? The enemy would cut off his bow fingers, or a more vital part of his being. The soldier may have been thinking of the dead, the ghosts of companions and enemies alike who could haunt one's dreams and waking hours in equal measure. *The screams and the silence.* When Fordham had spoken to Cooper a week ago he had said that he wanted this to be his last campaign: "I've been ankle deep in mud, blood and corpses for too long ..."

Robert Cooper stared into the fire and thought of Grace. The swirling flames reminded him of her bright red hair, fluttering in the breeze as she cocked her head back and laughed. Grace was his chance of a peaceful, good life. Of a wife, children and farm. So far the archer had only brought death into the world. Death had been his duty. And death would be his sole legacy, should he die tomorrow, he mournfully thought. Grace represented life. Hope. He loved the way she had a dimple on one side of her face, but not the other, when she smiled. The way her freckles bloomed on her cheeks on a summer's day. He loved that she was kind and intelligent, free from affectation. Grace could always bring Robert out of a gloom and make him laugh. He wasn't a soldier when he was with her, rather he was the man he wanted to be. The archer loved her cooking and the way she could name every flower and plant she encountered on their walks together. He loved her ...

Another log cracked on the whistling fire. Walworth slapped his tree-trunk thigh and laughed at a joke he told to Hall. The adolescent bowman devoured another piece of greasy crackling and grinned ear to ear at the jest. A carthorse whinnied outside in reply to a hound baying at the moon. The serving girl's dress rustled, as she sat on Fordham's lap and clasped her arms around his neck. But Robert Cooper was in his own little world. He offered up a silent prayer that he would survive the campaign. That she would say "yes" when he asked Grace to marry him. Cooper wryly hoped that God concerned himself with the fate of bowmen as well as kings.

3

Morning.

Thomas Chaucer entered the King's chambers, fatigued from a sleepless night. He was about to kneel and formally greet his sovereign but Henry made a subtle movement of his head to dismiss such ceremony. The King prized efficiency over flattery.

The chamber, situated in the King's palace in Kennington, was well lit and well aired. Clouds scudded across the horizon outside and parted to let in the buttery light. The agent's eyes flitted around the room, absorbing and collating his environment as well as checking that no one else was present. Official correspondence and books lay piled upon a large, cedar wood desk which had once belonged to Edward I. Chaucer squinted and noticed that Henry had been reading Virgil and Saint Augustine. A large Bible also lay on the desk but unlike other editions Chaucer had encountered in the houses of noblemen and churchmen the book was open. Three of the four walls in the room were lined with tapestries and paintings, with maps – of France – on the other. A sword was also mounted on the wall, which had once belonged to Edward of Woodstock, the Black Prince. Below the weapon was a plaque with his motto inscribed upon it: *I serve*. Chaucer noticed a harp in the corner. Henry had been in continual practice since boyhood, but he had still to master the instrument. "Should you hear me play then you will realise just how mortal and imperfect a king can be," Henry would comment.

Henry was of medium height and slim build – a marriage of elegance and athleticism. A taut, sinewy torso lay beneath his clothes – a spring waiting to uncoil. His hair was brown and straight and it was shaved half-way down, so that Henry resembled a monk as much as a monarch. His head was narrow, shaped like a coffin. His nose was long and slender, like a blade. Ink stained his fingers from writing letters and his hand was calloused from sword practice. Henry's face was smooth and unblemished, save for the mark of a scar from when the then prince had been wounded by an arrow at the battle of Shrewsbury. The arrow, deflected off a nearby helmet, went halfway through his head but Henry fought on, not wishing to diminish the morale of his troops by abandoning them. One of the most skilled surgeons in the country, John Bradmore, removed the arrowhead and admired the prince's capacity to endure unspeakable bouts of pain whilst doing so. God had spared the prince, many commentators noted. Before the surgery however many opponents of Henry declared how God had fired or deflected the arrow, in order to strike him down. The scar was still noticeable by the side of his nose but it failed to disfigure the young man's handsome face. Henry's demeanour was often serious but seldom severe – although Chaucer had twice been witness to the usually imperious King breaking out in a rage. His nostrils would flare out like a dragon's and he looked as if he were about to spit fire; the just King's eyes blazed with something harsher than justice.

Henry wore a simple, white linen shirt and brown breeches. His regal bearing stemmed from his character rather than his wardrobe. He was comfortable in society, whether drinking with his archers or discussing theology with churchmen, but he also enjoyed his own company.

Henry smiled – briefly, politely – before speaking. He was amiable without being overly warm or affectionate. His speech was clear and measured. The King embodied two – almost opposing – qualities: youth and wisdom.

"You look tired, Thomas – somewhat worse for wear."

"It's been a long night," the agent replied. His eyes were half closed and red-rimmed. Chaucer tried – but failed – to suppress a yawn. "I've been at the Tower."

"Then someone must look even worse than yourself this morning, I warrant. Should I be worried about anything?"

"You pay me to worry for you. I apprehended Edmund de Lacy last night. He is the son of Roger de Lacy, who sided with Percy at Shrewsbury. A source informed me that de Lacy could be involved in a plot against the crown so I questioned him."

"Did he talk?"

"Everybody talks," the agent said assuredly. Despite the protestations of some members of the clergy torture worked as a method of securing intelligence and preventing crimes against the state.

Edmund de Lacy, who had recently matriculated from Oxford, had started talking before Chaucer and his attendant, Glanvill, had even commenced the torture. As de Lacy hung in chains, whilst Glanvill readied the accoutrements of his trade, he confessed to everything he knew, whilst he soiled himself and whimpered. Having served as Speaker of the House Thomas Chaucer was used to people lying to him and, although he believed de Lacy was telling the truth about the prospective plot to overthrow the King, the agent believed in being thorough. First he asked Glanvill to use a branding iron on the youth's genitalia. Next he instructed the attendant to cut off one of the prisoner's ears. When de Lacy lost consciousness a surgeon was called for to revive him. Chaucer then threatened to slice off both of de Lacy's eyelids. Whether out of mercy, or fatigue, the agent and attendant only removed one. The truth was wrung out of him as if he were a sponge. Chaucer urged the conspirator to confess everything, for the sake of his soul, but both knew that de Lacy was more concerned with preserving his bodily parts. Chaucer also promised that the truth would set the traitor free – but that was a lie. Edmund de Lacy still remained in the Tower, ready to be tortured again or executed. The agent raised the corner of his mouth in a smile, recalling the moment when, on being told that he could still keep his life and his lands if he cooperated, de Lacy had also begged that no one would confiscate his fur gowns and collection of hats.

"It seems he had something to confess, given that you were planning to be on the road back home to Oxfordshire this morning," Henry said, as he sat down, picked up a knife and commenced to sharpen a series of quills on his desk.

"Unfortunately the young de Lacy appears to be a small link in the conspiracy's chain, but nevertheless he is still connected to the plot. Firstly, he confessed that a French agent, one Reynard of Troyes, is currently bound for Lothian, carrying a consignment of gold. He is due to meet Walter Bane there. The reputation of the agent precedes him. Reynard is as guileful as he is fanatical. There is little he puts his mind to which he doesn't achieve. He has the ear of the Burgundians and Armagnacs, as well as the Pope. Reynard is not to be underestimated. Rumour has it he is the only man in France who John the Fearless fears. He is self-educated and self-made. His ambition is to rekindle the old alliance and pay Bane to encourage his kinsmen to invade England while the army is mustered in the south, ready to disembark for France. Reynard intends to draw Owen Glendower and the disaffected English nobles into his conspiratorial web too, in order to effect a coup. Our prisoner confessed that the French agent is bringing a special gift with him as well, but couldn't specify any more than that I'm afraid."

Henry pursed his lips and a storm swirled in his usually equitable brown eyes. Again he bowed his head, either in prayer or thought. *Uneasy lies the head that wears the crown.* Agents of the King had come to him with news of similar conspiracies and would-be coups before. His father's reign had been plagued by plots to seize the crown – to usurp the usurper. Henry had inherited the crown – and its enemies. Indeed Henry would be more worried if he *didn't* hear news of some ambitious or fanciful conspiracy to overthrow him.

It is a fool's errand to try and please all of the people all of the time.

"I cannot be too distracted in my cause by this latest conspiracy Thomas," Henry stated. *We have no more thought in us but France.* "But nor can I afford to ignore it. I will need you to tug at this thread some more in order to unravel things. Ride up to Lothian. Take your company of archers and men-at-arms. Confront Bane if you have to. The man is odious. Few will mourn the death of Reynard, should your paths cross. Put out the fire before it starts. Even I might break out into a smile if you are able to secure any French gold. Let our enemies pay for their treachery. Your father would appreciate the poetic justice."

Thomas Chaucer smiled at Henry's comment but inwardly sighed. He had hoped to spend time with his wife and family at his house in Ewelme, before joining his King in Southampton and sailing to France. Home life nourished his soul, whilst his existence in London ate away at it. But he would do his duty to his King because he was his sovereign – and equally so he was his friend. Before the spy had left for London his wife had (half) joked how he was married to his work – and she was his mistress.

"There is something else, Hal. The prisoner revealed that he was tasked by Reynard with paying an assassin recently. Unfortunately Reynard did not give his lackey the name of the assassin's target, although he did say that 'the country cannot afford to go to war without the man.' You may wish to alert and increase your personal guard," Chaucer warned.

"I will endeavour to play my harp some more, to keep any assailant at bay. But I will do as you suggest, Thomas. Should you worry less about me then I may then be able to subsequently pay you less. But tell me, how came you to question and apprehend the young de Lacy?"

"The jeweller, Herbert Molyneaux, contacted me – out of loyalty or fear. He was commissioned by de Lacy to produce a number of ornate badges, in the design of the white hart of Richard II. He rightly thought that he should inform me of the transaction."

"Reynard has met his match. You must uproot any weeds before they look to overrun our blessed plot. Our greatest hope is that Bane, even more parsimonious than his countrymen and more duplicitous than the French, will pocket the gold himself. The French or Scottish may look to blow us off course but my compass is set and my cause is just," Henry announced, his voice and features forged with steeliness as he stared across the room at a painting of his flagship, the Trinity Royal.

After discussing the mission to Scotland further the King allowed Chaucer to take his leave. Henry stood alone for a moment, peering out across the expansive sky as if an ocean lay before him, the future both set and unreadable. The sunlight pouring through the window like honey was inviting. It was a fine day to go riding and hunting. But the King proceeded to call in his clerks and work his way through his correspondence and accounts. He first composed a number of letters. Some he dictated, some he wrote in his own hand (occasionally doing both at the same time). Among others Henry wrote to Sir John Holland, thanking him for his hospitality at a dinner he gave in honour of his majesty. He also reiterated to Holland the preferred ratio of taking three archers for every man-at-arms as the nobleman put together his company for France. He next wrote to Richard Courtenay, thanking him for his gift of the first ever printed copy of Chaucer's *Troilus and Criseyde*. Henry was tempted to pass the book on to the author's son, but the bibliophile could not bring himself to do so. He told himself that such an act would bespeak of ingratitude towards his friend Courtenay. Next the King called for his cook and settled on the menu for his forthcoming dinner with Richard Whittington, the financier and former Mayor of London. "We must finely furnish the dinner table. Spare no expense, in hope that our friend will spare no expense and finely furnish our war chest."

Henry then turned to his accounts and the arrangements for his campaign. Before recruiting a single soldier the King had gone to war against the culture of corruption and incompetence that was rife throughout the procurement officers and clerks who served the crown. "Every penny and every goose feather will be accounted for," Henry had expressed, leaving no one mistaken about the sincerity of his conviction.

He scrutinised purchasing orders, tax receipts and all manner of invoices. He would dull the edge of any sharp practises which looked to short change the crown or country. Embezzlers and rogue traders would be weeded out and punished. The King, unlike many of his predecessors, hoped to tax fairly and spend any revenues prudently. The heaviest tax burden fell upon those who stood to profit most from the campaign. He sometimes felt like he was more of an accountant than a monarch – but stoically bore both roles. Money was the lifeblood of the crown and for too long, under both Richard II and his own father, the state had haemorrhaged capital. And so Henry had appealed to parliament to fund his cause. He offered royal jewels as surety to captains in his army. Towns, as well as individuals, provided Henry with loans. The entire country, rather than just the army, was going to war and investing in the campaign. He would take tax revenues and, alchemist-like, turn them into war booty. Masons and carpenters had been employed to fortify the southern ports. Men and material would be accompanying soldiers across the channel: fletchers, surgeons, blacksmiths, farriers, miners, engineers, clergyman, minstrels ...

A procession of courtiers and clerks came and went. Some were thanked and praised, some were chided and instructed to amend or improve their performance. Few commanded the King's complete attention however as he worked on through the morning. He drank some fine ale and some wine mixed with water, but ate little. His hand developed a cramp as it scratched its way across parchment after parchment, but still the clerks continued to feed him documents and his eyes devoured their contents. Henry only paused when he reached a document accounting for the cost of the floors and ceilings being reinforced at certain border forts in the north, so they could support the weight of artillery pieces.

Scotland. The old enemy was about to re-forge the old alliance. Henry had calculated the odds of an invasion from the north when he departed for France – and had fortified and garrisoned the border towns accordingly. Before this morning though he had discounted the threat. Scottish independence and antagonism towards the English had bred indebtedness and isolation. A notable number of Scottish people had grown tired of a political class who desired blind subservience towards an increasingly bloated state. Both the peasants and mercantile classes were being taxed to death. Scottish lords, through terror and conceit, had cleverly created a state of affairs where to criticise them meant you were committing treason against the Scottish nation itself. The problems of Scotland were laid at the door of the English, or Westminster in particular, to hide their own sins. Scottish lords played on their differences with their neighbours rather than working on how they could unite in a common cause. The English were to blame for everything wrong with their nation, or indeed the world. But Henry believed that the English would be safe from its northern neighbour. More than any other nation the Scots were good at defeating themselves, through in-fighting and a lack of planning and funding. Henry had no intention of attacking the Scottish in a pre-emptive strike. If he poked the fire he was liable to be burnt. Henry was wise enough to know that nothing united the various Scottish factions like the common enemy of the English. But would Reynard and his French gold be able furnish them with a sufficient war chest to cause an invasion to succeed?

I would have the Scotsman as my brother but should he attempt to stab me in the back then my cause will be fratricide.

"Bad diet will kill the enemy off or their wives will nag them to death … They're as envious as they are indignant. Greater numbers will come south looking for a job rather than a fight," Thomas Chaucer had argued – and Henry had wryly smiled to himself at his friend's satirical humour.

But then his majesty's smile faltered as the dangers and gravity of the campaign came to the fore again, oppressing the King's soul. In his bid to win the French crown would he lose his own?

Henry solemnly prayed.

God and Saint George go with you Thomas Chaucer – and also your goodly archer Robert Cooper… The game's afoot.

4

The sun's rays pounded through the window onto the anvils of Edward Fordham's eyes. His head throbbed from the Bordeaux and his limbs ached from the serving girl's voracious lovemaking. His brain throbbed too from trying to remember the young woman's name. It was Mary, he thought. The gap between her teeth, which showed when she smiled, only heightened his fancy that he had just bedded a young Wife of Bath. Her constant laughter yesternight had been endearing, but now it grated on his soul.

"Compose another poem for me," Mary brightly remarked, looking up from resting her head on his chest. The night before, to further seduce the maid and amuse himself, Fordham had recited a number of poems to the enamoured maid. He pretended that they were original compositions, in honour of her, but in truth the poet had recited a couple of his previous works and some lines from John Gower's *The Lover's Confession*.

"I'm afraid I'm spent, in more ways than one," the man-at-arms replied, unable to raise a smile or anything else. Fordham was more tired now than he had been after the battle of Shrewsbury.

"Perhaps I could inspire you," Mary mischievously whispered, as she kissed his chest and slid her hand beneath the sheets. She coiled her leg around his. Her heart-shaped face had housed a look of innocence last night but her mind was less than pure, Fordham mused.

The gentleman-soldier was too tired to engage with the woman anymore, yet too chivalrous to abruptly ask her to leave. Before the jaws of his dilemma could swallow him up Fordham was saved by a knock at his door.

"Come in," he called out, his voice betraying a bit too much eagerness.

Stephen Hall entered. The young archer's features crimsoned on seeing the naked woman sprawled across the bed. His gaze initially darted around the room in an attempt not to ogle her, but ultimately his eyes drank in her sunlit figure. He clasped the small wooden cross around his neck. Fordham thought that Stephen might well clasp something else later upon remembering the comely maid. The adolescent eventually bested the catch in his throat and spoke.

"Thomas Chaucer has returned and asked me to fetch you. We're downstairs," Hall said. For a moment he stood, frozen to his spot, as Mary caught his eye and grinned, half amused and half charmed by the well-proportioned soldier.

"I'll be with you anon," Fordham remarked, relieved that the bowman had provided him with a means of escape.

Hall nodded at Fordham in reply. As if he were a gentleman at court and she a lady the young archer bowed at Mary and took his leave.

Mary pouted at her lover having to leave her. She traced a finger across Fordham's muscular and scarred body in the hope that her well-off man-at-arms would crave one last bout of pleasure. But it was to no avail. Fordham told her he needed to put his duty towards his King before his heart's desires, whilst putting on his boots, shirt and breeches.

"Will I ever see you again?" the serving girl asked, her pout having returned.

"Yes. I'm beginning to miss you already," Fordham charmingly answered, as he wrapped his arm around her lithe waist and kissed her deeply for the last time. They both knew the soldier was lying but neither wanted to spoil the mood.

*

Chaucer, Cooper, Walworth and Hall were all sat around a table in a private room when Fordham joined them. Bowls of steaming beef pottage and fresh bread were brought in. Cooper smirked to himself, as he rubbed tallow into his bow to prevent it from drying out and cracking, envisioning the kind of night his friend had endured and enjoyed. Fordham's unkempt hair stuck up at the back as if it were a half-finished thatch. His eyes looked like two piss holes in the snow. No doubt the serving girl was smitten with the soldier-poet, but by the end of the day Fordham will have forgotten about her. Cooper just hoped that the girl was cleaner than Walworth's jokes.

His fellow archers looked similarly worse for wear as they nursed their heads in their hands, their eyelids half-closed. A nasty bruise and lump marked John Walworth's forehead from where the tall archer had bumped his head on a door frame last night. It wasn't the first or last time it would happen. The uncomplaining bowman fed the beast of his hangover by downing a large cup of ale with his pottage. Stephen Hall had imbibed half the amount the veteran had consumed last night, but appeared twice as wasted as he pushed the bowl of pottage away and made a face like he was going to vomit.

Thomas Chaucer waited for Fordham to be seated and he checked the serving staff had departed before commencing to speak.

"There's no rest for the wicked gentlemen, I'm afraid. The King has commissioned me – and therefore you as well – with a task. You will not be travelling to the south coast tomorrow, as originally planned," the agent remarked, hoping to infect his men with a sense of intrigue and enthusiasm.

"We're not being sent to Wales I hope, to track down that bastard Owen Glendower again. We'll have more chance of finding a fucking unicorn."

"No, John. Owen Glendower – and the unicorns of Wales – will be safe from us. For now. I'm well aware that you would all follow me into hell. But unfortunately I'm about to ask some of you to follow me to somewhere far more inhospitable – and colder. Scotland."

Edward Fordham rolled his eyes and winced, thinking of the cuisine and women available north of the border. He had travelled to Scotland a few years ago and vowed then that his first visit would be his last. Half of the Scots he encountered had despised the English, nearly as much as they should have despised themselves, he judged.

"You're in for a treat, lad. The Scots are the only people I know who the more they drink the unhappier they become.

They'll tax you for pissing and sneezing and they'd rather welcome the bloody flux into their home than an Englishman," Walworth expressed to the untraveled Hall, screwing his face up in disgruntlement at the prospect of crossing the border.

Robert Cooper considered Chaucer's words – and recalled one of Edward III's mottos: *It is as it is*.

"We are to go hunting again, this time for a fox. A French fox, to be precise," the agent continued, as he brushed away a few crumbs of bread from the part of the table where he was sitting. He knew that his men would not be pleased with the mission, but he also knew that they would carry out their orders.

"You mentioned that you would only be asking some of us to join you," Fordham said.

"Yes. You didn't just get lucky last night Edward. I'll need you to remain in the capital. John, you will also be staying in London. I have a special job for you both, the details of which I'll divulge later this evening. The rest of us, along with the remainder of our company, who are lodging in less salubrious lodgings, will ride north tomorrow. You can stay here. I trust you won't drink them out of the Bordeaux, Edward. Whilst I trust you won't drink them out of everything else, John."

*

The two friends shared another jug of ale, after the rest of their companions departed. Robert Cooper laughed as Fordham recounted the story of his recent seduction of a nun.

"... And why not? At least with a bride of Christ you're unlikely to hear the sound of a husband's footsteps charging up the stairs ... But enough of my conquests. What do you think are the chances of Henry succeeding in his campaign against the French? I warrant he is capable of winning any battle – but incapable of winning any war on foreign soil. The King may not run out of gold, but the army will run out of food and arrows at some point. Sooner or later we will have to retreat back to Calais and then England. In terms of the sacrifices he will have to make and the constant fighting I can only conclude that Henry is going to war as a rehearsal for married life ... I do not believe that even Chaucer is privy to the King's intentions and plan. He is still negotiating with both the Burgundians and Armagnacs. We do not even know which group of cowardly and treacherous Frenchmen we'll be fighting alongside."

"Perhaps it will be neither and we'll fight them both," the archer answered, seemingly unperturbed by the prospect of defeating two forces – or one grand army.

"Then Henry is as mad as his French counterpart. I have heard that Charles sometimes believes he is made of glass. If only our monarch were as transparent, we might be able to divine his strategy."

"His strategy will be sound. I have faith in our King, cause and the ability of our bowmen to pierce any armour. France is divided and vulnerable," Cooper said, with confidence rather than arrogance.

"But she isn't weak and our campaign could prove a catalyst for the Burgundian and Armagnac parties to unite together under one banner. Henry is playing with fire. Sooner or later he'll get burnt, I fear."

Robert Cooper was thoughtful as he listened to his friend's reasonable comments. He recalled his encounter with the King, many years ago, during which he first heard Henry talk of going to war with the French. Henry had asked Thomas Chaucer to lend him his bowman for the day in order to improve his archery skills. Unfortunately Henry was as accomplished a performer with a war bow as he was with a harp.

The two men had loosened arrows into a target, positioned at the end of the King's garden at his residence in Kennington. Occasionally they had been interrupted by the arrival of an official or servant. Henry had dealt with them briskly but not impatiently. The archer had been in earshot of the King previously during his service in Thomas Chaucer's company. More experienced soldiers dutifully followed his orders not just because of the authority of Henry's rank but because of the wisdom of his commands. As much as his sovereign was independently minded he still surrounded himself with noted diplomats, churchmen and warriors. Thomas Chaucer gave the King a good report too, before he formally introduced his bowman to his monarch. Like his father before him Chaucer was more inclined to satirize than praise a man but the agent genuinely admired his sovereign.

"... The King possesses advisers but not, like Richard II and Edward II, favourites. Henry has conscientiously studied the lessons of history in order not to repeat his predecessor's mistakes ... He is a man of many talents and virtues, some he has propagated for show but most are ingrained and authentic ... He is honourable, pious and diligent. Henry is as much a patron of poetry as he is of ecclesiastical scholarship. He has forged himself into a man of war because he values peace. He values merit over entitlement and holds all men as being equal – whilst he can look down on them all at the same time ... But as much as I might list his virtues and vices Henry is made of such stuff that he will always defy and dwarf such a list ..."

It had been a spring day, with the wind just about strong enough for the archer to employ the breeze as an excuse for his King's wayward shafts. Cooper was tempted at first to miss the target on occasion too, in order not to embarrass his sovereign, but professional pride wouldn't allow him to.

"I would that I had ten thousand bow arms of your ilk, Robert," Henry had said, as he placed another arrow upon his stave. "France may then simper as opposed to goad us. France is a bully. And like a bully we must give him a bloody nose – then he might think twice about wishing to accost us again. France – in its constant raids on our south coast, in landing troops in Wales to foster revolt there, in supporting Scotland's border incursions – wishes to humiliate me as it did King John. But I will have the last laugh. They will neither erase our language nor our sovereignty. I will return the territories justly won by Edward to us and I will not lease this land out to France as though we were some vassal. France. We'll bend it to our awe or break it all to pieces," Henry had vowed, as he pulled back the string further than he had done so before. There was mettle in his looks and an even harder cast of iron in his soul, Robert judged. "And the best form of defence will be to attack."

For the first time one of the King's arrows had struck the centre of the target.

"Good shot, Sire."

"It may have been more good fortune than good judgement. But rather than a great king give me a lucky one," Henry had remarked and smiled slightly, pleased with both his comment and shot. "As your father served the Black Prince, Robert, I would ask you to fight alongside me when I sail across the channel with an army which'll cleave both the sea and dukedoms of France apart. I possess a number of old letters, by Edward, which commend your father. Others at the time attested to his courage and skill as a soldier as well."

"You may well know my father better than I. He spent most of his life on campaign, as opposed to being at home. I barely saw him when I was growing up," Robert had replied, recalling the hole in his childhood caused by his absent father. At first Cooper idolised his soldier father from afar but admiration eventually turned to resentment. Brave men can also prove to be selfish men – and unfaithful husbands.

"Your father would be proud of you now. And you are not the only son of a soldier to lose his father to the army. Ironically there were moments when Richard behaved more like a parent to me than my own. It was only after I joined my father on his military campaigns that he grew to esteem me. I earned his respect by being on the battlefield. Any time spent in a library was time wasted, he argued ... My father tried to be a good king and sometimes he succeeded. But he was haunted by the ghost of Richard. And as much as you may hear myself lauded as the son of Edward III or the Black Prince I am my father's son – and I have inherited some of his sins. Most notable of which is pride. During the end of his reign, when I was eager to inherit the throne, we were akin to two magnets, unable to come together and unite in regards to any cause or opinion. We seldom saw eye to eye, indeed his eye would sometimes pass over me altogether in favour of my younger brother ... And I have sins of my own, that I cannot just pray away, which I'm unable to lay at my father's door ... But do not believe all you read about me in chronicles or hear whispered about me from snake-like courtiers, Robert. According to some my youth was spent floundering around at the bottom of a jug of ale – and I straddled more whores than I did tournament horses. My arm may be untrained with this bow but that is because I was too busy holding a book or sword. I am as a king that which I was as a youth: the hundredth best swordsman in the land, its thousandth most accomplished scholar-cum-harp player and its worst archer. But I have said too much or, if you were my confessor, too little. Yet taken all in all do you believe that the bowmen of England would follow me, should I give the call to arms and go to war with the French?" Henry had said, staring so intently into his eyes that Robert had believed his King was trying to divine his soul. With a wave of his hand Henry had dismissed an approaching attendant.

Cooper fancied they were more likely to follow their sovereign if they could be assured that their wages would follow them around too, but he had declined to voice this thought.

"I would not wish to speak for all of the archers of England, your majesty, but you have my bow, for all that it might be worth."

And Robert Cooper, as he listened to his friend's doubts in *The Parfit Knight*, was still determined to honour his vow to Henry – whether the campaign proved to be an historic triumph or a fool's errand.

5

The following day.

The afternoon heat warmed rather than stung. Boisterous swallows darted in and out of leafy trees on either side of the rut-filled highway. Robert Cooper heard more birdsong in an hour in the countryside than he had during a month in the capital. He breathed in the fresh air, filling his lungs. The archer's heart swelled too, with Grace.

What with half of his soldiers already mustered in Southampton Thomas Chaucer had brought along a dozen archers and ten men-at-arms to accompany him on his mission. At the King's expense Chaucer was able to provide a mount for each of his men. The weather had been fine and they made good time. Although it was not the quickest route north the party journeyed to Scotland via Oxfordshire and his estate at Ewelme, so that the agent could see his wife and children.

As the company of men travelled north they met a host of soldiers and tradesmen – walking, riding or perched on the backs of rickety carts – venturing south. The country was answering Henry's battle cry. Old friends and brothers- in-arms greeted each other. Chaucer heard one bowman cry out, "Death or glory". The promise of booty and fame shone in their eyes like gold coins, but most of the soldiers were likely to die from the bloody flux rather than from a sword thrust by a valiant French nobleman. *Is it because I am getting older that they seem to be getting younger?* For a moment or two the pinched expression on Chaucer's face betrayed how he was already mourning the procession of men travelling south.

"First come the drinking songs but then, ultimately, come the dirges," his father had once told him. Thomas Chaucer shook off the memory of his father and certain maudlin sentiments. He turned his attention towards the mission ahead.

Reynard of Troyes. Rumour had it that the agent was the illegitimate son of the Bishop of Troyes and for a while he had been known as Reynard the Bastard. His other nickname had been Reynard the Poisoner, both for his preferred method of dispatching his enemies and also for his practice of whispering poison into the ears of royalty and courtiers. His love of France was only matched by his hatred of the English. A source had informed Chaucer that a company of English archers had raped and murdered Reynard's grandmother during one of Edward III's campaigns, though a rival intelligence report claimed the French agent fabricated the story in order to justify his cruelty towards his enemies – and propagate resentment towards English bowmen.

Thomas Chaucer was wise enough not to underestimate his counterpart and, although he hoped he would be able to reach Lothian before the Frenchman landed, he would plan for the worst. Chaucer knew he would need more information and men before facing Reynard and Walter Bane. He commenced to weigh up his options for allies in the region. He couldn't afford to allow the French spy to instigate any plot and escape.

Who will be the spider and who will be the fly? I need to be the architect rather than the victim of a trap.

Robert Cooper trotted alongside Stephen Hall. At first he had been amused by the young man's expression as he shifted nervously in the saddle on his skittish chestnut mare. But as the horse settled down Hall's face still betrayed flinty shards of apprehension. Cooper realised that it was the first time the adolescent would be so far away from his home. And, as usual, Chaucer was being guarded as to what their mission would entail.

Laughter from the men behind Cooper and Hall broke the silence as several archers and men-at-arms shared jokes, songs and wineskins.

Owen Morgan, a ruddy-faced Welsh bowman Chaucer had recruited after capturing the enemy combatant during a failed attempt to track down Owen Glendower, led the joke-telling.

Beside him was the former thief, Jack Mercer. Chaucer had offered to save him from the gallows, in return for serving in his company. The roguish Mercer had replied at the time that only God could save him. Chaucer countered however that God would be unwilling to give him a warm meal, a warm bed and an even warmer whore that evening. Mercer signed a contract and claimed that the only things he now stole were "maidens' hearts".

Behind Mercer rode the elderly Cornishman, Andrew Tanner. His hair was now more grey than black and he could no longer shoot as far or as true as he once had, but the agent was loyal to those who were loyal to him, and he had recently contracted Tanner to serve with his company for another year. Andrew Tanner had now lost most of his teeth and it took a while to penetrate his Cornish accent (though when one did it was apparent that the archer had little to say). As much as most of the company struggled to understand the former brewer from Cornwall he still rambled on and told old war stories at any opportunity, to the point where Chaucer had nicknamed him "Nestor".

Next to Tanner rode Percy Badby, who was by a long shot the worst shot in the company, but the mild-mannered son of a Suffolk thatcher was one of the finest fletchers in the country. Badby was also a skilled carpenter, bowyer and blacksmith. He could more likely be found with his head in a copy of the Bible than in a cup of ale. Cooper also noticed how Badby often blushed rather than laughed at the jokes Morgan and Mercer told.

As well as his archers riding behind him Cooper heard the booming voice and laughter of George Clifford. Such was his powerful build – he was equal in size to John Walworth – Clifford was often mistaken for a bowman but, in the absence of Edward Fordham, he served as the captain of Chaucer's men-at-arms. The illegitimate son of a nobleman, Clifford called himself "more bastard than gentleman", although his father had funded his training. Although he was good humoured amongst his comrades the Yorkshireman was vicious and vocal in the heat of battle. Instead of a broadsword he armed himself with a giant pole-axe and would make a small mark on the handle for every man he killed. Suffice to say the long piece of oak was now heavily scarred. George Clifford had started – and ended – more tavern brawls in his time than Cooper cared to remember, but the whole company was grateful the mad dog fought with them rather than against them.

"Have you ever travelled to Scotland before?" Hall remarked, keen to learn more about his friend and the land he was heading to.

"Aye. The landscape is God's own country, but they fight like demons. Expect us to be eyed with suspicion. We'll be the butt of the odd jibe and comment too. But not everyone holds a torch for a burning antagonism of the English north of the border. There's a silent majority that wishes to trade and have healthy relations with us. They do not bitterly blame the English for all the ills which afflict them, nor do they slavishly follow the self-serving lords and rabble rousers who preach a religious hatred against us. England will remain secure from invasion when the army travels to France. The fractious Scottish factions are too impoverished and disorganised to come together and cause great harm. As much as they'd like to they couldn't arrange a piss-up at a brewery. But keep your blade sharp. As much as this foxhunt might turn into a wild goose chase we could have to cut through more than just the morning mist to get back out of the country alive," Robert said, not knowing if his words would lessen or increase his young friend's apprehension.

"Do you think our mission will be to capture or kill this Reynard of Troyes?"

"Knowing Chaucer, we'll probably have to do both."

"How far left till we get to Chaucer's estate?" Stephen Hall asked, on behalf of his stomach.

"Not long," the archer replied, recognising an orchard and mill from previous visits to the agent's estate in Oxfordshire.

"What's his wife like?"

"She's a good woman, a lady ..." But Robert answered as if caught in a daydream. The soldier's thoughts lingered on not his employer's wife, but rather his housekeeper, Grace.

6

A homely smell of fresh bread and wildflowers filled the air of the kitchen.

"She could prove too much of a distraction," Thomas Chaucer said flatly, his brow knitted, as he covertly peered out of the window and looked at Robert Cooper and Grace sitting together in his garden. His wife had just revealed that she thought the archer intended to propose to their housekeeper. Chaucer immediately regretted allowing Robert to stay the night at the main house, as opposed to billeting him with the rest of the company in numerous cottages across his grounds. "His mind needs to be on the mission and imminent campaign. Now is not the time for him to marry."

"But Grace will give him someone to fight for," the agent's wife, Matilda, argued. She liked both Grace and the archer. It would be a good match.

"He has a king for that."

Chaucer stroked his beard and continued to stare intently outside. His eyes flickered, darting between the two of them. When he heard the couple laugh he pursed his lips in disapproval even more.

"Our King may be great in many ways, but even he cannot perform the all the duties of a loving wife."

Matilda's fair comment and fairer smile lightened Chaucer's gruff mood, though he still frowned somewhat at the prospective match between his best bowman and only housekeeper. One of the reasons why Thomas Chaucer could manage affairs of state and his complex network of informants so effectively was because he had no need to worry about the management of his own household, due to his wife and good staff being in place.

"I am thinking of you also, Matilda. How will you cope if Grace decides to keep her own house instead of ours? How and when did this courtship occur? I am able to keep abreast of events throughout the four corners of Europe, yet I am unable to keep track of what is happening in my own home it seems. I am clearly more suited to dealing with matters of the state than matters of the heart. Given how Robert kept this affair secret, perhaps I should employ him as a spy instead of an archer from now on."

Chaucer turned to his wife, his expression a mixture of bewilderment and disgruntlement. He was unaccustomed to not being in control and not being informed. It was his brief to know things first. The spy was used to shaping events, not reacting to them.

"Now promise me, Thomas, that you will not meddle. Let nature take its course. They deserve a portion of happiness. Robert has spilled enough blood and Grace has scrubbed enough floors." Matilda sidled up to her husband. Chaucer could smell her scent and was unable to detach himself from her gaze. Her fine turquoise eyes were a blend of silk and steel, charm and determination. His frostiness melted before her touch. Thomas Chaucer adored his wife. She was his friend, confidante and lover. To those who said that he had married above his station he replied by agreeing with them. Her character was imbued with poise, intelligence and compassion. Her dress was elegant but not ostentatious. Time had started to line her face a little but Chaucer still found his wife attractive, and had remained faithful to her throughout their marriage, despite various temptations. Her round face and upturned nose could sometimes project pertness, sometimes pugnacity. Matilda often spoke her mind and was not afraid to disagree with her husband. She supported him, although she was, unlike many women who attended court, not overly ambitious for him.

Chaucer sighed and resigned himself to fate. Or his wife's arguments. He had to concede that, as opposed to a distraction, his own wife and family did give him something to fight for.

It may all come to nothing anyway. Love doesn't conquer all.

"I promise not to meddle. Just so long as I do not have to scrub the floors or cook if we are left without a housekeeper."

"If you do the latter then your nickname may well become 'the Poisoner'. Promise me as that you will take care when you ride north. How dangerous is this Reynard of Troyes you seek?"

"It will probably prove the case that our paths will never cross. It will be like looking for a needle in a haystack. The weather may not agree with him – nor will the disagreeable Scots – and Reynard will turn his ship around as soon as he lands," Chaucer said humorously, wishing to alleviate any anxieties that his wife might be feeling.

But the sage woman was neither amused nor satisfied with her husband's dismissive response.

"That's not what I asked," Matilda replied. Steel eclipsed the silk in her eyes. The agent's wife knew all too well how her husband could obfuscate. Matilda knew, better than anyone, when he was lying to her or himself.

Thomas Chaucer knew his wife could extract the truth from him even more effectively than Glanvill could at the Tower.

"He's dangerous ..."

But so am I.

*

Tufts of coral-white clouds drifted across a lustrous blue sky. Fragrant summer flowers encircled the small herb garden like ribbon. A gentle breeze rustled through the leaves of a nearby pear tree.

Grace wore her finest linen dress, the one she normally saved for church on a Sunday. Matilda had encouraged her to wear a belt, to accentuate her enviable figure. The mistress of the house also loaned her housekeeper an attractive sapphire brooch which matched her bright blue eyes.

Her pretty, freckled face seemed incapable of scorn or beguilement. Her long, flame-coloured hair was neatly pinned upon her head, although the soldier preferred it when Grace let her hair down. She fingered the necklace and silver cross around her neck. Grace believed that the thoughts she had, in relation to Robert, were sometimes sinful. But she also told herself that she would be absolved of her sins. Because, hopefully, one day they would be married.

Grace had first met the bowman a year ago. She caught his eye – and he hers – from a distance when Chaucer had invited Cooper to stay at the cottage on the southeast corner of the estate. The following day the housekeeper had taken a trip to Oxford. On a street located just behind the market the maid was accosted by a trio of students. The young men came from titled and entitled families. They were dressed in the latest fashions and could neither hold their drink nor their tongues. They believed money could buy anything, including a woman's virtue. When Grace refused their advances they started to abuse her and the leader of their pack grabbed the woman's wrist. It was at this point, having heard a cry for help, that Robert Cooper came around the corner and confronted the students. At first they warned the "peasant" man that he should mind his own business. The archer decided to teach the students a lesson. The lead student snarled and threw a limp-wristed punch at the bowman. Cooper caught the youth's hand and broke his forefinger. The snarl quickly turned to a snivel. The soldier, quite literally, kicked the arrogant student's arse as he scampered away, followed by his acolytes. As a result of his injury the student was unable to sit his exams, but his father made a donation to the college and he duly matriculated – with honours.

Robert escorted Grace home that afternoon and later on in the evening she cooked dinner for him at the cottage. "The fastest way to a man's heart is through his stomach," Matilda advised her housekeeper before the meal.

Grace enjoyed Robert's company. They shared a sense of humour and a sense of ambition. He told her of his hope to form his own company of archers one day. Grace found that she could open up to the bowman. Robert didn't judge the housekeeper for her humble background and he encouraged Grace in her ambitions to learn to read and improve herself. He was a welcome tonic to the attitude of her parents, who on more than one occasion had deemed their daughter "good for nothing" and openly declared how they would have preferred having another son. Grace had heard about the reputation of soldiers – and archers in particular – but she realised Cooper was different. She loved him for listening to her and remembering what she said. He never frowned upon her speaking her mind, unlike her family and past suitors. She loved the way that he had met the King, several times, but was modest about it. She loved the way he held her in his muscular but tender arms.

Robert sat next to Grace on the bench in the garden. His palm was slightly clammy as he held her hand. The archer had shaved and put on his best (cleanest) shirt and breeches. He smiled gently and his demeanour was serene, but thoughts buzzed like hornets in his mind and his heart galloped. He felt that there were more butterflies fluttering around in his stomach than there were flying around in the garden.

You need to ask her today. Now … But what if she says no? But I cannot leave tomorrow without knowing. I feel like half a man without her.

His throat was as dry as the bark on the surrounding trees. Robert Cooper was more terrified than on the morning of a battle. He knew what he needed to say but the words were stuck in his mouth.

"What's that?" the archer asked, referring to a large board and cloth bag next to Grace on the bench. Matilda saw Grace as a companion as well as a housekeeper. She encouraged the young woman in her quest to educate herself and gave her blessing to her relationship with the archer.

"It's a present from the mistress, to help me with my letters. She first bought it for her daughter, Alice," Grace replied, as she picked up the wooden board and bag which contained numerous wooden tiles with letters painted on them.

Robert inspected the board and bag but his thoughts were focused on how he could bring up the subject of marriage. For years the bowman's sole ambition had been to lead his own company of archers. But now the only company he needed was hers. He had recently passed smallholdings in the county and pictured himself living there with his prospective wife and family. If she said "yes" then France would be his last campaign.

"How is young Alice? Does she still spend her time dreaming about marrying a lord?"

"Yes. I warrant that no one but a prince or king will be good enough for her though. She did ask after you the other day. The master of the house spoke highly of you too."

"If only his wages were as high as his praise," the soldier remarked, only half-jokingly.

"Will your mission be dangerous when you go to Scotland and France?"

There was a slight catch in Grace's throat when she spoke. She lowered her eyes, already consumed by worry.

I want to be a soldier's wife. Not a soldier's widow.

"The good thing about being an archer is that you stand away from the heart of the battle. I am not about to take any risks. I will be back here again soon. Your cooking has given me something to live for."

Grace beamed, outshining the lustrous sky, and laughed (although her fears were only outwardly dispelled).

She's too good for me ... But tell her how you feel before it's too late.

Robert sighed and remained sheepish and silent. He gazed at the blank board in front of him and fingered a wooden tile, a "D". His hand trembled a little as his mind and will were illuminated by an idea. He placed the tile on the board. His heart thumped, as if wishing to break free from the cage of his ribs. But he would finish what he started.

DEAR GRACE

The sweet-faced housekeeper appeared curious at first but then her heart began to beat faster, attuning itself to the man she loved sitting next to her.

WILL YOU M

The archer's large, strong hand trembled even more as he was unable to find another "A" and "R" to continue his message. His tanned complexion concealed his blushes. But he was saved by Grace. His companion, with tears of happiness glistening in her jewel-like eyes, calmly reached into the bag and pulled out a number of tiles.

YES

No other words needed to be said. Robert and Grace were unable to speak even if they wanted to, as their lips met in a kiss to seal the novel proposal.

7

"This tastes like it's been brewed in a drab's hole," John Walworth remarked to his companion, wincing at his cup of ale. He still took another swig however and devoured a couple more oysters from the large plate in front of him on the table.

"Any more of those oysters and you'll either be sick or want to fuck the next strumpet that comes in to view," Fordham said, amused and impressed by the size of his friend's appetite for the rumoured aphrodisiac.

"And who says I can't do both?" Walworth countered, with a grin and a wink.

The establishment they were drinking in, *The Boar's Head*, was a far cry from the *The Parfit Knight*. The tavern, situated in an alley near the Ludgate end of the Fleet River, was dimly lit and populated by lawless characters. *The Boar's Head* was renowned for being a hub for the buying and selling of stolen goods. The proprietor, Gilbert Swinton, prided himself on his ability to look the other way. He provided a hot meal and warm bed for any cutthroat and sharper in desperate straits. Just so long as their money was good.

Fordham was not expecting to encounter their quarry at the inn but he was hoping to find out more about him – and perhaps discover where he was staying in the capital.

Cheers and jeers erupted from a backroom where a bunch of half-soused patrons placed bets on a cockfight. A rhythmic creaking sounded from above. Fordham fancied that if all the whores worked upstairs at the same time the cracked ceiling may well collapse completely. Fordham looked askance at a large patron sitting adjacent to his table. Half his arse was packed in his breeches and half of it was spilling out of them. The man soon moved when a scar-faced fellow patron approached and instructed him, with a subtle nod, to vacate his chair.

The scar-faced man scowled as he sat down – moving his jacket to reveal the knife in his belt – and spat on the floor before speaking.

"It's not often we get someone dressed like a gentleman in The Boar's Head. Are you lost, my friend?"

The man was middle-aged but his voice was croaky with cantankerousness and from a lifetime of drinking rough ale.

"I'm not sure if that was intended as an insult or a compliment, John. And there was I thinking that I had sufficiently dressed down for the evening to fit into my surroundings," Fordham replied. He had, however, deliberately dressed himself in a fine and colourful outfit for the night in a bid to attract attention. It would have been little use trying to question any and everyone in the tavern about the assassin. Rather he would wait for one of the lead dogs in the pack to come to him.

"The name is Nicholas Poole. That may not mean anything from where you're from but it means something here. It means that I can give the word and have half a dozen men will put a blade to your throat."

Poole grinned, menacingly, revealing two dog teeth. He licked his lips, envisioning the stranger's throat being cut. Poole had long, greasy black hair and even greasier skin. His nose was red, puffy and veiny. His cheeks and chin were marked with scars and when he sneered he had the kind of face that any woman, even the man's own mother, would recoil from. The careerist criminal had started life as a pickpocket, graduated to housebreaking and now led a gang, whose crimes were as numerous as its members.

Edward Fordham merely yawned in reply and proceeded to scratch the mould off a piece of cheese in front of him. Nicholas Poole wrinkled his face up in resentment at the man's unexpected reaction towards being threatened.

"I'm not looking for any trouble, although I should warn you that we won't run away from any should we encounter it. Rather, I am searching for some answers to a few questions I have. If you are willing to be a help instead of a hindrance then I will be happy to pay you and your friends with their blades. For once you'll be able to earn some honest money," Fordham stated, placing a coin on the table as he did so.

Poole's eyes widened at the size of the unexpected bounty – and again the rogue licked his lips.

"You've got my attention stranger. But as much as you may hold the money I can still hold a dozen blades to your throat. So why don't we play a game? Why don't we toss that coin there? If it turns up heads then you get to ask your questions, of which I may or may not choose to answer. But if it doesn't then I keep the coin and you and your friend can fuck off back to where you came from, with your throats intact," the villain said, grinning with a pre-emptive sense of triumph. Nicholas Poole was still undecided as to whether he would slit the stranger's throat or not. On the one hand he, along with his large companion, looked like they could handle themselves in a fight. But on the other Poole suspected that the stranger had more money in his pockets. The Fleet was used to drinking down corpses. One or two more wouldn't end up damming the murky river, Poole figured.

Fordham turned to Walworth and raised his eyebrow, as if to ask what he thought of the offer. The big archer, after shovelling another two oysters down his neck, shrugged his shoulders.

Nicholas Poole turned around too and with a nod of his head called for his six cohorts, sitting in the corner, to join him. Other patrons gave them a wide berth as the half a dozen men, with cruelty and malice dripping from their expressions, stood behind their leader in a horseshoe. Hands wrapped themselves around cudgels and knives. Rings were placed on fingers in anticipation of a brawl. The rule would be that there wouldn't be any rules, Poole thought. The odds were in his favour.

"I thought I'd bring some friends along to make sure our game's played fairly."

The professional thug smirked, revealing his blackened pair of dog teeth again. His men would drink and fuck well tonight, if the stranger's purse matched his garb.

But Fordham's roguish grin in reply was just as wide, if not wider. The soldier confidently met the criminal's triumphant glare.

John Walworth tapped one of his oyster shells on the table twice. A smile lit up the archer's lantern jaw as eight men (his brothers and cousins), drinking in different locations around the room, congregated together behind the bowman.

"And I thought I'd invite my family along, to enjoy the show," the archer exclaimed, standing up to further enhance his intimidating figure.

Most of John Walworth's family, who were based in Bermondsey and Deptford, shared his build. Although none of them were soldiers they were still veterans of tavern brawls. When Fordham, judging that they may run into trouble during their enquiries, asked Walworth to recruit some trusted men to watch their backs, the archer knew who to call on. Most carried butcher knives, as the Walworths took their work home with them for the night.

Alarm clouded Nicolas Poole's self-satisfied expression. The odds were no longer in his favour. But he would not back down. Hatred and pride stoked the gang leader's dismal soul.

"Well we've got our audience. We may as well commence to play," Fordham remarked, picking up the coin from the table. His tone was jocular and conciliatory but it did nothing to remove the tension infusing the air as much as the pungent smell of rancid butter. Eyes flitted towards faces and hands as weapons were gripped even more tightly with sweaty palms. Prospective combatants thought about who they wanted to stand toe to toe with. Fear slithered down the spines of Poole's men more than Walworth's family. They were now outnumbered. A few thought Poole had got himself into trouble and it was not their responsibility to get him out of it. Money, not character, inspired loyalty for the brigands.

Onlookers stood enthralled but also ready to retreat, not wishing to be caught up in any violence. Whispers and murmurs grew, like the sound of the tide coming in, as to the cause of the disagreement. Few would mourn the demise of Poole, yet they were naturally averse to any strangers coming into their environment and unsettling the natural order of things. Rusty blades scraped out of scabbards. Poole's men seethed, or even snarled. John Walworth downed one more oyster and mouthful of ale. One hand remained close to the leg of the table.

Silence ensued and time stood still. Fordham flipped the polished silver coin upwards and it hung in the air in the candlelight …

*

A velvety night sky, studded with stars, shimmered above the men. Smoke billowed out from the main chimney of the house in elegant spirals. A brace of owls hooted in the distance. Moths and flies congregated around an oil lamp dangling from a branch close to where Chaucer and Cooper sat. They had just finished having dinner, along with Thomas' wife and Robert's wife to be. At first Chaucer was reticent about inviting the couple to dine with them for fear of muddying the waters between master and employee. But his wife insisted they celebrate their friends' engagement. The good food – and wine – soon softened Chaucer's mood and once pudding had been served Thomas opened a bottle of one of his finest vintages and invited Cooper outside to enjoy the cool night air and converse with him in private.

"King Richard gave this bottle to my father, many years ago. It was a good year for wine, though not for monarchs unfortunately. You should savour this, Robert, as you may not taste anything better for a while," Chaucer remarked, as he filled the archer's cup. As butler to the King Chaucer had cultivated relationships with the best wine merchants and vintners across the continent.

"We may not taste anything better than the dinner we just had either. We are more likely to find a happy Scotsman than we are a well fed one north of the border," Robert countered. He savoured the first two sips of his wine, out of politeness to his host, but he was soon downing large gulps as if it were ale.

"Indeed. But you are about to embark upon a campaign far more perilous than anything you might encounter in Scotland or France. Marriage. If ever you thought God almighty kept an eye on you Robert, it's nothing compared to a wife's scrutiny, I can assure you. A vengeful God can prove more forgiving than a wronged wife."

The archer smiled at Chaucer's comments.

"You seem to have a happy marriage. What's your secret?"

"The cynic in me would say that the secret to a happy marriage is spending plenty of time apart. Absence makes the heart grow fonder as much as familiarity can breed contempt. I also had the good fortune to marry a good woman."

Chaucer was smiling at the warm feeling instilled in him from picturing his wife in his mind's eye. Due to what the agent had seen – and done – over the course of his career his faith in God had been shaken. In the name of keeping the country safe he had endangered his soul. Life was cruel and unjust. And he could be cruel and unjust as well. Guilt and grief weighed upon the agent like a yoke, but when he went home his burden lightened. Matilda saw the good in him and she had the ability to make him see the good in himself too. Often in church Matilda noticed her husband tap his foot impatiently or roll his eyes upon hearing the sermons. His wife however would tenderly hold his hand and soothe him.

"You should still pray to God. As a diplomat you know the value of keeping a dialogue open," she argued.

"But what good can it do?" he said, despairingly.

"What harm can it do?" Matilda replied, kindly.

Chaucer had long known that his wife possessed more faith in God than he did.

Hopefully it's enough for the both of us.

A shooting star, like a celestial fire arrow, arced across the sky and caught Chaucer's eye, snapping him out of his reverie. Doubtless a propagandist close to Henry would be proclaiming how the shooting star was a favourable omen for the campaign ahead. Enemies of the King would be arguing the opposite. Chaucer breathed out, envying and admiring the universe's indifference, or insouciance, towards the base politics of men.

"But you are fortunate too Robert. Grace will prove a good wife. I should mention that Matilda has taken the liberty of moving your room to the rear of the house, close to your future wife's chamber. Noise carries in the property however, so I recommend that you move quite stealthily should you get up during the middle of the night, for whatever reason. If nothing else it'll serve as good practice should we have to sneak up on any of our enemies in Scotland."

The archer smiled broadly and gratefully – from both the wine and picturing his naked wife to be in his mind's eye.

Chaucer didn't know whether the soldier would have a good marriage or not. But he would have a good night.

*

Nicholas Poole stood, transfixed, as the coin continued to spin and climb in the air. He tilted his head towards the cracked ceiling. But before the coin fell to the floor Fordham grabbed the distracted gang leader by the shirt. He pulled the thug towards him whilst launching his head forward and butting his opponent on the bridge of his nose. The sound and sight of the injury made a couple of onlookers wince. Blood spewed forth and flecks of bone and cartilage glistened within the wound. A mixture of pain and drowsiness infused the still shocked Poole.

Walworth lost little time in picking up the table and launching it towards the men closest to his friend. Those that were not knocked over by the unorthodox missile retreated out of the way. The rest of the Walworth family were similarly quick to react and stood ready to attack or defend themselves, their weapons (knives and meat cleavers) held at arms' length. An unspoken wariness checked the gang members from rashly coming to Poole's aid. It was better that only two men spilled their blood as opposed to over a dozen. The ferocity and speed of Fordham's attack also gave them pause.

Fordham removed his hands from the gang leader's jacket and he duly slumped to the floor. Fordham stamped on his groin for good measure. Poole groaned – but he would soon talk.

"You can spit out teeth or spit out some answers to my questions. It's up to you. And if I'm content with what I hear I may just let you leave here with your throat intact. Some gentleman, eh?" Fordham remarked, thinking that he could still get back to *The Parfit Knight* for last orders.

Nicholas Poole talked. *Everybody talks.*

Fordham gave the rogue descriptions of Edmund de Lacy and the assassin. As to the former Poole said that he had seen him once at the tavern, meeting with the latter. The nobleman had stood out, through his dress and manners. He remembered him for being "a wrong'un". As to the man de Lacy met with

Poole confessed that he had seen him a few times, accompanied by two other men – "a short, bald man and a young, rake-thin youth". He once overheard the adolescent call the man with the black hair "Pierre". "Pierre" had spoken passable English but he couldn't wholly disguise his French accent. Poole hadn't seen any of the men in the tavern for weeks, however.

*

Fordham was back in his room at his lodgings, after sharing two or three more goblets of wine with John Walworth. His head throbbed and he sighed with exhaustion. Their visit to the tavern this evening had narrowed down their odds of finding the assassin. But only just. Fordham had more chance of bumping into Gawain's Green Knight or the ghost of Thomas A Beckett on the streets of London than finding the Frenchman before he chose to reveal himself.

Fordham spared a thought for his friend Robert Cooper and hoped that he would have better luck with locating his target. He recalled their discussion yesterday afternoon, about Henry's chances of success in France. Part of the satirical poet was amused and appalled by his friend's blind faith in the King. *Such blind faith will get him killed.* Fordham could also come up with arguments to annul the naïve archer's belief in God. *Religion – everything – is a conceit. All is vanity under the sun. Knowledge erodes faith. How can one love a deity who is responsible for starvation, the bloody flux and the food at The Boar's Head? To see is to believe – and I do not see anything worth believing in.* But the tragic – or comic – truth was that part of him envied his friend for his devotion and faith. Part of him wanted to live for – or die for – a noble cause. To believe in something or someone.

As a poet I should at least believe in chivalry. But I am only a sometime poet…

There was a knock on the door. Fordham let Mary in.

8

Clement weather – and a soldierly attitude to get on with the task – meant that the company travelled north quickly, like a sharpened blade scything through soft earth. It rained but not excessively – and mostly at night.

They passed by rolling, lush green hills with the bodkin-like spires of village churches thrusting upwards in the background. The sound of yew trees being cut down, to fuel the demand for war bows, could occasionally be heard in the distance as they rode through forests. Endless torrents of soldiers migrated south, towards Southampton. Towns were populated by numerous people – and smells. When they stopped off at inns along the way the company would often encounter other groups of archers. Impromptu tournaments were arranged and wagers exchanged. Cooper's fame sometimes preceded him and when rival bowmen discovered who he was half of them were keen to challenge the renowned archer and half of them refused to chance their arm. He won most competitions easily but a few he nearly lost. With his winnings Cooper treated his company to an evening with some clean-ish whores.

It was not just the quality of the whores which prompted Thomas Chaucer to conclude that the country, even the north, was becoming more prosperous and civilised. Church building was on the rise. There was an increased amount of spicemongers, bookbinders, silversmiths and haberdashers in the market towns. One shop even sold chessboards with ornate, ivory pieces. The agent enjoyed the complex game of strategy and believed that sooner or later it would become popular throughout the realm. *Even the peasants might play it ... one day.* People quoted his father's works and *Piers Plowman*.

Perhaps more than anything Chaucer appreciated the variety and quality of food which was now on offer in the towns and countryside alike, compared to when he was a child. Inns no longer just served the ubiquitous dishes of eel pie, pottage and salted herring. Rather the company feasted on spiced mutton, chicken in breadcrumbs, swan with ground pepper and venison with mustard. Fish courses were available inland, instead of just on the coast. The company could order sea bream, pike in onion gravy, lobster and smoked salmon. Rather than the usual watery ale Chaucer washed his food down with Spanish and Rhenish wines, cloudy Kentish ciders and honey-coloured meads.

Law and order prevailed (for the most part). Goods could be moved more securely between towns. As the crown no longer extorted money out of the aristocracy, the aristocracy no longer extorted money out of the people. Chaucer was amused when he witnessed a vintner being pilloried for selling a bad wine. He was doused with the offending "vintage" and then made to drink the dregs. Peace, prosperity and the English language were flowering throughout the kingdom, Chaucer considered with some pride and satisfaction.

Soldiers, clergy and farmhands alike toasted the King up and down the country. Gone was the tyranny of Richard's reign and the uncertainty of Henry IV's. As much as "good King Hal" might be taxing the country of late the people knew that the money was being spent upon the army, rather than purchasing silk robes and baubles for royal favourites. Chaucer deliberately assessed the mood of the tavern, the soul of England. Henry was Edward III re-made, or he would fulfil the promise of the Black Prince. Henry was a devout monarch – and God and Saint George would be on his side. Greybeards began to glory in their tales of Poitiers again, as the beardless spoke of travelling to Southampton and signing up to a company.

The agent spoke to non-combatants also during his time "talking to the nation". He endured rather than enjoyed making the acquaintance of a couple of young men travelling south, who were due to attend Corpus Christi College in Cambridge. Chaucer had known Frenchmen to be less arrogant and pretentious. They were keen to talk about themselves and keener still to spend their (parent's) money as if it were going out of fashion. Suffice to say he thought they would feel right at home at the university. With their smooth complexions and boyish features they would also go down well with some of the tutors. One of the students wanted to be a diplomat and the other an actor. Chaucer advised them that the former involved being the latter.

The journey north was long but far from arduous.

Forests filled with yew trees eventually turned to ones filled with scots pine.

*

Midges congregated overhead but then parted as a kohl-black hawk swooped through the air and gracefully landed on Donald Greyson's forearm. The bird of prey, with eyes like two black pearls, looked as if it could rip off a finger as easily as it could a vole's head. Mercer imagined that the demonic-looking creature had probably been trained to rip off an Englishman's head. The middle-aged man nodded approvingly at the bird as if it were a dog or small child. He was mounted on a fine black charger and wore a well-cut black leather jerkin, with a mail shirt beneath. He had a round face and ruddy complexion. From his red eyes and redder nose it was clear the man liked to go drinking, even more than hawking, Cooper surmised. He also suspected that the ageing knight could still swing his broad sword as well as lift a cup of ale. His flat expression was far from friendly but the archer expected little else north of the border. Behind him, seated on similarly handsome mounts, a group of stony-faced-looking warriors spread themselves across the road, barring Chaucer and his company's way as they approached the crossroads. Their clothes and beards may have been bedraggled but their weapons were of a high quality and well maintained. Many of the Scots were from Celtic descent and their copper-coloured hair shone in the sun. The bowman casually cast his eye over the nobleman's retinue and estimated that, in terms of numbers, they were nigh on equally matched. Cooper shared a glance with George Clifford – and both men wordlessly communicated that they would be up for fight rather than flight. Although their proximity to each other and the narrow road meant that the archers would not be able to bring their bows to bear they still all carried short swords and daggers. The archers, however, were not used to fighting on horseback. But Cooper had confidence that Clifford and his men-at-arms could even any odds. Experience told him that they could defeat their prospective enemy but it also told him that they would lose, at best, a third of their force to achieve such an outcome. There would be no artillery, no flanking manoeuvres. Fighting would be chaotic, at close quarters. Bloody. Their best hope would be to hit them hard and fast – and force them into a quick retreat.

A chill wind blew through the surrounding trees and kicked up some dust on the uneven road. Neither opposing party of men wished to move aside for the other. Grins and glowers were traded, as a prelude to the trading of blows.

The black-cladded nobleman fleetingly smiled as he affectionately stroked the imperious looking bird of prey along his neck and breast, before addressing Chaucer, who had positioned himself at the head of his company. His voice was deep and gruff as if some of the gravel on the road had made it into his throat.

"You men appear to have taken a wrong turn," he said, with the hint of a smirk showing beneath his bushy beard. Cooper was now half expecting the Scot to demand a toll for using the road or demand a fee for providing directions. Outlaws – and landowners – had extorted money from travellers for years in such a fashion. The men who judged themselves to be Robin Hoods were merely just bullies and criminals, akin to King John and the Sheriff of Nottingham. "You are now in Scotland. And Scotland has its own laws and customs."

"I can swallow your laws. It's just your cuisine I can't abide," Chaucer replied, his smooth, polished English accent was in stark contrast to the tone of the Scottish nobleman, who now trotted towards the agent. Cooper rolled his eyes a little in exasperation at Chaucer's barbed comment and stiffened his muscles in anticipation of a fight. He had hoped that the diplomat might endeavour to talk them out of trouble – not into it.

A few of the horses, from both parties, scraped the ground and whinnied – either from anxiety and excitement at the prospective combat. But the whinnies soon resembled laughter as the two men clasped each other on the shoulder, smiled warmly and shook hands. The release of tension between the two companies was palpable. Tight, hunched shoulders were relaxed and hands moved away from weapons. Even the combative George Clifford puffed air out of his cheeks, relieved to avoid a fight.

Chaucer had sent a messenger ahead to inform his friend and political ally that he would be visiting his estate – and the host had ridden out to meet his guest.

"Gentleman, this here is Donald Greyson, the onetime scourge of the English in these parts. But now, thankfully, an ally. Donald has the best chefs in Scotland on his estate, although they do not have much competition," Chaucer turned and announced to his men in good humour.

"And, lads, this here is Thomas Chaucer, son of the poet. Don't let his fine, womanish clothes fool you. He can wield a blade as deftly as his father wielded a pen," Greyson posited, clapping his friend upon the shoulder again. "So, I imagine that thing are bad, seeing as you're travelling this far north whilst the rest of the country is heading south to Southampton and then France. Or has young Alice sent you north in order to find her a prince worthy of her ambitions?"

Donald Greyson picked a piece of ham out from between his teeth and laughed at his own joke. An avuncular smile replaced his former dour, affected expression. Greyson had been a fearsome squire and an even more fearsome knight in his prime at the turn of the century. He had won fame and fortune in tournaments as well as on the battlefield. A well-struck marriage had furnished him with lands and one of the finest estates in the south-eastern part of the country. During Henry IV's invasion of his homeland over a decade ago Greyson had fought against the King. It was partly due to his authoritative voice that the noblemen of Scotland adopted the tactic of remaining in their strongholds against the English King. When Henry realised that he would be unable to force a decisive pitched battle he returned home, with both his people and parliament doubting the virtues of his martial prowess and decision making.

Thomas Chaucer appreciated talent and, instead of deciding to eliminate the redoubtable knight, he chose to recruit him when Henry V ascended the throne. First the agent provided the Scottish nobleman with assurances that Henry had no intention of invading his country – and then he provided him with gold to purchase his loyalty and influence. But the professional soldier and patriot wasn't swayed by gold alone. He believed that he was saving, not betraying, his nation by working with the English. "We should look to emulate our neighbours, as opposed to eliminate them." Scotland had lessons to learn in fostering trade, collecting taxes and looking outwards as well as inwards. Scotland was defeating itself and an alliance with France could deliver a fatal blow. French envoys promised Scotland the world (or parts of northern England). But the French would stab the Scottish nobility in the back as soon as they had secured their aims.

Chaucer and Greyson thought as one in regards to strengthening the common ground between England and Scotland. The actions of the past, of Edward I and William Wallace, should not condemn the present and future. Peace bred prosperity. Together the two countries could prove greater than the sum of their parts and stave off any subjugation to France and Europe. Chaucer and Greyson had also developed a personal, as well as professional, relationship over the years. On more than one occasion Greyson and his family had visited Chaucer's house at Ewelme and conversely the agent was no stranger to the Scot's hospitality north of the border. The two men played chess together and shared a taste for vintage wines.

"Things may well indeed be bad. But I'm here to stop them from getting any worse," the agent said, humour absent from his usually wry tone.

"Well let's get you all watered and fed first, before we discuss the business at hand. You have been riding for days. Your arses must be as sore as a Cambridge graduate's," Donald Greyson said, smiling at his beloved hawk as though the bird understood the joke too.

9

A fair number of Chaucer's company considered Scotland to be just a backwater of England, but even they were impressed by Edward Greyson's palatial house and grounds.

After the stable hands had taken their horses the members of the company were ushered into a building which was called the barracks, but which was more like an inn. The soldiers were offered food and wine, but many spent the afternoon sleeping. They knew that there would be a long night of revels ahead.

Come the evening the Englishmen were invited into the great hall of the main house. Trophies, both from hunting and tournaments, lined the walls – along with various decorative shields and weapons. Two large tapestries also adorned the walls, one depicting Bannockburn and the other the Battle of Sluys. Greyson was proud of his ancestors, who had fought at both. A roaring fire heated the high-ceilinged chamber. The light, from more tallow candles and lamps than any sober soldier could count, shone off the polished silver tableware. Jack Mercer's eyes lit up too, tempted by the rich pickings (although a fear of being caught – and even a slither of a sense of honour to not steal from his generous host – tempered his actions).

Edward Greyson welcomed his guests and had two barrels of Kentish ale set down, issuing a challenge. He made a bet with Chaucer that his men could finish off their barrel faster than the English company. And the prize for the company which finished first would be a second barrel.

The ale and good humour flowed, the rivalry was friendly – and after an hour or so the competition was forgotten as the English and Scottish drunk from each other's supplies. The two sets of countrymen soon realised how much they had in common. Owen Morgan unsheathed his best (dirtiest) jokes and Laurence Firth, the captain of the Scottish company, told a story about a prioress, a crucifix and screams of ecstasy which reached all the way up to heaven (or down to hell). Out of respect for the old soldier they allowed Andrew Tanner to tell a story and both the English and Scottish contingents let out a laugh even though neither wholly understood the punchline (or what preceded it) due to Tanner's Cornish accent and slurred delivery.

Halfway through the evening the soldiers were joined by a number of serving girls and local women from the nearby village. Stephen Hall's grin was as long as his war bow by the morning. George Clifford couldn't quite decide which girl he wanted to spend the night with so, out of diplomacy and desire, took them both to bed later that night. Laurence Firth praised Scottish women to his new friend Owen Morgan: "They're bonny and clean, but often come with filthy minds. Don't become too enamoured with them. When our maidens get married these blessings can become a curse and you'll be more likely to die from her blade than any Frenchman's. Scottish wives can be colder than our weather – and nastier. I once had a friend from the Orkney Islands who fucked his wife and his cock fell off from frostbite."

Despite being situated in a small dining room over the other side of the house Chaucer, Greyson and Cooper could still hear the booming laughter of George Clifford and his boisterous drinking companions. A half-eaten feast (of brawn with mustard, roasted turbot, garlic chicken and stewed apples) sat in front on the three men. Donald Greyson patted his stomach in satisfaction and licked his bearded lips after downing another large mouthful of one of his favourite vintages. He then replied to Chaucer's question, concerning Walter Bane.

"I trust him about as far as I can throw him – and he weighs more than two barrels of ale. There are plenty of Scotsmen I know who would sell their wives if they could. But Walter would sell his own mother too if it meant that his purse would clink that little bit louder. I'm not sure how silver-tongued your French agent is, but his gold will be able to do enough of the talking to win Walter's support. I have heard that he needs a new source of income. He invested the majority of his capital in purchasing lamp oil, believing that the price would remain high and stable. But as much as the swine can be calculating his figures didn't add up.

"Unfortunately Walter and his jackals have the will and ability to cause trouble for England once his army sets sail for France. They will head south and raid as much as they can. For years they have been calling for both a political and military campaign against the English. They talk of rescuing and restoring James I but in truth they long to depose him. 'Scotland for the Scottish and freedom,' they cry, too busy lusting after power or hawking out the nation to France to appreciate their irony or hypocrisy. And some of my countrymen have lapped-up their poison. They believe England is to blame for their penury and discontent. Westminster Palace is hell and Henry is the devil incarnate. And they brand anyone who doesn't share their warped view of patriotism to be a traitor to their country.

"I am ashamed to say that some of my countrymen have swallowed their bait. But thankfully far from all of them have. Yet aided by French gold and more troll-like foot soldiers their influence may increase. Their boorish and boring followers already extort money from the people and shout down their opponents at town meetings."

When his host jabbed his fork at the remaining chunk of salted beef on his plate Cooper sensed that the old soldier might have been thinking of stabbing Walter Bane in the eye as he did so.

Greyson remembered his most recent encounter with his neighbour, during a local hunt. He had made sure the lord had overheard a joke he made at his enemy's expense (partly in hope of Bane calling the knight out and facing him in one to one combat).

"It seems that Walter got his fingers burned on his lamp oil investment," Greyson had remarked, to a chorus of laughter from the group of noblemen he was standing with.

As Bane had trotted off Laurence Firth spoke to his friend and paymaster: "Hopefully there'll be a stray arrow this afternoon – and it'll strike the arrogant turd in the neck," the soldier had said, half hoping that Greyson would instruct him to shoot the "stray" arrow himself.

"Such is the size of the fat bastard that it'll be impossible for any stray arrow *not* to hit him."

Thomas Chaucer also recalled his last exchange with the treacherous nobleman. It had been in London, outside one of the capital's most exclusive brothels. The Scotsman had been just leaving as the Englishman was entering (for the purpose of asking the owner if he had any new, influential patrons that the agent should be aware of).

"We should have dinner together soon, Thomas. Your father and my father used to regularly drink together. Or perhaps your father was just spying on mine, if the rumours are to be believed about him," Bane had remarked, with a raised eyebrow and a look which expressed a knowledge of the son's true profession as an agent of the crown.

"My father never drank regularly with anyone he didn't like," Chaucer had replied. "And you shouldn't believe everything you hear. If all the rumours about yourself were true then I would be honour bound as an Englishman to run you through right now."

A crescendo of song sounded in the background from the great hall as the English archers let out a spirited version of a ballad about Robin Hood, lifting Chaucer from his reverie. He paused briefly before speaking: "As calculating as Walter may be he is but a pawn compared to the bishop's son. Have you heard any news pertaining to the arrival of the French?"

"I'm afraid not, but the good news is I can be confident as to where the French ship will land. Part of Walter's estate rests on the coast and encompasses a fishing village, called Aberlady. The village is home to both a pier and harbour which could accommodate a small French ship. If the vessel has already arrived it will be moored there – and if it is still due then the village will have been forewarned. I can provide you with guides to take you near to the village, although we should not have them travel all the way with you. If captured then our alliance will be exposed.

"I understand," Chaucer replied, half engaged with the conversation and half engaged with his own thoughts.

"War is like a game of chess is it not, my friend?" Donald Greyson posed, as he refilled Robert Cooper's wine cup.

"Aye, it is," Chaucer replied, dwelling on the whereabouts of Robert of Troyes as he attempted to think two moves ahead of his shadowy, wily opponent.

10

Stephen Hall's young limbs ached like those of a man three times his age. But any pain now had been worth it in exchange for the bouts of pleasure he had experienced with Katherine. The serving girl had kept him up, so to speak, all through the night. He grinned to himself like a village idiot, as he pictured the girl's coquettish eyes, full lips, long glossy auburn hair ... and other body parts. He yearned to see her again and hoped that his mission would come to nothing so they could return immediately to the estate. He would be like a knight errant and she his lady. Her laughter rang in his ears and he could still feel the touch of her fingertips – and tongue – on his skin. His countenance seemed serene but his heart beat wildly – like a smooth river with turbulent currents beneath its glassy surface.

Is this how poets feel when they write about love?

The moonfaced archer seemed caught up in a dream as he tramped through boggy puddles, slimy leaves slapping against his face. It had rained earlier in the day and the canopy of trees had prevented the sun from drying out the forest floor. If a wild boar gorged his leg it was unlikely that the distracted adolescent would even notice. Stephen had promised he would capture a French knight for Katherine – and they could live off his share of the ransom. Katherine in turn promised the soldier that she would wait for him, be faithful to him.

Thomas Chaucer, followed by Robert Cooper, led the way through the dense and mossy wood. The three men had parted company with Laurence Firth and the two other guides an hour or so ago. The Englishmen would soon come through the forest and survey the village and harbour beneath them.

Chaucer, tired of letting Reynard of Troyes dominate his thoughts, mused upon the far more attractive mettle of his wife. During the morning he had composed a letter to Matilda. When the agent was engaged on a mission he always wrote a missive to her as if it would be his last. He declared his love and passed on some words of affection and wisdom to share with their daughter too. Chaucer was mindful, however, not to communicate that his life might soon be forfeited and the words expressed in the letter could indeed be his last. Thomas wanted – needed – Matilda to know how much she meant to him.

Cooper may be here to protect my person but she has saved what little soul I have. What is better than wisdom? Woman. And what is better than a good woman? Nothing.

Robert Cooper composed a letter to Grace too, for the messenger to take back to Ewelme that morning. The letter may have been less eloquent, but it was no less sincere or ardent as the son of the great poet's correspondence.

Cooper half focused on following Chaucer's trail in front of him and waving aside low branches and clusters of insects, but he also pictured the woman he loved in his mind's eye to ease the unpleasantness of his surroundings. He remembered the last time he and Grace had been together as he mounted his horse to travel north with the company. She gave him a cloth bundle, filled with bread, ham, cheese and freshly-baked oatcakes.

"Promise me you will be careful," Grace had said. Sunlight had danced across her freckled features. Fondness was entwined with sadness in her voice and eyes. "You now have to think of two people, rather than just yourself."

The archer had been tempted to reply that he was looking forward to caring and thinking about three people or more – implying his desire to start a family. Fordham had recently told Robert how he would never retire from his profession, he had "soldiering in the blood". But now he had Grace in his blood as well. "The aim of a professional soldier should be to earn enough money not to be a professional soldier," Cooper had said to Grace, reassuring her of his ambition to live the quiet life. "I won't always be an archer."

"What do you want to be?" Grace had replied.

He had paused but then smiled.

"I want to be – with you."

Cooper had recalled a couple of lines from Geoffrey Chaucer, although he felt too awkward in reciting the words out loud to Grace. He had first heard the couplet from listening to the priapic Fordham seduce a nobleman's wife. The lines had helped usher the man-at-arms into the lady's bed.

One flesh they are; and one flesh, so I'd guess,
Has but one heart, come grief or happiness.

Let there be more happiness than grief, Cooper prayed.

The sea air began to penetrate the gassy stench of the damp woods. As well as thinking about his last scene with Grace Cooper also recalled his departure that day, when he had bid farewell to a number of men from the company.

"Don't kill all the garlic-munching wankers yourself. Save some for us," George Clifford had said, shaking the archer's hand.

"If the cowards offer up the target of their backs as they run away it might prove difficult to keep such a promise," Robert had replied, smiling as he noticed all the love bites on Clifford's neck.

As the archer had mounted his horse Percy Badby had come rushing over, handing him a new quiver of arrows.

"They're fit for a king. I've included a couple of fire arrows as well. Chaucer asked me to produce a batch first thing this morning," the soldier-cum-fletcher had said.

"Try not to become too bow-legged riding while I'm gone Owen," Cooper had advised his friend.

"They'll be no fear of that. I've spent enough time on horseback these past weeks," the Welshman had replied, his body and wit sluggish from the previous night's revels.

"I wasn't talking about riding horses," Robert had drily remarked, to the amusement of the rest of the company. Owen Morgan went on to confess how his night's lovemaking with a serving girl had been cut short when he retched whilst still on top of her. "Some of the sick went in her mouth even. It was difficult for us to recapture the right mood after that."

The remembered sound of laughter jangling around in the soldier's mind was quickly replaced by the gusting, whistling wind. The three men came out of the woods and crouched upon a grassy overlook. Tufts of foam were spread out like petals across the metallic grey sea. The sound of screeching gulls could be heard in the background. The light was beginning to fade. Louring clouds on the horizon sailed towards them, but the three companions could still clearly make out the small fishing village beneath them. Boats bobbed up and down on the incoming tide. As well as fishing boats Chaucer and his men took in the medium-sized cog at the end of the main pier. The agent had travelled enough to know that the freshly-painted vessel was French.

Villagers went about their business. Many were dressed in little more than rags and even from afar Chaucer sensed the poverty and despondency of the hunched over inhabitants. Their landlord taxed them as regularly as the rise and fall of the tide, blaming the increasing taxes on the English for not offering him a fair price for his wool and lamp oil.

As well as the natives Chaucer couldn't fail to notice the finely dressed French soldiers among them. Some wore plate armour or carried crossbows. A small group seemed to be harassing a trio of young women, attempting to lift their skirts and blocking their way. The agent's eyes scanned the scene to no avail, searching for a figure that could have been Reynard of Troyes.

What the agent wouldn't have now given for the presence of the *Trinity Royal* approaching the harbour. The French cog would have gone down faster than a serving girl in Bankside, he mused.

The question of whether Reynard of Troyes had landed in Scotland had now been answered. But other unanswered questions steadfastly remained. Was the gold still on board the ship? And what was its value? Where was the French agent? What was the extent of the combined forces of the French and Walter's men? What were the details of the Frenchman's plot or plots? How many allies had Walter already recruited or purchased?

There are always more questions than answers.

"As curious as your mind should always be you must learn to live with not knowing everything, else you'll drown in the sea of knowledge," his father had once cautioned him. "Faith can be as powerful as knowledge. The greatest scholars are not always the wisest people."

Stephen Hall squinted and screwed-up his face in concentration as he attempted to count the number of French soldiers in view. Robert Cooper removed his bowstring from his pocket and hooked it around the horn-tipped ends of his weapon, pre-empting Thomas Chaucer's orders.

"We need to see more and know more. How do you feel about impersonating a Scottish fisherman?" Chaucer asked.

"Just so long as I don't have to sleep with a fishwife or suffer her cooking," Cooper replied.

The young archer next to him gulped in fear in response to Chaucer's proposal.

"We'll have to work our way down to the village unnoticed. There is a trail leading towards the beach there. Once on the outskirts of the village we can steal some appropriate clothing and blend in. There is also an argument for capturing one of the villagers and questioning him. Money talks," Chaucer remarked, patting the small purse on his waist.

"Shouldn't we go back and assemble the rest of the company, along with Greyson's men?" Stephen Hall suggested, wary of being captured himself. He was a soldier not a spy.

"There isn't sufficient time. Besides, as I once heard the King argue, 'The fewer men, the greater share of honour'," Chaucer said with a wink, as he attempted to bolster the adolescent's confidence.

*

Albert Garyn wore an expression of disdain on his face, which was directed at his fellow Frenchmen and his new allies of ill-dressed and ill-smelling Scottish people. Few failed to avert their eyes when the soldier glowered at them. The brawny man-at-arms stood on the pier next to the cog and oversaw the offloading of his master's trunks containing his papers and personal effects. The gold would remain on board the ship until his master said otherwise.

Long, thick brown hair was splayed, mane-like, along his back and shoulders. His countenance, even when not formed into an obdurate scowl, was far from pleasant looking. A large brow hung over hard, bony features. His eyes were dark, emitting little light or life. He wore a mail shirt, attached to which were segments of Milanese plate armour. His Genoese crossbow and Spanish sword were the finest that money could buy. The weapons had been used to great effect in tournaments, on the battlefield and in the service of Reynard of Troyes as an assassin all across Europe. The seasoned soldier walked with a swagger – giving off a well-earned air of superiority, intimidation and invulnerability.

Garyn, along with his master and a company of over three dozen French men-at-arms, landed earlier in the day. They were greeted by Walter Bane and a retinue of soldiers, brandishing pole-axes and surly expressions. They puffed out their chests and deliberately looked unimpressed at their French counterparts. But Garyn appeared even more unimpressed and snorted with derision. Whether carrying a sword, axe or crossbow he was confident of besting any of them in a fight.

From an early age Albert Garyn had realised that he had a gift for fighting and cruelty which could be put to good use through soldiering. The son of an ironmonger from Gascony, he had little desire to take up his father's trade. Although capable of following orders and absorbing the technical skills of a man-at-arms when he was let off the leash Garyn fought with a raw savagery which appalled and impressed his peers. He was different from other men-at-arms. Better. Nastier. Reynard of Troyes recognised the Gascon's brutality as an asset rather than liability and signed him up to his company of men. Garyn duly reciprocated his trust and loyalty. Despite lucrative offers from nobleman supporting the Burgundian and Armagnac causes Garyn refused to serve under any other master.

Out of the corner of his eye Garyn witnessed a number of carping gulls fly upwards along the coast, on the other side of a steep bank which led towards some woods. His hawkish eyes also noticed a faint cloud of dust proliferate the air, which was unlikely to have been made by the birds. His master had warned that their presence may attract spies – and his master was seldom proved wrong in such judgements. The soldier sensed something was amiss. Albert Garyn proceeded to march back along the pier and gruffly ordered a number of his men to follow him and prime their crossbows.

*

The three men had all lost their footing at some point during their cautious descent of the trail which ran towards the beach. The leaden clouds above resembled the dull, metallic-grey hue of the sea. The incoming tide rattled loudly on the shingle and the swirling wind drowned out all other sounds, including the approaching French soldiers.

The French men-at-arms appeared from nowhere and quickly surrounded the Englishmen in a semi-circle. Twelve versus three. The steely looks in their eyes conveyed their competence and lack of compassion. Once they were given the order, or if forced to defend themselves, they would shoot to kill. The crossbow bolts couldn't fail to hit their target at such close range.

Cooper knew the odds were against him but his reflex action was to reach for an arrow, but Chaucer raised his arm and shook his head, instructing the archer to stand down. There would be little honour in trying to fight back or escape.

"Now is not the time for heroics," Chaucer said to his friend.

Garyn's sneer and smile were one and the same expression. His goading look challenged the English archer to attempt to nock and fire an arrow, faster than he could aim and pull the trigger of his crossbow. Garyn walked towards Cooper, unflinching in his antagonism towards the bowman. Garyn shared his master's hatred of the English. He raised his weapon but Cooper refused to lower his gaze, despite wanting to turn his nose up at the smell of fish and garlic on the Frenchman's breath. Both men wanted to kill one another, but both also knew that now was not the time.

Stephen Hall followed the lead of his companions and relinquished his bow and short sword to the enemy. The colour drained from his face as the numerous steel tips of crossbow bolts loomed large in his eyes. His heart sank and a sense of terror rose up in his throat, preventing him from speaking. He would no longer be able to go back to Katherine as a conquering hero.

The mission has ended before it's begun...

The frightened youth began to pray. He had heard stories of the French cutting off the fingers of English archers – and torturing them by other means as well.

"You are spies. But now you are prisoners," the rough-voiced Gascon said, not caring if his captives could speak French or not. His master would be pleased. He would amuse himself with his prisoners and clinically extract from them any valuable information they might possess. His master would then dispose of his enemies, like a surgeon washing the blood from his hands.

Hopefully he will permit me kill this defiant archer for myself.

If they were playing a game of chess then Reynard of Troyes had just captured more than one significant piece, Thomas Chaucer thought.

11

The temperature dropped as sharply as Stephen Hall's hopes of survival. The night was drawing in. The blue skies would soon become as black as tar.

The strong wind slanted the rain into the soldiers' faces as they walked – or were dragged by the ropes around their bound wrists – along the track which linked the fishing village to Walter Bane's estate.

Garyn had ordered his men not to harm the prisoners. Yet. His master would want then untouched. Unspoiled. But that did not stop the Englishmen from occasionally being ridiculed or spat upon by the French and Scottish soldiers alike.

"You are a spy," one swarthy-faced French soldier issued to Robert Cooper in English, little disguising the enmity in his voice.

"I'm a spy? Does this mean I'm now entitled to a pay rise?" the archer drily replied, turning to Thomas Chaucer.

Before Chaucer could answer he too was addressed by the Frenchman: "And you are a dog and coward."

"I've been called worse. A 'politician', for instance," Chaucer remarked, little disguising the indifference in his voice. "Keep your spirits up, Stephen. All is going according to plan, trust me," Chaucer then said to the scared young archer next to him, with more confidence in his tone than in his heart.

The main house was built from a dark grey stone that not even the summer sun could cast in an attractive light. Smoke belched out from a couple of chimneys as servants looked to heat the house for the cold night ahead. Behind the house lay a large field, bordered on three sides by woodland. Chaucer noticed a few shapes in the distance, which he took to be archery targets. He also saw a jousting track in front of a small pavilion, which could house around fifty spectators.

Walter Bane walked, or rather waddled, down the steps of the main entrance to the house. A couple of spearman flanked him, as if they were lictors and he an emperor. His clothes were made from the finest materials but were just shy of fitting him properly. They stretched, or sagged, across his body. A gem-encrusted sword, which had witnessed far more ceremonies than battlefields over the years, hung from his hip and bounced off his leg inelegantly. His features could appear both flabby and flinty at the same time. His wispy hair yearned to cover the whole of his scalp – but failed. Liver spots mottled his temples and hands. Walter Bane was a man who desired to be obeyed constantly but commanded little natural authority. Staff and sycophants had laughed at his jokes and hung on his words over the years. They had convinced Bane of his importance, his greatness. He believed he was destined to lead "his" people to greatness too. Although he stated that his cause was to invade England in order to rescue his imprisoned King, James I, Walter Bane spent as much time working out how he could depose the King, once James was returned to his kingdom.

The self-satisfied grin across the Scottish nobleman's face was as long and curved as a scimitar, Chaucer fancied. Bane licked his lips and rubbed his hands together.

"What an unexpected pleasure to see you here, Thomas. Although what is not so surprising is to capture you as a spy. It seems that the apple did not fall far from the tree, given your father's calling as an agent of the crown."

Garyn grunted and moved his prisoner forward, to prompt him to address his captor.

"I met your own father on more than one occasion, Walter. He was well educated, decent and amiable. It seems that the apple has fallen into another orchard, in relation to yourself," Chaucer drily replied. His contempt for the Scottish demagogue strengthened his resolve not to be intimidated by him.

The smile fell from Bane's lips.

"It's good to see you have retained your sense of humour, despite your perilous situation, Thomas. There will be little opportunity for laughter, however, after I introduce you to my French ally. As triumphant as I now feel, I also cannot help but feel pity for you all too," Bane stated, shaking his head a little in regret. The nobleman, for a brief moment or so, appeared to feel genuinely sorry for his captives. The thought of what Reynard of Troyes would do to his enemies sent a shiver down his spine. The zealous French agent had venom running through his veins rather than blood.

Garyn grunted and pushed a frightened Stephen Hall forward. The young archer's legs gave way and he stumbled to the ground. A few of the surrounding soldiers sniggered at the enfeebled Englishman. A film of sweat glazed his pallid face. Fear gripped what little was left of his heart, as he anticipated the fate that awaited him.

Robert Cooper helped his friend to his feet.

"Don't worry lad, you'll doubtless get a chance to stick arrows into these bastards eventually. We'll get through this. I made a promise to your parents that I'd look after you – and I intend to keep that promise."

The bowman made another promise – to himself – that he would stick an arrow into the French, bullying bastard who had knocked Hall to the ground.

12

The prisoners could hear the rain spit against the stone walls outside. The cell was as damp and chilly as a church crypt, Chaucer gloomily considered. A couple of small lamps weakly lit the chamber. The agent and bowman were chained to the back wall, facing the heavy oak door. Casks of wine and ale lined the sides of the room. Insects crawled across the rough stone floor. The ceiling was low and arched.

An hour or so after the three men were imprisoned a guard entered, unchained Stephen Hall and escorted him out. Again Thomas Chaucer tried to reassure the frightened youth that all would be well and things were going to plan but his words brought little consolation.

The two men offered up little conversion after their third companion departed. Occasionally the sound of a clinking chain could be heard as one of the prisoners repositioned themselves on the floor, to try and find a degree of comfort. Thomas Chaucer thought about his wife, Matilda. Robert Cooper thought about Grace, hoping that she could one day still be his wife. God became closer, more real, for the condemned men.

They were suddenly jolted out of their reveries by the sound of wild, high-pitched screams emanating from a room along the corridor. Cooper flinched as if he were being tortured himself. His face hardened and his nostrils flared as anger fuelled his being. The first bout of screaming lasted for ten minutes but it felt like an hour. There were firebreaks to the unholy ululations as, at first, Stephen Hall could be heard shouting – or pleading – for the torments to stop.

"I don't know anything."

The walls muffled his voice but couldn't silence his despair and agony.

The torture continued. For hours. Occasionally there were periods of eerie silence during which Reynard of Troyes ordered the attendant to revive the prisoner again.

Stephen Hall screamed out that he didn't know anything more. The French agent had extracted every sinew of available information from his victim. But he would continue to torture the young Englishman for sport, and for the benefit of his companions. The adolescent, caught up in a game which he could little comprehend, soon clung to the promise of death more than life. His body and spirit were mangled. He could no longer recall the image of Katherine, or his parents and friends.

Robert Cooper writhed in his chains, clenched his fists till his hands ached and looked as though he was about to snort fire – as each scream scorched his ears and soul. God seemed more distant. Thomas Chaucer merely clenched his jaw and suffered stoically. The usual humour and verve in his expression were absent. He too, on occasion, had tortured prisoners in the earshot of their confederates. Chaucer found himself silently praying for the young archer's end – to deliver him from a fate worse than death – and his prayers were eventually answered.

*

A short time later two mail-shirted, blood-besmirched soldiers entered carrying oil lamps, which they placed either side of the cellar. Reynard of Troyes followed them in and then, with a nod of his head, ordered them to leave. The infamous French agent appeared younger and healthier than most men in their fifties. His hair was cropped short and tonsured. His eyes were narrow, reptilian, and seemed to smile slyly of their own accord. His face was tanned, close-shaven, aside from a moustache and goatee beard. His features were handsome and distinguished. He wore a long, black surcoat of fine cloth (having removed his gore-soaked butcher's apron before entering). He was dressed like a priest, Cooper thought. And like many a priest Reynard of Troyes' zeal was fired by hatred more than love. As a boy he had hated his absent father and his peers. The latter he judged as being frivolous or sinful. He had then developed a hatred towards the English. Reynard of Troyes told himself that he loved France and his King, but he detested most of his fellow Frenchmen and believed his Charles VI to be mad or, worse, incompetent. He loved women, when the mood took him, in a carnal sense – especially young girls, who could look up to him as a priestly figure.

"Good evening gentlemen, my name is Reynard. But you have probably already surmised that," he issued, with a brief, polite smile. "I apologise for not meeting with you earlier but, as you can especially understand Thomas, I had business to attend to."

The Frenchman's English was excellent, his accent neutral. His tone was smooth, silken – persuasive.

"I understand you only too well, Reynard," Chaucer said evenly, his insides churning with wrath and grief.

"We have met before Thomas, although you may not remember the occasion. It was last spring. I was posing as an alderman and I introduced myself to you at Henry's court, out of a sense of curiosity and amusement. You are a more than competent agent Thomas, though you should have remained south of the border this time. But I am keen to get to know my English counterpart. I hope you are suitably flattered by me deeming you a rival. We spoke about wine, your father's poetry and, as all Englishmen do, we discussed the weather. How is your wife, back in Ewelme, by the way?"

The French agent laughed, a little effeminately, after he spoke, as he observed the slight surprise on Chaucer's face. Reynard paced up and down as he talked. He peered at the labels on the casks along the wall and fastidiously removed pieces of fluff and dirt from his surcoat. There was no word or gesture from him which didn't seem deliberate, no matter how insignificant. Reynard of Troyes was conscious, to the point of obsession, of appearing to be in control. He was religiously well-mannered. He could be polite, right up to the point of slitting a man's throat.

Before Chaucer could reply he was distracted by the two mail-shirted soldiers returning – and dumping the corpse of Stephen Hall on the ground. His once sweet face was bloody, pulpy – almost unrecognisable. Flesh wounds and burn marks criss-crossed his torso. A brace of flies already buzzed around the cadaver. Robert Cooper leapt forward like an enraged lion, but the thick iron chains checked his attack. He yanked them repeatedly and for a moment the agent's eyes betrayed a flicker of distress. He believed the archer might pull his shackles from the wall. But the shackles and wall mounts held. Amusement replaced distress as the dispassionate Frenchman allowed the vengeful soldier to tire himself out, physically and emotionally.

Reynard of Troyes showed how bored he was by Cooper's display by unsheathing a slim dagger and scraping away dried blood from beneath his fingernails.

Cooper had such hatred and vengeance swelling in his expression that Chaucer thought a cannonball might explode out of his chest and lay waste to all in its path. For his part Chaucer merely stared at the Frenchman with simmering disgust.

"You may eye me with a portion of displeasure and disapproval, Thomas, but we both know you have blood on your hands too. You shouldn't have let this pup run with the wolf pack. I have informants at the Tower who tell me you are also keen to be present when one of your prisoners is questioned. You may well consider me a kindred spirit. Few people can know you like I know you. From one tradesman to another, so to speak, I should tell you a bit about my session with your young archer. I first sliced open his nose with this knife, which was given to me as a gift by the dauphin. Phillipe here, standing to my left, then branded the inside of his thighs and – how do you say it? – genitals. Your companion relieved himself at this point. The truth will out, as will the contents of a man's bowels. He also unburdened himself of information, though that hardly tempered our zeal.

"Once we revived the boy, after he passed out, I inserted a bodkin into his eye, from an arrow from his own quiver. Phillipe then flayed him and we sealed up the wounds using hot wax and a branding iron. As you can imagine, I have worked up quite an appetite. As such I would like to invite you to dinner, Thomas, or to what passes for dinner here. I am starting to regret not bringing my cook along on this assignment. We may both be tortured this evening.

"As for you, archer, you should stay here and save your strength. You will be putting your skills to the test tomorrow. You will be pitching your longbow against my lieutenant's crossbow. Albert is much looking forward to besting you. Perhaps we could strike a wager, Thomas, in regards to the competition. I know how fond the English are of betting, as exemplified by your own monarch, who is about to gamble away his own life and kingdom."

Again the Frenchman laughed, or rather tittered. Partly he was amusing himself in earnest, but partly it was an act. For years Reynard of Troyes had considered himself to be an actor upon a stage, whether he was playing the part of the neglected bastard, the brilliant but modest theology student, the obsequious courtesan or the cultured diplomat. He enjoyed creating and manipulating peoples' perceptions of him, inspiring thoughts and emotions in them.

Despite Troyes' proclivity to conceal his true character and intentions he desired to be honest with the English agent, to flex certain muscles in his make-up which he so seldom exercised. Thomas Chaucer, given the similar role he played in life, might be one of the few people in the world capable of sympathising with him. He also knew that by the same time tomorrow Chaucer would be dead and any secrets he shared would go with him to the grave.

13

The dining room was well lit. Even the mean-spirited Walter Bane felt he could be profligate with lamp oil. The damp-streaked walls were decorated with fading tapestries and rusty weapons. The host often told his guests that the latter were trophies won by his antecedents whilst campaigning with Robert the Bruce. But really they were just rusty weapons.

Reynard of Troyes and Thomas Chaucer sat either end of a long, pine table which had been painted black.

"Two's company, three's a crowd, as your saying goes," the French agent amiably remarked, making reference to the Scottish nobleman's absence. "Not only was I not keen to spend the evening in the company of our tedious host but he also would have spent half the night glowering at you in silence – and then the rest of the night berating you and your countrymen. Walter considers himself a knight, but really he is just a pawn. His one virtue is that he doesn't realise it."

Thomas Chaucer nodded in reply and looked at the two guards, flanking the Frenchman. They stood stone-faced, gargoyle-like. He would have to be as swift as Mercury and as brave as Hector to retrieve a sword from the wall, defeat the men-at-arms and slaughter his enemy. The image of Stephen Hall's disfigured countenance haunted his mind's eye still.

I'll kill the bastard. But not yet.

*

There were few people in England Henry admired more than Richard Whittington. Whittington had travelled to London from Gloucestershire with next to nothing to his name. But through his industry and amiability the mercer's apprentice became Mayor of London and a friend and financier to three kings. Whittington made his fortune from the import and export of silk and other goods. He then became a prosperous moneylender. Whittington was an astute reader of the market – and people; he knew which businesses would flourish and who could, and would, pay back a loan. Henry – and his father before him – greatly admired Whittington's character and judgement. The financier engendered trust and confidence, which made him as rare as he was precious amongst his peers. Friends became business acquaintances and business acquaintances became friends. His wealth helped free him from a culture of corruption and cronyism. The mayor couldn't be bribed and similarly had no desire to bribe anyone else. Richard Whittington was ambitious but his drive to create wealth was matched by a desire to redistribute his profits through good causes. He funded the building and restoration of a number of London's churches, financed a special ward for unmarried mothers at St Thomas' Hospital, improved the capital's sewerage system and invested in the arts and education. Whittington often gave copies of Geoffrey Chaucer's books to foreign merchants and dignitaries, as he believed in exporting English culture, along with English wool. His legislation as mayor was progressive, compassionate and costed. Whittington represented the best of London and Londoners were proud to have the banker represent them. He had served as mayor of the capital on four separate occasions.

A fire murmured in the background and wax candles, lining the finely-crafted walnut table, bathed the chamber in a welcoming glow. A neat pile of documents sat next to an ornate silver ewer. Before dinner the King and financier had discussed business matters, most notably how much the crown already owed Whittington and how much more money it could borrow. Henry expressed his sincere intention to repay the loans (not only because of a personal sense of honour, but also because he knew if he lost the trust of his friend he could also lose the trust of the aldermen in the City of London). A portrait of St Augustine hung opposite the fireplace and dominated the room. Well-attired servants entered and unobtrusively filled wine cups or took empty plates back to the kitchen. Henry and Richard sat either end of the table in a small, intimate dining room at Henry's palace in Kennington.

Whittington's build was neither imposing nor puny. He was a man whose deeds, rather than his features or clothes, were remarkable. His voice, despite his advanced years, was strong and authoritative – but never harsh. The light from the candles reflected in Whittington's bright, intelligent eyes, yet time and sorrow lined the rest of the older man's features. Or was it grief? Whittington had not quite been the same since his wife, Anne, passed away. Their marriage had been childless, but far from loveless. Whittington had endeavoured to fend off his sorrows through work, but at the end of the day he would come home to his grief. "My marriage to Anne was the best contract I ever entered into," Whittington had once declared to his friend, hoping to encourage the then young prince not to marry just the first princess – or dowry – which came along.

"I must apologise again for the misunderstanding with my exchequer," Henry said, referring to Richard being asked to pay tax twice on a consignment of goods he had imported. The customs officer had been as zealous as he was incompetent and Whittington had appealed to Henry to intervene.

"I do not blame you. Perhaps I should not blame your exchequer either. A taxman who doesn't want to tax would be akin to him questioning his own existence. And he lacks the wisdom to do that, I dare say," the merchant remarked. Whittington had recently argued to Thomas Chaucer that taxation, more than anything else, is the enemy of peace and prosperity – a rapacious dragon, which is never satisfied, turning enterprise and industry to ash, but he prudently failed to share this view with his King. "All is well now. As much as your exchequer may have been lacking in good sense please pass on my compliments to your cook. The spiced partridge and cherry compote were particularly fine. I am, quite literally, eating like a king. Thank you."

There were few people in England Richard Whittington admired more than his King. At the beginning of his career the merchant had supplied Richard II with the finest silk robes for his wardrobe, as well as financial advice. Unfortunately the King only treasured the former. Whittington didn't mourn too much when Henry Bolingbroke replaced Richard on the throne. It was during this period when Whittington first noticed the young prince. He was inquisitive and personable, displaying a rare diligence in his studies and military training. Despite brief periods of waywardness, during which the prince took advantage of the pleasures of women and wine, the young Henry displayed a remarkable amount of laudable traits which led Richard to believe he would become a worthy monarch. "He's worth investing both time and capital in," Whittington had confided to his wife. "Wine and women no longer weaken his sense of purpose, indeed rumour has it that he has remained celibate since his coronation. His piety is genuine, as is his talent for military leadership. Henry will eclipse his father – and maybe even his great-grandfather."

The aged merchant stared at Henry across the table with avuncular fondness. The two men hosted one another for dinner half a dozen times a year.

"I should be the one thanking you, Richard. Without your loans and patronage my soldiers would not be able to eat in the forthcoming campaign," Henry said, grateful for the merchant's support. Not only did the former mayor pledge money for Henry's war chest, but he encouraged other financiers in the capital to loan money to the crown at a fair rate of interest.

"Is there no chance of peace?" Whittington asked, already mourning the loss of life and commerce. He understood the arguments for war but still couldn't celebrate the outbreak of the conflict. He had seen too many wounded, destitute soldiers populating the streets of London over the years. Too many women who had been widowed and too many children who had been orphaned. Wars still have a lease of life – and death – after the fighting stops, Whittington lamented.

"I am bound for Winchester tomorrow to meet with French peace envoys. They will put forward a proposal and I will put forward a counter proposal. We will both parley but both know that there is nothing more to be said. War is inevitable. The army will be on French soil within the month," the King said, with a measure of resignation, relief and resolve.

Whittington nodded but inwardly sighed.

War is inevitable. Like death and taxes. If we do not attack the French the French will attack us...

"God intends me to unite the kingdoms of England and France," Henry added, talking to himself as much as his guest.

Whittington was not so sure God was concerned with such earthly matters. Yet he believed Henry concerned himself with God. Was it a curse or a blessing? Time would tell.

*

Reynard of Troyes waited for the servants to leave – after they had placed the food on the table and refilled the guests' pewter goblets with wine – before speaking again. No doubt their host had charged his staff with reporting back anything they heard, the Frenchman thought. He briefly pursed his lips, as he considered the lacklustre cuisine in front of him, before summoning the strength to slice off a piece of leathery beef.

Thomas Chaucer paused too before eating. For whatever reason he heard his wife's voice in his head, saying grace. The agent wanted to pray too, but couldn't.

"You are not eating Thomas? I hope you do not think that I am intending to poison you. If you wish I will swap plates with you. I dare say, such is the palatability of the food, you would not know if there was poison contained in it or not. As for the wine you might yearn for it to be poisoned after tasting your first mouthful. You may then be spared from drinking anymore of the swill. Doesn't the cuisine in this sodden country ever improve? I understand if you are hesitant in trusting people. My father was the most distrustful person I ever met. He was a man of God, though he was much more devoted to himself than any deity. His soul was black, unfathomable. Like mine, you may now be thinking. He took many secrets and sins to the grave. Even on his deathbed he remained resolutely unrepentant. My father revealed he had a saying, regarding confiding in people, which he lived by, but he never trusted anyone enough to divulge it."

Reynard of Troyes remained solemn-looking for most of his speech but then broke out into a smile, amused by his own joke. As Reynard smiled Chaucer noticed a set of clean, white, sharp teeth. He thought there wouldn't be a coffin large enough to contain all the Frenchman's secrets and sins.

*

Pierre Montbron gazed out of the shutters in his room, which overlooked the Thames. The river slapped and sloshed against the weathered timbers below. A pungent smell of sulphur, mixed with ordure, filled his nostrils, but the assassin's expression remained unchanged. Tonight would be the night. His employer had sent a final, encoded confirmation – along with reliable intelligence as to the location of his target. Transport back to France, in the form of a fishing boat for him and his two confederates on the south-east coast, had also been arranged.

Montbron was neither tall nor short, portly nor slim. He was dressed neither poorly nor richly. His only distinguishing mark was a sickle-shaped birthmark on his forehead, which was concealed by a fringe of long black curls. He looked ordinary – and anonymous. Montbron and his men – Jean Villon and Bertrand Mauny – had posed as wool merchants. They paid their bills to the innkeeper, but otherwise kept out of sight and out of mind. It was a shame, however, Montbron fancied, that he had been unable to experience more of the city. London – and its populace – intrigued him. The capital was a patchwork of menace, squalor, affluence and industry. People in London seemed to walk and talk quicker than their counterparts in the country. The grimness of city life bred a grim sense of humour, to help combat misfortune. Ale, as much as the Thames, flowed through and sustained the heart of the English nation. It would be tempting to stay for the spectacle of the funeral, Montbron fancied.

But our job is to end his life, not mourn or celebrate it.

The assassin wryly smiled to himself as he recalled his meeting with Reynard of Troyes. The agent had employed him before. He called Pierre "a loyal servant of France and Charles VI". The spymaster could call Montbron anything he wanted so long as he got paid. Charles VI would truly be mad if he thought that the former soldier would work for nothing. He would be loyal insomuch as he would honour the contract.

A tendril of smoke from a house situated on the opposite bank of the Thames reminded Montbron of the way smoke spiralled up out of his chimney at home, on his farm just outside of Bernay. A pang of sorrow slid through the assassin's ribcage as he remembered – and missed – his wife and children: Isabelle, Arnaud and Gilles. Montbron consoled himself with the thought that the income from the current contract meant he could spend the remainder of the year with his family. He could also afford to purchase the field bordering the north-west corner of his farm. Pierre Montbron was as much a sheep farmer as an assassin. The discrepancy between his two livelihoods didn't trouble him. Indeed there was more chance of Montbron losing sleep over too little rainfall than the thought of slitting the throat of a woman or child he was contracted to kill. Half his year was spent being a loving husband and devoted father. He also took care of his aged parents and looked after his niece and nephew, who had lost their parents to the plague. Back home his closest friend was the village priest. They would share a bottle of wine and stay up at night, debating the nature of good and evil or playing dice. Montbron's generosity funded a small school and repaired the spire of the local chapel, which had been struck by lightning. He was a good Christian, by all accounts, for six months of the year.

The room was spacious enough to meet their needs. The assassins had few clothes and possessions, aside from those needed to complete their mission.

Montbron instructed his companions to check and recheck the actions of their specially designed small crossbows. Swords and daggers were sharpened, one last time. The trio had killed before and they would kill again. Their hearts were as hard as the tips of their crossbow bolts.

The three men donned their grey, hooded cloaks and nodded to each other to convey their readiness.

Tonight would be the night.

*

Reynard of Troyes mopped up the blood from his slab of beef. Afterwards he wiped his mouth with a white, silk-inlaid, linen napkin which he had brought over with him from France. Chaucer noticed how well maintained his beard was. The Englishman rubbed his fingers along his own beard and promised himself he would trim it once the mission was over.

If my head hasn't been somehow trimmed off before that time.

"You are an educated man Thomas, a man who hopefully values rationality over prejudice. Surely you must see that England will be a safer and more prosperous nation once it becomes a vassal of France? You will have a greater voice in trade matters with the rest of Europe. What will it profit you to separate yourself from the continent and become a little Englander? Henry is like some petulant son, rebelling against his father, in his desire to do battle with France. Does he believe himself to be some kind of Prometheus? You are a young nation – in many ways the father of your nation and its culture was Edward III – and with youth comes folly," Reynard of Troyes argued, sneering a little as he mentioned the English King's name.

"You have forgotten about a monarch before Edward, Alfred the Great, who helped to forge little England originally. And you are underestimating Henry. Sometimes sons eclipse their fathers, as you yourself have done I dare say," Thomas said, offering up his own knowing yet polite smile. "Despite all your machinations I still believe Henry will make it to France and unseat your masters. Edmund de Lacy spoke of your plot to assassinate Henry or have others depose him through a coup. I should tell you that I have increased the guard around him, to thwart any plans to assassinate him."

The French agent tossed back his head and laughed, whilst also clapping his hands.

"Thomas, I thought better of you. Even if I am underestimating Henry I can say with some confidence that you have underestimated me. The capture of Edmund de Lacy has proved as much of a blessing as a curse. Not only, due to him, do I now have the pleasure of your company, but the charmless whelp was a wonderful unwitting conveyor of false intelligence. You underestimate the scope and ambition of my mission. The gold aboard my vessel is not just purposed to pay our host, in order to fund a Scottish army to cross the border. Some will be set aside for the fugitive Owen Glendower, so he can continue the fight from the west. Bane has also been tasked to purchase the loyalty of the Percies to foment rebellion. Yet even without my prompting a plot to oust Henry is already afoot, involving Sir Thomas Grey and Lord Scrope. They will offer bribes to a number of noblemen and captains in the army to turn against their King and side with the Earl of March – the true successor to the English throne. Henry will soon be dead or deposed, I warrant, with little assistance from myself.

"But I have had a hand in other schemes. Even St George will not be able to slay the amount of dragons I am about to set loose across this cursed isle. A civil war will bleed this country dry. But should Henry somehow manage to muster a defence of his realm and sail to France then the white sands of my country's beaches will turn red with English blood. My informants have been able to secure copies of a number of contracts, between Henry and his captains, which reveal that his fleet will sail for Gascony. Preparations are being made so that Henry's troops will fall into the jaws of the French army. I find it ironic somewhat. Richard II lost his kingdom whilst on an ill-considered campaign against the Irish. When he returned the usurper Henry IV had taken advantage of his absence. Now it could prove the case that the usurper's son will lose his crown from leaving his kingdom for an ill-considered campaign against France. The sins of the father will indeed be revisited on the son. And if Henry returns he will discover a new usurper occupying the throne...

"Your face is a picture Thomas. I only wish I could have brought a competent artist along with me to preserve your confounded expression for posterity. Did you believe that the likes of the Earl of March and Lord Scrope were loyal to Henry? Surely not. Loyalty is a commodity, like timber or grain. It can be bought and sold. Your weakness, it seems, is that you still possess a kernel of faith in God or, worse, the divinity of men. I, however, do not deal in faith. I deal in knowledge. To see is to believe. The Bible tells us that 'He who increases knowledge increases sorrow', but sorrows will be heaped upon England and Henry because of a lack of knowledge, not a surfeit of it...

"Your silence speaks volumes, Thomas. I thought the son of the great Geoffrey Chaucer might prove more talkative. You are as mute as the young archer in the cellar. My apologies. That was a joke in poor taste. But you must feel akin to Sisyphus. You have pushed your rock, or plans, up a hill only to see them tumble back down and come to nothing. But, please, tell me your thoughts before I unveil one last surprise. I feel like I have been lecturing you all evening. Tell me something. You have the stage. Lecture me, Thomas," Reynard of Troyes exclaimed, the wine and sense of triumph fuelling his buoyant mood. Troyes wanted to defeat his counterpart in every way possible. He wanted to break Chaucer's spirit before breaking his body.

"You should have more faith, Reynard. That's my advice. Your paid-for traitors and mercenaries may take up arms against Henry, but the rest of England will stand by him. There may be battles to be fought, but there will be no civil war. Henry has mobilised a nation, not just an army. The country has fed off his industry, not lies. He commands respect, not fear. You could offer myself – or my other archer in the cellar – all the riches of Croesus but you know full well you would not be able to purchase our loyalty, as if it were a commodity. You are still underestimating Henry – and the English," Chaucer said, with iron in his soul and equanimity in his voice.

"As you will soon see Thomas, you have underestimated myself far more than I have Henry," Reynard of Troyes posited. "Philip, would you fetch our most royal guest?" The gargoyle immediately sprang to life at his master's command.

Chaucer heard the heavy footsteps across the tiled floor. Accompanying them was the lighter tread of another figure. Chaucer was genuinely intrigued about the Frenchman's mystery guest. Had the agent captured a significant royal personage? Would he hold him for ransom? Had he secured the allegiance of a foreign prince?

Reynard bowed his head over his plate but subtly turned his eyes upwards to register the reaction of the English spy.

For a brief, haunting, moment Thomas Chaucer believed he was seeing a ghost. His jaw dropped, his cutlery fell out of his hands. A feeling of the sublime rose up in his chest, choking him of the ability to speak or think clearly. He knew that the figure standing before him couldn't possibly be Richard II but …

"Thomas, let me introduce you to your once and future King, Richard of Bordeaux, eldest son of Edward of Woodstock and Joan of Kent, grandson of Edward III. Your knee doesn't seem to be kissing the ground. Or perhaps you know the man as Gilbert Radcliffe, an actor I discovered during a performance of a satirical play I watched in one of your ubiquitous market towns a couple of years ago. Gilbert was of course playing the part of the tragi-comic Richard. I immediately hired the man for the role of his life. As an actor Gilbert will play any part should the fee be substantial enough. For the past two years he has been schooled in the life, mannerisms, tastes and character of Richard. I have arranged for him to attend court and note several key persons the King will need to know and recognise. He can write a passable counterfeit of Richard's signature. He can recall key episodes of Richard's childhood and reign. Staff and courtiers have been bought to bear witness, upon the Bible and the souls of their children, that the man before us is Richard of Bordeaux. I dare say that Gilbert can even quote your father's poetry better than you, Thomas. There will of course be doubters that Richard has returned from hiding. But enough supporters of Richard – and enemies of Henry – will rally to the standard of the white hart. I still have to finalise his wardrobe and write his lines for his first few appearances, but once my actor makes his entrance on the stage news of Richard's return will spread across the country faster than the plague," Reynard of Troyes proclaimed, gazing with pride at the false King.

The regal-looking figure in front of Chaucer wore an expensively dyed purple coat with embroidered cuffs. His fine, curly hair shone in the lamplight. *All that's missing is a crown.* Chaucer shook his head slightly in disbelief and awe. The mystery behind Herbert Molyneaux's commission to produce white hart brooches could now been explained. The French agent was right. People would flock towards Richard's standard. His likeness alone would be proof enough for some of the population. Henry's authority would be undermined. Two words scythed through Chaucer's heart, like a bolt of lightning.

Civil war.

"But you must also hear my mummer speak, Thomas. Say something," the beaming French agent instructed, turning to Gilbert Radcliffe – who stood awaiting his cue.

"A monarch should never be bidden to speak, but rather he bids other people to," the former pantomime player smoothly and haughtily remarked, arching his eyebrow and peering down his slender nose.

"Excellent, excellent," the Frenchman enthused, applauding the actor. "Well done Gilbert, or rather I should say Richard. I have no right to force a sovereign to attend upon me so enjoy the rest of your dinner in your room, though the cuisine is scarce worthy of royalty." The agent waved his hand, directing the actor to exit his stage.

Thomas Chaucer had encountered Richard II on a number of occasions, having first accompanied his father to court in his capacity as a poet and agent to the crown. It had now been fifteen years since Richard's passing (rumour had it that Henry Bolingbroke poisoned or starved his cousin to death so as not to provide any physical evidence of his murder). Should Richard have lived he could easily have looked like the actor standing in front of him. Radcliffe possessed the same fine, almost feminine, features of the late monarch. He was the same height, and had cultivated Richard's regal bearing and supercilious demeanour. Richard had been a great patron of the arts, a loving father and had shown great personal courage in his youth during the Peasant's Revolt. Yet he had not fulfilled his early promise, indeed his early triumph seemed to sow the seeds of conceit and arrogance into his character. The young monarch had proclaimed himself an instrument of God when, in reality, he had acted more as an instrument for his own interests and those of his favourites. His personality became increasingly unstable and vindictive, his reign tyrannical. Richard had antagonised sections of the aristocratic, mercantile and peasant classes alike. The country had desired to throw off the yoke of its sovereign and, in Henry Bolingbroke, it found its champion. Yet the King was the king and a number of his noblemen – and beneficiaries – called the usurper a usurper. Some plotted against Henry – in the name of the true sovereign and Plantagenet line – and some proclaimed that Richard of Bordeaux was still alive. Some even drew parallels between Richard and Christ, with both figures condemned to death at the age of thirty-three. But both would also rise again, they believed.

"It seems I have underestimated you. You deserve even more applause than your actor companion. Not only do you possess a pawn, in the shape of Walter, but you have managed to insert the piece of a king onto the board, under your control," Chaucer said amiably, still somewhat dumbfounded by the French agent's audacious powers of manipulation and infiltration. He was also scared, for Henry and his countrymen. Reynard wanted to condemn to death his sovereign, language and laws. Wipe England off the map.

"I am pleased to see you haven't lost your sense of humour over my reveal, Thomas. That really would have been a tragedy. The danger, of course ,may be that I have too many pieces in play on the board. The Earl of March, Walter Bane, Owen Glendower, Richard II, the Dauphin, the Percies – who will be crowned sovereign next? Yet though my stratagems may seemingly contradict one another my ambition remains simple and consistent. At present I do not much care who sits on the throne of England, just so long as it isn't Henry. Let me quote Cicero: "Money provides the sinews of war". The gold I am using to form my alliance against Henry was originally set aside to fund a peace agreement and Catherine Valoir's dowry. Your so-called "wise" king has forsaken peace and a queen in the name of satisfying his dreams of military glory – of scratching an itch. For such folly he deserves to forsake his kingdom," the French agent said – almost hissing in disdain as he did so.

"And what of the kingdom of Scotland?"

"Indeed. What of it? The country is filled with inebriated savages. The women are as hard-faced as granite. France will civilise it. Firstly its people will be made to speak French. At least then the rest of Europe will be able to understand them. Scotland wishes to rid itself of the English yoke by enslaving itself to the French. Any such kingdom deserves its fate. We call it 'the old alliance', but that does not mean it is a partnership of equals. You should be thankful for Walter and I turning the Scottish against the English, otherwise it would have always been akin to a whining, costly wife. You must know that your two neighbouring nations will never have an entirely happy marriage. A divorce now will be of mutual benefit," the agent argued, believing that France best knew how to manage Scotland – like a wife, the country needed to be governed with a firm hand.

"Marriages can and should endure, even if they are not entirely happy ones. As much as Walter may claim to be capable of leading his people he does not represent them. I will be the first to ridicule a Scot – I have not lost my sense of humour – but he should not be put in the same stocks as our ignoble host. Walter is rapacious, mendacious and pompous. In stark contrast I have found most of his countrymen to be prudent, plain-speaking and affable. They are God-fearing, as opposed to Walter who considers himself to *be* a God. The Scottish can fight hard, work hard and drink hard. Walter is only capable of the latter. You may well be underestimating the Scottish people as much as you are Henry."

Reynard of Troyes yawned in reply to his Chaucer's comments but then forced a polite smile. Inwardly he sighed. *He has too much faith. He's a lost cause. What a shame.* A part of the bishop's son had hoped to convert the Englishman to his crusade. He could have been a valuable asset. Chaucer had the ear of the King. *But he is too virtuous. Too foolish. I do not have the time and energy to break his spirit. I will have to be content with breaking his body instead.*

*

The temperature dropped a little and Henry called for an attendant to stoke the fire. The King offered his guest a blanket but Whittington replied that he was fine. He didn't wish to cause a fuss or be treated as an old man too much. A small table containing a jug of wine and jug of milk (the latter of which Whittington asked to take home to give to his cat) stood between the two men as they sat around the hearth and continued to discuss the imminent war with France.

"I do not doubt that you have spent a great many years planning the campaign against France. But winning any war may prove to be not even half the battle. France is already a divided land on the brink of civil war. Its gentry bleed the people dry and the church tax what little money they have left. The crown is heavily in debt and the merchant classes are treated with suspicion – or downright contempt – by the aristocracy. The Burgundian and Armagnac factions could either unite against you, or force you to fight on two fronts if you win the French crown. I know you to be a keen student of history. Blood begets blood. Wars beget wars. Your campaign in France may turn into a conflict without end. Ask yourself this question: should the French King land upon these shores would you expect the people of England to ever wholly submit to him? Would they not oppose him until he sails back to France – defeated? And you will still have to attend to your own people – and enemies – here. As tall as you are, even you cannot bestride the sea like a colossus and rule two kingdoms at the same time," Whittington warned, emboldened by his King's instructions to speak freely.

Henry hung his head and nodded. The sense of burden closed around him again, as if he were putting his head in a noose. He appreciated his friend's candour and pragmatism. Henry harboured every doubt – and more – that Whittington had about winning the war and equally winning the peace. But he had faith...

"When I was a boy my uncle, Thomas, gave me a set of painted wooden knights on horseback. I played with them so much that the paint rubbed off against my fingers within a month. I would endlessly move my troops into battle and outflank an imagined enemy, or relive the campaigns of Caesar and Charlemagne. I would gallop the wooden horses in and cheer as my forces, inevitably, won the day. I can understand how some might deem me a warmonger or a conceited brat, just playing at war. But I am no longer a boy and I would be doing my soldiers a great disservice if I thought of them as mere toys for me to play with.

"France wishes to dominate Europe and subjugate England. Our enemy conspires against us on a daily basis, fuelling discontent in Wales and Scotland, raiding our ships, bullying foreign diplomats and merchants to act against our interests. This country's fate will not be to serve as a jewel in a French empire. I must draw my sword against France before she draws her sword against me. But my ambition is to free her rather than destroy her. As you have said, France is divided. I can unite her.

"First I will take possession of those lands in Normandy and Aquitaine which were taken from us. The region can then act as a beacon to others, of good governance and prosperity. I can win a battle with a sword but not a country. Trade, laws, institutions and merriment must win over hearts and minds.

And the people must be given more than just bread and circuses. I know that there are those at court who cynically sneer at the ideals of chivalry and patriotism. They would argue that the idea of Englishness is outmoded and should be consigned to the history books. But we should carry our sense of history with us, like a lamp to guide our way. It is an Englishman's love of duty and liberty which will put fire in his belly to defeat the French – and similarly temper the excesses of his own King.

"But being the King I must lead. I once spent an afternoon in the company of Geoffrey Chaucer. I was just a boy. He drank and spoke freely to those present. The former diplomat was too old to care about offending people. No one could quite tell when he was being satirical or in earnest – and I warrant it amused him to confound his audience in such a fashion. But he took me by the shoulders towards the end of the day and spoke to me solemnly. He told me that nobility has its responsibilities – and that noble traits are earned as opposed to inherited. He said I would one day be in a position to lead men. I should be responsible for their standard of living, as well as their lives on the battlefield. 'Be the best that you can be,' he said. 'If gold should rust, what will lead do?' Of course after Chaucer spoke he dismissed his own words of wisdom, citing that it was just the drink talking. Wine truth. Which he added was the most enjoyable type of truth."

A rare smile lit up the sovereign's sombre features. As he spoke the fervour in his eyes rivalled the brightness of the fire, Whittington fancied.

He is right. France should not be allowed to dominate Europe. No one kingdom should. Perhaps it is England's role in Europe to hold the balance of power rather than be the ruling power. He is worth investing in ... Not bankrupting.

"I want you to know that it is not the wine talking now, Hal. If I never earned another penny again – and lost four-fifths of all my wealth – I could still live comfortably. I know that you have paid me interest, so to speak, over the years. But I have also paid an interest in you. I know that you have provided capital and goodwill to a number of the good causes I have funded. You have behaved honourably towards the church and City of London. Two institutions that, I am all too aware, do not always value a sense of honour. I know how, at the time of my wife's passing, you ordered your physician to attend upon her. Although the gesture did not mean much to the disease which took her it meant a great deal to me. A king with a conscience comes along once every century. Which is why I dread what may happen after your passing. I have dedicated half of my life to improving the lives of Londoners. I do not want my legacy to be that of bankrupting a king and country. These loans have given you the means to conduct your campaign against France. But, though loans sometimes appear to grant a man his freedom, they too often become burdens. It is the province of God to absolve you of your sins but thankfully it lays within my power to absolve you of your debts," Whittington said, lifting the bound pile of documents from the dining table and throwing them onto the fire.

Henry's mouth and heart lay open. The fire, as if knowing how much wealth the papers represented, came to life. The King sat, stupefied, as the flames curled, crimpled and blackened the documents. Just when Henry believed he couldn't be more grateful to his friend, he was. More than the roaring fire, the portrait of St Augustine, or King himself, Richard Whittington dominated the room. Though most remained, some of Henry's almighty burden was lifted.

Henry rose to his feet and then bowed down before Whittington on one knee and warmly clasped his guest's hand.

"Surely, never had a king such a subject," Henry exclaimed, touched and overawed. Tears welled in his eyes.

"Surely, sire, never had a subject such a king."

*

The light from the oil lamps was fading when Thomas Chaucer was returned to the cellar. The body of Stephen Hall remained in the middle of the room. Blood had oozed out of the body and then congealed. More than two dozen flies now swirled around the corpse. A fetid smell, like rotten cabbage mixed with rancid fish, hung in the air.

Robert Cooper sat, slumped, against the wall. He stared into space and appeared so lifeless that many might have mistook him for a corpse as well.

His expression was vacant but Chaucer knew the man. His innards were a furnace, being stoked by vengeance and grief.

Chaucer was not the only one who had made a vow to kill the French agent. Revenge, more than hope or his love for Grace, was sustaining the soldier. Even more than to a merciful God to deliver him the bowman prayed to a just God to damn the French spy. Cooper had spent much of the evening gazing at his butchered companion – and remembering him at his best. If he remembered his friend then, in some way, he lived on, the archer reasoned.

Chaucer sat down next to his listless soldier. There was little, in terms of prospects or rank, separating the two men now. They breathed, grieved, as one. Cooper considered that there was scarce chance of them lasting the day tomorrow. He promised himself he would take at least one of the enemy with him if the Frenchman decided to torture and execute him.

"What are we supposed to do now?" Robert quietly asked after a long period of silence.

"Have faith Robert. Have faith," Chaucer replied, fraternally clasping his fellow captive on the shoulder. The hint of a smile played upon his lips as the agent spoke but it was quickly swallowed up by darkness as the last oil lamp died out.

14

Henry invited his friend to stay overnight in the guest wing of the royal residence, but Whittington wanted to return home. He had work to catch up on in the morning. As much as he was happy to forgive Henry his debts he had no intention of writing off those of other merchants and financiers.

A polished, bulbous moon hung in the clear night sky. It was late. Even the nightingales and tawny owls were sleeping in their nests. The section of the road which ran from Kennington to London Bridge was largely free from travellers. Whittington lived on the north side of the river. The road was well maintained as the King often used the highway. As well as being accompanied by the driver of his pageant wagon Whittington travelled with two attendants, who doubled up as guards. They rode on horseback, flanking the carriage. The pageant wagon was comfortable and sturdy but not, like those in fashion with the gentry, gaudy or ostentatious.

Whittington sat up with his driver, with a cloak around his shoulders and a blanket across his lap. The driver's name was George Page. He was the son of the merchant's previous coachman. The Page family had now been in his service, in one way or another, for nearly three decades. Page was a Londoner, born and bred. No matter what the weather he always wore a sunny disposition. There was an even greater glow about George Page of late due to his wife having given birth to their first child, Peter.

"Perhaps I will live long enough to have young Peter drive me too, one day," Whittington wryly said, with a wink, as the two men made conversation. The merchant knew that there was little chance of him living for another ten years though, let alone more than that.

My time is nearly up. The bell will toll, no matter how much we would like to turn a deaf ear to it.

But the prospect of his death did not frighten him, for heaven would indeed be heaven if he could see his wife Anne again, Whittington mused.

*

Pierre Montbron was satisfied with the horses he had arranged. He had ridden better specimens in his time but the three sorrel mares would suffice. They just needed to keep pace with the wagon and get them to the coast in good time.

Although Montbron was initially troubled by the news of Edmund de Lacy's capture (he was less troubled by news of his death) the assassin reasoned that the English were unaware of his target, but he still took the precaution of ordering his men to change their appearances slightly (by shaving their beards, where applicable, and cutting their hair short).

Montbron had ordered Mauny to ride ahead and keep watch at the palace. His instructions were to ride back when Whittington was about to mount his coach. Montbron knew his quarry, having stalked the old man on more than one occasion, and believed that he would return home for the night rather than stay with the King. Like most people the merchant was a creature of habit. He also predicted that Whittington would be travelling with just his coachman and two attendants.

Montbron waited with his confederate, Jean Villon. Villon had dismounted from his mare and began to sigh audibly and pace up and down as he waited for the return of his comrade. Villon had argued, more than once, that the merchant would now be staying the evening with the King and it was pointless to tarry any longer. Montbron, growing impatient with his fellow assassin, offered him a hard, withering look. Villon pursed his lips but stopped sighing and pacing.

Tonight would be the night.

Jean Villon's short, stocky figure meant than he was almost comically dwarfed by his horse. The man's ongoing gambling debts meant Montbron could always call upon the former soldier when he needed him. Villon's rough, leathery features were as unappealing as most of his character traits. As Montbron sat on his horse, towering over the short assassin, he couldn't help but notice how much the moonlight gleamed off his confederate's bald head.

In contrast to his fellow assassin Bertrand Mauny had such a slim, willowy build that Montbron sometimes fancied that a gust of wind might blow the young man over. In some ways the youth was serving an apprenticeship with Montbron. Mauny was willing to learn and dutifully followed orders without complaint. The former medical student realised that he could earn far more money taking lives than saving them. Montbron soon noticed Mauny enjoyed killing. He often volunteered to deliver the killing blow – and there was a strange light in his eyes as he stabbed or shot his victims. He enjoyed the power. He enjoyed being vicious. Montbron had even once observed Mauny lick his lips, with relish, as blood from a target had splattered across his face. But as long as the young man's professionalism outweighed his viciousness the assassin would allow his apprentice to have his fun.

Bertrand Mauny rode back towards his paymaster and breathlessly communicated that Whittington and his men were approaching. Montbron reiterated that their first attack, using their crossbows, should concern itself with eliminating Whittington's driver and guards. The old man would be incapable of fight or flight once his attendants were dead. At the end of Montbron's speech Mauny requested to be the one to slit the Englishman's throat and cut off his finger (to retrieve his ring and seal, which they needed to pass over to Reynard of Troyes). Montbron assented to the request but added that he should kill the old man quickly. Not only did Pierre Montbron appreciate efficiency but, in a rare concession to compassion, he had no desire to see the merchant suffer unnecessarily.

*

The clip-clop of horses' hooves reminded Whittington of the sound of his new-fangled clock at home. It would soon be his time. After thinking about his death – philosophically doing so, with little or no gloominess – Whittington turned his attention to his will again. He did not regret absolving Henry of his debts, indeed he wanted his wealth to create and sustain an even greater legacy. Some men desired to die owing money to everybody. But Whittington wanted his capital outlive him. He believed that money could be a force for good. He would set up a fund, through his trade guild, for the purpose of helping good causes and good people in London long after his death.

The former Lord Mayor was distracted from his thoughts by the sound of horsemen approaching.

*

Bertrand Mauny's nostrils flared as he rode towards the wagon and his victim. All three assassins kicked their heels into the flanks of their mounts. They held their reins in one hand and their crossbows in the other.

The guards' eyes widened in alarm as they saw the silhouettes of the weapons. There would be no time to turn the wagon around and retreat to the safety of Henry's palace. They would be unable to outrun their assailants, but they were sufficiently devoted to their paymaster not to want to desert him. Page flicked the reins of his team of two dapple-grey horses and Whittington's guards drew their swords. But it was too late.

The first crossbow bolt, fired by Mauny, struck the coachman's shoulder. George Page, with little regard for his own life, had been about to throw himself across his employer's body to protect him. The bolt buried itself through flesh and the wooden backrest of his seat. The shock and pain of the injury caused the driver to lose consciousness.

Montbron and Villon kept their heads as Whittington's guards galloped towards them, their polished swords glinting in the night. Their battle cries (briefly) permeated through the air. There was little chance of the veteran assassins missing their targets – and they didn't. The short missiles shot out faster than a serpent's tongue and bit into the chests of the guards like fangs. The two attendants fell from their mounts. Silenced.

The coach slowed to a standstill. The assassins trotted towards their target. They didn't feel the need to reload their crossbows, save for Mauny. The merchant was all but a corpse as well. Whittington's wrinkled countenance grew pale in the moonlight but he did not cower in the face of the assassins, whom he mistook for common thieves and murderers. He closed his eyes briefly, in resignation and prayer, but then opened them again to take in the landscape of the city he loved so dearly. Save for seeing his wife again, it was unlikely that heaven would hold a fairer vision for the old merchant. London had been both a father and a son to him over the years. Whittington had helped shape the capital, and the city – and its wonderfully diverse inhabitants – had helped shape him in return.

A strong gust of wind howled through some nearby trees as if nature were rehearsing to mourn the great Englishman's death.

The pimple-faced Bertrand Mauny carefully placed the crossbow bolt along the slight groove on the top of the weapon. He cranked and set the deadly machine. He wiped his sweating palms on his dusty, russet-coloured breeches. His grin seemed as wide as the width as his crossbow as he stared at the elderly merchant. The assassin was torn between savouring the moment and satisfying his homicidal urge. He imagined the sound of the weapon springing to life, the hiss of the bolt in the air and the thudding noise as it found its target. The light would be extinguished from his victim's aspect and his body would slump down, as if Mauny had cut the strings on a puppet.

Richard Whittington closed his eyes and spoke to God. He pleaded to the Almighty that he would be see his late wife again and thanked him, believing that he would.

*

Henry lay on his goose-feather mattress. The chamber was decorated with two, large tapestries – one depicting the Battle of Lincoln and the other narrating the life of Edward the Confessor. A pomander and bowl of rosewater stood on the oak table next to his bed, along with a triacle, a plate of fresh fruit and a dagger. Henry wryly smiled to himself. He had been surrounded with the trappings of decadence for far too long. Instead of ornate statues, gaudy paintings and perfumed flatterers the soldier yearned to be on campaign, surrounded by hauberks, bucklers and plain-speaking men-at-arms.

Dear God, let me be worthy of you and my people. Too many kings have besmirched the annals of our history. They were thieves and tyrants, letches and cowards. They lavished the crown's riches on mistresses and favourites instead of tending to their people. They manipulated the country or were manipulated by fawning courtiers. Let me write a chapter in our history, in your name, which can be sung like a hymn and re-read with pride through the ages. If this chapter must be written in our blood, let it not be too much blood. But blood must be spilled, I know, to secure our freedom and kingdom. May this campaign save, rather than damn, us...

Henry also prayed to God to bless and protect his friend, Richard Whittington.

*

"French fuck," John Walworth proclaimed, after firing off the arrow which buried itself in Bertrand Mauny's breast – killing him instantly. Walworth's own chest was puffed out in pride as he congratulated himself on the difficult shot, taken in the dark, under pressure. The assassin had been on the cusp of killing his target. Walworth had dismounted before shooting, otherwise not even his friend Robert Cooper could have hit the mark.

Thomas Chaucer's instructions to Fordham and Walworth had been to keep a close watch on Richard Whittington – but to also keep their distance lest they alarm the merchant or scare the assassins off. Chaucer ideally wanted to capture one of the enemy. Although Chaucer had arranged for the guard around the King to increase he was confident that the monarch was not the target. It was not the custom of kings to order the assassination of fellow kings. But financiers were fair game and, more than any other candidate, England could not afford to go to war without the support of Richard Whittington.

Whilst his companion dismounted to take his shot Edward Fordham drove his chestnut rouncey on. The man-at-arms waved his sword and offered up a loud battle cry in order to attract the attention of his enemies – and distract them from their task of assassinating the aged merchant.

The sight of the long, ash arrow cutting Mauny down struck fear in Villon's own breast. English archers were the scourge of the French and Villon had experienced their murderous, mass volleys on more than one occasion. The stocky Frenchman squinted to try and see the numbers they were facing, but he quickly gave up the task when another shaft whooshed past his ear. Enough was enough. As much as the mercenary owed loyalty to Montbron he had an even greater loyalty towards his self-preservation. The taking of the English merchant's life was not worth his own demise.

"We should go," the gruff assassin shouted. He did not wait for a reply. Villon wheeled his horse around and commenced to gallop away from the danger. Rather than ride back to the capital the Frenchman decided to cut across a field, which bordered the road, to make his escape.

Montbron ignored his retreating companion, scrivener-focused as he was on the approaching horseman. He discarded his crossbow, knowing that he would be unable to reload the weapon before his enemy was upon him, and drew his perfectly balanced sword, made from Spanish steel. Montbron sized his opponent up. The Englishman appeared to be no stranger to combat, but he was confident of besting his enemy. In the background the assassin saw a large archer giving chase to Villon across the field. It barely troubled Montbron whether the bowman would catch and kill him. His main concerns now were to complete his mission, receive the rest of his money and get back home to his wife and family. The sword-wielding English horseman stood in the way of his aims – but not for long, Montbron vowed.

The ground shook as the two men thundered towards each other. No quarter would be asked for or given. The combatants made two passes at each other before engaging one another close to. Montbron attacked with both savagery and skill, but Fordham matched his opponent blow for blow as the two men slashed their swords at one another. Richard Whittington was an audience of one as he remained on the coach, confused as he was perturbed by events. He flinched with every loud, clanging clash of blades.

The deadlock was broken as the Frenchman kicked his opponent backwards and then stabbed the flank of Fordham's horse. The rouncey suddenly reared up on its hind legs and threw its rider. Fordham's sword span off in an unknown direction. The man-at-arms landed on his back – slightly disorientated and winded, his pride more wounded than his body. Thankfully his mount remained on its feet – Fordham had known more than one soldier who had been crushed to death by a falling horse.

Pierre Montbron looked down upon the defeated Englishman. A wisp of a smile played upon his thin lips. His opponent had fought well – but not well enough. The assassin was tempted to finish him off, before finally dealing with the merchant, but the decision was made for him as Fordham rose to his feet and sped away.

The assassin wheeled his whinnying mare around and faced Whittington, sidling up to the coach, his sword glistening with fresh blood in the moonlight. Tonight would still be the night.

"For France," Montbron exclaimed, in his native language, as he was about to thrust the point of his blade into the merchant.

"For England," Edward Fordham countered, as he fired Mauny's crossbow. The Englishman had only fired such a weapon a few times throughout his life, but at this close range he was unlikely to miss. The bolt went clean through the assassin's sword arm and pierced his side. Montbron dropped his blade and roared in pain, but the attack had only wounded him. He knew he could only manage flight, not fight, now. Before Fordham had an opportunity to reload the crossbow or retrieve his sword Montbron kicked the flanks of his horse and rode off in whatever direction the mare would take him. He gritted his teeth and forced himself not to pass out. He would live through the night and make it back home. Tonight would not be the night he would die.

Fordham muttered a curse beneath his breath as he realised he had cracked a rib, but he also gave thanks that he was still breathing. The Frenchman had bested him, but he was walking away alive and in possession of the assassin's fine sword. Fordham also offered up something resembling a prayer of thanks on seeing the figure of John Walworth riding towards him in the distance. "The little bastard made a small target, but I managed to stick an arrow in him in the end," the burly archer would soon report to his friend.

Richard Whittington breathed several sighs of relief. The danger seemed to be over, though a sense of confusion lingered.

"You have my gratitude, sir," the merchant said to the stranger. "Let us first concern ourselves with taking my injured coachman back to the King's palace. We may yet save his life. You can then hopefully enlighten me as to what just occurred."

"I will explain as best I can," the soldier replied, a little breathlessly. "Just know that it sometimes takes more than a cat to drive vermin away."

15

A mustard-coloured light shone through clumps of cloud as white as bleached bone. Wildflowers freckled the emerald green field. The Englishmen waited within a cordon of numerous armed guards. Condemned men. Reynard of Troyes was determined to have his fill of amusement with his prisoners. His champion, Albert Garyn, would challenge Chaucer's archer to a test of strength and skill. Longbow would contest crossbow.

Robert Cooper watched Thomas Chaucer squint. Were his eyes strained by the searing blue sky and midday sun? Was he looking at the archery target, positioned in the distance? Or had something caught his eye in the treeline of the woods that bordered the field? Robert Cooper was impressed, and confounded, by the agent's blithe air of calm – considering it was likely they would be tortured later in the day. Or executed.

Chaucer had instructed Cooper not to do anything rash when they woke up in their cell together that morning, despite their desperate situation. He was fully aware of how much Cooper wanted to kill his captor and endeavour to escape should the opportunity arise.

The pavilion, which looked out over the jousting track and grassland where Walter Bane's tournaments were hosted was abuzz with anticipation. Walter Bane had promised his friends a spectacle. Spectators ranged from French knights and crossbowmen to Scottish noblemen and their wives – or mistresses. Although a number of minstrels and acrobats amused the crowd spectators were eager for the main competition to start. French soldiers positioned themselves on the right of the stand, facing the competitors. Either through a sense of loyalty, or knowing the French agent would somehow rig the outcome, no one placed a bet on the Englishman. The Scottish lords and ladies occupied the central part of the pavilion and Bane's men-at-arms were sat to the left of them. Some of the latter were already half-drunk – and even those who were sober began to jeer at the English bowman and ran their fingers across their throats when their doomed enemy turned towards them.

Trumpets and cheers out-sounded the jeers however when the crowd saw Reynard of Troyes and Walter Bane make their way over to the Englishmen from their places in the pavilion. They were accompanied by Gilbert Radcliffe and the crossbow-wielding Garyn, who wore a scowl more menacing than usual. Radcliffe wore fine, white linen trousers and a silken, brocade-decorated jacket. Chaucer had seen the real King Richard wear a similar jacket many years ago. The impostor also wore long pointed shoes, which had been the fashion in Richard's court, during his reign. As the actor stood next to Chaucer he realised Radcliffe was wearing the same perfume as the late monarch. The devil is in the detail.

Walter Bane, his lips stained with wine, approached the English spy.

"For all of the lies you've told and games you have played over the course of your career, Thomas, it must particularly gall you to be on the losing side. It proves that our cause is just. Long live Scotland," the rotund nobleman said, relishing his moment of triumph. The Scot had spent half the previous evening awake in bed, thinking of how he and his new allies would divide up England, once defeated. As much as he often vilified "Westminster" and "London" in his speeches Bane would demand to have a residence there in any settlement. But Scotland would finally be free, though the country would still wish to use the currency of England. And it would, of course, submit to French laws, where their allies saw fit.

"Long live Scotland indeed. I am of course unable to exclaim, with the same measure of conviction 'Long live Walter Bane'. I dare say I am not in a constituency of one either in this regard," Chaucer drily replied, as he gazed over at the pavilion, half-concentrating on assessing the combined force of the French and Scottish soldiers.

"You always have a joke to hand, Thomas. But I can assure you I will have the last laugh. I have requested to be on hand when Reynard interrogates you this evening. It will be a long night for you, considering how many secrets you must be privy to," Walter Bane said, letting off a solitary cackle.

"Would you please excuse us, Walter? I wish to speak to our friend alone," Reynard of Troyes exclaimed, cutting into the conversation.

"Certainly," the Scottish nobleman said. "I have things to attend to." Bane nodded and took his leave – to attend to the remainder of the game pie he had left back at the pavilion.

Reynard of Troyes was dressed in a similar black surcoat to that which he had worn the previous evening. His hair was perfumed and oiled – and he had trimmed his beard again. He smiled at the Englishman – the very soul of civility. Meanwhile his mind amused itself with the methods of torture he would devise, in relation to the captured spy, during their interrogation later.

"We are nearing the moment of truth Thomas, are we not? I am not talking about your interrogation but rather the competition. Which will triumph, the crossbow or longbow? Is this the era of the French man-at-arms or the English archer? I am confident that your man will acquit himself ably. The outcome, after all, will decide whether he lives or dies. My Albert has never been defeated in such a contest. Should your archer defeat my man it will of course be reported that the crossbow proved victorious. You understand the need for such propaganda more than most. Whether you like it or not you are my mirror image. We are two opposing sides of the same coin. I am the best, or worst, of you," Reynard argued.

"We may be similar in some small part, Reynard, but it is so small as to be insignificant. I should thank you for the comparison. When I look upon you I am entitled to think to myself how much goodness and honour I still have left in me. I have had cause to come across many Lollards over these past few years. Some consider the Pope to be the anti-Christ, as you doubtless know. I warrant I should introduce them to you however, in order to refute their argument and offer them another candidate to fulfil the role."

Reynard of Troyes let out another short burst of laughter, genuinely amused.

"Now you are just flattering me, Thomas. I do believe that I will miss you. Would you care to join me in the stands, to watch the competition unfold?"

"Thank you but I would rather remain here with my bowman. I will try to offer him what little encouragement and advice I can provide. It is, after all, part of our brief to know which way the wind is blowing."

The French agent had instructed Gilbert Radcliffe to play the King at every given opportunity in order to immerse himself in the role. The actor royally approached the archer and decided to give him some words of encouragement.

"The best of luck to you today," the mock-king exclaimed, munificently.

"Go fuck yourself," Cooper replied, slightly less regally.

*

Reynard of Troyes returned to the pavilion with the others who had stepped out with him onto the field. The cordon of guards around Cooper and Chaucer dissipated too and joined the crowd of spectators.

A table was brought out by an attendant, along with the Englishman's bow and five arrows, which he stuck in the ground by the archer's feet. Upon the table he placed a jug of water and a jug of ale, as well as five crossbow bolts, a number of items used to maintain his weapon and a second crossbow of a slightly different design to the one Garyn was carrying.

Walter Bane stood up and gave a long speech. He loved the sound of his own voice nearly much as he loved his food. He thanked his distinguished French guest and explained the format of the competition. Each competitor would take five shots. They would score ten points for hitting the centre circle and five for the outer circle. Just when the audience were starting to grow restless from the length of the speech the hissing sound from a suckling pig on a spit attracted Bane's attention and he brought his oratory to a close.

Robert Cooper didn't feel the need to rub tallow into his bow. He did not care if it cracked in the future for its next French or Scottish owner. The archer merely stared intently at the centre of the target, seventy paces away. Finally he removed the hemp bowstring from his pocket and hooked it around the horn tips of his weapon. He felt a pang of remorse, believing that it would be the last time he would do so. He thought of Grace – but then his target. Out of the corner of his eye he noticed his opponent standing at the table, eyeing up his crossbow bolts and weapons like a stonemason assessing the tools of his trade.

The Frenchman took the decision to shoot first. The heavy crossbow seemed light in the burly soldier's hands. He placed the well-crafted bolt on the stock, cranked the mechanism to its maximum strength and buried the butt of the weapon in his shoulder, looking along the top of the flights – following an imagined trajectory of the bolt into the target. Cooper had seen many a man knocked backwards – or even knocked off their feet – after firing such a large crossbow, but there was a power and smoothness to his technique. The weapon didn't jolt or rear up once the bolt was unleashed.

The missile struck the target's outer circle but it was close to the inner so, as per instructed by the French agent, the scorer awarded his countryman ten points. Suffice to say he was instructed not to afford the same level of generosity, or poor eyesight, to the Englishman. A flurry of applause and cheers greeted the score.

Garyn offered up a monosyllabic grunt in response to his effort, accompanied by a snort which sent two projectiles of phlegm out of his nose and onto the grass, close to where the Englishman was standing. Cooper stared at the brutal-looking man-at-arms. His nose had been broken more than once. Both his ears had the bottom of their lobes missing and his jerkin contained a patchwork of stains – mostly red wine and blood.

The cheers turned to jeers again as Cooper plucked an arrow out of the turf and moved to his mark. He inspected the shaft for any flaws – or sabotage – but the arrow was true. The archer thanked God for small mercies – he had been given his own arrows, produced by Percy Badby, to shoot.

Cooper's fingers were like talons as he commenced to draw back the powerful yew bow. His barrel chest tightened. His eyes narrowed – and sucked in the centre of the distant target. The jeers and curses increased in the background but the archer concentrated on the task at hand. His taut, muscular arms drew back the bow so his fingers were now level with his ear. Archery came as easily and naturally as breathing. Habit, as much as conscious thought, directed the bowman in choosing the angle and strength of trajectory. Henry had once told Cooper how, before every battle, he offered up a prayer to God and St George: "But I also give thanks to Edward III for making the country practice archery every Sunday."

Practice makes perfect.

The shaft sang through the air and perfectly hit its mark, dead centre of the inner circle. The scorer, with a pinched expression of disappointment on his face, signified ten points. The impressive display of skill by the Englishman fuelled rather than dampened the spectators' vociferous attitude towards him. But their base hatred only stoked the bowman's determination. He would defeat the Frenchman, even if it meant hastening his own demise.

Whilst Garyn reloaded his crossbow and took his second shot Thomas Chaucer surveyed the pavilion. Walter Bane's mouth and chin glistened with grease as he wolfed down another plate of food. The soldiers, both the Scottish and French contingents of troops, were becoming more animated as the ale and banter flowed. Several punched the air when Garyn scored another ten points. In contrast Reynard of Troyes appeared oblivious to the drama of the tournament. The militaristic entertainment being played out before him was not to his taste. As needful as they were the agent considered most soldiers to be savages – and expendable. Instead the French agent, sitting behind a pillar, read over several documents handed to him by his secretary. Sitting several places to his right was the actor. Radcliffe smiled and waved to a number of people around him (particularly young women). Chaucer was confident that, sooner or later, the impostor would forget his lines and the mask would slip. But by then it would be too late …

Chaucer tore his gaze away from the pavilion as he spotted a large black bird wing its way across the sky. To assist his archer he bent down and picked up a few blades of grass, tossing them in the air to assess the strength of the wind. At the same time he picked up a short, pointed piece of wood and concealed it within the sleeve of his coat.

Chaucer proceeded to walk towards Cooper. He whispered in his ear. Garyn let out a couple more deep-throated grunts, to try and hurry proceedings up, but the two men continued to whisper to one another. Garyn then spat out a curse, which contained the word "bastard" three times. Chaucer finally stepped away from the archer. The final words he uttered were loud and clear: "Now is the time for some heroics."

Robert Cooper looked around thoughtfully, taking in the line of guards standing thirty paces away and assessing the soldiers populating the pavilion. The bowman placed another arrow on the stave and lined himself up with the target. The audience, enthralled by the competition, leaned forward slightly in anticipation. Just when they believed he was going to loosen the arrow the archer quickly turned towards the stand. It only took a few seconds for Cooper to pick out Gilbert Radcliffe and fire the arrow into his chest. The mock king was dead.

Shock and silence temporarily infused the atmosphere – before all hell broke loose.

A trumpet sounded in the background, from the treeline.

Cooper ran towards the lead-footed Garyn and jabbed him in the face, catching his eye with the horn tip of his bow. The man-at-arms screamed in agony as he staggered backwards. Cooper lost no time in moving in the opposite direction, retrieving another arrow out of the ground, and firing the shaft into his disorientated enemy. Albert Garyn's face was contorted in disbelief as the arrow buried itself in his throat. He gurgled before falling to the ground.

Thomas Chaucer caught the guard next to him unawares, coming up behind him. Blood gushed like a drunk vomiting as the agent lodged the point of the stick into his jugular vein.

A cacophony of sound issued forth from the French soldiers in the pavilion. Some let out curses and a call to arms. The jingling sound of mail shirts and clang of plate armour could be heard too. Yet these sound were soon eclipsed by the dreaded noise (but welcome to the English) of a swarm of arrows infecting the air and afflicting the French. The contingent of English archers fired upon their enemy as soon as they darted out from the woods. Panic ensued as the French men-at-arms attempted to grab what weapons they had and clamber over the benches of the pavilion. But it was too late. The deadly missiles, fired with relentless accuracy and rapidity, rained down upon the enemy and decimated their ranks. Within a minute most of them were wounded or slain. The needle-sharp bodkin arrowheads pierced any segment of armour the soldiers wore. It was the era of the English archer.

Walter Bane's men panicked and retreated as best they could, despite not being under direct attack. Many were without weapons and armour, judging that they wouldn't be needed for the day. They lacked leadership and cohesiveness. There was little will to join forces with their French allies and arrange a defence or counterattack. Bane cried out to his soldiers to protect him, as he hid himself, cowering, behind a pillar.

Robert Cooper nocked another arrow and scanned the pavilion, searching for the prime target of Reynard of Troyes. But the agent had disappeared into thin air, like the devil.

The ground reverberated as Donald Greyson, mounted upon his majestic black charger, led a cavalry attack. Those soldiers who had raced towards Chaucer and Cooper – in order to capture or kill them – were caught in open ground. Ribbons of blood patterned the grass as Greyson and his men sliced open the torsos and faces of their enemies.

The force of English and Scottish men-at-arms was commanded by George Clifford and Laurence Firth. Few of the enemy rushed out to face the well-equipped and well-marshalled professional soldiers. Those who did were met with a volley of hunting spears. Once they closed upon their opponents the order was given to break ranks and charge the retreating, routed, enemy.

George Clifford's pole-axe shattered a man's jaw, nearly taking his head off. The tip of the nightmarish weapon was dripping with gore as he vigorously stabbed and slashed with it. Firth fought beside his new friend using his shield as an offensive tool to push his opponents back and knock them over. Once grounded the Scottish man-at-arms then thrust his sword into his enemies' groin, heart, neck or face.

Many of Bane's supporters abandoned their wives and mistresses. The enemy surrendered or retreated and the carnage subsided. Donald Greyson praised his troops and encouraged them to raid the main house and grab some deserved spoils of war. Jack Mercer led the way.

"You may want to leave most of the wine," Chaucer recommended to Greyson. "Unless your kitchens are in need of more vinegar."

Greyson was pleased to see his friend unharmed and duly dismounted and hugged the Englishman.

"I still cannot quite decide, Thomas, whether you are a genius or just damn lucky. Your plan worked."

"It's not all over quite yet. If your men come across our friend Reynard have them detain rather than kill him. I look forward to hosting him in the Tower. As much as he revealed his plans to me I may be able to glean more information from him. He's a spider – and spiders spin more than just one web. Also, where are Badby and Morgan? I will need to borrow some horses and a few of your men. You have some work to do yet, Robert. You still have one last target to shoot at."

16

Sweat marbled the horses in the sweltering afternoon heat.

Thomas Chaucer rode hard for Aberlady. Time was of the essence. He couldn't be sure if Reynard of Troyes had been able to send a message out instructing the French cog to disembark. Both agents knew that Scotland could not afford to go to war without France's gold.

The plan had worked. Knowing that he would be unable to extract and trust the information given to him by Reynard of Troyes, if he managed to interrogate the wily agent, Chaucer had allowed himself to be captured. Laurence Firth and the guides had been ordered to follow them and then alert Greyson as to their location. Chaucer deliberately kept his ruse from his archers, lest they be tortured. The strategy was a gamble but the stakes were sufficiently high. Reynard revealed his plans willingly, believing that the Englishman would take them to the grave. The arch confessor confessed. Not only would the Frenchman's plots now fail but Chaucer had learned his own piece of misdirection and false intelligence had succeeded. The English agent had deliberately created contracts with soldiers citing that their destination would be Gascony. Henry's army would now be able to land safely.

The original plan concocted by Chaucer was to have Greyson and his men raid the main house the day after their capture, in order to free them. The tournament had worked to their advantage however, trapping all their enemies in the same place. The appearance of Greyson's hawk had signalled to Chaucer that his friend was ready to attack. Chaucer had been tempted to instruct his archer to assassinate the dangerous French spy, but Cooper had no line of sight to take the shot – and the figure of the impostor king could have proved a greater threat to Henry's reign.

Things could still unravel however, Chaucer thought to himself. The French gold could still be distributed to Henry's enemies if he didn't reach the fishing village in time. Also, how grave was the threat to depose Henry and proclaim the Earl of March as monarch? Chaucer cursed Lord Scrope, in particular, for his treachery but he also believed that most of the nobility – and more importantly the army – would not desert Henry.

Owen Morgan rode behind the agent. At first the Welshman had cursed his fate when Chaucer ordered him to join the party of men bound for Aberlady. Most of his companions were about to loot the nobleman's estate. When the bowman heard about the prospect of purloining a chest full of gold coin, though, he drove his horse as hard as any man. Morgan was flanked by Cooper and Percy Badby, the latter carrying multiple cloth bags of specially-produced arrows. The archers were followed by over a dozen of Greyson's soldiers.

Cooper replayed Chaucer's words in his head. "All has gone according to plan," he remarked to the archer, with a sense of relief and triumph. But then he remembered Stephen Hall and remorse tempered his tone. Was his death worth the cost of the intelligence the spy had gleaned? Chaucer would have argued that it was. Cooper was not so sure. As much as he regretted his decision to have Hall join them on the mission he knew that, if just Chaucer and he had been captured, the French agent would have tortured and executed him. Chaucer would soon be writing a condolence letter to Grace and compensating her with a year's wages, instead of doing so to Hall's parents. Guilt and grief scoured his soul.

I should feel fortunate. But I don't.

*

The French agent believed he had ridden fast and far enough away from the danger. In response to the attack he had quickly retreated from the pavilion and ordered a messenger to tell his ship to disembark without him and prevent the gold falling into English hands. He had then commanded a handful of his soldiers to ride north with him. They now congregated in a clearing in the forest. Their tired horses drank from a creek and rested. His soldiers were demoralised, defeated, but they dared not offer a word of complaint for fear of the unforgiving agent's reaction.

Sweat glazed Reynard's sunburnt complexion. His mouth was dry, his head throbbed. His limbs ached. His whole body yearned for a cold bath and warm massage. He had instructed his secretary to burn any official or personal papers he carried with him, but as such there wasn't enough time for his attendant to secure certain personal items, such as his comb, silk embroidered handkerchief or small jar of perfume.

Reynard recalled the scene of the attack. He hated himself for experiencing a womanish sense of fear. He detested soldiers and war. He was more a student of Byzantium than Rome. *Man is little more than a beast*. He disliked not being in control, and he hadn't been since the English archer had shot the actor. Reynard of Troyes shaped events. Events didn't usually shape him. Less than immaculate looking, Reynard was now like any other mortal. He was reliant on fortune, rather than his own will, to determine his fate. He could but hope that his ship escaped in time, but he refused to debase himself and pray to a god who didn't exist.

The ice-hearted spy felt no remorse for the (dim-witted) actor. Sooner or later the agent would have poisoned the man himself, not just to conceal his true identity but also to plunge England into civil war between various claimants to the throne. But he did grieve over all the wasted time and resources he put into producing his creation. Reynard of Troyes also refused to mourn for Walter Bane. He was a vindictive demagogue, enamoured with the idea of being powerful and respected. He was a pied piper who would happily lead people to their deaths.

Bane can perish. I hope you survived the skirmish though, Thomas. Just so I can torture and kill you myself one day. Soon. I underestimated you. But I won't make that mistake twice. There will be a second act to the drama we have been written into. All is far from lost.

Rays of sunlight poked through the trees and chequered the forest floor, like a chess board. There was gold in the agent's purse and venom in his thoughts. Reynard of Troyes smiled, serpent-like, and took consolation from the fact that he had at least fooled Chaucer into believing that the King was his assassin's target – and not a financier.

*

The newly painted French cog the *Halygast*, had left. Reynard's messenger had been and gone. But the vessel was still in sight and still in range. Cooper and Morgan raced to the end of the wooden pier. The smell of brackish sea water filled their nostrils as they fastened their bowstrings. Chaucer and Badby followed them, a little way back. The agent was carrying a brace of lanterns whilst Badby was laden with his arrow bags.

Thankfully the wind was not strong enough to speed the enemy ship away, although there was a sufficient breeze for the fire to spread, Chaucer thought.

The archers pulled back their bows and Badby and Chaucer lit the specially modified arrowheads. Morgan missed with his first missile but used it as a range finder. He cursed as he did so, but one couldn't be sure whether he cursed because of missing the target or because he would now be sinking instead of saving French loot.

Cooper's first arrow thudded into the side of the hull, just below the gunwale.

The bowman – and the men lighting the tips of their arrows – quickly settled into a proficient rhythm as the missiles, like lava spewing out from a volcano, rained down across the defenceless *Halygast*. The shafts began to ignite the hull, deck and sails. The blazing sun helped incubate each small flame.

The French vessel was manned by a skeleton crew as most of the agent's men had accompanied him to Bane's estate. There was an absence of leadership and method in combating the terrifying attack. The paint began to blister, the wood began to burn and crack. Each arrow was a hornet's sting, helping to bring down a mighty beast. Smoke began to fill lungs. The fire began to heat and scorch skin. Tongues of flames commenced to lick the sails and rigging. Some tried to rally their shipmates and attempted to fill buckets or stamp out the incendiaries. Some called out in vain to their attackers to have mercy and that they would surrender. Some called to abandon ship and a few jumped into the sea, estimating that if they did so now they could still manage to swim back to the shore.

Cooper and Morgan ignored what was happening on the ship as they focused on sustaining their accuracy and rate of fire. Cooper's heart – ire – burned as fiercely as the arrowheads he was shooting. Beads of sweat ran into and stung his eyes. His expression, however, was that of a marble statue of a Roman stoic. The archer loosened arrow after arrow – not in the name of England or for his paymaster but for Stephen Hall and to damn the French agent.

The sailors soon realised they were fighting a losing battle. The blazing ship resembled a Viking funeral vessel. Roaring, amber flames writhed and danced against the teal sea and azure sky. Chaucer ordered Greyson's men to commandeer a number of nearby fishing boats and rescue the French sailors who had leaped overboard.

Eventually the *Halygast* started to lurch to one side and plumes of steam were thrown up as the glowing timbers kissed the water. The cog burned – but it would soon also drown.

The soldiers stood, entranced, as the ship was sucked down into the frothing sea.

Now it's over.

Thomas Chaucer felt both exhausted and uplifted. The King would be pleased. But more so he thought of how his father would have been proud of him. They would have been prouder of him still if he had been able to return with the gold. But not everything can go according to plan. The sea was deep and would be reluctant to give up its new found wealth, Chaucer fancied. He would be unable to organise the necessary diving team swiftly enough and the strong currents in the water could spirit the booty away in numerous directions.

Time and tide waits for no man…

EPILOGUE

Whether his actions were borne from loyalty or fear the Earl of March, Edmund Mortimer, chose to betray his conspirators rather than King. Mortimer rode in person to his sovereign and revealed the plot against him. Henry acted decisively and mercilessly. Lord Scrope appealed directly to his sovereign, arguing that he had joined the plot in order to gather more intelligence and foil the plot from within its ranks. Henry would have laughed at such a line of defence had he not been so hurt by his old friend's betrayal. Edmund Mortimer was pardoned but the remaining conspirators were arrested, tried and executed within little more than a week – as efficiently as possible. Henry didn't want any further delays to his fleet setting sail.

The King received Thomas Chaucer's message, delivered by Donald Greyson's most accomplished horseman, about the conspiracy a couple of days after Mortimer's confession. He read the remainder of his report with a sense of wonder and relief.

Henry held the message in his hand now as he received Edward Fordham in his cabin on the *Trinity Royal*. His newly scoured armour was piled upon a table, gleaming in the coppery light pouring in through the stern window of his flagship. Also on the table was the Black Prince's sword, newly engraved with his motto: *I serve*. On the large desk by the window there was, piled equally high, sheaves of correspondence, lists and financial documents pertaining to the campaign. Henry's ink-stained fingers attested to the fact that he was, at present, still more of a clerk than soldier. But that would soon change.

Fordham bowed in front of his sovereign. Although the sea was relatively calm the ship had still lolled about too much for Fordham's liking. "I don't mind a woman moving about beneath me but I like the ground I walk on to remain still," he had confided to John Walworth the evening before. The two companions spent the night drinking and toasting the success of their mission, but they had been worried about how Cooper and the rest of the company were faring. No news was bad news.

The companions spent the morning after in an ale house, overlooking the port and sea of ships about to set sail from France. Fordham lost count of the number of vessels sprawled across the dark turquoise ocean but he estimated that the total exceeded a thousand. The sea was more ship than sea. The fleet was varied with cogs, galleys, carracks and ballingers. Single and double-masted crafts. Some constructed in England, some leased from foreign powers such as Holland. Some ships were fitted with turrets on their bows and sterns and a great host of boats had been converted into transport vessels for the thousands of horses needed for the campaign. The scene of the animals being hoisted on board made the soldiers laugh and wince (and tragedy nearly ensued for beast or handler on more than one occasion during the dangerous operation).

The fleet was also a giant menagerie in the form of the heraldic creatures – leopards, swans, stags – painted onto the hulls and banners of ships. The Trinity Royal, at five hundred and forty tonnes, dwarfed all the boats around her. And two colourful banners rippled in the wind on her mast against a cobalt blue sky – one of St George and one of Edward the Confessor. Fordham considered how the King was the son of those two fathers – or he wished to project such an impression for propaganda reasons. Such was the scale of the operation – and the multifarious people populating the human tapestry – that it seemed like the whole country was present. England had never witnessed such a sight before and it may not see the like again. The grand scene was awe-inspiring. "We ask that God help us but, seeing what I see before me, it's the French who will need God's help," Fordham had remarked to Walworth. The scene had also stirred anxieties, for if the entire country was going to war then how much would remain if Henry's gamble did not pay off?

The soldier was about to kneel when Henry told him to remain at ease. "You will need all your strength for the coming campaign," he said. Fordham couldn't quite tell if it was said in jest of not. And he was unaware of what the etiquette was in regards to grinning or laughing in the sovereign's presence.

"I received a letter from Richard Whittington yesterday. He gave me a full account of your conduct on the evening of the assassination attempt. He has asked me to commend you. Richard also states that he is in your debt: you may well be the only man in England who can say that Richard Whittington is in your debt, as opposed you being in his debt. I seem to recall that we met once before, the day prior to the battle of Shrewsbury. You are Roger Fordham's son, are you not? Your father kindly contributed to the campaign. You are also a poet, if memory serves? I hope you are following the example of Thomas' father and composing verse in English?

"Unfortunately, your majesty, that's the only thing our verses have in common," Fordham answered, wishing that he could have just a tenth of the talent of the author behind *The Canterbury Tales*. He was somewhat taken aback by the fact that the Henry remembered him after all these years, having only conversed with to him once. Fordham had had lovers who hadn't remembered as many details about him. Although in fairness the soldier had courted many a mistress in the past whom he couldn't even remember the name of now.

"Indeed ... I have not just called you here to pass on a commendation. I thought you might like to know that Chaucer and the rest of your company succeeded in their mission. They should be joining our ranks in a day or two. My attendant outside will arrange a cask of ale for the company and a vintage Bordeaux for Thomas. You are a good man, Edward. With a few more soldiers like you and Robert France may fall before the leaves do in autumn.

Fordham was grateful for the drink and news. A weight had been lifted. He and John would have yet another thing to toast later. He also started to realise why the King had made such a favourable impression on his archer friend. Henry possessed an air of majesty but also had the common touch. Maybe the two things were one and the same, Fordham mused. If God had any sense or taste he would be siding with the English monarch during the forthcoming war.

The man-at-arms was at pains to remember if anyone had ever called him "a good man" before. But when the King said it Fordham wanted to prove him right.

Perhaps Robert is right. Henry is worth having some faith in.

Sunlight scythed through the window of the royal cabin, bejewelling motes of dust. The two men shared a jug of ale and conversed for longer than either man had expected before their meeting. Henry made a promise that, once they were in France, he would invite Fordham, Cooper and Chaucer to dinner.

As the soldier took his leave he noticed a large, vellum map pinned to the wall, next to a portrait of Edward III. The map outlined the north-west coast of France. Several place names had been written on the map but only one had been circled: *Harfleur.*

*

The English countryside. Clement sunshine gilded the pastoral scene.

Thomas Chaucer and Robert Cooper rode at the head of the company of men. As much as they had enjoyed the hospitality of Donald Greyson and had made friends with their Scottish brethren they were all pleased to be back home. The golden green contoured fields, bountiful orchards, rich brown hedgerows and Arcadian forests of England were appreciated anew. Bells in village churches chimed out the hour. Packs of hunting hounds occasionally bayed in the distance. Strangers conversed about the weather and wished each other good day as if they were old friends. Laughter and songs rang out from teeming ale houses. The smell of fresh hay – and fresh dung – filled the air.

The archer took another bite out of his crunchy ruby-red apple. Juice ran down his chin, which he wiped away with his sleeve. His body ached not from being imprisoned or from fighting – but from being in the saddle for days. Cooper's acute heartache stung him more, though. He yearned to see Grace again. Hear her laugh and have her talk about everything and nothing. He pictured her long, flame-coloured hair ablaze in the sunlight and her guileless, freckled face.

"I was tempted to keep it as a surprise Robert, but I imagine that you have had your fill of surprises these past few weeks. There is a fork in the road up ahead. We will turn off for Ewelme whilst George leads the rest of the men down to Southampton. I don't want to leave these fair shores without seeing my even fairer wife," Thomas Chaucer exclaimed, as he worked out in his mind what dish, accompanied by what wine, he would ask his cook to serve them that evening.

The bowman's usually neutral expression immediately brightened and his body and heartache disappeared more quickly than snow from an iron foundry's chimney.

"But what about the King? Did he not order us to travel directly to Southampton after completing the mission?"

"He did. But you will soon learn in life that it's one thing to cause displeasure to your king and another to your wife. A wife can make a husband's life a misery with just one word or, far more ominously, she can say nothing at all when displeased ... I need to see Matilda again and you need to see Grace."

"Does this mean that you are giving me your full blessing in marrying Grace?"

"Yes, I suppose it does. Sometimes love conquers all," Chaucer replied. He realised that, although Cooper was not the richest or most chivalrous man he knew he was one of the noblest. When the agent had first signed the bowman to his company Chaucer believed that he could teach the lowborn Cooper about honour. But, far more than teaching the archer, he had learned from him. *He's a good man. And he will make a good husband.*

"I would ask a favour of you, Thomas, before we reach your home. Would you mind keeping the details of the past few weeks to ourselves? I don't want Grace to know what happened. She would fret too much about me when we're in France."

"There is no need to worry on that front. I'm no stranger to keeping secrets… I must confess that I am a little surprised by you wanting to keep things from your bride to be though. But it augurs well. I have learned over the years that happy marriages, much like spy networks, are built on secrets and lies. Ah, secrets and lies. How could we live without them?" the agent cheerfully posed.

HARFLEUR

"A mighty flame followeth a tiny spark." Dante

"My power has not been laid so low and the hand of God is not yet so weak that I cannot with his grace prevail over my enemy." Edward III

1

It looks like the end of the world. Or, at the very least, the beginning of the end, Thomas Chaucer, agent to the King, thought to himself as he took in the grim scene in front of him. The white walls of the French port of Harfleur were pockmarked from where English cannons had fired stone missiles against the redoubtable defences. *Girded Harfleur*. Stubbly patches of grass still mottled the landscape but for the most part the earth was pitted and churned up, like a scab failing to cover an open wound. Red clay marbled the soil. The muddy ground was strewn with rubble, pieces of half-burnt timber and a smattering of rotting corpses. The town's suburbs had been razed to the ground so Henry could move his artillery and trenches nearer to the town. Gulls pecked and plucked the flesh from arrow-ridden bodies. A cloud of flies swarmed above the carcass of a once handsome black courser. A springald bolt jutted out of the animal's swollen chest. Its mouth was contorted in a gruesome grin. Had the noble horse, at the end, been able to smile in the face of death, or was the creature laughing at the folly of the English for continuing to besiege the defiant town? The putrid smell of death and excrement filled the air, as did the unholy sound of another cannon blast.

The afternoon heat beat down on Thomas Chaucer — the son of the lauded poet — cooking him in his Milanese plate armour, but he bore his discomfort with stoicism. He was the soul of civility, even when torturing an enemy of the state at the Tower. For years his duties had included being the Speaker of the House and serving as the King's butler, helping the royal household purchase its wines. But now Chaucer found himself advising his monarch on military matters. Instead of ruby-red vintages he held the lives of thousands of soldiers in his hands. The spy, who was no stranger to death or violence, had been taken aback by the scale of suffering already spawned by the campaign. He recalled the words his father had spoken concerning war, many years ago.

"War is one of the great necessary evils in the world, along with taxation and the church. The living may regale you with stories of chivalry and gilded triumphs but if the dead could speak they would report tales of cowardice, butchery, inept leadership and the bloody flux. Disease and starvation slay three times the number of soldiers as those who die in combat. You need to arm yourself with more than just a sword and buckler if ever you go to war, Thomas. Keep your wits about you and be capable of compassion and cruelty, as they will both be called for."

Chaucer sighed, from exhaustion and relief. He missed his wife, Matilda, his children and their home in Ewelme, Oxfordshire. He realised that, more than for his King or country, he was fighting to get back home. Capturing the port was just a means to that end. *I have no desire to be written into the annals of history. I just want to be a husband and father again. Drink a fine vintage. Play chess. Read a good book. Sleep in the same warm bed as my wife.*

He suddenly remembered a passage from one his father's poems, *The House of Fame*:

"For when your labour is all done,
And you've made all your reckonings,
You hasten home without delay,
And, as dumb as any stone,
You sit and read another book
Till completely dazed is your look."

Out of the corner of his eye Chaucer glanced at Henry — his captain and sovereign. His lips were compressed together, sealed shut like the gates of Harfleur. His slender face had grown even thinner, gaunter, over the past fortnight. Thomas couldn't remember the last time he had heard Henry laugh. Henry sat up, his back arrow-straight, on his horse despite having the world on his shoulders. His polished cuirass gleamed majestically in the honey-tinged light, but his eyes had lost their lustre. His hand clasped his sword — he was anxious to draw the weapon. Chaucer greatly admired Henry.

The young King was wise beyond his years. Chaucer's faith in God may have been shaken over the years, but he believed in Henry. Yet was Henry losing his faith in God and himself?

"The wolves are out. They will be lambs to the slaughter," Thomas, Duke of Clarence, the King's brother, remarked as he surveyed the doom-laden scene from afar. A party of audacious French crossbowmen had rushed out from behind the walls of the town, intent on attacking a group of miners. The plan had been for the miners to dig beneath the foundations of the town's defences and collapse the wall, creating a breach to attack through. Previous mines had failed, however. The first, constructed by the *Leure* gate, was foiled by a deep moat. The mines by the *Montivilliers* gate had successfully been countermined (the French having dug the other way, collapsing the enemy's tunnel). It seemed that Raoul de Gaucourt, the wily commander of French forces at Harfleur, was now looking to not just destroy the half-constructed mine, but to slaughter the English and Welsh miners as well. The crossbowmen ran across the ground between the town and mouth of the mine (protected by a wooden sow which shielded the miners from missiles whilst they worked). Gaucourt had offered each man a small reward for every enemy he could kill. There were no mounted troops in sight to protect the miners and cut down the crossbowmen. The pack of wolves would devour their prey and then retreat back to the safety of the town, ready to rain down further crossbow bolts on any pursuing, vengeful English force. It would be a small victory for Gaucourt, again.

2

Robert Cooper encouraged the miners around him to flee. It wasn't their fight. Besides, the sight of a routed enemy might distract the French and encourage a number of the crossbowmen to fire their weapons rashly and prematurely. The English archer rolled his head on his neck, stretched his arms and flexed his hands. Sweat and grime besmirched his flat, hard face. He smiled to a new recruit to instil confidence in the nervous looking youth. He recalled how a grey-haired ventenar had done the same to him, many years ago, to bolster his courage. *Just stand your ground, aim true and everything will be fine lad.* Cooper briefly thought about Stephen Hall, the last young archer he had taken under his wing, but then forcefully shook the image of his mangled corpse out of his head. Duty called. It was almost time to spring his trap.

"Now?" John Walworth, Cooper's friend and fellow archer, asked. The burly Londoner was keen to both start and end the fight. "It's about time French soil tasted some French blood."

"Not quite. I want all the bastards out in the open. Some might be tempted to turn tail and run back to the safety of their defences," Cooper replied.

A dozen or so archers stood before him, their shirts and jerkins emblazoned with the cross of Saint George. They were concealed from the enemy behind the wooden sow, waiting on the order to attack. Many were familiar, trusted, battle-hardened faces. Owen Morgan: a veteran bowman from Wales who was always ready to fill a man's cup with ale and his ears with a bawdy joke. Jack Mercer: a common thief who, to save himself from the gallows, turned professional soldier. Mercer was in France searching for gold rather than honour. "Chivalry can't put food on the table or a whore on your lap," he had quite rightly argued when crossing the channel. Percy Badby was also among the group of bowmen. His skills as an archer may have needed honing but the company couldn't ask for a better fletcher.

Bowstrings were attached and arrows rested upon staves. Each man carried twenty or more arrows in a cloth bag, which hung over his shoulder. Cooper had given orders for his men to line up in small groups of three and pick their targets as a group. Although one archer could miss his enemy it was unlikely that all three would. Hopefully the crossbowmen would make it easier for them by coming together to create a bigger target to aim at. Conversely by lining-up in groups of three the archers wouldn't be providing their enemy with too great a target to fire at. Only he and John Walworth, positioning themselves either side of the entrance to the mine, would stand apart.

The bowmen had entered the mine under the cover of darkness. Over half a day went by with the soldiers concealed beneath the sow, not knowing if their enemy would take the bait and advance on their position. But Gaucourt judged the mine too great a prize — and a successful raid would further injure English morale, as surely as their enemy chipped away at the town's white walls with their cannons.

Cooper had discussed his ruse with Chaucer and both men had then presented their plan to the King.

"The army could use a victory, however small," Henry had asserted, pleased with the proposal. "And I am all for having fewer crossbowmen attacking us at the breach. So far we have been target practice for them. It's about time we had them in our sights. They will think twice about further attacking one of our mines once we give them a bloody nose... Fine work Thomas. Take some of the good stuff from my personal stores and share it out among your company once the mission is over. I must commend you too, Robert. You're proving as invaluable to me as your father was to the Black Prince."

Cooper's heart swelled with pride as recalled his sovereign's words, but he also recalled Chaucer's advice, as the two men had left the King's tent: *"Be careful that he doesn't put you on too high a pedestal Robert, as it may well lead you to dig your own grave. A man can only survive so many suicide missions."*

Cooper took a breath and addressed his men. Some of his hounds were straining at the leash. It was time.

"I don't care how much you get the scent of blood in your nostrils don't break ranks and give chase. Let your arrows do the work, not your legs. If you get too close to the town you'll be fired upon. Now let's give these bastards such a fright that, even if we fail to hit the mark, we'll scare them to death."

"Aye, they may not be suffering from the bloody flux yet, but let's make them shit themselves," John Walworth added.

The English archers swarmed out of the mine, fanning themselves across the ground, clustering into groups of three. Most of the French stuttered in their advance, unsure whether to continue their attack or retreat. But the bowmen did not falter. Once in position they pulled back their longbows, almost in unison, and loosed a volley of broad-headed arrows. Anguished screams swiftly succeeded the sound of the swish of polished shafts flying through the air.

Cooper quickly surveyed the killing ground and selected a target — a lone crossbowman about to fire at a trio of archers, led by Owen Morgan. Usually, when formed-up in battle, he would have pulled his bowstring back past his ear and aimed upwards in order to hit his distant target. But his quarry was in too short a range. Cooper looked along the top of the arrow's shaft. The hemp string cut into his fingers. The familiar smell of tallow, which Copper had recently rubbed into his bow to prevent it cracking, filled his nostrils. His muscular arm bulged in the blazing sun. He controlled his breathing and the missile sprang from the bow, almost with a sigh. The arrow flew flat and fast, like a bird skimming across the ocean, and struck the enemy's sternum. Without stopping to admire his work Cooper pulled out another arrow and selected a new target.

As was his custom John Walworth uttered a curse, either out loud or under his breath, each time he fired off an arrow.

"Garlic chewing bastard," the butcher's son exclaimed, as he watched the broad-headed missile punch through the skin, flesh and bone of a crossbowman's thigh. His barrel chest expanded as he pulled back on the war bow once more and shot at a bushy-bearded Frenchman. "Hairy bastard ..."

Jack Mercer skewered his target in the stomach and wondered how many of the enemy Owen Morgan had successfully wounded or killed, as the two friends had struck a wager on who would score the most hits (both had marked their shafts accordingly so they could verify the outcome).

A few of the French raised and fired their weapons but their eye wasn't in and they snatched at the shots. Some made the fatal decision to try and reload their crossbows but for every bolt they could fire, as they cranked the mechanisms back or pulled on their stirrups, an English archer could shoot over half a dozen arrows. Fight or flight brought death however, as Cooper's men were all too willing to bury their arrows into the backs of the retreating Frenchmen. Some darted from side to side, like deer attempting to avoid a predator, but to little avail. A few of the enemy fell with two or more broad-headed shafts sticking out of them, ending up as human pincushions.

Many of the archers were possessed with a sense of proficiency rather than viciousness. They ignored the dull aches in their shoulders and they tuned out the occasional piercing scream which would have set most other men's teeth on edge. Their hearts remained dispassionate, but a few of the bowmen grinned sadistically as they triumphed in the pain they were inflicting on an enemy who had slaughtered their comrades and jeered at them from the walls of the town. They were agents of justice and vengeance, redressing the balance.

A handful of the French raiding party made it back to the town's gate but the rest lay dead or dying. Raoul de Gaucourt stood on the rampart, surveying the disastrous scene. The French commander repeatedly banged his fist against the top of the stone wall and cursed the English (as well as privately admiring their deadly professionalism). The archers had lived up to their fearsome reputation, again. Gaucourt wished for just fifty bowmen of their calibre. He would then be more confident of holding the besieged town. For too long his country had been obsessed with believing that horsemen held the key to victory on the battlefield. The French aristocracy — knights themselves — believed that knights were the pride of their army. Yet how could a knight alter the course of a battle whilst lying in the mud, impaled by half a dozen arrows, before he even reached the enemy's lines? How many French souls had to perish before his paymasters learned the lessons of Crécy and Poitiers? Gaucourt shook his head in mournfulness and disappointment at the failed raid, but he was as determined as ever to hold off the perfidious English before the Dauphin and his army could arrive and relieve the town.

But time — and food — are running out.

Robert Cooper held his bow aloft and gave the order for his men to cease firing. Most had already done so. There was no one left to shoot at. Cooper did a quick headcount and was relieved to find that none of his men had been injured or killed. Had they been lucky or had they made their own luck? A few of the archers turned the tables and jeered at their counterparts on the walls. Jack Mercer and Owen Morgan clapped one another on the shoulders and commenced to check how many of their specially marked arrows could be found sticking out of French corpses. John Walworth, fearing that few of his comrades had the stomach to do the honours, mercilessly slit the throats of the French wounded. He rummaged through their clothing afterwards. The men would pool any spoils of war. Cooper thought he might leave the fallen to rot within view of their countrymen, to serve as an example. It might encourage some to surrender or goad them into sallying forth again. Out of the corner of his eye he noticed a fallen French soldier similar in height to himself, wearing a well-made pair of boots. His own were in an unenviable state and it was unlikely that St Crispin, the patron saint of cobblers, would answer his prayers and provide for him. He unburdened the dead crossbowman of his fine, leather footwear and slipped them onto his feet.

On top of the ridge, Chaucer squinted and attempted to make his own headcount. Henry patted his whinnying horse before turning to him and nodding in satisfaction. Corpses littered the scorched land like some kind of macabre shrub-life, blooming from out of the ground. Yet, despite gaining a minor victory, the stench of death was still stronger behind the English lines. The bloody flux was proving more deadly than any contingent of archers.

The sun continued to pulsate, rippling the air and reddening the faces of the living and dead alike. A brace of cawing crows began to circle the killing ground, between the mine and white walls of Harfleur. Chaucer darkly mused how the birds would have fuller stomachs than most Englishmen or Frenchmen come the evening — and during the days to follow.

3

Writhing, golden flames from the campfire licked the night air. Cooper and a small number of his men — John Walworth, Owen Morgan and Jack Mercer — had found a quiet spot in the woods, away from the noise and sickening smells of the army's main camp. Chaucer had supplied his archers with salted pork, some cheese and a large jug of ale.

At first the brothers-in-arms raised a toast to fallen comrades. Five men from their company had died from the flux in the past week, including George Clifford. Whether the impulse was borne out of courage or madness the bastard son of a Yorkshire nobleman had always fought at the vanguard of a battle, or in a tavern brawl. The handle of his giant poleaxe was scarred with numerous notches, one for every man the weapon had cut down. Clifford had been good humoured, brutal and built like an ox. But the bloody flux broke his body and spirit within just a few days. If the flux could kill the mighty man-at-arms — swatting him like an insect — then it could kill anyone. But despite the danger of contracting the dreaded disease Percy Badby had tended to his friend, to make his death as comfortable as possible. Badby spoon-fed him, changed his bedding and prayed for his fellow soldier, but it seemed that not even God could hear the goodly fletcher's words over the thunderous cannon fire.

Cooper also silently remembered Stephen Hall, the innocent archer who had been tortured and murdered by the French agent, Reynard of Troyes. Henry had ordered Chaucer, Cooper and a number of other men to travel to Scotland. Their mission had been to scupper a French plot to fund a Scottish army to attack the north of England whilst the King campaigned in France. The mission had ultimately been successful but Hall had been captured, interrogated and butchered by the zealous

French spy. As Cooper downed another cup of ale he spared a thought for the two vows he had made in the past month: to marry Grace and to murder Reynard of Troyes.

The friends peered through the canopy of maple trees and watched clouds of smoke mushroom into the air. It was difficult to know whether the smoke was coming from campfires or mass graves, as the army incinerated its dead. To combat the mournful atmosphere Owen Morgan lightened the mood by filling everyone's cup and asking about French women. The conversation then turned towards whores — and the best ones they had ever slept with. Morgan was as vocal as ever and led the discussion: "Like all the best women she was Welsh," the archer proudly asserted.

"I suppose she had a great singing voice," Jack Mercer chipped in.

"I couldn't tell you how good a singer she was. Her mouth was too full from playing on my pipe," the Welshman posited, grinning from the memory. "I saw her a few times. She even gave me a discount. Now if that's not love I don't know what is. But c'mon Jack, you've spent more time in brothels than you have in church. Which whore stole the heart of a thief?"

Jack Mercer pursed his lips and paused before speaking. A procession of female faces paraded through his mind. There was Margaret, the fishmonger's daughter. She had a lazy eye but everything else about her was willing. And then there was Plymouth Sally, a comely whore who allowed her clientele to pour honey over her body and lick it off. The bowman cringed however, when he recalled the image of Sally scraping the excess honey off her skin and putting it back in a jar, ready for her next customer. He smirked slightly as he remembered his kissing cousin, Mary. She would carry a sprig of mistletoe around with her, even in summer.

"Well back in my housebreaking days my partner and me would always celebrate a job by making a beeline to the local brothel. Because I'm more of a gent than most the owner asked me to break in a new girl. Her name was Constance. She was a pretty thing — with tits that begged to be squeezed and an arse that you could happily get lost in. She'd recently been thrown out of a convent and needed to put food in her belly. She was shy and sweet. I gave our novice a religious experience. She certainly called out to God on more than one occasion during our night together. We spent as much time talking as rutting though, and come the morning she asked if she could stay with me. She offered to cook and clean for me — and serve me in various other ways. Perhaps it was due to the fact that she was straddled over me at the time but I suddenly got the urge to settle down and make a home for myself, instead of breaking into others people's houses. I said to her that I had another job to do in the next town but that I'd return in a fortnight. I gave her my word but her life had been a patchwork of broken promises. We're all liars and bastards. It's just that some of us are worse than others. I think she only half believed I'd come back. I only half believed me too."

Mercer began to hypnotically stare into the fire as he spoke. An element of the philosophical crept into the usually cynical rogue's voice.

"What happened?" Morgan asked, leaning slightly forward, intrigued by his friend's story.

"A week after I left, some drunken caitiff slit her throat. They hung the bastard. And that was that. But I don't want to sadden you all so much that you'll want to cut your own throats. Tell us about your best whore, John, before the ale runs dry and fire dies out."

Cups were refilled, washing away the gloom. Walworth spoke: "Her name was Alice. The brothel was on Bankside. She didn't have the prettiest of faces. She had a lopsided grin and one ear seemed to be larger than the other. Her front teeth were missing but she turned that affliction to her advantage when bending down on her knees and plying her trade. Her stamina was greater than any shire horse. I stumbled into her little room drunk at midnight, but by the time I left at dawn I was legless for a different reason. I was less exhausted after the battle at Shrewsbury. My bones ached from supporting her weight and heaving her into position. The grin on my face though, when she finally let me leave, was as wide as her arse. God bless you Alice — and all who sail on you!" Walworth raised a cup to the absent, buxom whore.

"It's a shame that our friend Fordham can't be here," Owen Morgan remarked, making reference to Edward Fordham, the poet turned man-at-arms who also served in Thomas

Chaucer's company of soldiers. "He's fucked more women than Badby's made arrows." Although Fordham was the son of a Norfolk landowner and higher in social rank than the archers he still drank the same ale and spilled the same blood as the men sitting around the fire.

"I doubt Edward thinks it's a shame not being with us tonight, given the company he's in. Now there's a filly I'd like to ride," Jack Mercer added, with good humour gleaming in his eyes as he pictured the achingly desirable Marie Nouvel.

"Aye but any horse would have an even longer face, should you try and mount it," Owen Morgan joked, before a chorus of drunken laughter rang out amongst the ribald bowmen.

4

Thankfully the smell of the food and burning lamp oil overpowered the other odours inside and outside the large tent. Thomas Chaucer had given Edward Fordham the use of his billet for the evening, in order to host the French female agent and conduct negotiations with her. Chaucer had also arranged for Henry's personal cook to prepare a meal, and had begrudgingly sacrificed one of his finest vintages for the cause.

Fordham and Marie sat opposite one another around a table. A veritable feast lay before them: capons in garlic sauce; sturgeon coated in breadcrumbs; roasted hare; glazed apples and apricots. Yet the couple feasted more upon the sight of one another.

Marie was the daughter of Charles Nouvel, a merchant and ally of the English. Nouvel paid lip-service to Henry's cause but he passionately believed in his own campaign of making as much money as he could before he died. Even before landing on French soil Chaucer had contacted the merchant to provide the army with intelligence and supplies. Nouvel had sent his daughter to finalise the terms of the contract. She had arrived four days ago, accompanied by a small retinue. Charles Nouvel had instructed his daughter to assess how parlous a state the English campaign was in — and to raise his fees accordingly. Chaucer in turn had asked the handsome and personable man-at-arms to attend to their ally and negotiate as favourable terms as possible.

"He usually gets his way with women," the agent had remarked to the King.

"Aye, his wicked way I imagine. Just make sure that our seducer isn't seduced himself. I have heard that Nouvel's daughter is a beauty of some repute. More importantly than securing a fair maiden Fordham needs to secure a fair price," Henry had replied, his brow knitted in worry from the latest reports by his quartermasters. The besiegers, as well as the besieged, would soon begin to starve.

Marie Nouvel narrowed her almond-shaped eyes slightly and surveyed the room. A number of books and correspondence sat upon a desk in the corner, though Chaucer had removed any important documents from prying eyes. A spare saddle, along with a sword and basinet, occupied another corner next to a stool with a silver basin on top of it. Above them hung a cross. Marie was surprised at the item, as she considered that the worldly agent wasn't a follower, or victim, of religion. The cross however had come from his bedchamber at his house in Ewelme. Chaucer's wife, Matilda, had asked him to take it on campaign with him, to remind him of her and bolster what little faith he had left.

Edward Fordham narrowed his gaze too and took in, again, Marie's bewitching beauty. Her sun-burnished skin was as smooth as Persian silk. Her long black hair had the sheen of polished ebony and hung down to her breast. Her sharp features could sometimes appear haughty, but they were always alluring. Although the agent often wore riding breeches, with a dagger fastened to her belt, Marie had, on this last night with the Englishman, put on a fine dress — the neckline of which plunged down to the ends of her hair. The crimson, embroidered cotton garment clung to her lithe figure. She wore a small, gold pendant around her neck and a diamond-studded brooch. Both gleamed in the candlelight, but failed to shine as brightly as she did.

Fordham recalled what Thomas Chaucer had said when he had spoken to him about the merchant's daughter:

"Women are often deemed to be angels or whores. Marie Nouvel is both. The more beautiful the rose, the harder the thorns. Priests are torn between damning her soul and saving it. Her tongue is as sharp as the knife she wears around her waist. And she's not afraid to unsheathe it. Her English is faultless and she can speak passable Italian and Spanish too. She is familiar with every aspect of her father's mercantile business and is as niggardly as Charles when it comes to setting the terms of any deal. Yet I have heard plenty of stories

of her charitable works. She funds a local school and provides employment and shelter for war widows and orphans. You will fail to wholly understand her Edward, which will compel you to want to understand her all the more. Our French Cleopatra can be lovely one moment and scornful the next. She has never been married but I warrant that she has received more proposals over the years than we've hurled millstones at the walls of Harfleur. She has seduced squires, knights and aged husbands alike, in the name of business or for her own amusement and pleasure. Past lovers may curse her name but many would also willingly go through the whole affair again. You will not be able to take your eyes off her — so watch yourself Edward."

Rain began to fall on the roof of the tent. Fordham thought the sound similar to that of when Marie had drummed her nails upon the table, in tedium or impatience, during their first meeting. Her frosty manner had thawed though since their first encounter. They had spoken about literature, history and shared something of themselves. They had made love. *But had it all just been an act?* Fordham wondered. *Were they both just playing a part?*

"I must leave tomorrow. This will be our last night together. We may never see each other again. Will you not grant me a token, as if you were a chivalrous knight and I a chaste maiden?" Marie remarked, with a playful smile on her lips. Her voice was as clear and beautiful as cut glass.

"Would you like me to give you a token?"

"No. I have too many already cluttering up my home. Most are fit for the fireplace. They burn quicker than a man's desire for a lady, after he has satisfied himself."

It was Fordham's turn to subtly smile, as he recalled something he had said to his friend Robert Cooper a day ago: *"Words can trip from her tongue like honey — or acid."*

"You are not an admirer of chivalric love?" the soldier asked, filling Marie's cup and then his own.

"In my experience most men like to bow before a woman in order to catch a greater glimpse of her legs. I have lost count of the amount of noblemen who have pledged their undying love for me, especially when they find out the value of my father's estate. But when they are no longer welcome in my bedchamber their undying love dies out quicker than a candle can be extinguished," Marie replied, whilst pinching the light out from the candle next to her on the table. "Love is just a transaction is it not; a business deal? Although both may believe in the trade they are making one party always benefits more than the other. The bonds of chivalry are just that — fetters. A sovereign uses chivalry to bind his knights to him. A knight will use it to subjugate his tenants and mistress. Love is a joke is it not, Edward? And you can laugh and play along with it more than most men, I imagine."

Marie's eyes darkly glowed like burning coals as she spoke. Her beguiling features could scold or seduce at will. A part of her longed to meet a man who could prove her cynicism wrong. She wanted to love someone, marry and have children. But to be a wife was to be a slave, the educated woman firmly judged. "I have been courted by countless princes. But all I've kissed are frogs, toads, asses, dogs and pigs," she had confessed to Edward the previous evening. There had been sadness and humour in her tone. Marie surprised herself by how open she could be, when talking to the equally satirical Englishman.

"I am not sure what love is. I just know that it's rare — and therefore precious," Fordham remarked, somewhat wistfully. He briefly thought of Chaucer and Cooper. One was happily married and the other about to be. *But love and happiness are not for me.* Fordham had lost count of the number of bedchambers he had crept out of over the years, the perfumed letters he had received which remained unanswered and the broken promises to serving girls. Some had truly believed that the prosperous man-at-arms would save them from penury and a loveless marriage to someone who would treat them ill.

"Perhaps you could write to me, even if we are unable to meet again soon?" Marie proposed, and for the first time in a long time the manipulative agent genuinely meant what she said. Part of her resented the Englishman for making her favour him and ask something of him. But desire eclipsed any feelings of vulnerability. He was unlike any man she had ever encountered before.

Fordham replied that he would do so and for once in his life he intended to keep his word, although he was unsure how much the bewitching woman was just teasing him.

Love is an act.

"But let us not talk of chivalry or love anymore. Tell me — how do you feel when you kill someone in battle?" Marie asked, her eyes peering over the rim of her cup as she sipped her wine. There was a blend of curiosity and playfulness in her voice.

"I feel thankful that I am alive and my opponent isn't — and that there is one less person in Christendom who wants to kill me or my friends."

"You seem to be a good man and a good soldier, Edward."

Fordham was unsure whether the woman was asking a question or asserting an opinion. Or mocking him.

"It's a rare thing to be both, like being a rich poet. But I am a better soldier than I was a poet, unfortunately or not. I dare say my readers, all four or five of them, would also agree."

Lust and amusement shone in Marie's expression. She ran her tongue around her lips, perhaps to catch any wine upon them, and tucked her long kohl-black tresses behind her ears.

"You are wickedly funny. And the more wicked you are the better. But is there anything that you are serious about? Duty? Honour? Or are they just mere words to you too, like chivalry?"

The light reflected against the sun-kissed skin of her neck and breast. Fordham's heart beat faster, echoing the tempo of the rain thrumming upon the tent. There would be no more talk of the price of flour or or the fees for maps of the French countryside. Fordham no longer wondered whether he was seducing her or she him. Their lovemaking yesternight had been carnal at first but then sensual and tender; well-practised but then intimate. Marie sighed — a lover's sigh. She had given instructions to her attendants not to disturb her for the rest of the evening.

"I am being serious when I say that I am going to stand up, plant kisses on your throat and carry you over to the bed, as if it were a duty and honour to do so."

"And what do you think will happen then?" Marie playfully said, her expression awash with pleasure.

"Well then I will be in your hands, my lady. Or at least part of me will."

5

Thomas Chaucer waited for the morning light to slant into the room (Henry had allowed his agent to billet in a spare room of the house that the King had commandeered at the start of the siege). Unfortunately the light was accompanied by the distant sound of sawing, hammering and cannon fire.

His limbs ached from sleeping on the stone floor — and his head ached from having stayed up late with Sir John Holland. The knight was a formidable soldier, and an even more formidable drinker. Chaucer calmly closed his eyes and pictured the peaceful scene of his garden back home, of an emerald lawn freckled with flowers, apple and pear trees laden with fruit, the smell of freshly baked bread coming from the kitchen, and the sound of his daughter's voice ringing in his ears. Chaucer let the warm sunlight and visions wash over him, in an attempt to smooth out the creases of his aching body and soul, before commencing to write a letter to his wife.

Chaucer had married Matilda for love and money, although he would not now part with his wife for all the riches of the world. She understood his moods better than anyone and provided a haven from the intrigues and interrogation sessions of his life in the capital. His wife never bored him, which put Chaucer in a minority amongst husbands, he judged. Their marriage had endured the tyranny of Richard II and the tensions of Henry Bolingbroke's reign. Matilda had patiently suffered her husband's change of career and frequent periods away from home, either in London or foreign lands. Perhaps, Chaucer mused, it was due to his absence that his relationship remained strong.

As was often the case when he wrote to Matilda the agent was torn between being honest and protecting his wife from the harsh realities of the world. She would want to know how he and the campaign were faring, and she would trust his report more than any news she received from others. But a husband cannot tell the truth all the time, Chaucer considered. If nothing else it would prove too exhausting, for the husband and wife.

"*Dearest Matilda,*

I am safe and well. Please pass on the news to Grace that Robert is fine too. My thoughts are often with you and the children. If only the rest of me could be present as well.

The crossing was, thankfully, uneventful. We landed unopposed. When reaching the shore Henry fell to his knees and prayed, giving thanks to God. He also kissed the ground, like Edward III. It was difficult to tell whether the King's performance was borne from reverence or for propaganda reasons. With Henry, there would have been no contradiction if it had been both.

The first order of the day was for our soldiers to mark the red cross of St George on their chests and backs, so as to distinguish ourselves from any enemies we might encounter. Some might say that we have been branded like cattle, and some may posit that we will be slaughtered the same way.

Henry proved his mettle as a just king by issuing orders that looting was forbidden. Women and children are not to be abused. Like Caesar Henry realises that clemency will garner more support than cruelty.

We soon surrounded the town but not before our enemies flooded the valley, creating a situation where we can only attack Harfleur from two positions: the Leure and Montivilliers gates. Unfortunately the flooded valley slowed our advance and before we could encircle our target the town was reinforced by several hundred seasoned soldiers and a competent commander, Raoul de Gaucourt.

After refusing to peaceably surrender Henry, claiming his authority from God and the laws of Deuteronomy, threatened Harfleur with all manner of punishments should the town defy him. Perhaps the promise of violence and retribution strengthened the townspeople's resolve rather than weakened it. Fishermen and dyers have become hardened fighters, pouring scorn, hot oil and lime upon our troops.

The suburbs of the town were razed to the ground and the siege engines advanced. Our cannons spit out more missiles than our children used to spit out my cooking. But one cannot bombard a town into submission. Our attacks have been repulsed and our mines have been counter-mined. As much damage as we seem to inflict upon the town each day the defences are patched up come the following morning. A large barbican stands at the entrance to the Leure Gate, like St Peter guarding the portals of heaven. There have even been occasions when Gaucourt's troops have sallied forth to capture or destroy our artillery pieces. We had planned and provisioned to take Harfleur within eight days but I sometimes dread that it will now take more than eighty. And all the time the Sword of Damocles hangs over us in the form of the arrival of a French army, sent to relieve the valuable port.

The town is more tightly sealed shut than a Jew's purse. But there is hope. The men remain loyal to the cause. There have been few words of dissent or outbreaks of lawlessness. One of our mines could still reach the walls and create a breach. Our enemy may have the stomach to fight, but soon that will be all that's lodged in his belly as their food reserves are lower than ours. I have also received reports that the Dauphin is reluctant to send a force to relieve the town.

Harfleur will eventually fall but we must half-destroy that which we prize. It will now take time and capital to rebuild and garrison the town.

But as each day passes the burden weighs heavier on Henry's shoulders. He is a model of industry and purpose but the strain is beginning to tell in his features. Worry lines have formed, like marks on a map, around his eyes. Please save your prayers for him, not me. I fear he may lose his faith in the campaign, or God. Both are wedded to one another in his mind. The death of Richard Courtenay has also diminished his soul. Courtenay was a goodly man and a loyal friend but the bloody flux holds no respect for such virtues, it seems. Courtenay used his position as Bishop of Norwich — and an adviser to Henry — to enrich the kingdom rather than his own coffers. He was a scholar and a gentleman. Henry himself attended to his close friend during his passing. He bathed his feet, held his hand and reminisced about shared hunting trips.

Courtenay often looked up at Henry and smiled, as if he were a child. But then his gaunt features would contort, in agony, as the disease ravaged his body and mind. Attendants burned incense to lessen the stench of sweat and ordure. Henry continued to speak to his friend, even when he fell into a sleep and died. The King closed his eyes and kissed his forehead, before ordering that his friend should be taken back to England and buried in Westminster Abbey. The whole scene softened the hardest of hearts. Mine included."

Chaucer put down the goose feather quill and flexed his fingers, in order to fight off the growing cramp in his writing hand. Part of him felt like he was shriving his soul by writing to his wife, sharing the burden. His grief and despair of late had prowled around in his chest, like a caged beast desperate to break free. But Chaucer was a cold pragmatist and knew that a problem shared was not a problem halved. Sharing information on food shortages, the height of the town's walls and the number of men dying from disease would do nothing to annul those problems. He briefly thought of Fordham. He had signed off on the contract with Marie Nouvel last night. The problem of food shortages at least would be halved, once the merchant delivered the produce.

What we need now is faith, not despair. We also need to take the barbican, then town. And move on from this God-forsaken place. I will re-draft the letter later. Tell virtuous lies. Keep in the letter that you are well. That the army landed safely. That morale is strong, despite some set-backs. Tell her of Courtenay's passing, if only because she will suspect that something is amiss if you do not include some bad news. And tell her you love her and are looking forward to coming home. That truth remains sovereign over all other secrets and lies.

Chaucer recalled the scene earlier, just before the dawn. He had been woken by an anxious looking attendant, with the news that a knight had been struck by a bolt of lightning on a hillock away from the camp the previous evening, during the storm. Chaucer immediately sent for the squire and man-at-arms who were with the knight at the time of the freak accident. The agent explained to the two men that the knight had perished from falling from his horse. Chaucer vowed to reward their discretion if they refrained from divulging the true sequence of events. The truth needed to be contained, like a disease. The feeling remained unspoken, but hung over the camp like a black cloud, that God was not now on the side of the English. For some of the more superstitious soldiers — of which there were many — the bloody flux was a pestilence sent by the Almighty to punish the transgressing army. They were fated to fail in their campaign. The French were the righteous ones. The story of a nobleman being struck down would only add credence to their irrational thoughts. Some men needed to be lied to, like children. *Ignorance is bliss.*

6

Fordham closed his eyes and breathed in Marie's scent. She laced her fingers in his and ran her toes along his muscular leg beneath the sheets. Their breathing returned to normal once more, after the breathlessness of another bout of lovemaking. Cannon fire had woken them an hour or so ago, but they had kept each other awake since.

Fordham bemoaned that they would likely be disturbed soon but Marie, sumptuously smiling, explained that she had instructed her attendant (who also doubled as her bodyguard) to stand sentry-like outside of the tent and not admit anyone. Fordham pictured the dour-faced Henri keeping watch. He had the build and charm of a bullock. The burly Gascon was protective of his charge and also jealous of all her lovers.

"How did you know that I would want you to stay the night?" Fordham asked, his features askance in a piratical grin.

"In my experience most men are only interested in two things: sex and money. And I'm not altogether sure they're interested in the latter."

Fordham sighed, recalling the night before. Marie had straddled him and deliberately, tenderly, kissed all the battle-scars marking his torso. Her body had been taut with desire, entwining itself around him like ivy.

"At least I can claim to be different in some respects then. I am interested in you for your intelligence — and your grain stores," Fordham wryly stated.

Marie let out a burst of laughter, as sweet as any song. She cupped his unshaven face in her hands and planted a succulent kiss on his wine-stained lips.

"I should have included a clause, obtaining you in the contract. Or perhaps I can still entice you away. You could stay with me. I would seduce you, like Calypso did Odysseus.

And you would never want to leave," Marie softly uttered, as she fleetingly thought of how she would have preferred to be his Penelope. Faithful and good. Loved. "Or are not all beautiful women more like Circe, blessed and cursed to turn all men into bestial slaves? My father once called me Circe, as a pet name." The smile abruptly fell from Marie's face when she mentioned her father. She let go of Fordham's hand.

"What's wrong?" he asked. It was rare for concern to oust out glibness in his tone. It was a strange but not unwelcome sensation.

"Nothing," Marie answered, half distractedly, turning her head slightly away from him. For the first time since arriving in the camp she flinched at hearing a cannon blast.

"Nothing can come from nothing. I've become intimate with every inch of your body. You can tell me what's on your mind too."

After closing her eyes for a few seconds, Marie took a breath and began to speak, as much to herself as to the man lying next to her.

"Happiness is so fleeting, is it not? It has, at best, the lifespan of a mayfly. Happiness can flit in and out of sight so quickly that we start to doubt if it ever truly existed. I am a victim of my own success. My father dearly wanted a son and he educated me as such — and I am not ungrateful for it. I have a chamber full of silk garments, gems and love letters. But I treasure my books more than anything else. He used to regularly call me his asset and greatest weapon.

"I was thirteen when he first introduced me to a member of his merchant guild. His name was Jean Bouvet. My father wanted to purchase the man's shares in a tin mine. He was far from unpleasant. I have slept with men with more years to their name and fewer grey hairs on their heads. He took me for walks and bought me dresses and a gold hairpin, with a bejewelled butterfly on the end of it. I listened to my father's instructions and played my part. On the evening of signing over the shares to my father, Bouvet took me to bed. My mouth was so dry my kisses could not have been much to speak of, I imagine. He was gentle and respectful — at first.

"Since then I have been called many names: Jezebel, She-wolf and the Whore of Caudebec, among others. I have been a frequent asset to my father since that night. I have served him and countless suitors. I have served myself too, I cannot lie… My father says he is not keen on my marrying yet, until the price is right. Happiness is fleeting. If only unhappiness could similarly be over within the blink of an eye."

Fordham pulled Marie towards him and she buried her teary face in his chest. The cynical soldier couldn't quite tell whether Marie was being sincere — or if it was all an act to the beguiling French agent.

*

Robert Cooper stood on top of a grassy slope, which overlooked the camp. A phalanx of tents occupied the muddy ground. Smoke from dozens of campfires spiralled up into the air. Acrid, black smoke also belched out from the fire pits, which incinerated the dead. Men, wearing muddied and bloodied apparel, trudged around, ankle deep in the mulched up earth. When the army had first landed there had been a mood of purpose and expectation. Soldiers, smiths, carpenters, farriers, masons, armourers, quartermasters, fletchers and others had come ashore with a lustre in their eyes and their chests puffed out in pride. But careworn expressions, hollowed out cheeks and slumped shoulders would greet Cooper if he ventured down into the heart of the army now.

Cooper recalled Fordham's comments from a couple of days ago: "It seems that the four horsemen of the apocalypse have joined us on our campaign: War, Famine, Pestilence and Death."

Cooper's thoughts turned again to Grace, his intended. The archer had recently asked Thomas Chaucer's housekeeper to marry him. He was still somewhat in shock that she had said yes.

I don't deserve her. But I want to be deserving of her.

Cooper had made a promise to himself — and Grace — that this would be his last campaign. He had saved up enough money, which Chaucer had kept for him and invested wisely with, to purchase a small farm. He wanted to start a family and be there for them, unlike his own father who had been absent for most of his childhood. When his bowman father had finally come home, after spending over half his life on campaigns, he was a dramatically changed man. War, and the death of his friend and commander Edward of Woodstock — the Black Prince — plunged him into a funereal gloom. Cooper had come to believe that peace was harder for his father to adapt to than war. The veteran archer often stared into the distance as though he had left part of himself back in some foreign land. Matthew Cooper took little interest in his wife and child, even when it became apparent that Robert was displaying great progress as an archer. Drink sometimes softened or enlivened his mood, but then he would drink too much and become angry or violent. On more than one occasion he would come home from the tavern, his face marked from brawling, and on more than one occasion he would come home and beat his wife.

Henry, along with others in the army, had praised Robert's father as a hero. But Robert Cooper was determined that the last person he wanted to emulate was Matthew Cooper. Only at the end did his father display some semblance of remorse. Matthew Cooper had seized his son's sleeve and drawn him closer. In a rasping, breathless whisper he spoke: *"You've done the hard part son, by becoming a better archer than me. Now you just have to do the easy part, by being the better man..."*

Robert Cooper let the massaging rays of the late morning sun pour onto his face. He thought of Grace, rather than his father, and his heavy heart was lifted. Cooper could capture and ransom the wealthiest knight in all of France but he knew the real prize was waiting for him back home. This would be his last campaign, the archer resolved once again. *I've spent enough seasons in hell.*

7

Henry was pacing around the room, throwing a worn tennis-ball up in the air and catching it, when Thomas Chaucer entered. The agent was about to kneel before his sovereign but Henry gently shook his head to signify that there was no need to indulge in any ceremony.

"If your knee must kiss the ground, let it be in a prayer to God instead of in deference to your king," Henry said.

Chaucer briefly nodded and stood, attentive, before his commander. Although still relatively youthful, Chaucer noted the crow's feet perching on the corners of Henry's eyes (eyes which some deemed intelligent and others cold). His slim face appeared more lugubrious than usual, Chaucer thought. Grief still occasionally haunted his countenance. Time may heal most wounds but the pain of Henry's great friend's death was still raw. The King's dress was plain and his slender frame belied a body which had been work-hardened through years of soldiering. His muscles were as taut as a bow string. A small star-shaped scar next to Henry's nose, from a wound received during the Battle of Shrewsbury, could not despoil his fine, regal features.

The room possessed an air of austerity. The furniture was functional, as opposed to ornate. Two large barrels, filled with bran and the King's plate armour, stood in one corner. The cereal helped to keep the metal polished and oiled. The food on the table was little different to the food the King's soldiers ate. The only real decoration adorning the chamber was a painting depicting the Black Prince surveying his troops before the Battle of Poitiers. A large table ran along the back wall and housed several books: a bible; a copy of Saint Augustine's *Confessions*; *Concerning Military Matters* by

Vegetius; and Julius Caesar's *The Gallic Wars*. The latter lay open.

"This ball was a gift from the Dauphin, would you believe? His envoy delivered it, along with several others of its kind, some time ago," Henry remarked, throwing the ball up and catching it one more time. "I have kept this ball — and the missive which accompanied the gift — to remind me of my enemy's arrogance and folly. The Dauphin wrote that, as such a young king, I should confine myself to merely enjoying my sport. I wish the Dauphin would take up my offer to play with me, either in the form of single combat or to have our two armies meet. For every ball he has gifted me I will bat back a hundred gun-stones. I will turn his tears of laughter to tears of woe, as he mourns the loss of the French crown," Henry stated determinedly.

Chaucer had been present at court when the Dauphin's envoy had presented his underwhelming gift. The supercilious diplomat read out a statement, making subtle reference to Henry's licentious days as a young man. Henry's reply was infused with wit, authority and barely veiled anger: "*For many a thousand widows shall this make a mock of their dear husbands, mock mothers from their sons, mock castles down, and yet some are yet ungotten and unborn that shall have cause to curse the Dauphin's scorn. But this lies all within the will of God, to whom I do appeal, and in whose name tell you the Dauphin I am coming on to venge me as I may, and to put forth my rightful hand in a well-hallowed cause. So get you hence in peace.*"

The envoy had retreated, Chaucer recalled, as had the blood from the diplomat's face.

"To some it may seem that the Dauphin is having the last laugh," Henry added, his hand now gripping the ball like a talon. "Harfleur stands as securely as it did before our army even landed. Indeed we are in peril, far more than its townsfolk. Every day we lose men to disease, whilst every day the Dauphin adds to his ranks with new recruits and knights, answering the call to serve under the Oriflamme. We trade artillery blows, like two punched out pugilists. As you know it is my custom to disguise myself and venture out into the camp, in order to measure the morale and temper of the men. I did so yesternight and sat around a campfire with a group of half drunk and half starving archers. They were worried that, like Caesar at Alesia, we may soon be surrounded by a larger army — and at the same time the forces in the town could attack us from the other direction. I reminded them that Caesar was victorious at Alesia, which allayed their fears but a little. The flagon of ale I produced lifted their spirits far more, I warrant, but it will take more than just one flagon of ale to lift the spirits of the entire army. How fares our negotiations with Nouvel's agent?"

"The terms are fair, though far from as fair as his daughter," Chaucer answered, wondering if Fordham had had any effect on softening Marie Nouvel.

"Take your company of men and deliver payment to Nouvel personally. Pressure him for prompt deliveries of the supplies. Soldiers can live without hope but they won't last long without alcohol. God willing the ale we'll receive can be used for toasting victory. I have been in negotiations with Gaucourt, through letters passed between us. I have allowed him to send a message out to the Dauphin. Gaucourt believes that the Dauphin will send a force to relieve the town. In return, if the French army does not heed his call then he will freely surrender the town, by the end of the week. I believe the coward will wait and amass a greater army — and sacrifice the port — before daring to face us."

"And can we trust Gaucourt that he will keep his word?" Chaucer asked. His latest reports affirmed Henry's conviction that the Dauphin was willing to sacrifice Harfleur to the English.

"Only if he as honourable as he is wily. But Gaucourt, our very own Vercingetorix if you like, could as easily go back on his word as a man can put bat to ball. I must still look to take the town by force. Diplomacy alone cannot engineer a breach in those stone walls. At the very least force will give diplomacy some teeth. Though we may be bogged down in the mud, we will fight on. England will not submit to France, her laws, language or customs. Saint George still has a dragon to slay. But you have heard me say such things before, Thomas. If you must lose your life to this campaign, it should not be through me boring you to death. Tell me, have you heard from your wife at all?"

"I am in the process of writing to her now. I will doubtless receive a letter from her soon. She will instruct me to come back from the war alive, else my life won't be worth living," Chaucer said, smiling fondly, as he pictured his wife in his mind's eye.

"I remember a line from one of your father's poems, when I think about conjugal bliss: 'The woe that is marriage'. Did not the wise Justinus, in *The Merchant's Tale*, considerer marriage to be purgatory on Earth?"

Thomas Chaucer nodded. His father had always been a distant figure, geographically and emotionally. The agent had grown up in Lincolnshire with his mother, whilst his father lived a largely separate life in London and then in Kent, either working for the government or writing at home. Towards the end of his life however, Thomas, using his new-found wealth and influence, arranged for his father to live on the grounds of Westminster Abbey. They saw each other more often, but it was too little, or too late, for father and son to truly reconcile. Geoffrey Chaucer was a finer poet that he was a husband and father. *But he was a special man.* Time spent with his father had been precious to Thomas, because it was rare.

"I wouldn't adhere to my father's wisdom too much in regards to marriage, else you might die a lonely, old man. And a king needs a queen," Chaucer argued, thinking how Matilda and his small estate in Ewelme had provided him with a portion of paradise on Earth. But home felt lamentably far away right now.

"I am much too wedded to my cause to turn my attention to marrying at the moment. But because of my cause I will look to secure the hand of Catherine Valois, in conjunction with securing the peace. The union between two people will hopefully inspire an accord between two nations. Should she prove as ugly as sin then I will just have to lie back, shut my eyes and think of England. But thankfully I have heard that Catherine is pleasing to the eye. Once she learns the rudiments of English then she will be pleasing to the ear too," Henry remarked, and the feint light of a smile could be seen behind the cracks in the King's usually adamantine demeanour.

"Speaking of things which may prove pleasing to your ear, I have just received some intelligence regarding Reynard of Troyes," Chaucer said, making reference to the French agent who had been the author behind various plots to unseat Henry, including funding a Scottish invasion and championing the cause of a false, puppet, Richard II.

"The Dauphin and his French paymasters were far from impressed with his failure to sow unrest. The King himself, I was informed, chastised the agent, in a rare moment of sanity and authority. Reynard also lost a significant sum of money belonging to the French treasury. As a consequence his stock has gone down as quickly as the gold which sunk to the bottom of the sea off the south-east coast of Scotland. His malevolent halo has lost some of its lustre. He is out of favour and Reynard has a number of enemies at court who will be whispering into the Dauphin's ear to tarnish his reputation some more. Certain personages and factions were already unhappy that a commoner held too much influence at court. Fear secured Reynard's powerbase, more than devotion. Should I encounter the bastard then I'll sheathe my sword in his chest but it may transpire that, before I can do so, Reynard will receive a French knife in his back," Chaucer stated, believing that such an outcome was worth dirtying one's knee and praying for.

"Let us hope for the best and plan for the worse. I suspect that we have not heard the last of Reynard of Troyes. A wounded animal can sometimes be more dangerous than a healthy one."

8

A muggy, festering heat swelled in the insect-laden air. A triumphant shout — accompanied by a low groan and curse — could be heard in the background as a few archers played dice. The charcoal grey ribbons of smoke, from the incineration pits, still unfurled across the sky. Some soldiers slept in their tents, others were awake, restless, yearning for something to happen, and some were dreading the thought of the French surrounding them.

Robert Cooper and Edward Fordham shared a bowl of pottage and half a jug of watery mead. Cooper rubbed tallow into his large yew bow whilst Fordham let out a yawn, before continuing the conversation.

"So it seems it was just *au revoir*, rather than goodbye, when I saw her off this morning," the man-at-arms remarked. Marie and her retinue had departed that morning, but just after she left Chaucer asked Fordham to accompany him in delivering payment to Charles Nouvel at his estate situated to the east of Harfleur. "It's a shame you and John won't be joining us and enjoying the merchant's hospitality. But Chaucer mentioned that Henry deliberately wants you to remain with the army to help him break the siege. It's a double-edged sword, earning the admiration of the King. Just remember that a monarch's favour, and gold, are worth nothing to you if you're six foot under. If you're caught in the crossfire of a breach let somebody else be the hero for a change, Robert. You've got a wife-to-be waiting for you at home. Grace must be itching to nag you till your ears bleed, hide the ale and spend all your hard earned money too. It will be her wifely duty to do so, no?"

Cooper smiled broadly at his friend, who never seemed to tire of turning his satirical humour towards marriage — and love.

"I just want to be there on the day when you find happiness and the love of a good woman Edward. How dejected you'll be, at being proved wrong. But perhaps love's dart has already hit its target. You have an unmistakable look in your eye when you talk about this French woman," the bowman said, half in jest and half in earnest.

"I like to think that I am too fleet of foot to end up being shackled by the bonds of marriage. Not even Cupid's aim is good enough to strike me down with love's dart. But it will indeed be a pleasure to see Marie again and do my bit for Anglo-French relations. I will keep my end up, so to speak," Fordham said with a wink, whilst topping up his companion's cup.

"You shouldn't underestimate Cupid's arm. Even you might marry one day. Church bells will ring out, along with the sound of a hundred female hearts breaking. And a hundred husbands, married to wayward wives, will breathe a collected sigh of relief."

"We'll see. But that's enough talk about my conquests. How do you think the campaign is faring? Men seem to be dying in greater numbers than the trees we are cutting down for our siege engines. Yet still the town's stone walls remain as hard as my heart. If God is on our side, he has a funny way of showing it. Perhaps the King should sheath his sword and make a tactical retreat. There have been other failed campaigns and crusades. England will still be able to feed itself and get drunk each night if we return now, empty handed. The army is beginning to run short of some provisions even at this juncture. We will not be able to endure a winter, even if we march to Calais tomorrow. Kings and their armies need victories. But we cannot defeat an enemy which doesn't come out to fight. England can wish for no finer leader, given its recent history. But a fine leader can still lose a kingdom. Is it a sense of honour which keeps Henry here — or a sense of vanity? It seems like the bloody flux has already won one battle against us. If we stay, it could win the war. It's clinging to us and spreading like moss upon a tombstone. The road to hell is paved with good intentions," Fordham argued, his brow as creased as his off-white linen shirt.

"You know you could be hanged for such seditious talk," Cooper replied, more in jest than in a warning, but he was still somewhat disappointed by his companion's lack of loyalty towards the King.

"Just do me a favour and make sure that my last meal is better than this pottage, if I am found guilty."

Fordham sometimes envied and admired his friend's faith in his commander — and God — but at other instances he believed his stance to be confounding and contemptible.

"You shouldn't treat everything as a joke. This is a just war. The French have been funding our enemies, raiding our coastline and plotting against us for years. The ruling elite of France gorges upon its own people, as well as those of other nations. It desires to force its language and laws upon us, as if England should be a vassal state of France. If we continue to defy them then so might other countries. No one power should hold mastery over the continent. Whether Henry is acting out of honour, vainglory or something else we need to believe in him and our cause."

The soldiers had rarely exchanged a cross word over the years — indeed, throughout the uncertainties of war, their friendship was one of the only things the two Englishmen could rely on, but a steeliness and heat crept into the archer's tone. Fordham was tempted to reply in kind — and belittle the cause — but wisely thought better of it. The enemy was sitting on top of the walls of Harfleur, not sitting next to him. Cooper was about to be thrown into the breach and Fordham was due to travel through enemy-held territory. Fordham experienced a cold presentiment, which trickled down his spine like an icy bead of sweat. He mournfully thought that he might never see his old friend again. That one of them would die.

9

Grey clouds marbled the darkening sky as the metallic clang of swords rang out in the air. Two armour-clad knights, encircled by an engaged audience, fenced with a mixture of technique and ferocity. Aside from a few senior centenars, who commanded their own companies, Robert Cooper was the only archer present. Instead, knights and squires dominated the hundred strong group of men (Thomas Chaucer was absent, preparing for his departure in the morning). Cooper found himself standing next to the brave and high-spirited Sir John Holland, the famed knight who had led the first party ashore during the invasion. Sir John Cornwall stood a few paces away as well. Cornwall was a grey-haired veteran, whose fine manners at court masked a warrior's savagery on the battlefield. The knight had amassed a fortune over the years from tournament wins and the ransoming of prisoners.

Cooper judged that the larger of the two combatants must have shared his own build beneath his mud splattered armour, but the armour — a composite of pieces bought from Milan, Cologne and trophies won on the tournament circuit — caused the soldier's build to be veritably turret-like. A sword, according the chivalrous French knight Geoffroi de Charny, should be a symbol, "to defend right, reason and justice on all sides without being false to the Christian faith", but in the hands of the hulking English knight a sword appeared to be little more than a sharp club, to bludgeon an enemy to death with.

In stark contrast his opponent, wearing a suit of elegant but practical Milanese armour, relied on speed rather than strength. The large knight swung his weapon from his shoulders, through his powerful arms, whilst his slender combatant directed his broadsword from his wrists, whilst at all times moving his feet.

The two men suddenly converged, their swords pressing against each other, like two rams locking horns. Cooper was impressed by the slighter man's strength, who was managing to hold his combatant at bay. Yet he suddenly staggered backwards as the larger knight whipped his elbow around and struck him upon the side of his helmeted head.

The spectators, gripped by the bout, gasped, but the slender fighter quickly shook off the blow and resumed his rhythm of parrying rather than thrusting forward. Cooper realised that the swordsman was aiming to tire his opponent out, and the strategy seemed to be working. The larger knight soon lumbered forward. When he came near the archer Cooper thought he heard the man breathing heavily. Frustration fed his aggression and aggression fed his frustration.

The swifter knight moved inside but then deftly moved backwards. His opponent was already committed to a big, clumsy swing of his weapon. Once the tip of the blade moved harmlessly past the nimble swordsman he advanced again, brought his foot up and planted it square into the larger man's groin area. The large knight staggered backwards and fell to the ground. He was now as vulnerable as an upturned tortoise. With his combatant's blade at his throat, the fallen knight duly yielded.

"Bastard," he roughly exclaimed, with the curse directed at himself more than the victor. Not only was the professional soldier smarting from defeat, but the participants had wagered their second best coursers on the outcome of the bout.

The King took off his helmet and helped his friend, Sir William Talbot, to his feet. As the spectators applauded the swordsmen, Cooper noticed how Henry clasped a fraternal hand on the knight's shoulder and whispered a few words into his ear. The archer had no idea what the words were but Talbot's disgruntled expression softened itself into a smile, and he nodded his head in appreciation at his sovereign's comments.

Sir William Talbot was one of Henry's most famous knights. The former mercenary was now a landed gentleman at court. Talbot had first made his name as a squire on the tournament circuit. The son of a Norfolk stable master, he had already been an accomplished horseman when Sir Stephen Evesham bought him into his company. Talbot soon learned how to joust and fence, and more importantly how to fight when knee deep in mud and gore. He further learned siege craft, gaining experience in defending towns and also razing them to the ground. Soldiering was a source of wealth, rather than honour, to the ambitious mercenary. When his rank and estate afforded him to do so Talbot set up his own company of mercenaries and spent the next two decades on the continent. If the money was good enough then so was the cause. Over the course of his career Talbot had fought for both the French and Roman Popes, as well as the Armagnacs and Burgundians. He was paid by Milan to attack Florence and, the following year, he was paid by Florence to attack the Milanese. The joke was that Talbot's company had killed more men, in more countries, than the Black Death.

Talbot was known for being a stern disciplinarian, as well as for rewarding his soldiers well. *"It's one thing to strike fear into an enemy and make an example of people, but it's another to behave like savages, or the French at Soissons. I'm all for soldiers getting their end away, but let them pay for it in a tavern, like any civilised human being."*

After fighting for Henry IV against Owen Glendower's forces, Talbot decided to settle in his native county, purchasing the estate his father had once served as stable master to. Talbot was given various honours and invited into the Order of the Garter, though he would laugh, scornfully or good humouredly, whenever anyone called him "chivalrous".

Although Cooper had served in a couple of battles which Talbot had also fought at this was the first time that he had seen the knight up close. A thick mane of greasy black hair, streaked with grey, fell down to his shoulders. Like Cooper, Talbot was the wrong side of forty but it was difficult to judge his exact age. His face was tanned and weathered but he had a glint in his eye and a boyish grin. A fork-shaped scar resided beneath a large dimple on his chin. His nose had been flattened and broken more times than the veteran soldier could care to mention.

Henry called for an attendant to bring over some wine for himself and his thirsty opponent. Sweat glazed the King's face but his expression appeared far from lugubrious, enlivened as it was by the heat of the competition. Henry had offered Talbot a chance to best him in a fencing bout as he knew that the knight, unlike some others, would give his all to defeat him, not only from professional pride, but out of greed as well. Not only had they publically wagered their second best coursers on the result but in a private wager Henry had said that he would offer Talbot his best courser, and a gem-encrusted dagger, should he be defeated. The fight had been a close run thing for the King. He arms ached from having to parry Talbot's hefty blows and Henry had nearly lost his balance on more than one occasion when being forced on the back foot by the determined knight. The King later confided to Cooper that he would have lost to Talbot, back in the days when the knight was in his prime – but there was no shame in that. During his time when he had participated in tournaments people had said that Talbot was "William Marshal reborn". During his time as a mercenary however — be it a compliment or curse — Talbot was judged to be "John Hawkwood reborn."

Henry summoned Cooper to join him, as the King fended off various congratulations for winning the hard-fought contest.

"Robert, I would like you to meet Sir William Talbot, the most unchivalrous knight in all of England. But I wouldn't trade him for Sir Gawain himself. William, this is Robert Cooper," the King remarked, handing a cup of wine to the archer.

"One of the best shots in the whole army, I'm told," the knight exclaimed, sizing up the man in front of him. "I once served under a Sir Lewis Scalby, who served alongside your father and the Black Prince. Scalby claimed that your father possessed one of the best bow arms in the country. The apple hasn't fallen far from the tree, it seems. I'm surprised that Henry here hasn't asked you to knock out a load of bastards, so they can grow up into a company of archers one day. I certainly reckon your bloodline is far more valuable than the piss which runs through the veins of some of the folk I see here around me."

Henry pretended not to hear but Cooper noticed the King smile into his cup. Henry was all too aware of how Talbot liked to shock people. It was his way of testing a man's mettle and sense of humour. One needed both to get through life, the veteran soldier believed.

"I wanted to introduce you to one another, as you will soon be working together," Henry said.

"What would you have us do?" Talbot replied, confused and intrigued by his King's words.

"Nothing too impossible. Just end this damned siege."

Cooper nodded and tried to appear dutiful. William Talbot, however, let out a burst of laughter and took a large swig from his wine cup.

"Well, my new friend," the knight smilingly announced, whilst clapping his gauntleted hand on the bowman's shoulder. "What are we fucking waiting for?"

10

The saffron sun spread its light across the undulating, rustic landscape. Leafy woods skirted grassy fields, teeming with wild flowers. Swallows, starlings and chaffinches darted across the scene, sewing songs into the canvas of the landscape. Thomas Chaucer breathed in the fragrant air, welcoming a respite from the stench, din and clutter of the army camp. The sight of hedgerows reminded him of the English countryside. The thought of home was the sharpest of double-edged swords.

The agent rode alongside Edward Fordham at the head of a party of men-at-arms and archers, escorting a wagon carrying a chest of coins. They were bound for Charles Nouvel's estate, situated just outside of Caudebec. The Englishmen were now in enemy territory but Chaucer was confident that the party was safe from attack. Any large groups of men, capable of taking his company on, were travelling in a different direction, heading towards where the Dauphin was amassing his army, and any small contingent of French soldiers would lack the courage to challenge his archers and mounted soldiers.

The company made their way along a narrow, rutted road. Poleaxes vaunted up in the air from saddles. Watered down ale was gulped down. The clink of armour could be heard with each step. A number of soldiers towards the back of the party — ones who had consumed more ale than most — joined together in singing a rendition of a ribald ballad, which contained unimaginative rhymes for the words "pit" and "muck".

Despite the safety in their numbers Chaucer, as was his custom when travelling through hostile or friendly territory, nevertheless ordered two archers to scout along the road ahead, and two to screen the rear of the party. The gold coin and, to a lesser extent his life, he wryly judged, were too valuable to act with complacently in regards to security.

Edward Fordham seemed to take in the appealing scenery surrounding him, but as Chaucer glanced at his smiling, somewhat moon-faced friend he considered how the soldier may have been dwelling more on the figure in his mind's eye than enjoying the landscape. Fordham had cleaned his boots and was wearing his best jacket, a leather jerkin lined with mail. He had also polished his best sword — a fine Toledo blade — which he had taken from a French assassin during an attempt on Richard Whittington's life.

"So how did you find Marie Nouvel in the end? Are you looking forward to seeing her again? More to the point perhaps, will she be looking forward to meeting you again?" Thomas asked, raising his eyebrow and the corner of his mouth in a knowing fashion.

Fordham snapped out of his reverie and replied: "She was impressive during negotiations. She knew her brief and was firm but fair on certain points of the contract. Daughters should be permitted to run the business affairs of their fathers more often. It's preferable to wayward eldest sons wasting their fortunes on wine, women and song."

Fordham knew that the agent was fishing. Chaucer wanted to tease out of his friend whether Marie had cast a spell over him. But the man-at-arms wasn't biting. Not only did he wish to keep his feelings private, but Fordham partially felt vulnerable and ashamed. Marie had indeed somehow cast a spell over him. Had she seduced him? His heart seemed to beat in time with the brisk clip-clop of horses, when he thought of the French siren.

"I have never heard you describe wine, women and song as being some kind of a waste of life before. Perhaps Marie has indeed inspired a change of heart in you pertaining to some matters, Edward," Chaucer said, unable to disguise his amusement.

"I would argue that it would be difficult to change something which isn't there."

"Marie could have put a heart in place without you realising it. Women are known for such alchemy," Chaucer posited. He pictured his own wife, and how marrying Matilda had changed him, for the better. "I was once not unlike you. For all of my reading of poetry and tales of chivalry I considered love a fancy, something which versifiers made up to sell their books. Poetry was something to be quoted to get a woman into bed. And I believed marriage to be a contract, with various hidden clauses. Or it was a death sentence. I used to imagine that, on my wedding night, the door to the bed chamber would shut as heavily as the door to a gaol. But, should you find the right woman Edward, love and marriage are sacrifices worth making. You get to be part of something bigger than yourself. Love is a campaign which is far nobler than any act of military conquest. When I am away from Matilda I feel like I am missing a limb. To have a loving wife is to have a friend as loyal as John Walworth — but a John Walworth who's prettier and a better cook!"

Fordham laughed at his friend's jest but was still torn between the specular promise of love and its actuality. Or rather its lack of actuality. How many women had he seduced who, more than actually being in love, had been enamoured with the display of being in love?

"But how do you know when love is real? And how can a man know that the object of his affection feels the same way as he does? I can see this horse, those chestnut trees and the sun in the sky. But I have more chance of seeing a generous Scot or oath-keeping Frenchman than I do of seeing love. Of knowing love exists."

"I once borrowed a book from the King. Henry is a keen annotator of his texts. He inserts comments in the margins in reference to agreeing or disagreeing with points and also he underlines passages in order to memorise them. The book was a collection of the writings of Saint Augustine. The following line, which I duly committed to memory, was the only passage which Henry underlined twice in the volume: 'Faith is to believe what you do not see; the reward of this faith is to see what you believe.' Wickedness seems all too real and prevalent in this world, Edward, but love and goodness have to be taken on faith. Know this: I have never known Marie to look at a man in the same fashion as when she stared at you yesterday morning, whilst her party was preparing to depart," Chaucer said encouragingly, recalling Marie's expression.

"Marie asked me if you had a wife, or anyone special, back in England waiting for you. It may well be the case that she is merely feigning interest in you, but you can afford to nurse some hope, even if you think you cannot afford her. Marie is someone special. The thickest and finest Milanese plate armour is no defence against her smile and wardrobe. She may have, at any one time, a thousand would-be suitors willing to kiss her feet and declare their devotion to her, but I sense that Marie considers herself to be alone in the world. She also considers you to be special, I warrant. And it's about time you secured a wife for yourself, instead of securing other men's wives."

Fordham was, at best, only half listening. He still didn't know if Marie harboured the same feelings as him; if she felt different, finer, when she was with him. Fordham dejectedly imagined that Marie could just be playing with him, as he had similarly toyed with his lovers' feelings over the years. *She's not a reward for the good life but a fitting punishment for my sins.* The devout sceptic wanted to laugh at himself, at his folly, but for once the laughter didn't come.

11

Sir William Talbot's billet was one of the largest and most luxurious tents in the camp. Robert Cooper entered. Light fanned out from the entrance and reflected off an array of weaponry resting against one wall of the tent: swords, poleaxes, lances, targes, greaves, spaulders, helms, gauntlets and freshly sharpened halberds. As impressive as the display was Cooper knew that it wasn't all just for show. Every piece of armour had been worn at a tournament or battle. Every weapon had tasted blood and killed a man.

Cooper's gaze was drawn towards the bed, and the slender female thigh which hung out from the furs. The girl's long auburn hair half covered her face but Cooper could still discern that she was, at most, half the knight's age.

"Ah, that there is Eleanor. I think that's her name. Fucks like a bride on her wedding night. My French is *merde*. Not sure if she called me a pig or a prince last night. Probably the former. And she'd be right of course. But let's allow the sweet little strumpet to sleep for now. She's earned her rest. And she earned her fee... I know there is an ordnance forbidding the fairer sex but when in negotiations with Henry it was unwritten, though not unspoken, between us that there would be one rule for me and another for others. Henry knew that if he wanted my company of men he'd have to permit me some female company on the campaign," William Talbot exclaimed. The knight was dressed in leather boots, leather breeches and an embroidered linen shirt. The muscular soldier filled out his clothes. An old lion is still a lion. He wore a silver cross around his neck, which he kept salt in to flavour his numerous meals. He was sitting on a throne-like oak chair, the legs of which had been carved to resemble dragons' feet. The table next to it contained a pitcher of ale, a flagon of mead and a jug of wine. Cooper, no stranger to long drinking sessions, had been astounded and impressed the night before by how much of the good stuff the knight was capable of consuming, whilst still keeping his wits about him.

"In my line of work you have to be able to hold your drink and have eyes in the back of your head. A count or cock-loving bishop may invite you to a banquet in your honour in order to pay you or betray you," Talbot had asserted the previous evening, as he had clinked cups again with Cooper and John Walworth.

"And this here is Stephen Latimer, my biographer," Talbot said, interrupting Cooper's thoughts. He introduced the pale-faced, squinting figure sitting to the left of him. Latimer was a young, well-read copyist who Talbot had commissioned to chart his rags to riches story and record his victories. Latimer sat hunched over a piece of parchment on his lap, his twig-like fingers stained with ink. He forced a nervous smile and politely nodded his head at Cooper. Despite having been in Sir William's employ for nearly a year, the scrawny writer still seemed ill at ease and intimated in the company of coarse soldiers.

"What's good enough for the Marshal is good enough for me," Talbot said, making reference to the great William Marshal who, after serving under five English kings, had also commissioned a biographer to record his eventful life for posterity. "My detractors, of which there are quite rightly many, will argue that I am writing my life up out of pure vanity. But I'm not just writing this book to secure my fame for when I'm in the next life, I want it to make me some money in this life. I'm working on a chapter at the moment about how I came back to England for Henry IV to fight against Owen Glendower's forces. My chronicler here wrote that I heard the call to arms from the King as if I heard the angel Gabriel's trumpet in my ears. The truth was that I heard the sound of gold coins clinking together. I know that the old King had a difficult reign, but oftentimes he made it more difficult for himself. Thankfully the son is twice the man his father was. Our Henry will get the job done, with or without divine intervention. We'll go to see the King soon, to discuss our prospective intervention," Talbot affirmed. The knight turned his head and spat out a gobbet of phlegm into a bronze bowl on the floor, several feet away.

Cooper and Talbot had spent a large part of yesternight discussing how best to break the siege. To begin with Talbot had boasted about past successes. He had taken towns both by force and guile during his long career.

"On one occasion I had an archer shoot an arrow over the wall into the mayor's courtyard. A note was attached, offering him a substantial sum of money to open the gates during the dead of night to let our forces in. We received an arrow back. He couldn't possibly betray his own townsfolk for such a paltry sum of money. Suffice to say we doubled the bribe and the bastard betrayed his people quicker than a teacher will whip a schoolboy. Sometimes you have to starve them out but sometimes you just have to throw a load of poor, vicious souls into the breach and paint the town red..."

By the end of the long night the two men had formed a plan of attack to take to the King.

*

Henry briefly closed his eyes, perhaps in the vague hope that when he opened them again the nightmare would be over, but the town of Harfleur still stood resolutely in front of him. Henry again recalled with stoicism the motto of Edward III, his great grandfather: *It is as it is.*

"War without fire is like sausages without mustard," Henry said. He had once proclaimed those words with relish and vengeance ablaze in his eyes, during a previous siege when campaigning on the Welsh border, but now his tone was wreathed in ruefulness. It had been his intention to seize the town without the loss of a single life, on either side. It had been his intention to, like Caesar after crossing the Rubicon, conquer with clemency.

Henry sighed and nodded in agreement to Cooper and Sir William, who had just presented their plan. The town would only fall after the formidable great barbican, positioned outside the main Leure gate, was destroyed. They had to burn it down; mining would not work. They would be unable to recruit an ally on the inside to open the gates. Henry would have preferred to keep the bastion in place, as he would need the structure when it came to the English defending the town from the French. He knew that he would lose men in the attack on the barbican. "Every soldier here is a piece of England, so every soldier dying diminishes England and me," Henry had pronounced to his inner circle of advisers the other day. But desperate times called for desperate measures.

The King missed the counsel and company of his friend: Richard Courtenay, the man whom he had shared his doubts with when he had ascended to the throne. Henry recalled one of the last conversations he had with his friend, before the bloody flux took possession of his bowels and soul:

"When I was a boy, I used to play with a set of wooden toy soldiers. Every day I would picture the lush green contours of a battlefield and position my knights, archers and infantry accordingly. Suffice to say I never lost an engagement. One day though, in a fit of envy, my brother Thomas burned some of the beautifully carved pieces. After hunting down my brother and burning his favourite shirt I went back to my toy army and discarded the burned pieces. I believed that charred bodies had no place upon a battlefield. How wrong I was. Today I saw the gun-stone strike the church steeple of the town. The odds of it doing so must have been a thousand to one. Some of the men punched the air and cheered but most, including myself, remained silent. I felt a devout sense of shame. The church bells ringing out upon the hour were welcomed by both sides. I think that the sound reminded some of our soldiers of home. How could the Almighty smile upon such an action on my part? The people of the town must judge me an instrument of the Devil rather than God. I was supposed to liberate them from misrule, from a mad monarch and self-serving prince. For too long in this land it has been the culture that a knight will punitively tax a farmer so that he has to sell his cob in order that his master can buy a new courser... Starvation eats away at the sallow-cheeked faces of my soldiers. Or is it the bloody flux? My enemies are calling the scourge a God-sent plague — a divine punishment afflicting the unrighteous. Too many good men have already been cut down before their prime. I will do my duty and try to provide some consoling words to the parents and children of the fallen when I return to England. Yet nothing I say will be able to bring back their loved ones," Henry had confessed to the sedate and sympathetic Courtenay.

The burden of command is ultimately a solitary experience. It hung upon Henry's shoulders now like a prisoner's yoke. Yet still he kept his back ramrod straight, to keep up appearances and morale. *One must bear one's lamentations with fortitude.* Nothing he could say would bring his friend back. *It is as it is.*

"Commence the attack tomorrow evening," the King firmly ordered, hoping that the darkness would conceal their approach.

12

The light was fading but Chaucer and his party could still make out the rich farmland and herds of cattle in the distance as they neared their destination. Charles Nouvel's home could have been considered a small castle or large house. The property was encircled by steep grey walls, quarried from the wealth of stone on the eastern fringes of the merchant's estate. A newly built stable complex stood outside of the walls. A bell tower and chimney vaunted up out of the main buildings, with the latter unfurling a tendril of silver smoke into the air. The house dominated the landscape and was a rival, in size and expense, for any in the region.

Seeing the estate again reminded Chaucer of Nouvel's desperate need to project his success and impress the French aristocracy. The self-made merchant enjoyed lording it over his often debt-ridden neighbours, scions of the great noble families of France, but he also desired to be a part of their world. Nouvel craved their respect, envy and favour — a three legged stool which was hard to construct and even harder to sit comfortably upon.

Chaucer waited patiently at the entrance to the house as the great oak doors, reinforced with iron, were unbolted and unbarred. "The more you have means the more you have to lose," the prudent merchant had once remarked to the agent, as he boasted of his estate's defences. A beetle-browed attendant, Arnaud, greeted his master's guests. Sweat soaked his temples and Chaucer thought the man seemed over anxious. There was something forced in his manner. Yet the English agent considered that he too would be somewhat nervous if a party of French soldiers arrived at his house, in Ewelme. Arnaud requested that Chaucer's men take their mounts to the stables, so that they could feed and water the horses. He would then escort Chaucer to his master, whilst the servants served ale and roast pork to the English soldiers in the courtyard.

Chaucer and his company assembled in the courtyard as the gates were locked and barred for the evening. Torches were lit to compensate for the dying light. Ramparts looked down on the oval-shaped space. Servants, equally as sheepish and skittish as Arnaud, brought out a long trestle table. Pitchers of ale also appeared. The smell of roasted pig filled the air, ousting the body odours of horses and men, and the soldiers licked their lips. All was well.

The attendant led Chaucer and Fordham into the main house. Waist-high, marble statues of Charlemagne and Pericles stood at the bottom of the ornate staircase facing the front entrance. Rather than heading up to the first floor however Arnaud walked towards the back of the house, towards the main hall where their host was waiting. The corridor was lit with costly beeswax candles, illuminating the faces of saints and Roman emperors in the paintings which hung on the walls. Though the French merchant spent half his time projecting the state of his wealth on the world, Nouvel often pleaded a state of poverty when it came to negotiating business deals. Chaucer had known the merchant now for over a decade. Rather than believing in the greatness of France or England, Nouvel believed in the power of trade, to enrich himself and others. Nouvel wasn't a bad man, Chaucer considered, it was just that he wasn't a particularly good man either. In exchange for intelligence and favours Chaucer arranged for the merchant to receive exemptions from certain customs and excise duties on his goods. As hard-nosed and self-interested as the Frenchman could be in settling upon the terms of an agreement Charles Nouvel always honoured his word. All would be well. Henry would be able to feed his army again.

Fordham was even more anxious looking than Arnaud as they approached the door to the main hall. The soldier wiped his palms on his breeches several times, not wishing to have a clammy skin should he have to take Marie's hand and formally kiss it. His mouth suddenly became as dry as a leather purse left out in the sun all day. His ribcage tightened and he had to fight to catch his breath. Fordham wondered how familiar he should be with his lover in front of her father. Marie did not know he was accompanying Chaucer. The soldier would be able to see in her eyes immediately, if she was pleased to see him again.

A now profusely sweating Arnaud opened the door. Fordham had expected to be greeted by Marie, Chaucer had expected to be greeted by the elder Nouvel. But as the two men entered the chamber, warmed by a roaring fire, they were greeted by four swarthy looking soldiers, holding crossbows, and an old enemy.

"Abandon hope, all ye who enter here," Reynard of Troyes exclaimed, his voice a mixture of mirth and menace.

13

Reynard of Troyes knew that his enemies at court were revelling in his disgrace. Before disembarking for Scotland he had promised King Charles and the Dauphin Louis that Scotland would invade England, Henry would be deposed and a French puppet would be sitting on the English throne. But the agent's plans were all in ruins. He had even discovered that his intelligence, concerning where the English army would land in France, had also been false. Thomas Chaucer had out-witted him on that front as well.

Although unrepentant in his heart Renard of Troyes had nevertheless played the penitent when he presented himself at court. He was told that the King refused to see him (though the spy was unsure whether this was because he was out of favour, or if the unstable monarch was out of his mind again).

Reynard had been summoned to appear before the Dauphin, to explain his failure, and also the loss of a large sum of gold coins, which instead of being used to fund a Scottish army was now lying at the bottom of the sea (the English having sunk the vessel, which carried the war chest, through the use of fire arrows). The Dauphin had not disguised his displeasure at the outcome of the mission. He seemed to take great pleasure in shaming and humiliating the over ambitious agent.

Reynard still bristled in recalling the scene. The Dauphin had made sure his haranguing of the spy was public, with courtiers and knights flanking the prince. Reynard could still smell the wine on the Dauphin's breath and feel the royal spittle on his cheeks. He could still see his enemies smirk and hear the laughter of their mistresses behind the arras. *Whores.* Reynard silently vowed to slice out their tongues. How sweet would their laughter sound then? Usually he was the author of whispering campaigns at court, not the victim of them.

Behind a remorseful expression the once influential agent had gritted his teeth. The court had conveniently ignored his past successes. He would not forget their ingratitude though.

"If you were any sort of a man you would ask me for a dagger instead of forgiveness. You started to believe your own reputation and got caught up in your own web of deceit. In your attempt to injure our enemies you have wounded France," the Dauphin had shrilly exclaimed, gesticulating like a bad actor. Even before the Dauphin's humiliation of the agent Reynard of Troyes found little to admire about the princeling. He spent more time combing his hair than swinging a sword. He had a womanishly high voice, and an even higher opinion of himself. He treated his hunting dogs and goshawks with more humaneness than his subjects and seemed obsessed with outward shows of majesty, like a courtesan obsessed with her wardrobe.

A number of senior advisers and knights had also rounded on the agent, including the Constable of France, Charles d'Albret, and Marshal Boucicaut. For far too long, some of the nobles considered, the low-born spy had wielded too much power in the affairs of state. They now owned the perfect opportunity to denude the agent of his wealth and status. Reynard did not doubt that some were happier to see him fail rather than see France succeed. The best of French society were envious, ignoble and ignorant. They no more had the French peoples' best interest at heart than a Spanish milkmaid did.

"Wars are won through valour and military prowess, not through hiding in the shadows. Cowards scheme. Brave men fight. When two great beasts meet each other in the forest the snakes just get trodden upon," Guy de Artois had exclaimed, looking down his aquiline nose at the dismal agent. The supercilious count was not alone in savouring in the powerful spy's downfall.

They had insulted the bastard son of the bishop and impugned his honour, perhaps hoping that Reynard would throw down his gage and challenge one of them in a trial of combat. Yet the silver-tongued diplomat merely took his punishment, praising the wisdom of his betters, whilst venomously cursing them all beneath his breath. What little defence Reynard put up fell on deaf ears. They did not care that their Scottish ally, Walter Bane, was not fit for purpose. As for Thomas Chaucer, the English spy should not be blamed but rather be admired for his resourcefulness. "He has made you look like a fool, Reynard. It seems he has toyed with you like a cat with a mouse," Charles d'Albret had proclaimed.

The prideful agent's face had crimsoned in indignation, though his audience had assumed him red-faced with shame. He had noted the names of all who spoke against him. Vengeance bubbled in his stomach, like boiling pitch. Hatred nourished him like mother's milk. He had studied long and hard to out-perform all those who had bullied him and called him a "little bastard" at school. Ambition married itself to his sense of resentment and it drove him on, whipping him like a coachman would his horses. He learned languages, studied under an apothecary to learn about poisons, created an intelligence network, bribed or blackmailed people of influence — all to become the best agent he could be. Better than any high-born spy. Reynard believed in the superiority of himself and of France (in that order).

The Dauphin had received applause and a number of vigorous nods of approval when he decreed that Reynard's lands and possessions to be forfeited to the crown, as compensation for the coinage he had lost on his mission. A number of oleaginous noblemen had questioned the spy on the loss of the chest of gold, implying that he may have stolen it himself.

Reynard of Troyes' cold heart had tried to temper the fire in his blood as he bowed his head before "the royal whelp" and exited the chamber. He seethed, wishing that their whores would give them a pox. He desired for Henry to call the Dauphin out in single combat — and for the wretched Englishman to fillet him like a fish. His soul — and future — felt as black as the night.

But it is always darkest before the dawn. The following day Reynard received intelligence that the merchant, Charles Nouvel, was negotiating a deal through Thomas Chaucer to provide foodstuffs to the English army. The spy immediately summoned his lieutenant, Pierre Montbron, and ordered him to recruit a small force of mercenaries. They would ride to

Nouvel's estate near Caudebec. Even if they couldn't catch Nouvel in the act of colluding with the enemy he could extract a confession from the merchant. Nouvel's treachery would mean his lands and wealth would be confiscated by the crown, instead of his own, God willing. Should the devil, as well as God, move in mysterious ways, then he might also be able to deliver the prize of Chaucer himself to the Dauphin. Reynard's reward need only be that he was given the opportunity of interrogating Henry's spymaster.

"Forgive me Thomas for quoting Dante over your esteemed poet father," Reynard remarked, clearing savouring the moment, and the perturbed expression on his enemy's face. His narrow eyes were slightly upturned in a serpentine smirk. *Who was the cat and who was the mouse now?*

Thomas Chaucer — spy, diplomat and former Speaker of the House — prided himself on maintaining his sangfroid in the face of any drear circumstance. Yet even he widened his eyes slightly at meeting his French counterpart again. Chaucer had thought he would somehow encounter Reynard of Troyes again one day, through chance or providence, but each scenario he had painted in his mind had given the Englishman the upper-hand over the French agent.

Unfortunately Reynard appeared all too real to be mistaken for a ghost. Chaucer felt a sense of bloodcurdling fear and blood boiling rage. He had vowed to kill Reynard for being a dangerous enemy of England, and also for being the man who had murdered a young, innocent archer from his company.

"Pierre, you may now give the order to take care of our guests, waiting outside in the courtyard."

Pierre Montbron momentarily nodded to his paymaster but then turned his attention to glaring at the English soldier again. Fordham had foiled Montbron who, on Reynard's orders, had attempted to murder Richard Whittington, the former mayor of London and banker to the King. Fordham had not only wounded Montbron during their encounter but he had also stolen his sword, which the Englishman now wore by his side. Montbron satisfyingly considered how the man-at-arms wouldn't be in possession of the weapon much longer.

Fordham met the Frenchman's challenging gaze and dared to wryly smile. If he felt his stomach churning with fear then it was in relation to Marie. He needed to know if she was still alive, and he needed to know she hadn't betrayed him. If she had then Fordham would never trust a woman again (not that he had trusted them much before having met the merchant's daughter).

Montbron walked with purpose up the flight of stairs in the corner of the room, clutching the pommel of his sword.

"I can well believe, Thomas, how the shock of my presence could momentarily stun you into silence, but do you not have anything to say? You seemed to have an answer prepared for most of the things I said to you when we last met, in that Godforsaken country of Scotland," Reynard remarked, before pursing his lips and brushing a smattering of dust off the sleeve of his garment.

"I am afraid that I have been too busy preparing for the invasion of your Godforsaken country. I have been preoccupied with not losing any of my treasury's gold, not witnessing my ally's defeat and preserving my influence and honour in regards to my King. You yourself must know what constitutes success and failure in relationship to a campaign." Thomas replied, his voice imbued with sarcasm and defiance.

Reynard of Troyes smiled in response to the Englishman's barbed words, distant sounds of screaming interrupted his response.

"Of course, as I am sure you will agree Thomas, the principle responsibility when planning a campaign is to care for the wellbeing of one's soldiers. Unfortunately your men are being slaughtered as we speak. Crossbowmen are firing into them from the ramparts. After which my lieutenant, Montbron, will be leading a force of mercenaries, armed with spears and halberds, to finish off the wounded. How fitting, for Englishmen to die with cups of ale clasped in his hands."

The English howls of pain were replaced by triumphant French cheers. Chaucer's blood was up but his heart sank. Too many good men had just been needlessly slaughtered. He observed a stern-faced Fordham edge forward a little, his hand inching towards his sword. But Chaucer gently placed his fingers on his friend's forearm to dissuade him from acting rashly and sharing the fate of the rest of the company in the courtyard. This was not the time for heroics.

14

The sound of the large doors opening and closing as Charles and Marie Nouvel entered reverberated around the opulently furnished hall. Painted yew beams criss-crossed the high ceiling. The walls were skirted with ornate oak panelling and artworks from the four corners of the continent. Polished silver candlesticks and bronze braziers reflected the firelight. Richly designed Persian rugs covered over half the wooden flooring. A Greco-Roman mosaic, depicting a scene from the Aeneid, decorated the far corner of the chamber. In the other corner, beneath an oval-shaped stained glass window, stood a harp, the elegant curves of which matched the figure of its mistress.

As Charles Nouvel and his daughter came into view Chaucer knew that they had not been complicit in his capture. The merchant's once sharp, angular face was swollen and bloody. A large patch of blood also stained his neck and linen shirt from where Reynard had cut off part of his left earlobe. The merchant had confessed to everything even before the infamous agent had commenced to interrogate his prisoner. As Reynard instructed Montbron to torture the whimpering Nouvel he took a perverted, but welcome, sense of pleasure in picturing his counterpart, Thomas Chaucer, sitting in the merchant's place. Pleading for mercy and then screaming, alternately, as the session progressed.

Nouvel raised his bowed head, briefly, to look at Chaucer as he hobbled into the room. The merchant's usual confidence was absent. His right eye was circled by a large, fresh bruise. His nose was split. One of his front teeth had been extracted. The merchant was shoeless, revealing several broken toes on his left foot. He stood, hunched over and leaning to the side. Chaucer suspected that he had a number of broken ribs.

The pitiful sight reminded Chaucer of the way his antagonist had tortured Stephen Hall. Reynard was a butcher. A man was just a piece of meat to him, to be seared or tenderised. Although the English agent was no stranger to giving the order for an enemy of the state to be tortured, he took no pleasure from the experience. Chaucer told himself, again, how different he was from his French counterpart.

"Sorry," the disorientated Nouvel mumbled, drool running down his besmirched chin. He slurred his words and Chaucer couldn't be sure if he was talking to himself, his daughter or the man who had interrogated him.

"I am afraid that our friend used up all his garrulity last night — and again this morning. Nouvel confessed everything, to the point where I will not even need to fabricate any testimony to prove his treachery. Given his present physical condition, Nouvel has asked me to take over negotiations on his behalf, in regards to the goods and services you wish procure. As you know, I would rather deal with Satan himself and the minions of hell than help feed Henry and your stricken army," Reynard said, curling his thin lip in disdain as he made reference to the English monarch.

Fordham was astounded by the Frenchman's English. He had mastered both the accent and diverse vocabulary. But he spared little time dwelling on the nefarious French spy. He turned his gaze towards Marie. Although her face was drawn and her eyes were red-rimmed from tears it seemed she hadn't been harmed physically. Yet. Marie held her father's arm, either to console him or hold the broken man up. She had glared at her captor but her features softened upon meeting the Englishman's glance. The wave of solace which Fordham felt, in knowing that he meant something to someone and that he loved them in return, was undercut by his grim feelings of helplessness and dread.

As much as Fordham wanted to convey how much Marie meant to him in his expression, he knew that there was a danger in doing so. If Reynard knew how much he was devoted to her — and she him — then he would use it against both of them.

But the truth will out. Their glance lingered for too long and betrayed too much intimacy.

"What's this?" Reynard remarked, amused and intrigued. "Much like a poodle can sniff out a truffle I can sniff out love — or its more common bedfellow, lust. Have you been sleeping with the enemy, my dear? Perhaps I shouldn't be so surprised. You would sleep with a leper, would you not, if your father told you to?"

Before Marie or Fordham could reply they were distracted by the return of Pierre Montbron. The assassin was of average height and build and concealed his most distinguishing feature, a sickle-shaped birthmark on his forehead, by growing his fringe long. Blood spotted his cheek and jupon from where he had taken part in the massacre of the English soldiers. His men were currently slitting the throats of the wounded, searching their pockets for any valuables and drinking the ale which had been brought out for their enemies.

"It's done," Montbron remarked, business-like, to his employer. Killing was a job for the assassin. He neither gloried in the deaths of his victims nor felt remorse, though the recent events in England had caused a certain personal animus to develop inside him. Failure to kill Whittington, and having his sword taken by the English man-at-arms, had damaged his professional pride. He was also still suffering from a wound in his arm and side, from where the Englishman had shot him with a crossbow bolt.

Montbron's face tightened into a scowl when he stared at Fordham again. As unhappy as the Frenchman appeared at seeing his enemy he was, in some ways, glad to encounter the soldier. Honour — and his debt to his employer — could now be repaid. On returning to France, Reynard of Troyes told the assassin that he still owed him a debt of service, and if he refused Reynard would consider him an enemy of the state. As brave as Montbron was, he wasn't foolish. He would do the spy's bidding. But, as dutiful as he would be in his service, Montbron longed to return to his family and farm. He wanted to make love to his wife, taste her cooking again and teach his son how to hunt. Being good at his profession only made sense if it afforded him the chance to be a good husband and father too.

The sooner the English died the better.

15

The sun had long fallen off the edge of the world. Torches dimly illuminated the evening. A chill wind bit into Chaucer's face. He tried to remain impassive as Reynard led him out into the courtyard. The French agent, for once, didn't say a word. He just took a sublime pleasure in observing his counterpart's reaction to the macabre scene, breathing in the stench of the English dead as if it were a fine perfume. The Englishman didn't want to give his tormentor the satisfaction of seeing the grief and desperation he felt in his heart chiselled into the lines of his face.

Flies congregated over the gory bodies in a dance of death. The ambush had been swift but brutal. Some of his men had been able to draw their weapons but none were stained with the blood of their enemies. Crossbow quarrels and spearheads still lay lodged in chests and stomachs. Teeth were bared, in anger and agony. Throats were cut. Nouvel's servants had been ordered to start putting the corpses onto carts. "Bury or burn the dead," Reynard instructed. "It's all the same to me and them."

A rat gnawed upon the cheek of one Hugh Kempton, a goodly archer who Chaucer had recruited to his company several years ago. Kempton had thoughts of retiring before the campaign but his paymaster convinced him to sign a contract with him, one last time. Chaucer had promised him that Henry would lead them to victory, and that his arrow bag would be filled with booty by the end of the campaign. He knew Kempton's wife would blame him for her husband's death.

Chaucer had lost men before but he still lamented the tragic sight before his eyes. If this was all part of God's plan then he wanted no part in it. Even if he did believe in an all-powerful deity, he had no desire to serve a being who would allow such cruelty and suffering to exist in the world. He had been written into the plans of a godless Frenchman, but, God willing, Reynard would pay for his sins.

Chaucer stood in silence, noting every dead face. Remembering and revering each man. Reynard also stood in silence for some time before speaking: "Now imagine this pile of bodies multiplied by a hundred, heaped upon one another before the walls of Harfleur or strewn across a lush, green field. That will be the fate of your army, if Henry decides to prolong this campaign. He thinks he is digging a trench but really he is digging a grave for himself. Even kings are not immune to the most common of sins, pride. This campaign is pure folly. It may well be an equal piece of folly to try and convert you to my position, Thomas, but I feel I must try. It is also my duty to deliver you to my sovereign," Reynard sombrely remarked.

"If we are talking about the madness of kings then I will of course defer to your greater experience of such a phenomenon. Does Charles still believe he is made out of glass, or has someone finally shattered that delusion? Does he still deny he has a wife? It's the most convenient excuse to take a mistress that I've ever yet heard of. Even if Charles could somehow regain his wits then I dare say he would be driven to madness again by his court's fractious infighting," Chaucer replied, scorn lacing his tone like poison. If Montbron had not confiscated his weapons, Chaucer might have been tempted to stab his enemy there and then (regardless of the fact that the nearby soldiers would have cut him down shortly afterwards).

"Should you be held captive for the next decade then we might then have sufficient time to debate the madness of kings, but instead let us discuss the issue at hand. You have been an agent of war. You now have an opportunity to be an ambassador for peace. You have your sovereign's ear. You alone may be able to cool his hot temperament. How many more lives must be sacrificed on the altar of a convoluted bloodline and ancient, man-made, claims to a heavily indebted throne? Victory will elude you, as sure as night follows day. The Dauphin is mustering an army. Having created such a weapon he will want to use it. He may even amass an armada to turn his army into an invasion force. But if you persuade

Henry to tactically retreat now and give me some semblance of a victory then honour would be satisfied," Reynard judiciously pleaded. If he was instrumental in forcing the English back onto their ships then Reynard would be redeemed, made powerful, again. France could win the war with the flick of a pen upon a peace accord, without having to draw its sword. Henry would never be able to raise the funds and men again to threaten France.

Chaucer pensively stared up at the cloudless, majestic firmament. The stars twinkled more brightly than any gem upon a crown. Its beauty was both immediate and remote. Chaucer was all too aware of the game his counterpart was playing — and his motives. Peace had its virtues, but he had perhaps more chance of plucking a star from the sky than of altering Henry's determined course.

Yet Chaucer would play along with Reynard's game, for now. He had little choice but to do otherwise. Even if he could get a message out Henry would not be able to send a rescue party in time. He would be taken to Paris. The Dauphin would ransom or torture him.

What will be will be — unless I can do something to improve my fate.

"Come Thomas, let us discuss things some more inside. I have had Nouvel's cook prepare a feast for us. Our last meal together was under somewhat different circumstances. The cuisine and atmosphere will be more palatable this time, I hope."

16

Marie Nouvel lay on her bed, her knees almost tucked up to her chin, and dried her eyes. She finally stood up, combed her hair, smoothed her dress down and opened her jewellery box. She pinched her cheeks to put some colour back in them. She crept out of her room and stood at the top of the main staircase, waiting for the French agent's voice to retreat into the dining room. She then ventured along a narrow coffin-shaped corridor to enter the wing of the house where Fordham was being detained. She wanted — needed — to see him.

Two guards stood outside the locked door. The first was mole-faced, with bloodshot, covetous eyes. He leered and licked his lips on seeing Marie approach. The second — a grey-bearded mercenary with a skin complaint — puffed out his cheeks and let out an appreciative grunt.

Marie unsheathed one of her most amiable smiles and forced the light back into her eyes. The two soldiers were a little intimidated by the startlingly attractive lady, and they were soon charmed by her as she arranged for a servant to provide them with some food and wine. They saw no harm in allowing the merchant's daughter to visit the prisoner, especially after she offered them a ruby-encrusted gold earring each as a thank you. The mole-faced mercenary demanded that he search the woman however, just to be sure she wasn't concealing any weapons to give to the English man-at-arms. The lascivious Frenchman was thorough and ran his groping paws up and down Marie's body several times, much to his and his friend's amusement. His breathing grew heavier, excited. She forced herself not to recoil as she smelt his rank body odour. His teeth were as black as his fingernails and, she thought, Cerberus had sweeter-smelling breath (and a larger vocabulary) than the creatures guarding the door to her lover's room.

But they allowed her through.

Marie wordlessly fell into the soldier's arms as she entered the chamber. Neither could have told one another how long their nourishing embrace lasted for. Fordham held her with a strength and tenderness that, a week ago, he would have thought himself incapable of.

The bedroom was small but comfortable. A half-eaten plate of bread and cheese lay on a table. An oil lamp dangled from the ceiling, swaying gently in the breeze which whistled through a gap in the shutters. Paintings of Saint Jude and John of God (the patron saint of booksellers) hung on the wall, directly opposite the bed which the lovers sat down upon. An accomplished copy of Duccio de Buoningegna's *The Healing of a Blind Man* hung next to the door.

Fordham asked after Marie's father. Tears moistened her recently kissed lips as she told him that her father was sleeping in his room. Arnaud had attended to his injuries as best he could.

"I know more than anyone that my father has been more sinning than sinned against over the course of his life, but he doesn't deserve to be a victim of that monster down there," Marie said, her face twisted in disdain. When Reynard had first arrived, accompanied by his brutish soldiers, the spy apprehended Charles Nouvel "in the name of France". Marie initially wore her best doe-eyed expression to soften the agent's heart and try to ply some mercy out of him. But his heart was as hard as obsidian. Reynard remained amused by Marie's attempts to seduce him. Realising her failure she then offered him a bribe. Money and sex are equally powerful temptations. But why would Reynard accept a small portion of Nouvel's estate when his intention was to seize it all? Marie finally tried to sway Reynard by threatening him, arguing that her father had influential friends at court, but Reynard replied that the woman was wasting her time and energy. Her father's fate was sealed.

Marie continued to recount the events of the day to Fordham, in a voice infused with bitterness and grief.

"He ordered my father's torture just because he could. He claims that my father is a traitor, in conspiring with the English. But would he try and condemn John the Fearless and confiscate his lands for the same crime? France is a gorgon, hissing at and biting its own face. I met the Dauphin once. His eyes crawled over the sight of me, like slugs. A curse on all men, except you. I do not want my face to scowl or my heart to harden too much," Marie said, pouring out her heart. "So much has happened in so little time. I can scarcely believe that I met you less than a week ago, and I cannot believe that I disliked you when we first met."

"I can," Fordham drily replied.

Marie's sob turned into a laugh, like sunshine bursting through the clouds.

"You were just another knight, I thought. Far more in love with himself than anything, or anyone, else. Another man who believed himself to be God's gift to women. But, for me, you were an unwanted gift. Perhaps Thomas thought you would be a colourful distraction, like a peacock, to help secure better trade terms."

"What caused you to change your mind about me?"

"It happened slowly. You made me laugh. I noticed how gracious you could be. And not just towards me, but to the lowliest soldier or attendant in your camp. It dawned upon me that we were similar, in some ways. We believe that certain codes of conduct do not apply to us. We have lived eventful lives, played a number of parts, but no matter what we do there is still a hole in our lives. We think that the hole is borne from boredom and we attempt to amuse ourselves. I could not sleep the night after I met you. I regretted some of my barbed comments and that I didn't let you get to know me. Because I wanted to get to know you more. And I lay awake last night too, regretting the things I failed to say to you. I wanted to tell you that you are not really suffering from boredom, but you are a prisoner of your sorrow and despair. No matter how many books you read, poems you write, men you kill or women you seduce, you can never fill the hole inside you or feel content. You may have sometimes thought that drink could fill this hole but you are just pouring everything into a sieve. Friendship is a far more substantial nourishment but it can only, at best, half fill the hole. Only God or a woman can truly give you something to live for. They equate to the same thing: love. I have never wanted to give my heart to anyone before, as I believed that I didn't have one to give. I cannot remember the last time I felt pity for my father, but I felt pity for him today. I wish this day would have never have begun. Yet, being here with you now, I wish it would never end. I barely know what I am saying. I just know that I could — or do — love you, Edward," Marie expressed, tears wending down her cheeks. She wanted — needed — him to say that he loved her back.

He had never had a woman talk to him in such a manner before. Indeed he had seldom spoken to himself with such feeling. Fordham felt like he had a thousand tiny horses galloping through his body. He had never said "I love you" to anyone and meant it. The sybaritic soldier had given women poems before, trinkets, nights to remember and an outlet for revenge against their unfaithful husbands. But Fordham had never given his heart. Love was real, he could finally attest. His cynicism, which he had nearly drowned under, had been washed away by Marie's tears. Love was real. And strong. And ennobling.

He didn't say it because he felt he needed to say it, or that Marie needed to hear it. He said it because it was true.

"I love you too," Fordham declared, simply and sincerely, as he sealed his confession with a heartfelt kiss.

17

Two corpulent guards stood, statue-like, at either end of the dining room. The fire crackled and hissed with seeming glee beneath the marble mantle. The smell of the acrid smoke in the chamber was tempered by the moreish aromas of the various plates of steaming food placed upon the table: rabbit stew; broiled venison in an onion sauce; salted herring; sticks of carrots on a bed of cabbage; cheeses and sweet pastries filled with figs and dates.

A whey-faced servant's hand trembled as he refilled the French agent's cup with wine. Reynard couldn't wholly conceal his smirk of amusement at the raw fear he was inspiring in the man. He dabbed his mouth with a napkin and continued to speak to Chaucer, sitting at the other end of the table.

"How's your venison? Fit for a king, is it not? My sovereign cannot be completely mad if he insists that his supply comes from this region. There is a forest, to the south-east of Nouvel's estate, which used to be rife with wolves. A local official, in his wisdom, ordered that the wolves should be culled to stop the deer supplies from decreasing. And do you know what happened, several years later? The deer nearly died out completely, as an unnatural rise in their numbers depleted their sources of food to such an extent that many starved to death. My point is that though the world may fear such creatures, or pretend that they do not exist, the world needs its wolves, Thomas. And we are the wolves — necessary evils for the good of society. People may condemn us for serving the ruling elite or for carrying out heinous crimes to preserve the order of things, but the populace would soon kiss our hands if our kingdoms started to fall into misrule and disorder. And we are capable of compromise and change are we not? Was I not due to torture and liberate your head from your body when we last encountered each other? But now I choose to treat you as a prize, and I would as soon as cut off my own head as I would yours," Reynard politely remarked, all the time hoping that, after having delivered Chaucer up to the Dauphin, he would be indeed be given the opportunity to torture and kill his adversary. "I suspect that you consider me a self-serving and rancorous man. But let us assess the scales of justice more carefully. I may have ordered the deaths of many, but did not those assassinations help prevent a war, where countless scores of men would have perished? I have also been responsible for disrupting trade between nations, but ruined economies cannot afford to go to war. Are political factions not best set against each other at court, rather than on the battlefield? We both do what we do because we have to. You consider me a devil, but really I am a scapegoat. If I am a weed in the garden, I am at least one which prevents other weeds from growing and taking over. Surely I am preaching to the converted? You have committed similar acts of espionage, have you not?"

"I'm not so sure I'm as much a devotee of your religion as yourself," Chaucer answered, unmoved by the Frenchman's arguments. All the rivers of Europe could not wash the blood from the agent's hands.

Reynard pursed his lips. Chaucer couldn't be sure if his look of disapproval was directed at him or the piece of gristle which he had found running through his piece of venison. He cut away the offending slither of unwanted meat with surgical precision.

"Still you see yourself as St George and view me as a dragon. I remember the first life I took. It was many years ago, in a seminary. His name was Louis, he was the second son of the Philippe de Meulan. Louis was fundamentally unpleasant — a bore and a bully. He purchased friends by paying for their wine and taking them to the nearby brothel. Louis was, all in all, such a base and vile soul that I believe he would have risen quite high in the ranks of the church. Suffice to say I poisoned him, out of both spite and pragmatism. Unfortunately I wasn't present when he died, but my imagination was able to furnish me with the images of him foaming at the mouth and writhing on the ground. His elder brother had his suspicions about his demise but was incapable of substantiating anything.

"Now your first reaction may well be to condemn me as a monster, or that my revenge was disproportionate to the offence. But as a result of Louis' death his former acolytes became less dissolute and concentrated on their studies. This heinous act became an unwitting act for good. Now I put it to you Thomas, that you may consider any act of disloyalty towards Henry — your sovereign and friend — to be wrong or even sinful. But how wrong would it be to convince your Henry that he cannot win this war? How wrong would it be to save the lives of countless Englishmen? The most treacherous act in your life could prove to be the most virtuous too. Your father would appreciate the irony. I will concede however — given our recent history — that I may be the last person to convince you to commit some form of treason against your King and country, though it is for the good of your King and country to do so. But you may soon come face to face with the reality of the situation in the form of our grand army. We have more knights, more men-at-arms, more horses and more cannons than your ever dwindling force. If you will not listen to me then at least listen to the dictates of logic. Henry cannot possibly win in the field, after the Dauphin mobilises the might of France. God is on the side of the big battalions," Reynard argued.

"Despite the noise, it seems God must have been sleeping on the days of the battles of Crécy and Poitiers," Chaucer wryly countered.

"Ha! A fair riposte. I could not possibly entertain the idea of disembowelling you, Thomas. It would be a waste of some fine food and a fine conversationalist as well." Reynard smiled, mechanically, but his eyes remained as black and dead as a shark's, glaring at its prey. The French agent had every intention of killing the Englishman. But Chaucer knew this, and had every intention of killing his enemy first. For the first time, Chaucer knew he would take a marked pleasure in taking someone's life.

18

It felt like the last day of summer and that it would be the year's last balmy evening. Fordham had opened the shutters to reveal a bulbous moon, shining like a polished silver brooch upon a widow's black, silk dress. Restless horses, perhaps missing their deceased masters, whinnied loudly from the stables. The sound of carousing soldiers, joking or cursing, could also be heard through the window as the mercenaries made the most of their host's wine cellar.

The lovers both knew that this could be their final night together. Such grim thoughts remained unvoiced, however, by unspoken mutual consent. Instead they talked long into the night, about any and everything, as if they wished to pack an entire relationship into one evening. They spoke of their childhoods, their failings and their hope for a future together.

"This used to be my second bedroom when I was young. It also served as a sanctuary on those nights when I needed to attend to one of my father's business partners. After they would fall asleep I would silently creep out of the bedchamber over the other side of the house and come back here, where they would never find me. I would arrange for a servant to put a bowl of hot, scented water in the room and I would wash my body and rub oil into my skin. I sometimes told myself that I was washing away my sins, and those sins committed against me. It sounds silly, I know, but I occasionally prayed, back then. I also had a dog, a russet-coloured hound called Hector, who I allowed to sleep at the end of this bed. He was a terrible hunting dog. My father wanted to put him down but I stood between him and Hector and challenged him to swing his axe. Hector may have been a terrible hunter, but a dog can be a girl's best friend. He was not the smartest hound in the world, but that only made him more adorable, in my eyes. It often heralded a better day when I would wake up to him in this bed. I trusted him more than any man in my life, which admittedly wasn't overly difficult. Hector had a window into my soul. He would growl at those suitors who I especially found odious. I preferred to be licked by him than kissed by dukes. We'd go on long walks, disappearing for most of the day. I think a piece of me passed away when Hector died. My heart became even thornier. I became a piece of glass, beautiful but cold. I want you to know that you are the first man I have ever laid next to in this bed. I want you to be the last man I ever get to lie next to as well."

Fordham asked Marie to come back to England with him. He promised himself that he would track down a russet-coloured hound when he got back home. One that wouldn't growl at him. Marie said that she would be happy to travel with the soldier back to England. The rain would dampen her clothes but not her spirits.

"I never thought that I would one day want to be half of an old married couple," Fordham remarked.

"Is that a proposal? I would, of course, scrutinise any marriage contract far more vigorously than a simple trade deal," Marie slyly replied, as she lay next to him, beaming from the thought that he wanted to marry her. "Would you love me even if I grew fat?"

"Of course. There'd be more to love."

Marie let out a burst of laughter, though tears of sorrow laced her tears of happiness.

"And would you come home early from the tavern each night if I asked you to, after becoming husband and wife?"

"We may need to negotiate that clause in the contract, it seems. I am only human after all."

Again Marie laughed and, to stop herself from sobbing, leaned towards the man-at-arms and kissed him.

*

When he was sure Marie was asleep Fordham's handsome, loving expression quickly turned into a pinched, pained one. They had planned for their future but Fordham couldn't even be sure if he — or Marie — would be alive come tomorrow evening. Not even Chaucer owned sufficient powers of diplomacy to talk them out of their fate, and even if Chaucer could secure their release, Fordham wouldn't leave without Marie. He understood now why Cooper, despite it being in his blood even more than his own, could give up soldiering. Fordham would swallow his pride if need be and ask his father for a job. He would become a clerk or copyist. Just so long as he could become a husband — and perhaps even father — too.

If I can somehow save her I'll be saving myself too.

The evening song of a warbling bird winged its way through the window, threading itself through the guttural voices of the drunken mercenaries. Fordham couldn't quite tell if the song was a cry of love or loneliness, triumph or tragedy.

19

Morning.

Half constructed trenches scarred the muddy ground. Not a patch of greenery remained. Soldiers, some with more energy and purpose than others, moved to and fro, their faces as worn as the crosses of St George on their tunics. The sound of orders being given, blades being sharpened and armour being knocked back into shape could be heard in the background.

Sir William Talbot jutted his chin out to take stock of the breeze and temperature. Coral-white clouds scudded across the horizon. Cooper, John Walworth and Talbot stood in a row next to a trebuchet, facing the Leure gate and its barbican. The formidable structure was ribbed with tree trunks, held in place by iron bands. Holes had been made in the walls of Harfleur to allow men to travel between the barbican and town. A defensive ditch, filled with water, lay before the small fortress, to further slow or discourage any assault.

"Let's just hope that it doesn't rain. I don't want God taking a piss and putting out our fires tonight," the gruff knight remarked, as a cannon fired a gun stone overhead. The missile fell harmlessly against the base of a thick part of the wall.

"Bloody artillery. They couldn't hit a prick in a brothel," John Walworth pronounced, rolling his eyes.

"Well said, my friend," Talbot posited. The professional soldier had been witness to the power and progress of cannons over the decades, but it wasn't a coincidence, he felt, that most gun teams named their cannons after women. The weapons were difficult to move, inconsistent and combustible. Also, as much as artillery could help kick down a door, Talbot knew that an army still needed a good supply of well-trained men to do the dirty — and bloody — work of streaming through the entrance and capturing the town.

The lowborn knight and roguish archer took to one another immediately, after being introduced by Cooper the day before. Over a campfire and suckling pig they matched each other drink for drink, curse for curse and bawdy joke for bawdy joke. "You remind me of old John Falstaff," Talbot declared, clapping Walworth on the back. "Except that you're twice as brave and twice as slim as that raucous sot."

Cooper surveyed the scene and agreed that they needed cloud cover to help conceal their approach under a full moon, but not rain. His heart beat a little faster, to the rhythm of a marching drum, in anticipation of the assault. Fear crept into his stomach and twisted his guts, as if he had been stabbed and his intestines were being wrapped about a rusty blade. The archer, in the shape of Grace, now had something to lose. His wife-to-be would perhaps chide him for leading the assault on the bastion, he mused. Cooper would argue in reply that the sooner he helped end the siege the sooner he could come home.

"So do you think we have enough good archers to keep up an accurate rate of fire? They need to take out any French bastard charged with putting out the flames. I also need you to put an arrow through the neck of anyone looking to pour burning oil or limestone over our heads. You will need to assign some archers to shoot at any of the enemy manning the battlements up there. We'll be an easy target for any crossbowmen looking to flank us."

"Most of my own company are absent but I know the best shots available and have already started to recruit them," Cooper answered. Quantity would matter as much as quality, but he could not amass too great a force as the enemy would hear and see them coming. Forewarned would be forearmed.

"I have a group of archers attached to my company. I'll arrange for you to drill them and you can pick out the best of the bunch. And don't be afraid to make them sweat. Work them harder than a whore works her —"

"Cooper, Robert Cooper?" a florid-cheeked squire remarked, walking briskly up to the veteran soldier. His ill-fitting plate armour clanged together like a carillon of bells.

Cooper nodded at the youth and thanked him, after delivering a message that the King wished to see him at midday.

As he was doing so Talbot turned to John Walworth. "Use your fire arrows to incinerate half that bastard of a barbican and I'll chop the rest down with my axe. It'll be a tough nut to crack, but I've cracked open tougher. I was once on a freebooting campaign in the region of Perugia. There was a town, smaller than this but similar to it as well. Its walls were high and a barbican sat, like an angry toad, outside the main gates. We made out like we were going to starve the cretins out but it was just a bluff. We barely had enough food for ourselves. So, on the fifth day of the siege, whilst the townspeople were asleep and the barbican only half manned, we assaulted their defences under the cover of darkness. We eventually opened those gates up like the legs of a limber drab. But the barbican was the key to unlocking the town — once we took that, the siege was over. Once we take down that big wooden bastard tonight Gaucourt will be forced to surrender. The town will be shitting itself by then — and not because of the bloody flux," Talbot asserted, as he glared up at a figure staring back at him from the battlements.

Perhaps it was Gaucourt, the knight thought. As much as Talbot had cursed his name over the past few weeks the Englishman felt a begrudging admiration for the French captain. He had fought successfully against the Turks during his career and also had experience facing English archers. It had been an act of courage to ride into the belly of the beast and reinforce the town, just as it was being surrounded. And the Frenchman had proved as resourceful as he was valorous. He had turned fishermen and weavers into effective soldiers, ones who could rebuff the English army's attacks and, on occasion, go on the offensive to sally forth from the town and destroy mines and artillery pieces. Gaucourt had also turned the townspeople into an army of engineers. Mounds of sand and clay acted as cushions to lessen the damage to the town's streets. Any small breaches in the walls were quickly patched up with earth, timbers and dung. The French commander used his artillery well. Any bridges that the English constructed at night, over the defensive ditches, were burned the following day, destroyed by flaming gun-stones coated in oil or pitch. "If France has ten more commanders of Gaucourt's mettle then Henry really will need God on his side to win the crown," Talbot had said to Cooper the night before.

"Sir William?" John Walworth remarked, trying to attract the attention of the knight, who appeared transfixed by a soldier on the ramparts.

"Apologies. I was distracted."

"If only the garlic-chewing swine could be similarly distracted, tonight," Walworth posited.

Talbot paused. At first he narrowed his eyes and knitted his brow in thought, then his features became taut, alive and alert. "Very well said, my friend. You're a veritable fucking Vegetius!" Talbot would share a flagon of one of his finest ales with the archer. It was the least he owed the bowman, for help planting the seed of an idea which would help the English take the barbican.

20

Reynard of Troyes had arranged a fencing bout for Montbron to defeat Fordham. He enjoyed Chaucer's attempted interventions and pleas. The Englishman implored him to show mercy, to which Reynard replied that he was far more concerned with being rewarded in this life, as opposed to the next. Chaucer then appealed to his enemy's avarice, arguing that he could be rewarded in this life by sparing Fordham. He was the son of a Norfolk merchant and could command a worthwhile ransom. But Reynard, affecting an air of righteousness countered, that his sense of justice was sovereign over his greed. "It is only just that my man be given the opportunity to right the wrong against him. You are English Thomas, surely you can appreciate my dedication to fair play?" the agent artfully remarked, unable to suppress an amused smirk. Chaucer knew that he would not be able to threaten, bribe or reason with his antagonist. It would all be in vain. Even if Fordham could best his opponent, the French would execute his friend.

Despite the martial spectacle on offer, many French soldiers remained in their beds, heavy-headed from the previous night's drinking sessions. A force of just under two dozen mercenaries occupied the courtyard. Bleary-eyed soldiers gulped down water whilst discussing the prospective bout and making wagers. Some sat around two long trestle tables positioned either side of the courtyard. Few were dressed in their armour and few carried a full complement of weapons, but a half a dozen soldiers, with crossbows, were rostered by Montbron to be on duty. A couple stood by the portcullised gate to the estate, a couple kept watch on the right hand side of the ramparts and the remainder flanked the door of the house.

Pierre Montbron stood on one side of the courtyard. The assassin ran a sharpening stone along the length of his polished sword as two attendants strapped his armour upon him: aillettes, couters, cuirasse, greaves, vambrace, gauntlets, cuisse, poleyns, sabatons and bascinet. Before donning his helmet, Montbron unflinchingly gazed at his opponent and sneered, looking to intimidate him before the contest even started. Montbron had assured his paymaster of victory that morning: "I have fought the Englishman before. I know his strengths and weaknesses. My wounds have healed sufficiently. If possible I will toy with him and he will die the death of a thousand cuts. Or if needs be I can best him quickly. Either way, he dies ..."

Experience, rather than arrogance, fostered Montbron's confident attitude. He was a seasoned soldier and swordsman. He could not remember the last time someone had bested him in a tournament or on the battlefield. As a youth he had drilled himself to master various weaponry, and to conquer fear. During their last encounter, the Englishman had wounded his pride as well as his body. He had easily out-fenced his opponent but the English cur managed to arm himself with a crossbow and injure the Frenchman. Fordham had prevented the assassin from completing his mission in London, and was therefore the cause of him still being indebted to the agent. Montbron hoped that Fordham's death would provide restitution and Reynard would allow him to return to his farm and family.

Thomas Chaucer stood a few yards to the left of Reynard of Troyes. A pugnacious looking mercenary, his large hand resting on his sword's pommel, had positioned himself between the two fork-bearded spies. The Englishman noted how the dagger hanging from the mercenary's belt was in reach.

Chaucer mournfully stared at his friend, who was being readied for combat. When Fordham proved too sorrowful a sight to take in his eyes surveyed every other part of the courtyard. A large space had been cleared in the middle for the combatants. Faint bloodstains still discoloured some of the flagstones. Casks of ale and wine sat all around the edges of the courtyard. Barrels of lamp oil were piled on top of each other on the left hand side of the ramparts. Various household and agricultural tools rested against the side of the steps which led up to ramparts. Chaucer judged that, even if he and Fordham could race up the stairs, the drop from the steep walls would cripple or kill them. For weeks the spy had wracked his brains in regards to the problem of breaking into a walled settlement. Now he needed to come up with a plan to escape from one. He noticed how the burly Henri still kept a close watch on Marie Nouvel. The loyal — and doubtless formidable — bodyguard would join in the fight if he felt that the woman was in peril. But even if every one of Nouvel's men took up arms against their unwanted guests they would still be outnumbered and outfought.

The attendants had finished strapping on Fordham's armour. He glanced down and noticed spots of blood and rust across the dented breastplate. He looked over towards his opponent. Montbron's armour was shinier and — far more significantly — lighter. Fordham's sword was heavier too. He observed how the blade he had been given had been blunted. The edge was about as sharp as a Welsh yokel's wits, he thought. The odds were increasingly weighted against him. Fordham recalled his encounter with the assassin, when he had fought him back in England. They had traded blows on horseback then. He tried to remember his technique and angles of attack, in hope of using the information to his advantage. Perhaps his opponent was still hampered by the wound he had suffered during their previous contest. The Englishman's one hope was that, if he could manoeuvre the fight towards where Reynard of Troyes was standing, he could run the French agent through. Although he would die shortly after, it was still the most likely way he could save Marie.

Thomas Chaucer approached his companion, believing that it would probably be the last time he would ever speak to him.

"I don't suppose you have a small army concealed on the horizon, as you did in Scotland, when you last faced off against Reynard?" Fordham remarked, a half-smile blooming and then wilting on his face. "Indeed I could almost wish myself in Scotland instead of here right now, given our fate. I say *almost* though. Things are not that bad yet." Cracks appeared in his voice as Fordham spoke.

Chaucer offered up an encouraging, but faltering, smile in reply. "Kill this bastard. That's an order. You've faced far angrier husbands baying for your blood, after you've slept with their wives."

"I'll do my best. If my best somehow isn't good enough though please pass on a message to my parents. Say to my mother that I always spoke fondly of her. The small lie will be a cause of some happiness and consolation to her. And to my father, mention that I spent half my life drinking and whoring — and that I squandered the other half. Tell Cooper and Walworth to hunt down Reynard, if they can. Send him back to hell, with an arrow stuck in his gullet. As for yourself, I am not sure how much it's been an honour to serve in your company, but it's been something far nobler — fun," Fordham exclaimed, as he warmly clasped a hand on his friend's shoulder. Chaucer had saved Fordham many years ago, by paying off his debts in return for joining his company. "But you must now excuse me. I have to muster one last goodbye."

Marie Nouvel was wearing a pleated, cream-coloured dress made from fine, Flemish wool. A silver cross hung over the high neckline of the garment and the sleeves were wide, serving a practical purpose. A sky-blue silk belt adorned her waist and accentuated her slender figure. Marie wore her hair long. It was often her habit to plait her hair but her hands had trembled too much that morning to do so. Fordham thought Marie beautiful, but not because of the way she looked.

They walked towards one another and met near the centre of the courtyard. Tears glistened, like jewels, in the woman's eyes. Fordham experienced an urge to remove his breastplate, so that he could hold her and feel her head upon his chest. Instead they laced their fingers together. There was so much that they wanted to say to each other, but there was also so much that didn't need to be said. Words are often poor ambassadors to the soul.

"I prayed this morning, for the first time in a long time," Marie said. She had woken that morning and, seeing the painting of St Jude (the patron saint of lost causes), had prayed to him to protect Fordham. Marie had bowed her head, shut her eyes and clutched her hands so firmly together than they ached a little.

"I imagine that God was listening. If I was him I wouldn't be able to keep my eyes off you."

"You always make me laugh when I should be crying."

"It could be worse. I could make you cry when you should be laughing."

"I have been told that I will be journeying to Paris, with Thomas. I am not sure when I will see you again. I am worried that you will not be allowed to walk away from this fight. Reynard promised that you could go free if you proved triumphant. But I do not trust the man. He is as Godless as a savage," Marie remarked. Although the sun beat down upon the courtyard she shivered a little, chilled to the bone.

"I promise that we will see each other again, whether it be in this life or the next, Marie. I give you my word." *You've given me something to fight for. To live for. And to die for ...*

21

The air was not holy. The King's store of incense had been used up. Burned out. The putrid stench of ordure and death entered his nostrils, as did the acrid smell of smoke from the funeral pits. Enough was enough.

Henry solemnly bowed his head in front of the simple wooden cross in his tent. A bible lay open on a chest-high lectern to left of the King, displaying an annotated verse from John: *If we say that we have no sin, we deceive ourselves, and the truth is not in us.* A desk, containing various writing implements (a quill, knife, awl, ink, seal and parchment ruler), stood to the right. Henry had been composing a letter to Richard Whittington. The former Mayor of London had been a loyal supporter of the crown over the years. Henry wanted to reassure his ally that the campaign was not in such a parlous state as it seemed, and that he was still worth investing in.

Rumour can spread more quickly — and viciously — than any contagion, but know that we stand more entrenched than the walls of Harfleur and that our spirits remain as high as the ramparts of the town. Like their king, the men are unbowed and unbroken. France still desires to be sovereign over us, to rewrite our laws, silence our English tongues and have us pay homage. I remember reading a letter once which William Montagu wrote to a young Edward III, in reference to taking action against Mortimer before he carried out his plan to usurp the throne: "Better to eat the dog, than let the dog eat you," Montagu advised. And the advice holds true in relation to ourselves and France now. To those who question my judgement in continuing to fight — to save England from tyranny or ruination — I will reply by quoting the motto of the Order of the Garter: "Shame on him who thinks evil on it".

Henry at first asked Whittington for his prayers, but by the end of the letter he was asking the merchant for more capital. The army needed more men, in light of the disease which was decimating its ranks. It also needed a greater supply of provisions. An army marches on its stomach.

Henry felt a slight breeze on the back of his neck and heard someone enter the tent behind him. Yet still he bowed his head and silently — devoutly — prayed:

Lord, make me an instrument of thy peace.
Where there is hatred, let me so love;
Where there is injury, pardon;
Where there is doubt, faith;
Where there is despair, hope;
Where there is darkness, light...

The King turned to Cooper and smiled amiably at him. The veteran archer stood attentive to his monarch and commander.

"Come Robert, sit down with me awhile," Henry said, as he led the bowman off into a corner of the tent. A silver flagon of ale sat on a table and the King poured himself and Cooper a cup. The soldier noticed how the smile had fell from his sovereign's face. He appeared world-weary when he believed no one was looking. His face was lined with worry, his complexion as grey as the cobwebs hanging off the oil lamps in the tent.

Cooper noticed a portrait, leaning against the side of the tent, by the table and chairs. The figure was mounted on a horse, carrying a sword. Riders either side of him carried banners of St George. His jaw was strong, armour polished and expression purposeful. Cooper might have thought the painting one of Henry, if not for the advanced years of its subject.

"It's a portrait of my great-grandfather, Edward III," Henry said, proudly. His fondness for the artwork also derived from the fact that the portrait had been commissioned by Richard Courtenay, a parting gift from a dear friend. "I am told that Charles V kept a portrait of Edward too, and that he could not help but look upon his adversary with admiration. I am far from confident however that the Dauphin keeps a painting of myself in his chambers. If he did so then I imagine it's probably been a target for pieces of rotten fruit by now."

The King permitted himself a flicker of a smile at his own comment but, like a candle, the flicker died out. The painting — and achievements of Edward — were a source of inspiration to Henry, but the portrait also inspired feelings of deficiency in the king. Henry had failed to emulate his antecedent. Whilst the "King of the Sea" had captured the great port of Calais, he was still bogged down in the mud outside of lowly Harfleur. Instead of feeling that Edward was gazing upon him with a source of filial pride, he had every right to chide his wayward descendant and look on down him with grave disappointment.

A cannon sounded in the background and Henry seemingly woke from his trance.

"I am surrounded by a legion of earls, dukes and knights, am I not? But when I mused to myself this morning who was the most honourable — or honest — man in my camp I could not help but think of you, Robert. I recall a scene some time ago. We were practising archery. I remember that I had more chance of hitting the moon that the target in front of me. You were a better teacher than I was a student. That I am a better harp player than I am an archer is all one needs to know, in regards to my ability with a bow. I put a question to you back then. I asked if you thought I possessed the loyalty of the bowmen of England — if they would answer a call to arms and go to war for me. You replied simply and honestly that you were unsure as to the loyalty of your fellow archers, but that I owned your loyalty and bow arm, for all that might be worth. I wish you would reply in a similar honest vein now, Robert. In my decision to still besiege the town, as opposed to move forward or retreat, how much am I proving to be a King of England or how much am I playing the fool? They might be one and the same thing, some might posit. But I ask this question every day: how much am I acting out of a sense of pride, and how much am I acting from a standpoint of honour?"

Henry leaned forward slightly, from an urge to confess and a burning desire to hear the archer's reply.

Cooper paused. He strategically picked up his cup and downed several mouthfuls of ale to give himself more time to consider his response. He was surprised and flattered that the king should remember a conversation they had several years ago, but the archer recalled the recent words of wisdom from Thomas Chaucer: "Honesty is not always the best policy, when it comes to those in power. Sometimes it's best to let them hear what you think they want to hear. Be ever mindful that a king can as easily separate your head from the rest of your body as he can pluck a grape from a vine."

"It's not beyond any man, whether he be a bowman or a king, to be both proud and honourable at the same time," Cooper said, squinting from the light that shone down from the gap in between one of the tent's poles and the canvas roof.

"As you once tried to teach me archery, I think Chaucer may have schooled you in diplomacy. But pride and honour will both be defeated this evening if we do not take the barbican. This is our last throw of the dice. Too many of our men are dying and every death eats away at the heart of England. And England is not worth sacrificing for the lesser prize of France. If the bastion still stands come the morning then I will make preparations to evacuate our troops and return home. One cannot wash away blood from one's hands by spilling further blood. But I still have faith in England, and your bow arm, Robert. Where there is despair, bring hope. We will take the barbican tonight, and we'll soon be celebrating victory in the town rather than commiserating in the hulls of our ships, sailing prematurely back to Southampton. An Italian nobleman once presented me with a letter, composed by Edward III. He was writing to one of his allies, the Doge of Genoa. Edward had just suffered a setback. But his faith — in himself, his army and his God — defeated his doubt and doubters. He wrote the following: "My power has not been laid so low and the hand of God is not yet so weak that I cannot with his grace prevail over my enemy.""

Cooper could not quite find the words to sympathise with Henry. Indeed he was perhaps closer to sympathising with the thought that enough was enough. Yet, like Henry, the archer did not like losing, and as much as he was keen to return back to England and Grace he did not want it to be at the expense of leaving his honour behind in France. A pause hung in the air between the two men. Before the bowman delivered his reply his attention was distracted by another portrait, sitting behind his monarch. The figure in the picture was of a young, finely dressed woman with equally fine features. Diamonds hung around her pale, elegant neck. The artist had captured the intelligence — and sense of humour — in her aspect. A sapphire and amethyst encrusted diadem crowned her head. Her hair fell down past her shoulders like silk.

She must be a princess Cooper thought.

"You are looking at Catherine of Valois, daughter of Charles VI. If all goes well my enemy will become my father-in-law," Henry remarked. Hope and a wry humour coloured his tone. Catherine had been offered as a bride by the French in order to temper Henry's will to go to war. The dowry offered had been more than a princely sum too, but still not enough. Yet the prospect of marrying Catherine had, unlike the thought of relinquishing his claim to the French crown, remained. She was a reputed beauty and wise beyond her adolescent years. Henry had, on more than one occasion, quizzed Chaucer about the French princess. "I have encountered plenty of modest princesses during my time spent at various courts on the continent. Most of them have a lot to be modest about, I dare say. But Catherine would be a fitting match for you." Henry had kept Catherine's picture in his chamber, at his palace in Kennington, and had subsequently brought it over to France. He was captivated by it, as he hoped that he would be captivated by her in the flesh. The war between England and France needed to be a prelude to peace between the two countries. A happy union between himself and the daughter of Charles VI would mark a happy union between the rival nations. Henry promised himself that, should he prove victorious, he would take Catherine's hand in marriage. The once sinning prince had become a celibate King, partly in honour of his vow.

"But I fear I must sleep in a soldier's billet for some time yet, before I experience the feather mattress and silk sheets of a royal marriage bed. I will once day embark on courting and winning the heart of the woman you see painted before you though. Thomas has warned me that not many men come through a campaign of matrimony with their pride and honour intact, but I should not speak so ill of the institution of marriage, Robert, especially since Thomas tells me that you are to be wed within the year."

"I am," Cooper replied, unable to suppress a smile as a picture of his intended replaced that of Catherine of Valois in his mind's eye. "Grace has even set a date for us to be wed." *Had she tempted fate in doing so?* he darkly thought to himself.

"It may not seem like it now, with the walls of Harfleur still standing, but I give you my word that I will get you to the church on time. We will both be married, Robert, for better or for worse," Henry asserted, as he got up and placed a hand on the bowman's shoulder, believing that his promise would be honoured.

22

Three clangs sounded out in quick succession, like a blacksmith striking his anvil, as Montbron attacked Fordham and forced the Englishman backwards. A smattering of cheers and applause went up from the soldiers viewing the one-sided contest. Some taunted or cursed Fordham. Some amused themselves by pushing the man-at-arms forward and watching him try to retain his balance within his cumbersome armour.

Fordham attempted to catch his breath inside his ill-fitting helmet. The damp leather lining let off a pungent, sickly odour which nearly made the soldier retch. He noted a few more large nicks in his sword. Not even the lowliest squire from Scotland — or Ireland even — would choose to wield such a blade, he thought.

Montbron had proved too swift, strong and skilful. The Frenchman could afford to toy with his opponent, before finally ending the bout with a killing blow. A smirk, akin to a curved blade, lined the assassin's face beneath his helm. He knew he had the beating of the Englishman. A fair amount of the Frenchman's youth had been spent taking part in tournaments. The competitions allowed him to hone his skills and also earn prize money. He had made even larger sums, however, in defeat at times. Wealthy merchants and aristocrats would pay the swordsman to deliberately lose to their sons. Pride was a costly commodity in the Frenchman's youth, especially when he needed to look after his ageing parents, so Montbron took the money instead of the glory. He could afford to put on a good show now, however. He had already inflicted a few hits on his opponent, adding a few dints and dents to Fordham's already battered armour.

Marie gazed on helplessly. Whilst others squinted in the afternoon sun her face was creased in anguish. Gasp succeeded gasp. She had attended a number of tournaments over the years, and on more than one occasion rival knights had fought each other to win her favour. She knew enough to know that the Frenchman owned the advantage. And so Marie willed God or fate for Montbron to lose his footing at an opportune moment. She needed Fordham to survive, a life without him would be but half a life, she desperately thought.

Again, Montbron unleashed a series of deft, attacking strokes. The Englishman could only parry rather than counter-attack.

I need to even the odds.

Fordham ran through a number of underhand tactics — ones used in a fight as opposed to fencing contest — but he feared that he couldn't get close enough to the Frenchman to butt him or lift up his visor and gorge his eye out. He had little faith in his sword being able to pierce or cut through Montbron's fine armour even if he could win a small advantage. His would be surprised if his blade could even cut through parchment.

"It is all but over, is it not?" Reynard of Troyes remarked, turning to a distraught looking Thomas Chaucer and feeding on his misery.

"You may well have thought the same when you kept me captive on Walter Bane's estate. But fortune's wheel turned then. As it still could do now," Chaucer replied, without wholeheartedly believing in his words.

"Touché. But fortune's wheel turns for everyone. I warrant that you thought I was as good as dead, given how events unfolded in Scotland. It is important to kill, instead of just wing, one's prey, else the supposed dead can come back to haunt you. Just look at us now. Did you ever believe that I would hold the whip hand over you, so quickly, after my reversal? My one regret is that your archer, who thwarted me in Scotland, has evaded justice. But your man-at-arms will presently pay his blood debt. I have given Montbron instructions to have his fun and humiliate your soldier, should he wish to, but I also told him to kill him."

Chaucer was lost for words, but the funereal silence was soon filled by a chorus of laughter ringing out from the watching soldiers, as Fordham lost his footing and fell to the ground. Montbron bid a couple of the house servants to help his opponent to his feet. The English soldier felt a rush of shame, as well as anger, course through his blood. Fordham judged his heavy armour to be a hindrance instead of help. It had been the second time he had fallen to the floor. There wouldn't be a third, he vowed.

Time to even the odds.

The Englishman first removed his bascinet and threw it beneath the nearby trestle table. He then removed his cuirass and various other segments of protection. By removing his armour he would improve his speed and movement, although any hit from the Frenchman now would draw blood instead of just damaging his armour. Fordham stared at his combatant. Without a word said the Englishman goaded the Frenchman into removing his armour as well. Montbron didn't want to lose face in front of his men.

The faintest of smiles danced across Chaucer's lips. Fordham had a glimmer of a chance. He remembered one of the first Latin phrases his father had taught him: *Audaces fortuna iuvat*. Fortune favours the bold.

For the first time in the contest Fordham went on the offensive. Although his sword still felt heavy in his hand he could move his limbs more freely. Montbron was equal to the task of parrying the attacks, however, and, as the two men drew breath, he nodded in appreciation at the Englishman's swordsmanship. As they were now unhelmeted Fordham decided to try and unsettle the Frenchman, by talking to him.

"How's the injury to the arm? That crossbow bolt back in London must have smarted, no? You probably couldn't pull yourself off for a week."

Montbron's smirk turned into a snarl. The swordsmen launched themselves at one another like stags, but with blades clashing against each other instead of antlers. Sweat glazed their faces. Their sword arms throbbed but — out of habit and necessity — continued to move with speed and power.

After a flurry of strokes and slashes, coming from various angles, Fordham decided to suddenly thrust at Montbron, in the hope of catching him unawares. But the veteran swordsman read his opponent. The Frenchman gracefully evaded the attack, and also swished his sword. The tip of the blade sliced through the Englishman's forearm. Blood dripped down from the wound, causing a fresh stain upon the flagstones.

Fordham winced in pain and muttered a curse underneath his breath, directed at both himself and his adversary. He quickly examined the extent of his wound. *I'll live.* There would be a scar, he judged, just above a previous wound. The old scar had come from when a former lover had lashed out and cut him, using a pin from a large brooch. His married lover could forgive him for courting a second mistress, but not if that mistress was her younger sister.

The snarl turned back into a smirk as the Frenchman goaded the Englishman: "I was told you used to be a poet. You should have remained one, it would have been far less painful for you."

"You underestimate how hurtful critics can be."

After catching their breath their swords clashed again, and metal teeth gratingly scraped across metal. Roars began to accompany some strokes as both men mined their physical and mental reserves, looking to find an edge or overpower their opponent through brute strength. Blisters began to form on their already calloused hands. Their footwork was less precise. Their muscular arms ached, as if they had been hanging on meat hooks, but they kept their blades aloft. Their lives depended on it.

Fordham went on the offensive one last time, sensing that his enemy was tiring. He forced the Frenchman backwards, putting every ounce of experience and strength he owned into the attack. But sometimes, when you give you all, it's still not enough. Fordham brought his weapon down upon his opponent in a wide arc. Montbron positioned his sword to deflect the heavy blow, and in the process of doing so the Englishman's blade detached itself from the hilt.

The Frenchman was quick to react. The tip of his sword hung just in front of the unarmed Fordham's chest. There would be no chivalric gesture of providing the man-at-arms with a replacement sword. The trial by combat was over. Execution remained.

A solemn silence, rather than raucous applause, emanated from the watching soldiers. The Englishman had fought well. But not well enough.

Fordham turned to Marie. He wanted to drink in her image one last time and instil a lifetime of love and devotion into a momentarily glance. He needed her to know how much she meant to him. He needed her to know that, ironically, she had saved him.

Love exists. Perhaps God and Heaven do too — and I will see her again.

Tears streamed down Marie's cheeks as if she were already a widow. She wanted to scream but her heart was caught in her mouth. If she could have traded her life for his, she would have. Their eyes met. Despite, or perhaps because of, the tragedy they faced, they smiled at one another. Each wished to gift the other some consolation.

"I love you," the woman mouthed.

A brace of crows, perched on the roof of the house, loudly cawed. Bells, from a village church, pealed in the background.

Sunlight glinted off the Frenchman's Toledo blade. He turned to his paymaster. Reynard nodded his head.

Montbron drew back his sword. His features remained neutral as he stared at his victim. Fordham gently closed his eyes. Maybe he would finally find some peace.

23

The steel tip of Owen Morgan's broad-headed arrow zipped through the air and skewered Pierre Montbron's heart. The Frenchman slumped forward, onto Fordham, and died before falling to the ground. Morgan immediately nocked another shaft and, along with Jack Mercer, cut down the two crossbowmen positioned on the opposite side of the ramparts.

"To me," Mercer shouted to his compatriots as he threw two barrels of lamp oil across the battlements and onto the courtyard below. His fellow archer continued to fire arrow after arrow, raining death from above.

Mercer tossed a lighted candle onto the pool of oil between the right side of the ramparts and himself. A quilt of saffron flames immediately burned before his eyes and acted as a defence for anyone wishing to attack the Englishmen from the right. Mercer also launched a candle down upon the puddle of oil pouring out from the smashed barrels across the flagstones. The former housebreaker grinned as the blaze danced before his eyes and the enemy sped off in all directions in an attempt to avoid the fire, like rats leaving a sinking ship.

Hell was breaking lose.

Morgan and Mercer had been the two men charged with riding at the rear of the company on the journey to Nouvel's estate. The archers reached the gates and heard the cries of their fellow soldiers being massacred from inside. Prudence formed the better part of valour and they retreated into the nearby woods in order to take stock of the situation.

The bowmen waited for the cover of darkness before approaching the house again and abducted one of the stable hands in order to glean more information. Nouvel had been tortured. Chaucer and Fordham had been taken prisoner. A company of mercenaries, led by Reynard of Troyes, had murdered the rest of their countrymen. Morgan and Mercer withdrew to the safety of the woods once more and debated how they should proceed.

"There's nothing we can do. The mission is over. We will be better served by heading back to camp. Cooper can report to the king and arrange a proper rescue party," Jack Mercer argued, believing that it would be pointless to sacrifice his own life in an attempt to honour the memory of the fallen or save his comrades.

"You heard what that stable lad said. The French will be leaving tomorrow for Paris and taking Chaucer and Fordham with them. There's not enough time to get back to camp and muster a company to take on the butchering bastards," the Welshman countered. "We shouldn't abandon them to be tortured and killed, Jack."

"Why shouldn't we?"

"Because they wouldn't abandon us. And if Chaucer dies then it's unlikely that we'll get paid all our dues."

Morgan didn't ask Mercer which of the two arguments persuaded him. The Welshman was just pleased that his friend agreed to help.

The following morning Mercer, aided by the stable hand Guillaume (who possessed more loyalty for his master than for France), liberated a ladder. The archers scaled the walls and appeared on the left hand side of the ramparts, behind various barrels of lamp oil. They watched as the prisoners were led out into the courtyard. Their hope was to engage the enemy at their weakest and make as much capital as they could out of the element of surprise. As events unfolded the bowmen formed a plan of attack. Fire was their friend, and their new ally, Guillaume, could help cover their escape. The blade at Fordham's throat compelled them to act.

"It's now or never," Owen Morgan said to his friend as he drew back the string on his bow.

There's the quick and the dead. Thomas Chaucer turned towards the Frenchman nearest to him and snatched the dagger hanging from his belt. He slashed the blade across his enemy's throat just as the Welsh archer was firing his second arrow. A fountain-spurt of blood slapped against the flagstones. Chaucer sheathed the knife in the dead man's chest before freeing the corpse's sword from its scabbard. Fortune's wheel had, perhaps, turned once more.

Marie Nouvel had originally intended the dagger, which she concealed in the wide sleeve of her dress, for Reynard of Troyes. But there was a chance now to help save Edward, instead of just avenge him. She drew the gem-encrusted knife (a gift from a former suitor, which for once was proving to be of value) and stabbed the closest mercenary next to her. Marie's next instinct was to run towards Fordham.

Henri's primary instinct, after crushing an enemy's windpipe with his brawny forearm, was to protect his mistress. He picked up the axe which belonged to the strangled mercenary and began swinging it, as if he were a forester cutting a trail through a wood, to clear a path for Marie to reach the English soldier.

Chaos reigned. The French, without Montbron, lacked leadership and purpose. A cacophony of confusing shouts and cries swirled about in the air, as did smoke from the burgeoning flames. Nouvel's servants immediately fled inside or scrambled to the corner of the courtyard which was furthest away from the blaze and bowmen. French soldiers ran from the danger. A few took cover behind up-turned tables and cautiously peered over them to gauge the strength of their adversaries. A couple of crossbowmen, their eyes beginning to sting with smoke, fired up at the archers but the bolts clanged harmlessly against stone.

Reynard of Troyes moved cautiously backwards towards the doors to the house and cursed the ineptitude and cowardice of his own men. His eyes darted upwards and took in the mere two archers creating havoc. He then surveyed the courtyard. A ribbon of fire cordoned off half his forces from engaging their opponents. An arrow sliced through a crossbowman's neck as he laboured to crank his weapon again. The French agent's gaze flitted about in an attempt to locate Chaucer. The Englishman was making his way up the stairs to join the archers. He must not be allowed to escape again, Reynard determined.

"Go inside and rouse the rest of the men, you fool," he hissed to the slow-witted mercenary standing to his left.

Fordham just about picked up Montbron's sword in time to deflect the attack from the weasel-faced French mercenary who aimed to crack the Englishman's skull with his mace. After countering the blow Fordham moved his feet and flicked his wrist so that the tip of his sword cut a furrow through his enemy's cheek, lips and chin. The mercenary immediately fell to the floor and howled in pain. His high-pitched screams mirrored those of a nearby compatriot who rolled around on the ground, looking to put out the flames eating their way through his clothes and skin.

Henri arched his back in agony as a mercenary stabbed him, with the tip of his halberd, from behind. But torment swiftly turned to rage and the bodyguard swung his axe around and buried the head of the weapon deep into his enemy's collarbone. Henri fell to one knee afterwards however, his strength giving way. His final act, before passing out and eventually dying, was to wave his distraught mistress on and encourage her to escape with the Englishman.

Reynard of Troyes flinched as the sound of an arrow thudded into the sternum of the mercenary next to him. He realised that it was time to retreat into the safety of the house. As much as the agent took pleasure in torturing a man he had no desire to engage in swordplay. The agent consoled himself with the thought that, even if Chaucer and his men fought their way out of the main gates, his soldiers would easily be able reach the stables and hunt them down. He would withdraw, but not until after he delivered a parting shot. The loaded crossbow on the floor, by the dying mercenary, proved too much of a temptation. Reynard had fired similar weapons before, during interrogation sessions.

Marie Nouvel's glossy black hair and cream dress attracted his hawkish eye. Despite the smoke and number of bodies occupying the courtyard he still possessed a line of sight. She was standing next to Fordham, close to the foot of the steps which led up to the ramparts.

Both Fordham and Marie were facing the agent as he fired the weapon. Marie acted quickest and placed her body in front of the man-at-arms. Shielding him. Saving him. The tip of the crossbow bolt entered the slender woman's back and poked out through her first and second rib. A rose-shaped blotch of blood began to surround the wound. Fordham held her in his arms, as her body became limp. Her lips were contorted in pain as she passed out.

Reynard of Troyes offered up a thin, cruel smirk before slinking back into the house. As he did so he was met by a wave of mercenaries — fastening on clothes and drawing weapons — who were about to stream out into the courtyard. The agent coldly judged that the reinforcements would soon overwhelm his enemies. The English had no chance of escaping.

Thomas Chaucer, who was now standing next to his bowmen, called out to Fordham to join him, and then coughed from the smoke billowing up into the air. As much as Fordham's legs felt like giving way, he carried Marie over his shoulder and commenced to climb the stone steps whilst Morgan and Mercer provided covering fire. As he neared the top of the stairs the Welshman gave instructions to Chaucer to roll a large barrel of lamp oil onto the bottom of the steps. The barrel shattered against the ground, soaking the immediate area in oil. Jack Mercer tossed a candle onto the glistening liquid. The instant blaze scorched the beard of an encroaching mercenary. Others gave the searing inferno a wide berth. Chaucer kicked another barrel down the stairs — as did Mercer — to feed the conflagration and form an unbreachable barrier of flames.

A few crossbow quarrels whistled past their ears. Morgan and Mercer still picked off their targets as Chaucer and Fordham (still carrying Marie over his shoulder) climbed over the battlements and made their way down the ladder. In between arrows Morgan bellowed out an order to Guillaume, who was positioned just outside of the main gates to the estate. The industrious stable hand, along with a couple of other servants loyal to Nouvel, had wheeled a large wagon around from an outbuilding and placed it in front of the house. The wagon, which had been doused in lamp oil, was also weighed down with plenty of flammable material. After Morgan gave the order Guillaume ignited the wagon. The French mercenaries would now no longer be able to exit the gates quickly, retrieve their horses and pursue the English.

Owen Morgan was last man to descend and he tipped the large ladder over so that his enemies couldn't follow them down. A pillar of smoke, from the formidable fire outside of the main gates, vaunted upwards. He just about heard the roars of frustration from the French above the flames as they opened the entrance. The Welshman judged that the obstacle would furnish them with enough time to make good their escape.

Morgan heartily thanked Guillaume, as the French youth handed him the reins to his mount. He advised the stable hand to disappear for day or two. Until it was safe to return to the house.

"Time to go," Chaucer ordered, after helping lift the still unconscious Marie onto Fordham's horse. He briefly stared back at the house, which was wreathed in smoke. His blood burned as intensely as any flame, as Chaucer thought of how Reynard of Troyes had evaded justice again. He lit a flame in his heart too, of remembrance for Charles Nouvel and the men in his company who had died in vain.

This won't be the end of the story… I will hunt him down — and kill him.

*

The party rode hard to put plenty of distance between themselves and Nouvel's estate. Chaucer eventually slowed their pace and found a clearing, next to a stream, where their horses could take on water. The respite would also give Fordham an opportunity to attend to Marie.

"I owe you two everything," Chaucer remarked to Morgan and Mercer as they led their mounts to the silver, murmuring stream. "I'm at pains to think how I can possibly repay you. I am in your debt."

Jack Mercer was tempted just to ask for any back pay and one of Chaucer's finest vintages but thought better of it.

"Did those bastards kill all the rest of our company, sir?" Owen Morgan asked, mournfully.

"I'm afraid so. I also owe Reynard of Troyes a debt," Chaucer said. He wasn't the only one, he thought, glancing over at his man-at-arms.

Fordham was hungry and bone-tired, his face besmirched with blood and grime. During the ride home the soldier had nearly passed out on more than one occasion. He leaned forward onto Marie, as much as she leaned back on him as she sat in front of Fordham, his arms clasped her and the reins. He prayed to God. He vowed that he would sacrifice any and everything in his life — except her — if Marie lived.

Sunlight poured through the birch trees overheard, chequering the ground in light and shade. Fordham carefully laid her down on the grass. Her heart beat was slow. Her pulse was weak. Her complexion was paler than her cream dress, which was increasingly turning red. Marie woke and roused herself a little. She smiled when she opened her eyes to the sight of a weeping Fordham and reached up to touch his cheek, thumbing a tear away.

"I'm so sorry," he said.

"You English are so polite. You have nothing to apologise for. I should be saying sorry to you as I may have lied to you Edward, when I said that I disliked you when we first met. The truth is, I have always been in love with you. With the idea of you. I just had to wait awhile before we actually met. I wish that we could have spent more time together. But then again an eternity might not have been long enough... Please remember me, Edward. There's no one else that I would want to be remembered by more."

Marie's voice became little more than a whisper. She suffered twinges of pain as she spoke, clawing the ground as she did so. Fordham leaned over her to catch every word. Summoning up what meagre strength she had left, Marie raised her head a little and gently kissed Fordham on the lips. Marie then closed her eyes, as if she were sleeping. But she never woke up.

24

The dead of night.

The evening air was bracing. The moon occasionally peeped through the gaps in the thick fleece of cloud which was draped over the besieged town. A gun-stone had just been launched against the walls again, to convey that it was business as usual.

Sir William Talbot crouched down in between Robert Cooper and John Walworth. Such was their advanced position that they could make out the silhouettes of the enemy manning the barbican and ramparts. Talbot's assault force — nobody wished to call it a "forlorn hope" — was enveloped in darkness, some distance to the rear.

"Is that there George Clifford's poleaxe you're carrying, John?" William Talbot remarked, turning to the heavyset bowman.

"Aye," Walworth replied, gripping the formidable weapon even more tightly. "George gave it to me it in his will."

"Clifford was a good man. We could have used him for this bloody deed tonight. If he wasn't so damned loyal to Chaucer I would've poached him for my company. The bastard once broke two of my lances, before I finally unseated him in a tournament. I trust you'll carry on George's tradition of putting a small mark on the axe for every mutt you kill with it? George was uncommonly fond of that weapon there, as I am of Margaret here," the knight remarked, making reference to his own poleaxe, which he fondly held in his hand. "That's right, I named this beauty. Although, instead of a great beauty, I named her after my first mother-in-law, who was capable of cutting down anyone with a frosty look or a barbed word. There's nothing wrong with naming a weapon, gentlemen. A good one is far more reliable than a lover and far cheaper to maintain."

"There are fewer French turds up there than usual. It looks like the fish has taken the bait, Sir William," John Walworth said, with a certain relief and satisfaction in his voice.

"You should give yourself some of the credit too. You planted the seed in my head to provide a distraction," Talbot replied.

On the other side of the town a large proportion of the Duke of Clarence's army were now formed up, in preparation to attack. Gaucourt couldn't afford not to reinforce the Montevilliers gate, at the expense of the soldiers defending the Leure. Even when Gaucourt realised that the Duke's advance was just a feint, or ruse, the damage would be done.

"I should tell you about my greatest ruse. I was on my horse, in the heat of battle. Our mounted company had been ambushed by a group of Italian cavalry, just outside of Naples. Victory and defeat hung on a knife edge. My men were already half exhausted from a raid on a village earlier that day. But we fought valiantly on and Italian blood, as well as ours, was being spilled. I hacked away at two vicious bastards near me, stabbing their mares to best them. I had a moment to draw breath, and with that breath I shouted, in Italian, "To horse". It's the command to retreat. Our enemy had no reason to believe that the instruction didn't come from their own side. They welcomed the order I dare say, as it gave them a chance to live and fight another day. But what's done is done. Let's concentrate on tonight. Are your men ready, Robert?"

"They're as ready as they'll ever be. They're just waiting on your order, Sir William," the archer replied.

"Well they won't have to wait much longer. Not that they shouldn't mind waiting. Waiting around is half a soldier's job. And more time spent waiting is often less time spent dying."

The three men withdrew and re-joined their lines. They were greeted by a few young, pale, anxious faces. Thankfully those looks were outnumbered by the ranks of bearded, determined expressions from seasoned veterans — bowmen and men-at-arms alike. There were more men who looked like they were going to kill than be killed. That was all the bowman could ask for.

"Have the men all been supplied with their quota of arrows?" Cooper asked, after greeting Percy Badby.

The archer-cum-fletcher nodded in reply. Badby had spent the day manufacturing fire arrows. Each arrowhead had been dipped in boiling pitch. Badby — and his helpers — then attached a clump of tow (greased hemp) to each missile before leaving them out to dry and harden. After his work was done Badby offered up a prayer to God — and St Sebastian (the patron saint of archers) — that the arrows would do their job. Percy was aware that it wasn't the most Godly of sentiments but the archer knew that, as much as he tried to be a Christian, he was a soldier rather than a saint.

As well as a cloth bag full of fire arrows Badby also gave Cooper his leather jupon back, after having sewn a number of metal plates into its lining at strategic points (so as to grant the soldier protection whilst not restricting his movements). After buttoning up the garment the bowman strapped on a short sword.

"You have already put in a shift today, Percy. You are relieved of any duty in taking part in the fighting," Cooper said, full knowing that, whilst Badby was one of the finest fletchers in the army, he was one of the worst shots.

"I could never forgive myself if I shirked my duty, to God and the company. I should stand with the men," Badby said, simply and determinedly.

"Well I want you standing at the rear then. Chaucer will never forgive me if something happens to you. Given your aim you'll probably miss the barbican completely and put an arrow through Gaucourt's eye as he's walking down the street."

*

Whilst Cooper liaised with Badby and Walworth to ready the company of archers Sir William Talbot had an attendant strap him into his armour. Despite a few scratches, revealing the steel beneath, the knight's armour was as black as the river Styx. Rumour had it that the suit once belonged to the Black Prince, and Talbot let people believe the lie.

Talbot marched along the front of the phalanx of men-at-arms. Many wore mail or cuirasses. He noticed earlier how the red and white St George's crosses, which they had painted on their jupons and surcoats at the start of the campaign, had faded and frayed. But the veteran mercenary noted that blades had been polished and sharpened.

"We are soon going to light up this night. We've got the best archers in the world at our side, covering us. And they have got the bravest, and most brutal, bunch of men-at-arms fighting alongside them. We're going to cook those French bastards and the oven will be that barbican over there. I see some anticipation and wariness in a few of the faces in front of me. But I'm putting that down to a trick of the light. Our King has charged us with helping to break this siege. God and St George are watching over us. If we take that bastion then you won't just be tasting victory. Come the morning you'll be tasting the King's finest ale and roasted meats. And there'll be gold coins in your palms, as well as blisters in your hands from grasping your weapons all night."

The troops in front of him, some sallow-cheeked and some jutting out their square jaws, nodded their heads appreciatively at Sir William Talbot's speech, which stoked fires of greed and glory in their guts.

Talbot, Cooper and Walworth came together once more.

"I heard that the priests were hearing confession before the men formed up. Were you not tempted to shrive your soul too, John?" the knight asked, as he surveyed the most strategic section of the ditch, in front of the barbican, at which to cross.

"I'd be there all night and miss the fighting, if I had to confess all my sins. But God go with you tonight, Sir William," the stolidly-built bowman replied, as his strung his large yew bow.

"It may well be preferable to have the devil on our side this evening, given our wish to create hellfire," Talbot exclaimed, before giving an order to the Dutch gunners to launch one last missile before his men advanced.

Whether the soldiers posted on the parapet of the fifty foot high barbican heard strange noises, or saw that something was amiss, they gave the order for their artillery in the town to fire two flares over the wall. They illuminated the ink-black night, only to highlight their doom. A significant force of archers and infantry were advancing.

The gun-stone struck the midriff of the bastion but it neither shook the structure or the resolve of its defenders. Talbot observed the impact, and its lack of destructive power. He was more convinced than ever that only fire could bring down the defiant wooden Cerberus, which guarded the gates to Harfleur.

Iron braziers were brought forward and put into position, next to the English archers. Their coals were lit.

Talbot gave the order for the trumpet to sound, signalling the start of the battle. The noise travelled around to the other side of the town, prompting the Duke of Clarence to begin his tortoise-slow advance and further distract Gaucourt's soldiers there.

Robert Cooper stood at the end of the rows of archers. His barrel chest expanded as he drew in air, before bellowing out his orders.

"Nock!"

Fire arrows were retrieved from cloth bags, placed across bow staves and dipped into the glowing braziers.

"Draw!"

Cooper had advised his archers beforehand to wrap a protective rag around their hands, to prevent them burning themselves. He also instructed that they should aim high rather than draw their strings back too far.

"Loose!"

A harmonious twang, swiftly succeeded by a whoosh, rippled through the air as a hundred or so fire arrows arced towards the barbican, lighting up the night like a shower of tiny comets. A tumult of thuds then sounded out as the missiles hit their mark, biting into the wood and then purring with satisfaction as the flames licked the bastion's timbers.

Without pausing to assess the success of the volley, Cooper issued the same orders — again and again — with calm, rhythmic authority: "Nock... Draw... Loose!"

Pimples of flames began to flower all over the large wooden structure. Smoke began to fill the noses and eyes of the three dozen or so French crossbowmen who mobilised themselves and commenced to fire their weapons at the enemy. From the high ground the crossbow quarrels easily hit their mark, but their meagre rate of fire was unable to halt or slow the English advance.

A gust of wind suddenly blew up, directing a blanket of smoke into French faces, causing them to cough and splutter.

"That's it men, where there's fire there's smoke. Choke the bastards. Strangle them, like you would a perverted priest or unfaithful wife," William Talbot proclaimed, as he marched his men forward, past the bowman.

A few hisses of steam began to fill the night air as the barbican was reinforced by men tasked with extinguishing the flames.

"French cocksucker," John Walworth growled, as he watched his arrow cut down an enemy, carrying a large bucket of water. Walworth, along with a number of other veterans selected from various companies, were occupying an advanced trench. They had been given orders to target the crossbowmen on the crenulations of the town, who could send flanking fire into Talbot's men-at-arms. So too any French attempting to douse the blaze were priority targets.

"You eunuch's prick!" Walworth cursed himself, rather than his enemy, as one of his arrows clattered harmlessly against Harfleur's walls, just below a crossbowmen. He didn't like to waste an arrow, and the Englishman had made a vow that he would kill twice the number of French during the attack than he had seen friends die in the campaign so far.

The arrows swarmed above Talbot's head, like giant fireflies. Another strong gust of wind fanned the flames on the barbican and blew another wave of smoke into the defenders' eyes.

Perhaps God — and the devil — are on our side tonight.

As well as poleaxes, swords and truncated lances, Talbot's men also carried faggots with them, long, bundles of wood tied together which they would use to fill in the ditch in front of the barbican. The knight encouraged his men to dump their loads in the water-filled trench, so as to cross over to the other side as quickly as possible.

The English were now at their most vulnerable. Crossbow bolts rained down upon them from various sides. They were in the sights of those standing on the barbican and also those manning the town's battlements. The enemy had also brought up a number of artillery pieces and began to target the attackers.

A stone boulder crashed down from a trebuchet and bowled over several men-at-arms, like skittles. Chests were staved in and skulls squashed like rotting fruit. Crossbow bolts pierced through plate armour, and then flesh. Smoke wreathed and bodies writhed. Some men called for their mothers, or for comrades to carry them back to safety. Some gritted their teeth and offered up silent prayers or audible curses. Tears cut through faces streaked with dirt and blood (their own or others). Corpses, as well as faggots, filled the trench as if it were a mass grave. A blood-curdling cacophony of screams, roaring flames and whistling shafts swelled in the air and assaulted the ears. But Talbot remained calm and assured. He was a fixed rock whilst the rest of the world streamed around him. He had seen — and survived — similar scenes before. It was war. Unpleasant. Horrific. There was nothing new under the sun. Soldiers died, some more needlessly than others. But needs must. And they needed to bridge the enemy's trench. The knight raised his visor and spoke, offering up orders and encouragement: "That's it, well done... Shore up the left side, there... Let others through... Onwards."

William Talbot was first to negotiate the shaky, make-shift bridge across the ditch. His men dutifully followed, desiring to complete their mission and also avoid the deadly crossfire of artillery and crossbow bolts which rained upon them.

Before Talbot got to within twenty paces of the barbican, he felt a blast of heat from the blaze. The small fist-sized orbs of fire from each arrowhead had joined up and now the flames snaked upwards, spewing out thick smoke. It was becoming increasingly difficult for the soldiers on top of the bastion to see their targets clearly.

The volleys of fire arrows had stopped. But still Cooper's men kept up a rate of fire as their longbows released wave after wave of normal broad-headed and bodkin-tipped arrows at the French lining the parapets of Harfleur.

Talbot's men were now too close to the walls to be in range of their enemy's artillery pieces (yet still crossbow quarrels thudded into the earth, and his men). Rocks and other missiles were also thrown down from the bastion.

Witnessing the barbican up-close, Talbot could see how much it been repaired from previous damage. Fresh pieces of timber supported old, like a patchwork quilt. But Gaucourt couldn't be allowed to salvage his prized defensive possession after tonight. The knight moved around to the side of the structure and hooked his poleaxe around one of the ribbons of iron which held the timbers in place. Talbot puffed out his sweat-soaked cheeks and yanked and pulled on the metal, prising it loose from the charred wood. His men did the same, and also threw bags filled with incendiary powders at the target.

"Burn and fall you bastard," the old knight exclaimed, coughing and cursing, his heart raging like the fires above him. Timbers hissed and cracked. Screams slashed through the air. The barbican began to lurch to one side. Sir William Talbot dared to think it: *Victory*.

But Raoul de Gaucourt was daring to think the same thought too, as he ordered for the gates to be opened and for his soldiers to attack the depleted ranks of the English men-at-arms.

25

Sir William Talbot turned his head to observe dozens of well-armed soldiers streaming out from the town's main gates. Veterans. Killers. Gaucourt had unleashed them, like a pack of wild boars with orders to gore or trample their enemies underfoot.

"Bastard," the knight exclaimed, cursing God and the French commander, as he watched the bulk of the force move towards him. A few men however, carrying torches and containers of oil, peeled away and headed for the ditch. Their intention was to set the bridge of faggots alight and trap any English soldiers on this side of the trench. The French could yet save and repair the barbican.

A swarthy French man-at-arms, equal in size to Talbot, stood at the head of the troops. He was clad, neck to knee, in mail and also wore segments of plate armour on his shoulders and thighs. His greasy black hair was as unkempt as his beard. His face was bony and scarred. The soldier had gained a certain amount of fame among the English, as he had led various parties of French soldiers who sallied forth from the town. He had even earned a nickname — Atlas. Atlas twirled a large poleaxe around in his hands, as if it were a short sword, before pointing the weapon at Talbot. Challenge issued and accepted.

The knight barked out an order for his men to form up and hold the line. As they did so though a coordinated volley of crossbow bolts slammed down upon them from the ramparts, halving the already thinned-out force. Despite being outnumbered the English still needed to attack, Talbot judged. Should they engage the French then they wouldn't fall victim to another volley of quarrels from above.

The two opposing ranks of men, one more sparsely populated than the other, closed in together like two giant waves. They would soon smash against each other, and one would wash the other away.

A mace-wielding Frenchman broke ranks and rushed towards the black-clad leader of the English. Cut off the head and the body will fall.

The French man-at-arms let out a yell as he swung his weapon to connect with the side of Talbot's head. But the knight had confidence in his armour and raised his forearm. The plate armour was as strong as any shield and deflected the blow. Talbot quickly stepped inside and powerfully butted his helmetless opponent. Flooring him. The Englishman then picked up the mace, lying next to the prostrate Frenchman, and smashed his skull in with the weapon. Twice.

The act enraged the French and gave the English heart. The two sides clashed. Metal clanged upon metal, like the sound of a dinner bell. Battle cries cut through the blasts of wind, along with shrill shrieks of pain.

The trio of French soldiers, sent out by their commander to burn down the makeshift bridge, reached their objective, but just as they were about to ignite the bundles of wood at their feet a flurry of arrows sang through the air and buried themselves into chests, abdomens and faces.

Robert Cooper had spied the danger and rushed forward, calling on John Walworth and a handful of other men to join him. The torches which the enemy held acted as beacons in the murky night for their arrows to find their way home.

The barbican acted as a giant beacon too, illuminating the fighting which was taking place close to the town walls. The English dead littered the ground. A few cinders from the blaze fell upon the fallen, like blossom. All seemed lost, but that spurred the archer on to aid, as opposed to abandon, his comrades.

"I think it might be time to put a few more notches on Clifford's poleaxe, John," Cooper said to his old friend. "I'm asking rather than ordering you to come with me though."

"I'd prefer to fuck a leper than cross this bridge, but Clifford would never forgive me if he thought I was running away from a fight. I wouldn't forgive myself either," Walworth remarked, as he unstrapped the poleaxe from his back and slung his bow around his ox-like shoulders in its place.

Cooper instructed the remaining archers with him to head back to the other bowmen and rouse their company. Many were armed with knives and short swords and, through sheer weight of numbers, the bowmen could tip the balance of the fighting and rescue the men-at-arms fighting at the gate. If there were any left alive to save by then.

"Leave some archers in reserve. Keep them firing at the walls so that those bastard crossbowmen keep their heads down. Better still, have them take their heads off."

Cooper drew his short sword and, along with John Walworth, advanced. They were followed over the trench by half a dozen knights, their drawn, polished swords glimmering in the moonlight from where the clouds had parted. The lead soldier in the group raised his visor and spoke to the archer: "Now you didn't think that I was going to let you and Sir William hoard all the glory, did you?" Henry exclaimed, grinning like a gourmand who had regained his appetite.

At first Cooper's mouth was agape in wonder, but then he gritted his teeth in determination. Determined to prove his mettle to the king. Determined that no harm would come to his sovereign. Determined that his side would taste victory.

The likes of Sir John Holland and Sir John Cornwall advanced by Henry's side. They were but a few against many. But a few would have to suffice.

"On, on, you noble English!" Henry shouted, raising his sword in the air as if he were Jove wielding a trident, about to catch lightning and scythe down his enemies. His voice carried to the men-at-arms ahead of him and stirred their reserves of strength and belligerence. If they died, they would die fighting. The King's voice could also be heard by the soldiers behind him and a shout went up from an archer.

"Cry God for Harry, England and Saint George!"

William Talbot spat out a curse as a crossbow bolt punctured his armour and sliced through his thigh. He fell to one knee, all the while watching the giant Frenchman walk towards him. Atlas slayed two men, swatting them like flies, who stood in his path. Blood and sinew dripped from the head of his poleaxe. Atlas was coming for the English knight. Coming to kill him.

Talbot breathed heavily, in between seething with pain. He heard the barbican crackle and hiss behind him. At least he might have fulfilled his mission. Various men slashed, hacked and shouted around the exhausted knight. But everything seem to darken or fade into the background. There was only him and the hulking Frenchman. Atlas was stalking him, like death.

But I'm not going to fucking die on my knees.

The belligerent Englishman dug his sword into the ground — having lost Margaret in the melee — and used it as a crutch to get to his feet.

William Talbot knew he hadn't led a good life. But he had led a successful one, if one tallied up his tournament wins and the wealth he had acquired as a mercenary. He took consolation from the fact that Latimer would finish his chronicle.

My name will live on. I'll survive this night, just not in the way I would've preferred.

Talbot planted his feet in the mud as firmly as he could but the Frenchman's first ferocious blow knocked the sword from his hands and caused him to topple over. The French soldier, offering up a gap-toothed smirk, stood over his enemy. Atlas raised his weapon — holding it aloft longer than he needed to — like a priest at a sacrifice. He wanted the Englishman to stare death in the face.

"You miss, I hit," the voice remarked. It was the voice of the King, assured and commanding. Henry stood several paces from Talbot, pointing the tip of his blade at the Frenchman. Challenge issued and challenge accepted.

The French man-at-arms grunted with derision. Who was this puny man, holding a puny sword? His armour was fine. He would fetch a good ransom if he could take the knight alive.

"You miss, I hit," Henry said again, this time in French, goading his enemy. His father had taught him the phrase. Henry Bolingbroke had explained to his young son that the Black Prince had often used the line during fencing bouts.

William Talbot lay on the ground, heavy limbed and heavy lidded. Despite the heat coming from the burning bastion he felt a chill on his skin. For a moment he thought he heard the voice of the King and the sound of the English rallying but he couldn't be sure. It felt like a dream. The sight of another wave of arrows flying through the air, their goose feathers shimmering like petals of light across a lake, brought the knight a whisper of comfort before he passed out.

The French man-at-arms held his brutal weapon at its end to increase its reach even further. Henry had removed his helmet. He wanted to see everything and feel the breeze on his face. Both combatants smiled at one another, as if they knew something that the other was unaware of. Atlas appeared confident of victory, as if he were a god contesting a mortal. He would deal with the brave, but foolish, Englishman who had challenged him, and then he would slay the already-defeated knight in black armour. The swarthy man-at-arms casually spat out a gob of phlegm but before the green missile hit the ground he quickly swung his weapon at waist height, aiming to cut open his cuirass and disembowel his enemy.

He swung. He missed.

Henry was alert and moved his feet and hips backwards to avoid the attack. Once the head of the poleaxe moved past his body Henry propelled himself, and his sword, forward.

A hit.

The tip of Henry's blade sliced through the Frenchman's mail as if it were gossamer. Henry drove the point on, through his ribs, lung and spine. Blood bubbled out of his mouth and poured down his wiry beard. The sword scraped against metal and bone as Henry freed it from the corpse.

Henry recalled a passage from Vegetius: "*A stroke with the edges, though made with force, rarely kills, as the vital parts of the body are defended by armour and bone. A stab however, though it may penetrate by a mere two inches, is generally fatal.*"

The seasoned English warriors attacked their opponents from the rear. John Walworth stood shoulder to shoulder with Sir John Holland and encouraged more than one enemy to retreat. As did the sight of a dozens of wide-eyed, blade-wielding archers crossing the trench. The French men-at-arms could also no longer see their champion towering above the enemy. Cut off the head and the body will fall.

Some of the French made it back through the gates but the rest were abandoned to their fate. The soldiers manning the barbican could not turn back the flaming tide either. The damage was done. The structure was beyond repair. The French retreated back behind the walls of the town, shoring up the holes which served as an entrance to the bastion.

Henry gave the order to fall back also. He had no desire to lose any more troops to the town's artillery and crossbowmen. Every soul was of value to the Christian. In some ways the campaign had just begun. Finally he would be able take the town of Harfleur, and move on. Gaucourt would surrender, sooner rather than later. The bastion was turning to ash, as were any hopes of the French prolonging the siege. Henry permitted himself to smile, briefly, on overhearing a colourful comment from John Walworth as they walked back to camp: "Now that we've removed the chastity belt of that damned barbican, we can fuck the maid at will."

The King instructed his personal surgeon to attend to William Talbot. When the wounded knight regained consciousness he was in bed, surrounded by Cooper, Walworth and his sovereign. When asked, by Henry, if the soldier wanted anything Talbot replied: "I want one of Chaucer's finest vintages, and a whore. And make sure she isn't as ugly as sin. Or Welsh."

Epilogue

Gaucourt surrendered. Henry was expecting a lion of a man before meeting the architect of the defence of Harfleur. Instead he encountered a gaunt figure doubled-over with stomach cramps, as Gaucourt suffered from the early symptoms of the bloody flux. "If the Dauphin cannot be bothered to fight and give his life for the town, why should we?" the Frenchman argued, caught between being embittered and philosophical about the loss of the town. "Enough is enough."

Henry treated his enemy with grace and favour, putting both his cook and physician at his opponent's disposal.

The royal standard and flag of St George were raised over the gates of Harfleur. As the King entered the town, his air was solemn rather than triumphant. Harfleur needed to be rebuilt, not razed to the ground. As Edward III had spared the lives of his enemies after the siege of Calais, so too the people of Harfleur would be shown mercy. "When lenity and cruelty play for a kingdom, the gentlest gamester is the soonest winner," the King replied, when one of his knights argued that they should make an example of the defiant town. Henry desired to be a ruler, not conqueror. His first order was that the bell tower of St Martin's church should be restored. He entered what was left of the holy building and, barefoot, prayed.

Many French swore fealty to the English monarch. Others were imprisoned and would be ransomed. Henry did not have the provisions to feed many of the women, children and infirm in the town so he provided safe passage for them, granting them an escort and five sous each to reach the nearby settlement of Lillebonne.

The King proclaimed that Harfleur would be garrisoned and become, like Calais, an English colony. A bridgehead. He declared that they owed their great victory to God, although Henry also individually thanked as many of his troops as possible and rewarded those who took part in the assault on the barbican.

Cups were raised and clinked together to toast the breaking of the siege. But cups were also raised in memory of the fallen. The siege had cost Henry a quarter of his force, through death and through those who had to be shipped back to England from disease. For a day or two the army wondered if all of them would now be sailing home. But no, they would march on. There would be no turning back.

"Even if our enemies enlist the greatest armies, my trust is in God, and they shall not hurt my army nor myself. I will not allow them, puffed up with pride, to rejoice in misdeeds, nor unjustly, against God, to possess my goods. They would say that through fear I have fled away acknowledging the injustice of my cause. But I have a mind, my brave men, to encounter all dangers, rather than let them brand your king with word of ill-will," Henry pronounced, signalling his intention to continue the campaign.

Not every soldier celebrated upon hearing the news. But they understood.

"Henry wants to glean more glory, in order to satisfy his pride," Owen Morgan remarked.

"Or more likely Henry needs to earn more gold, in order to satisfy his creditors back home," Jack Mercer replied, as he passed the pitcher of ale back to his friend.

*

Robert Cooper and Edward Fordham sat together around a small fire, away from their compatriots. Whilst the rest of the company drank and sang, Cooper and Fordham just drank. Chaucer had explained to the archer what had transpired during their mission. Cooper didn't quite know what to say to his grief-addled friend. There were only degrees of saying the wrong thing.

Fordham felt like his innards had been scooped out and replaced with the black bile of sorrow and the molten lava of hate. He stared blankly at the humming flames whilst he sharpened his sword. It seemed to Cooper that Fordham had spent over half his time since he'd been back sharpening his weapon. Preparing his blade and soul. The soldier's deep-set eyes were red with sleeplessness and drink. Fordham hadn't shaved for several days and already he wore a scraggly beard.

Fordham poked the fire again whilst his thoughts, memories, scorched his brain. He tried to recall fond images of Marie, of her laughter, their lovemaking and the declarations of the way they felt about each other, but eventually the shadow of her death darkened his reverie. The wound was still open, tender. In the dead of night, and when he awoke, part of him wanted to end things. But he could not bring himself to consummate the devout desire. Fordham still owed a debt in this life. He needed to atone for his sins, and honour Marie and his companions slaughtered in the courtyard, by killing Reynard of Troyes.

As well as drinking, the soldier tried to sleep as much as he could. It was as near as he could get to death. Yet often he would suffer nightmares. Marie would die in his arms again and again. But at least in his nightmares he could see her again. Hear her voice. Be with her. He pleaded with God to bring Marie back or promise him that they would be together once more, in a better place. Sometimes he also cursed God. He had cruelly shown him a glimpse of happiness and then snatched it away.

Cooper recalled how Fordham had once judged life to be a bad joke, but one which the man-at-arms could laugh along with. Yet Fordham hadn't laughed once, since his return. His heart, like the barbican at the Leure gate, was beyond repair. Cooper considered how he would feel should he lose Grace in similar circumstances. "Would you like another measure?" he asked, lifting the jug of ale, already knowing the answer to his question.

*

The fragrant and holy scent of incense filled the King's tent once again. Henry had just closed a meeting with his closest advisers. There was much to plan for: the garrisoning of Harfleur; the preparations for merchants and tradesman from England to populate the town; and the logistics of decamping the army and marching it through enemy territory, to reach the safe port of Calais in the north.

Thomas Chaucer remained behind, having requested a private meeting with the King. He walked towards a large table, covered with various maps, where Henry was sitting. Henry's leather-bound copy of Vegetius' *De Rare Militari* was perched on a lectern next to the Bible, and Chaucer couldn't help but note the underlined sentence on the well-thumbed page: "*For it is not numbers, but bravery which carries the day.*"

Chaucer mused on how the military maxim would need to hold true. The English army was about to advance through one of the largest countries on the continent, pursued by a force over three times its size.

The ever-observant Chaucer also noticed how the portrait of Edward III was now hanging on the wall, as opposed to sitting on the floor. Perhaps Henry thought now, after capturing Harfleur, he could look his ancestor in the eye.

Thomas Chaucer stood before his sovereign and put forward his case.

"Edward has a will, I believe, to cast off your crown and also cast down the lives of my loved ones. My desires to hunt down Reynard of Troyes and aid you in your campaign are not mutually exclusive. The one feeds into the other."

Henry pursed his lips in deliberation before replying.

"I will relieve you of your duties in regards to remaining with the army, Thomas, but I am too short of men to allow your company to join you on your mission. So as to prevent him from deserting, and carrying out a separate crusade involving the same end, I can spare your man-at-arms however. You mentioned that he developed genuine feelings for Mademoiselle Nouvel. Well if Fordham can fall in love then there is hope for me also," the King said, half-jokingly, as he wistfully thought of Catherine Valois.

Chaucer nodded and smiled, as he philosophically recalled the words of a previous monarch, Richard II: "*Love to Richard is a strange brooch in this all-hating world.*"

The English agent freed himself from considerations of love, however, as he stared down at the maps laid out across the large oak table. He began to plot his journey, in regards to the first part of his plan to defeat his enemy. Chaucer also took in the map of central France, which outlined the possible routes that the army could take to reach the port of Calais. Despite being well travelled many of the place names were unfamiliar to the spymaster: *Frevent, Maisoncelle and Agincourt.*

RICHARD FOREMAN

AGINCOURT

"It has often been noted that a small number of desperate men can conquer a large and powerful army, because they would rather die fighting than fall into the cruel hands of the enemy." Christine de Pizan

"Mine honour is my life; both grow in one.
Take honour from me, and my life is done.
Richard II, William Shakespeare

1

The sunlight was weak, like the colour of unploughed wheat. The clouds were off-white, like old bones. The archers — Owen Morgan and Jack Mercer — ran through the long, dewy grass of the field, pursued by the French. Morgan occasionally reached up to make sure that his leather cap, with his bowstring underneath, didn't fall off. His thighs started to ache and his chest began to burn but he didn't — couldn't — slacken his pace.

I'm going to die.

The mounted French patrol had spotted them, from a vantage point on a grassy incline, and closed on their enemy with every step. Morgan and Mercer needed to reach the river by an old barn up ahead, at the top of the field.

Pierre Guiche dug his spurs into the flanks of his black destrier and bellowed out to the six men accompanying him to pick up the pace. His armour gleamed brightly, even in the dull sun, and his long, blond hair unfurled in the wind, like a banner. His features were fine and sharp, like the sword he had just drawn from his scabbard. Although the two English archers were too poor and ignoble to ransom they were still of value for the information they might possess about the size, location and morale of Henry V's army. He would be rewarded, either with gold or prestige, for capturing the English soldiers.

Guiche was certain his victims were deserters. As Henry's army moved eastwards the two men had escaped westward, back towards the coast in order to find passage to England. Perhaps he would be rewarded with the opportunity of interrogating the bowmen.

Everyone screams — and everyone talks.

Guiche grinned, baring his off-white teeth, as he closed in on the archers. He calculated that he would be able to catch up with his quarry before they reached the river. He wished that his beloved brace of goshawks could be in attendance. The nobleman had trained the birds to attack men, as well as their usual prey. The peasants on his estate had the scars to prove it. Guiche paid them a generous fee for their pains — and his pleasure.

Owen Morgan could feel the ground shake as horse hooves thrummed against the soil, quicker than the beat of his heart. The sanguine Welshman had always believed — hoped — that he would die an old man, in his sleep. Corpulent and crapulent. He wanted to die in his bed with a young wife next to him (and it need not have even been his own wife, Morgan had jovially mused). The dream had been for him to capture and ransom a French nobleman, not suffer the nightmare of being cut down by one.

Guiche visualised the stroke. He planned to keep his blade low and slice the hamstring of the fleeing archer. He had practised the motion, as an esquire and then knight, countless times before. He readied himself to lean lightly across his freshly polished saddle.

A couple of French men-at-arms rode just behind Guiche. They would let their paymaster have his sport. The rest of the mounted patrol closed in on the second bowman. They had been given orders to bloody their blades, but not kill their quarry. They would obey orders. The French soldiers were well paid by the aristocrat and enjoyed being part of his retinue. Over the past few years the men-at-arms had spent more time with Guiche fucking in brothels than fighting in tournaments or on battlefields.

Girard Trau, a veteran mercenary, led the horsemen who closed in on Jack Mercer. The archer heard an equine snort behind him and felt the chestnut gelding's breath on the back of his neck. Trau held aloft a shortened lance, which he would use to stab the bowman and end the hunt. The Frenchman looked forward to slicing off the Englishman's bow fingers. He had ended the careers of other archers before, and enjoyed the sensation of his blade working its way through soft flesh and delicate bones. Trau drew his weapon back, in anticipation of the blow.

Jack Mercer offered up a vague and desperate prayer to the Almighty, which included more than one curse word. His prayer was answered as he heard the divine sounds of a bowstring twang and the swish of an arrow dart through the air. His guardian angels had revealed themselves, as Robert Cooper and John Walworth stood on the roof of the barn and fired on their enemies.

The hunters had become the hunted.

A bodkin-tipped arrow pierced Trau's plate armour, as easily as a seamstress' needle moving through a piece of linen. The Frenchman was knocked backwards off his horse from the force of the missile. Mercer heard a clang as his enemy hit the ground. He also heard the unmistakable snap of the man's neck breaking.

Robert Cooper placed another shaft on his yew bow stave. Neither hate nor anxiety shaped his flat features. The veteran archer was a picture of cold, hard assuredness. Nock. Draw. Loose. The process came as naturally to him as breathing — or killing. Cooper had fired off as many arrows over the years as a blacksmith had hammered in nails. His brawny arms and barrel chest filled out his tunic and leather jerkin. His short brown hair was turning to grey around his temples.

Cooper unleashed another arrow — and cut down another man-at-arms.

"French twat!" John Walworth exclaimed, as he shot down another soldier. The arrow punched through the Frenchman's leg, and wounded his mount. The distressed mare reared up and threw its rider, who landed awkwardly and broke his back. It was perhaps borne more from custom now than malice, that the son of a London butcher let out a curse each time he killed an enemy.

Guiche's men quickly gave up their pursuit of the English archers and looked to escape themselves. Bodkins were soon entering backs, as well as fronts, as a couple of soldiers wheeled their mounts around and attempted to ride back the way they came. The air was filled with the noise of whinnying horses, whistling arrows and the screams of Frenchmen.

Henry had tasked Cooper with capturing a French soldier in order to glean more intelligence about the size of his enemy's army and its objectives. He also needed to know which of the fords and bridges the French had secured along the Somme.

After spotting the mounted patrol Robert Cooper formulated his strategy. He would use bait to lure his prey into the open ground.

"Can you run that fast and far?" the veteran archer asked, after proposing his plan.

"Well, it looks like we'll fucking have to," Jack Mercer replied, pursing his lips and shaking his head. He kept his spirits up by telling himself that their enemies might be carrying some valuables, which they wouldn't have any need of when dead.

"Just don't miss when they come into view," Owen Morgan remarked to John Walworth, fearing that it might become a close run thing.

"I worry that I might become distracted by the comical sight of you running for your life," Walworth said, grinning.

"Well, if I do end up dying, then know I'll come back to haunt you. I'll start knocking over your ale in the tavern and every whore you tup will be riddled with the pox."

"Well, every whore I'll tup will probably already have the pox, but I wouldn't want anyone spilling my drinks, whether they came from this world or the next, so don't worry, Owen, I won't miss," the hulking archer exclaimed, as he placed a large but fraternal hand on the Welshman's shoulder.

Cooper had briefed his men beforehand that the Frenchman leading the patrol needed to be captured rather than killed. An arrow might mortally wound him or strike his horse, which could then throw the knight, so, instead of firing, Edward Fordham, an English man-at-arms, rushed out of the barn to secure the prisoner. Guiche had been caught unawares by the attack and was slow in bringing his horse to a halt and wheeling the large destrier around. As he was doing so, Fordham closed in and held his brutal poleaxe with its long spike and crescent blade at its head, close to his opponent's face.

"Yield, or die. It makes no difference to me," Fordham remarked in French, his expression and tone as cold and hard as the steel on his weapon.

Guiche sneered in defiance but reluctantly nodded. Even if he could evade the Englishman on the ground the bald-headed archer on the roof, who had him in sights, loomed large. The nobleman wished to live and fight another day, unlike the fallen soldiers in his retinue.

"You may have won this battle, Englishman, but the war isn't over yet."

Fordham let his opponent's words wash over him. The soldier had little concern for England, France or Henry's campaign anymore. His war would only be over once he had killed Reynard de Troyes, the French agent who had murdered Marie Nouvel — the woman he loved.

2

John Walworth and Jack Mercer checked the corpses for any loot. Blood smeared the coins and valuables they found, but that would easily wash off in the river.

"We've had worse days," Mercer remarked, commenting on their haul.

"Aye, but they haven't," Walworth replied, nodding in the direction of the two fallen soldiers at their feet.

The archers reined in any horses which hadn't bolted, with the intention of swapping their enemy's fine mounts with their own — somewhat haggard — mares.

Shafts of sunlight poured through the holes in the roof of the disused barn. Weeds sprung up from the ground, rising to knee height in the corners. Various agricultural implements, russet with rust, leaned against the walls. The air was thick with insects and the smell of decay. Cobwebs hung from the main rotting beam in the barn, as did the figure of Pierre Guiche.

Owen Morgan had stripped the French knight of his armour and bound his hands together. The prisoner now stood with his arms stretched out above his head through a length of rope slung over the beam. Vulnerable yet defiant.

"The English are deserving of all the curses the world throws at them. You are a pack of over-confident, warmongering drunkards. You are a bastard and belligerent race," Guiche remarked, in English, before spitting on the ground, his face as twisted as the rope above his head. As a child Guiche had grown up with tales of savage English soldiers raping and pillaging their way through the French countryside. The Black Prince had been a hell hound. The English razed villages to the ground and desecrated churches — and only returned home once their accursed archers ran low on arrows.

"As a Welshman, I couldn't agree with you more," Morgan said, smirking. "I'd even be willing to add to your list of insults, if it would make you feel any better. You will soon have cause to extend your list of reasons to hate the English, without any help from me though."

As Morgan stopped speaking the large, rickety door to the barn opened and Cooper and Fordham entered.

"You are fine to take a break, Owen. Jack has found some salted pork and a skein of wine in one of the saddle bags. I would get there quickly, as John has found it too," Cooper remarked.

The Welshman rolled his eyes, in anticipation of being left with the dregs of the wine, and departed.

"How good is your English?" Cooper asked the Frenchman. His tone was surprisingly amiable. He was dressed in a leather jerkin, covering a tunic which was branded with the cross of St George. Although clearly low-born, the bowman was also clearly a natural leader, Guiche considered.

"Good enough to have overheard what your name is, Robert Cooper. I suppose it is your intention to ransom me? You English crave gold, as bees do pollen," Guiche said, jutting out his smooth, pointed chin.

"Gold is all well and good, I grant you. But I am after something even more valuable than gold: wisdom. We have captured you not for what you own, but for what you know."

"I would rather die than betray my sacred country," the aristocrat proudly replied to Cooper, though his eyes sometimes nervously flitted in the direction of the brooding man-at-arms standing next to him.

"Be careful what you wish for," Cooper wryly countered.

"You would not dare torture me. I am not some mere peasant. I am of noble birth. Your King would punish you for spilling noble blood. My father would hunt you down, like the dogs that you are, if he heard of any maltreatment of his son," Guiche issued, his voice more shrill than usual.

"Our King has charged us with bringing back information, not prisoners. What happens in this barn will remain in this barn. My piss is worth more than your noble blood right now. My friend here will ask you a number of questions. If he is not satisfied with your answers — or if he suspects that you are lying to him — he will torture and eventually kill you. I hope my honesty makes up for any lack of nobility."

Without saying another word Cooper took his leave. The sound of the barn door slamming behind him reverberated like a cell door closing.

Fordham filled the silence by unsheathing his knife and running a small sharpening stone along its blade. Light glistened off the steel and shone into unresponsive eyes. Grief — and a lack of rations — had eaten away at Fordham's handsome features of late. His expression was devoid of pity and pleasure alike.

Despite a chill running down his back, causing him to shiver and writhe within his bounds, Guiche's countenance was glazed in sweat. His throat felt as dry as cracked leather.

"I am surely worth more to you alive and untouched. My father will pay any ransom you demand. You are a Christian, no? God will punish you if you harm me. I have a wife and two children. Do you have a wife and family back home?"

Fear crept into the Frenchman's tone. He pictured the gruesome scars of knights who had returned from the east, after having been tortured. He had heard stories of tongues being cut, genitals being burned and eyes being gouged out. The colourful anecdotes, which the young nobleman had occasionally jested about, now suddenly seemed very real. And terrifying.

For a moment there was a slight pause in the soldier's rhythmic scraping of stone against steel as Fordham pictured Marie again, her face bloody and contorted as she lay dying in his arms. His eyes narrowed and his nostrils flared in torment. Had Fordham have had Reynard of Troyes before him instead of Guiche, he would have buried his knife in his throat immediately, no questions asked.

The rope began to rub away the skin on his wrists as Guiche moved as far away as possible from the knife in front of his face. His life was worth more than information about the size of the French army, or where they were guarding certain fords and bridges. The French would overwhelm the English, no matter what he confessed, he judged. Guiche wanted to see his wife — and mistress — again.

Fordham remained impassive as blood began to trickle down the Frenchman's cheek (from where the Englishman had made a small incision beneath his eye socket) — and piss began to run down his leg. The Englishman remained menacingly quiet whilst Guiche screamed like a woman.

*

Robert Cooper sat with his back to the barn, brushing insects away from his face, and gazed out across a turquoise river and tawny fields. Occasionally the water lapped against the bank. The sound reminded him of the stream near Thomas Chaucer's house, where he and his wife-to-be, Grace, would take walks. A brace of martins darted across the scene. The archer had seen his last butterfly, he mused. Summer was over. The landscape would no longer be teeming with flowers, foliage, and food. For the past few days his eyes — and nose — had grown used to traversing through seemingly endless bogs and marshland.

Pain flared up in Cooper's shoulder again, like a garrotte. His body was telling him to retire, as well as his war-weary heart. The bowman gently closed his eyes, as a bird trilled upon the branch of a skeletal tree in the background. He pictured Grace in his mind's eye, felt her satin-soft flame-red hair on his chest. The thought of Grace delivered both consolation and despair. He was so close to her, yet so far away. Each day was supposed to bring him nearer to Calais and home, since the army departed from Harfleur. But each day they moved further into the heart of France. Every day the English grew hungrier, as every day the French army grew in numbers.

"Will you be content as a farmer?" Grace had asked, worried that he might resent her for taking him away from his company of archers when they were married.

"I'm not sure," Cooper had replied, as her lithe body slotted next to him in bed. "But I will be happy being your husband. It will be hard work setting up a farm, but after all I've experienced these past years, hard work is the last thing that I need to be afraid of."

"Why have you remained a soldier for so long?"

"I suppose that I signed on originally as an archer to prove something to myself, out of sense of adventure. There was little for me in the village where I was raised. I wanted to make some money and a name for myself, as my father did before me. I grew up in the army. Friends became family. The army made me a better man, I believe. And I'm not much good for anything else. Some folk consider the army to be a punishment. Yet for others, it's their salvation. But I've got another home to make now, another family to look after.

"My father joined the army at fifteen and left after he was fifty. Endless campaigning turned him into a broken man. He spent so long being a soldier that he couldn't adjust to normal life. Soldiering can change a man over the course of time, as a river will smooth a rock. Even the best bowstring will snap, sooner or later. War gnarled my father's bones and soul. There was a hardness to him that not even his wife and child could soften. Chaucer said to me once that to know only a life of soldiering isn't chivalrous or heroic, but tragic. I do not want to turn out like my father, Grace. These past few years have been marked with so much — too much — death…"

Stephen Hall, a young archer who Cooper had taken under his wing, had been tortured — and then killed in front of him. One of the bravest men he had ever known — George Clifford — had died of the bloody flux. The bulk of the rest of Chaucer's company had been ambushed and slaughtered by French mercenaries, on the orders of Reynard de Troyes. Cooper had also watched men fall, cut down in their prime, outside the gates of Harfleur. A jagged rock, fired from an artillery piece, had separated one man's head from his body. He knew death was closing in on him, like an archer getting closer to hitting the centre of the target with each shot he fired.

But there can be life after death.

Cooper broke off his reverie at the sound of approaching footsteps. John Walworth burped before speaking, after appearing at the back of the barn.

"The horses have been watered. Is Edward alone with that French peacock still? He may well slit the bastard's throat before he gets the chance to say one word. He's changed, since he got back. The death of that French lass hit him hard," the burly archer remarked, running his hand across his scarred, bald scalp and thinking to himself how he hadn't heard Fordham laugh once, since Harfleur. "Hopefully when we get to Calais he'll find someone that can turn his head and put the wind back into his sails. We'll soon be back in England. That'll put a smile on everyone's face."

"I'm not sure if Edward will be sailing home with us. At least not until he tracks down and kills the bastard who murdered Marie."

Or dies trying.

*

Edward Fordham didn't need to ask — or draw blood — twice. Guiche quickly unburdened himself of every piece of information he knew about the French army: its size, leadership and positioning. The young nobleman also divulged its intended tactics. Charles d'Albret, the French commander, intended to order his mounted troops to target the English archers: "Scythe them down, like wheat". Once the bowmen were routed — and removed as a force from the battle — it would then be easy to overwhelm Henry's small force of infantry.

After being interrogated by the man-at-arms, Guiche gave his word of honour — and parole — that he would not attempt to escape. Whilst Morgan fed and watered the prisoner in the barn, Cooper and Fordham reconvened on the bank of the murmuring river.

"We should take Guiche back with us. Henry will want to question him. Talbot can help us ransom the bastard as well," Cooper remarked, making reference to the veteran mercenary Sir William Talbot, who had captured many a French knight over the years. "We might all go back to England with some money in our pockets after all."

"His wife could pay us more to keep him captive, than return him to her, I imagine. He may well be the most cowardly French knight I've ever yet encountered, and he is not lacking in competition," Fordham replied. "But at least the information he has passed on to us will be of some use."

"Aye, if what he says is true, regarding the position of the main French army and which fords are being guarded along the Somme, then Henry's gamble will have paid off in marching further east. He should now have sufficient time to cross the river without being intercepted."

Fordham nodded in response, but knew Henry could only delay an encounter with the French army, rather than avoid it. Henry believed he would prevail, in emulating Edward III and marching through the heart of France as if it were his realm. He had faith — in God, his army and himself, but pride rather than faith was driving him, Fordham judged.

And pride comes before a fall.

"Are you not concerned with the numbers Guiche mentioned, in relation to d'Albret's main force? Henry's army could be swallowed up like Jonah. He may be as bold as Beauchamp, but he is also as doomed as Hector."

"At least Badby might finally hit the target, with that many troops amassed in front of him," Cooper countered, in an attempt to lighten the mood. Percy Badby was the worst shot in Thomas Chaucer's company of archers, but its finest fletcher.

Before Fordham could respond he was distracted by the dramatic sight of Pierre Guiche riding across the field, digging his heels into the flanks of a chestnut courser, his large linen shirt billowing in the wind like a sail. Cooper turned to take in the escaping Frenchman, but instead of firing off an arrow to cut Guiche down, he sped towards the barn.

Owen Morgan lay dead on the floor. Flies had already began to congregate over the body, like newly landed sailors hanging around a tavern. The genial smile which usually lined Morgan's face had turned into twisted rictus. Blood oozed out from the wound in his neck. Morgan's right hand rested on his chest, half clutching a wooden cross. Cooper hadn't ever thought of his friend as being a believer.

Every man finds God in the end, in one way or another.

After Morgan had untied the prisoner and given him food and water Guiche had approached him from behind and cut his throat. The French nobleman had retrieved a knife, concealed in his boot. Usually he used the blade to slice off pieces of cooked meet — or raw flesh — for his prized goshawks to consume. The preening aristocrat didn't value his honour, or the terms of his parole. Nor did he value the life of the bowman.

Guiche had cast a quick expert eye over the horses which were tied up, just outside the entrance to the barn. He swiftly mounted a spirited courser which had belonged to one of his own company, and galloped in the opposite direction to his captors. The accomplished rider reasoned that he would either receive an arrow in the back immediately or make good his escape, as the lowly archers, unused to riding, would not be able to make up the ground he would put between them.

When John Walworth rushed into the barn and saw his fallen comrade he stained the air with curses. He also picked up the nearest object — a rust ridden pale — and threw it against the wall. Jack Mercer, who had followed Walworth in, barely registered the sound however, as he fell to his knees beside his murdered friend.

Bitter tears welled in the eyes of the cynic and former thief. The two archers had sung the same songs, shared the same jokes, fucked the same whores and put arrows in the same enemies. Only now, when he was gone, did Mercer realise just how much the Welshman meant to him. He was his best friend, his brother. No one knew more about him. He had drunk with Morgan — and shared his thoughts with him — more than anyone else.

As Cooper, Fordham and Walworth made their way outside, to decide whether to pursue Guiche or not, Jack Mercer lingered next to Morgan's corpse. Grief pierced his being, like an arrow. His sorrowful mood soon melted like ice, however, as the flames of hatred fanned in his heart. He would mourn his friend, only after avenging him.

Leaden clouds hung low in the sky. A gust of wind whistled through the cracks in the barn's roof.

"We should hunt the bastard down. Now!" Mercer exclaimed, as he stepped outside.

Cooper watched the contemptible figure of Guiche make his way across a distant field. Fordham, on a good horse, might be able catch him, he considered. If they could get him within range of an arrow. The bowman had no desire now to turn the knight over to Henry, or ransom him. Justice is an eye for an eye, a life for a life — a death for a death.

Cooper also took in the sight of a number of horsemen — no doubt another French patrol — in the distance. They were lined up along the top of a shrub-filled hill, to the left of their position. Cooper owed a duty to Grace to come home to her, as well as a duty to his friend. He would not be honouring Morgan if, in the act of trying to avenge his death, others shared his fate. Cooper also owed a duty to Henry and the rest of the army, to pass on the intelligence he had gleaned about the enemy. The archer wanted to save lives, not lose them.

"We cannot risk going back into hostile territory and encountering other patrols. Night will soon descend upon us. We cannot have the French descending upon us too. Owen will go unburied for now. But not un-mourned. God willing, we'll soon do battle with the French and that piece of shit will cross our path again. Talbot may know how and where to track him down."

Mercer growled in reply. His blood was up. His face was as grey and hard as granite. But he held his tongue and resisted the urge to defy his captain. He knew that Walworth and Fordham would obey Cooper's orders too.

"He's a dead man. The fucker just doesn't know it yet," Walworth said determinedly, gripping his bow tightly in his hands. If it was possible, the stolid archer now hated France and the French even more.

Edward Fordham promised himself that if he came across the nobleman again, he would slit his throat. He felt a gnawing sense of regret that he had not remained with the prisoner whilst Morgan tended to him. He also should have tortured and killed Guiche when he had the chance.

The only good French aristocrat is a dead French aristocrat. Honour is just a word. A conceit. The only thing that is real in this world is wickedness.

The four men retreated back inside the barn, in order to say their final farewells to their friend. Cooper bowed his head and said a few words, echoing a few lines he had heard from a clergymen whilst attending church one Sunday with Grace. Before John Walworth placed a blanket over Morgan, Jack Mercer retrieved a dagger from his belt, vowing to himself that he would use the weapon to kill the Frenchman with, if ever he saw him again. Mercer could not bring himself to take the cross around his dead friend's neck and place it around his own. God felt too remote, like a dead father, who he had barely known whilst he was still alive.

The wan-faced Englishmen wordlessly mounted their horses and trotted away. Even their horses bowed their heads, seemingly in sympathy with their riders. Occasionally, Cooper turned back towards the dilapidated barn. He would now carry another death around his neck, like a cross, until he fulfilled the promise he made to himself to hunt Guiche down and kill him. He knew he would suffer another sleepless night, filled with ghosts and violence. Cooper only slept well when he was lying next to Grace. Only then did he feel a sense of peace, contentment and absolution.

The temperature dropped. Rain began to slant into their faces. They rode on, into a slight headwind. The night would be long. Already they missed their friend and the mood between the soldiers felt awry.

3

The night sky, mottled with dark purple clouds, appeared like a large bruise overhead. Henry squinted, just outside his tent, taking in the spectral figures in the distance who worked to repair the causeway leading into the ford, which had been partially destroyed. Progress was being made. A small flicker of a smile briefly animated Henry's lugubrious features and he sighed in relief. Finally they would be crossing the Somme.

The plan had been to reach Calais in eight days. Eight days had now passed. The King had watched his army snake along the river bank. The songs which his men had sung upon setting off on that first day had now turned to groans. Heads were bowed down, as if his soldiers were marching to a funeral. Henry's armour weighed heavier upon him. He was determined to only eat what his men consumed. The King's sacrifice eased his own conscience and — hopefully — earned him the respect of his troops.

Henry walked back inside his sparsely furnished tent. A small cedar wood chest sat in the corner containing a piece of the True Cross, which had been given to the King by a Welsh crusader on his return from the Holy Land. Henry's bible rested on a lectern but, for once, it was closed. A portrait of Edward III stood upright on a desk. A piece of cloth was wrapped around a painting of Catherine Valois. He felt uncomfortable when her kind eyes looked upon him now. In his mind she was a prize to be won — and a symbol of a new contract between England and France. Charles VI had offered his daughter's hand in marriage to the English king as part of a peace negotiation, before the war. Yet Henry yearned to court Catherine — marry her — out of feelings of esteem rather than political expediency. This conflict would all be for nothing if England — and his own heart — did not find a morsel of peace afterwards.

Henry had an attendant remove his armour. He asked for his sword to be sharpened, drank a small cup of diluted wine and sat down at a table to write a letter to his friend, Richard Whittington (the respected financier and former Mayor of London):

As you may have already heard, I sent a challenge to the Dauphin shortly before the army set off from Harfleur. I proposed a bout of single combat. Would God not approve if two men, as opposed to two nations, shed blood for their cause? I didn't expect a reply — nor have I received one. Louis is a physical and moral coward. His sword is a ceremonial one, his armour burnished to attract the attention of other men's wives. But his army will now know that he refused to fight for the honour of himself and his country. So why should they fight for his honour with wholehearted loyalty and devotion? Let us hope that this propaganda victory, authored by Thomas Chaucer, will not prove to be our only triumph.

There will be some people who will question my decision to prolong this campaign. We could have sailed home, with honour, after the capture of Harfleur. But the siege will be but a chapter, rather than the whole story, of this war. Why should I not march through lands which are rightfully mine? Why should I not put my trust in God, that the Almighty will not lead us to victory?

Like God, or Caesar, I have endeavoured to treat my enemies with mercy. Our army is under orders to pay for, rather than steal, supplies. We will not scorch the earth, as I hear the French have done. Women and children are treated with respect and clemency. Places of worship are as sacrosanct here as they are in England. We will not abuse the clergy, as much as they might have abused others. In regards to any fortified towns we have encountered, we have desisted from putting them to the sword in return for them donating provisions.

My intention was to follow in the footsteps of my great-grandfather. The plan was to cross the Somme at Blanchetaque and scythe our way through the heart of France to reach Calais. Should God have willed it, we would have scythed our way through the French army to do so. The fields of Crécy would have turned red with French blood once again. But, as a son will never wholly resemble his father, history never wholly repeats itself. Upon capturing a scout we learned that the French had reached Blanchetaque before us. An army, defended by stakes planted in the river and populated with crossbowmen and artillery, awaited us. We would have been target practice for our enemies. Even the French wouldn't have missed, or retreated, in such a scenario. Courage should never give way to foolhardiness. The Somme would have run red with English blood if we would have given battle at Blanchetaque.

And so we continued east. Often we would travel along the banks of the river, with our enemy shadowing our movements from the opposing side. Yet all the while the vanguard of the French raced ahead, seeking to guard or destroy any ford or bridge on the river where we could cross. They would have us cross the Somme at their choosing, and march into the jaws of their grand army.

But the river recently altered its course, preventing the French from mirroring our movements. We have finally found a workable crossing. Although we are not quite delivered, we are not quite as damned as we once were. I write to you from Voyennes, which houses a ford. We need only repair the causeway, and then the army will be free to move northwards. As the night sky is studded with stars, the army is still studded with hope. All is well.

As far away as England may seem I know that home is seldom far from our thoughts. I greatly look forward to seeing you upon my return, my dear friend. I should warn you in advance, however, that I may bore you with various war stories. I will try to bring back some vintage Claret for us to share over a meal. It is also my intention to return to the capital and repay all those who generously financed this campaign, including yourself.

Henry suddenly dropped his quill, as if it were burning his fingertips, and held his head in his hands. He wanted to let out a loud sigh, but was wary of being in earshot of someone. He could not let people know how desperate, or afraid, he was. A king needed to set an example. Henry remembered a line from Geoffrey Chaucer:

"If gold should rust what will lead do?"

He felt the pit of his stomach burn like a hot coal for the sin he felt at lying to his friend, but he had committed far greater sins over the past day or so. Henry had ignored his own ordinance that morning and given the order for a number of villages surrounding the town of Nesle to be pillaged and burned. Not only had Nesle refused to donate provisions but it had hung a make-shift flag — of the French Oriflamme — over its walls in an act of defiance. "I can stomach the insult but not the lack of victuals. Needs must," Sir William Talbot had argued, as the King deliberated on the situation. Some of his troops now had food in their bellies, but Henry had innocent blood on his hands. "To be a Christian monarch is a contradiction in terms," his father had once wearily told him. *Uneasy lies the head that wears the crown.*

All was not well. Hope was in short supply, as was food. The bulk of the army had been reduced to eating horsemeat and scavenging what nuts and fruits they could find from the surrounding woodlands. The cold nights seemed to freeze expressions — all manner of grimaces, scowls and drear frowns. *They look like death warmed up.* Emaciated faces and skeletal torsos haunted Henry's mind's eye. *Hunger eats away at a man's soul, as well as his body.* Some had started to embrace God, either fearing their end or asking to be delivered, but greater were the numbers who were starting to embrace godlessness. His soldiers were now pilfering from the French, as well as from each other. Henry could not turn a blind eye to one of his soldiers stealing a pix from a church. He gave the order for the culprit to be hanged.

This ignoble world will compromise the noblest of intentions, as surely as the finest blade will eventually succumb to rust.

Henry felt ashamed at not being courageous enough to tell Whittington the truth. His letter failed to mention the trickle of desertions which had recently taken place. How soon before hunger and desperation turned the trickle into a stream — and then a deluge? Thankfully most of the soldiers knew that there was safety in numbers.

The previous evening the King had smeared his face with dirt and donned a hooded cloak. He had wanted to move among his men anonymously to assess their gripes and spirit. The soldiers had spoken of wives — and whores — back home. They had spoken of the need to return to England with money in their arrow bags to provide for their families through the winter. They had darned clothes, played dice and drunk what little wine or ale they had left. Occasional arguments and scuffles had broken out, borne from frustration or deep-seated grievances which their empty bellies had forced to the surface.

The stench of ordure and sweat, as pungent as any apothecary's shop, still hung in Henry's nostrils and made him feel nauseous. The groans continued to reverberate in his ear from when some of his troops, still suffering from the bloody flux, retreated into the woods and emptied their bowels. He also heard prayers offered up through chattering teeth. Others would curse God, or the French, or the King, as they congregated around campfires.

The incessant rain dampened spirits too. A chill wind wriggled its way through the tent. Henry was no stranger to the privations and horrors of a campaign, but he keenly felt how he was responsible for the army's current fate, unlike before when he had ultimately served under his father's command.

Am I, like Moses, leading my people to freedom? Or am I more akin to the Pharaoh? Will I lead my army into a God-sent trap?

Henry flexed his fingers and turned his hand into a fist. His knuckles cracked, but his heart didn't. He sharpened his quill and continued to write to his friend:

You once said to me that "it is always darkest before the dawn". Our march along the Somme has sometimes felt like a descent into the underworld. Our backs may be as hunched over and curved as a longbow. Our feet may feel like they are encased in lead. Our wounds may feel like they will never heal and that we are fated to spend an eternity traversing the southern bank of the Somme, as the undead will wander along the banks of Styx and the Acheron. But I am reminded of a passage from Virgil's Aeneid: "Easy is the way down to the Underworld; by night and by day dark Hades' door stands open; but to retrace one's steps and to make a way out to the upper air; that's the task, that is the labour".

Henry knew that he was trying to convince himself that his campaign could still succeed as much as he was Whittington, but he was still in possession of his faith.

"Sire, Thomas Chaucer has returned," a beetle-browed attendant remarked.

Henry immediately stopped reading over his correspondence and rose to his feet. That his friend and agent had returned safely was good news in itself. He just hoped that Chaucer had further to report.

The tide needs to turn.

4

Thomas Chaucer's clothes hung off him, like they belonged to someone else. His face and figure were lean. The agent, who often promoted an air of confidence, appeared careworn. His beard was untrimmed, to the extent of being unkempt. His voice was lacquered with exhaustion and anxiety, and his eyes were red and heavy-lidded.

Chaucer had left Harfleur several days before the rest of the army. His principle mission had been to discover the whereabouts of Reynard de Troyes, the French spy who was an enemy of England (as well as a personal threat to Chaucer). The Frenchman had recently plotted against Henry to remove him from the throne. Reynard was also responsible for the massacre of Chaucer's company of soldiers, as well as for the murder of other people close to him. Chaucer now feared for his family back in England. Reynard had proved himself to be resourceful and merciless. The only way to ensure that his family lived was to kill the Frenchman.

Chaucer had found it relatively easy to locate his target. Reynard had decamped to his estate just outside of Troyes. The hard part would be besting the fortifications — and small army of mercenaries — which the French agent hid behind. But Chaucer had formed a plan. The enemy of his enemy would be his friend.

The English spy was able to travel through France undetected. He was fluent in French and familiar with the country's geography from previous missions. A purse full of gold meant he could purchase fresh horses, as well as pay for information regarding the leadership and composition of the French army. During his journey back to locate the English army Chaucer had gained as much intelligence as he could on the enemy, which he now duly reported to Henry.

"As you may already know Charles d'Albret, the Constable of France, has been granted overall command of the army. The King will not be entering the fray. The Dauphin has also decided to stay at home, which gives added substance to the rumour that he's a coward after all. D'Albret is a competent and cautious commander. He may choose to surround you without fully engaging us in a pitched battle, letting starvation and disease do his work for him. Such are his overwhelming numbers though — and the need for the French to rescue martial pride — that a pitched battle seems likely.

"D'Albret's second-in-command is the veteran knight, Marshal Boucicaut. Boucicaut is known for being daring and pugnacious. Together, though, they may prove less than the sum of their parts. Already there is tension between them. Every day they are joined by other senior soldiers and members of the nobility, who secretly or openly consider that they should be commanding the campaign. Our hope is that too many cooks will spoil the broth, and the French will be pulled in opposite directions," Chaucer posited before savouring a taste, as if it were a homecoming kiss from his wife, of the vintage on the table in front of him.

"And have you any information on the make-up of d'Albret's forces?" Henry asked, studiously absorbing his agent's words. The English would need to outthink, as well as outfight, the French if they wanted to reach Calais.

"The vanguard of the troops will be mounted knights and men-at-arms. The French aristocracy is in love with itself, leaving aside any jokes about incest. You will smell their approach from the perfume that they wear before you see them, I imagine. They consider that they have the right to win the battle and hoard all the glory. D'Albret will be unable to rein them in, even if he wanted to. For all of their weaknesses though, the French still possess strength in numbers. If you pay me to worry for you, then I should start claiming overtime," the spy drily remarked.

"A battle is inevitable, but it was ever thus. We were always going to return to England either having been defeated, or having run out of arrows, but defeat is not inevitable, Thomas. I have often spoke of having faith in God that we will endure and ultimately triumph, but equally I have faith in our men. I know that our archers could drink a jug of ale at night, yet still shoot straight in the morning. The likes of Talbot and John Holland have faced greater odds and still survived. There will be no retreat, or surrender. Our men-at-arms will plant their feet in the mud and stand as sturdy as oak trees. Robert Cooper is worth a dozen French knights. All we have now is each other, but that will be more than enough," Henry asserted, regaining something of his old self.

"Given that they intend to have their cavalry and armoured infantry attack first we should pray for rain at night, and then a dry morning afterwards. The sodden ground will hamper any advance and if the bowmen are able to keep their strings dry then they'll be able to shoot further and truer."

"God really would be smiling on us then, but perhaps not even God has the power to stop the rain in France during the autumn."

Chaucer's smile turned into a yawn as sleep called to him.

"This King does not possess the power to prevent you from falling asleep either. Take your leave. We can speak more in the morning. I know that you will be leaving again soon, when Fordham returns. He is a good man."

Chaucer was tempted to reply that he had been *once* a good man. Grief had turned Fordham's heart black. The goodness within him had died, as surely as Marie had passed away. Revenge now enveloped the man-at-arms, as the darkest of nights can swallow up the brightest of stars.

"Aye, he is a good man," the agent replied, with a tinge of mournfulness which Henry mistook for tiredness.

"You are a good man too, Thomas. My reign has been more secure — and the kingdom richer — as a result of your counsel. I will make sure that your family is provided for, should anything happen to you. If you wish me to pass on any correspondence to Matilda, I will arrange that as well."

"Thank you, but I have already arranged for a messenger to deliver a letter. I have advised my wife to marry an old, dull and moneyed nobleman should an accident befall me. On no account should she marry someone younger and more handsome than myself, who will alleviate his poverty by working his way through my savings."

Henry's sudden and unexpected laughter caused him to cough a little.

"Come back to us alive and well, Thomas. Consider it a royal decree. Who else will I be able to pay to worry for me, at such a competitive wage?"

Chaucer took his leave. He walked, or rather trudged, through the camp, his boots making a sucking sound in the mud. The agent flitted his eyes about and surveyed the state of the troops. Whey-faced archers mechanically tended to their bows whilst staring off into the distance, perhaps dreaming of home. Some wore clothes patched-up with various materials, taken from dead Englishmen rather than defeated Frenchmen. A grey bearded veteran rocked from side to side, shivering by a fire, and mouthed the words to a prayer. Another man curled up next to his dog and placed a stale piece of bread in its mouth. The sight of a rat caught Chaucer's eye as it scurried out of one soldier's trouser leg — though the man didn't even flinch.

Chaucer felt a twinge of guilt for some of the propaganda which had been sent out to towns and villages, calling upon young men — or boys — to go to war. For many it would be their first campaign. For too many it would also be their last. Yet Chaucer knew that many of the soldiers before him still wanted to take part in their own Crécy.

Would Henry have listened to me if I advised him not to declare war? Would we be here now if I had advised him to return home after capturing Harfleur? England will be about as well-guarded as a harlot's virtue in a brothel, should the French wipe this army off the map and then invade our shores.

Chaucer pensively recalled something his father had said to him, shortly before he died. Although estranged from one another for long periods the two men had eventually grown a little closer. Having secured a prominent position at court Chaucer arranged for his father to live close by, upon the grounds of Westminster Abbey. Eventually Thomas revealed to his father how he not only served the crown by being Speaker of the House but he had followed in his father's footsteps by becoming a diplomat and spy. A bed-ridden Geoffrey Chaucer had called his son to him just before he died. His skin had been snow-white, his voice strained, but gentle. Thomas had leaned over and his father had confessed how he was proud of his son, but he worried for him too: "Remember, your principle duty should not be to help win a war for your sovereign, but rather to prevent a war from happening in the first place. I have seen enough of war to know that I want to see the end of it."

5

The following morning Sir William Talbot and Sir John Holland crossed the river and, accompanied by a small force of archers and men-at-arms, secured a bridgehead. A large French patrol in the area launched an attack to try and drive the English back across the Somme, but they soon retreated. "The bastards rode away quicker than a nun would punish a novice once our archers fired off a couple of volleys," William Talbot remarked, relishing the victory.

Henry sat on his horse on the north bank of the ford and offered advice and encouragement as his troops crossed over. At midday he also knighted a number of his soldiers to reward their loyalty and hopefully raise morale. The men raised a cheer once the ceremony was over — the first cheer since Harfleur.

The King's mood was raised too when Robert Cooper returned from his mission. Not only was he glad to see the archer alive, but his intelligence confirmed and added to some of Thomas Chaucer's conclusions from the night before. Henry invited Cooper into his tent, along with Sir William Talbot, to discuss things further.

"I should be insulted that the French consider you, Robert, to be more of a threat to them than myself," Henry drily remarked, on hearing how d'Albret intended to attack the English bowmen first during battle. "To counteract their plan I want you both to spread the order that every archer should cut himself a stake the length of a man and sharpen the ends. One end should be placed in the ground by the side of him, at an angle, on encountering the French, whilst the other will loom large in any horse's eye. A horse will throw its rider before impaling itself. The size and momentum of their advance will work against them."

"But they have the numbers to defeat us," William Talbot stated, matter-of-factly, "and from what Chaucer has said, their army is still growing every day, as noblemen loyal to the Burgundian camp are rallying to their King's cause. Even John the Fearless is sending a company of men, although he himself is prudently holding back to see which way the wind blows, while technically keeping his vow of not personally bearing arms against you. The canny and cowardly bastard."

"It is not numbers, but bravery, which carries the day," Henry replied, quoting Vegetius. His voice rang hollow though.

"We could split our forces — and subsequently split theirs. We could send out a small, but tempting enough, force to halve their numbers. The mounted troops could lead them a merry dance. Our main army would then stand a better chance of combatting the enemy. Or we may even look to avoid a pitched battle. If we can put our backs between the French and Calais they may give up the chase, being relieved in the knowledge that we'll be heading home," Talbot argued. The veteran soldier would die for the King, particularly after Henry had saved his life outside the gates of Harfleur, but if there was a chance to save his own life — and that of the English army — by avoiding a bloody confrontation then he would grasp it.

"No, we will remain together. I will not sacrifice the few for the many, or the many for the few. When we left Harfleur for Calais I believed that we carried the numbers to defeat the French. I still believe that. We will not seek out the French army, but nor will we run from our enemy should it stand in our way. We must be as bold as Thomas Beauchamp, who in 1346 defeated over a hundred Norman knights with just a single squire and six archers at his disposal," Henry remarked, boldly.

*

Cooper and Talbot took their leave from the King at the same time. Talbot puffed out his cheeks in exasperation. He clasped his sword and smoothly drew half the blade out of its scabbard, checking to see if his squire had oiled the weapon. It seemed he would have need of it soon.

Cooper had only known the mercenary for a short while but there were few men in the army that he admired more. Talbot was, like him, from low-born stock, but the peasant's son had become a squire — and then a knight. He had fought as a mercenary all across the continent, selling his services to the highest bidder. Talbot eventually returned to England and purchased the estate that his father had worked as a stable hand to. "Some say I answered Henry's call to arms out of a sense of duty, or a love of gold, but really I came out of retirement because I was bored. I felt the itch again, and this time it wasn't because of the pox. I needed to prove to myself that I hadn't become a soft, old man," Talbot had explained to the bowman one evening, over a jug of cloudy Kentish ale.

"My hope is that the bastard French half-defeat themselves, and we just finish the job. Walk with me back to my tent, will you, Robert? I hear that you lost a good man, Morgan, whilst on your recent mission. I will have some wine sent over for you and your men. The swill may well taste as sour as a crab apple, but it's better than nothing. You should mourn Morgan's death, but also celebrate his life tonight. I met the man a couple of times. He always had a smile on his face, which probably means he wasn't married, so at least there's no wife and children to worry about," Talbot remarked, as much in earnest as in jest.

"He was murdered by a knight called Pierre Guiche. I thought you might have heard of the name."

"Aye, I have. I knew his father. We took part in a couple of the same campaigns. He and his company would stay back, and only enter the fray when victory was assured. He would always be first in line to claim his share of the glory and spoils though. I remember he had a talent for embroidery. The peacock would carry several handkerchiefs around with him. Shortly after meeting with a lady, he would sew her name into one and present it as a token of his affection. They would then swoon, or collapse, from the amount of alcohol he plied them with. I didn't know whether to condemn or compliment him at the time. I was no better, or worse, during my time as a chivalrous knight. I remember once an Italian countess asked me to compose a poem for her, on a perfumed piece of parchment she gifted me. In reply I gave her the blank scrap of parchment back and asked her to just write down how much it would cost me to fuck her for the night. It was more than I had hoped. I paid her the sum, but at least I didn't have to spend anytime courting her or writing verse. I should tell Latimer that story, before he finishes off the latest chapter of my biography. This book is going to be as long as a bullock's cock if I'm not careful. But to get back to Guiche — he must be an old man by now. Although it seems his son is carrying on his ignoble mantle."

"When this campaign is over we'll hunt the bastard down. He'll be the last life I take, before I sail back to England and retire," Cooper replied.

"Retire? Ha! I remember when I was your age and had dreams of retiring."

"I have made a promise to someone. I have some savings. My plan is to buy a small farm in Oxfordshire."

"Promises get broken, far more than yew bows snap. You're too much of a good soldier to become a good farmer. You have been given a calling, far more than any cock-sucking priest. You were not born to suffer blisters on your hands from ploughing a worm-ridden field. I promise you this: you will soon get bored if you unstring that stave. A good harvest won't quicken your blood. You will start to drink more, but it won't quench your thirst, or hunger, for what you really want. You will hope that someone in the tavern will start looking at you the wrong way. Brawls will take the place of battles. I've seen it before. You are also far too virtuous and faithful to take a serving girl as a mistress, Robert, and fend off boredom that way. You know that Henry won't stop campaigning either, no matter what befalls the fate of our army over the coming week. Maybe he won't *let* you retire. And maybe you'll thank him for it."

Cooper shook his head, yet his friend's words weighed heavy on his soul, as did a memory of when he and Grace were last together. Had she joked — or had she tried to gently confess the truth — how she sometimes felt that the army was his true wife and she was merely his mistress?

6

Edward Fordham watched, with a twinge of envy, as Percy Badby slept peacefully against an ancient sycamore tree. The fletcher's face glowed from the nearby fire. Occasionally, Badby stirred a little and made a motion with his hands, as if he were sharpening arrowheads, but for the most part he was wonderfully oblivious to the gloom, odours and squalor of the camp. Exhaustion — or an untroubled soul — meant that he could sleep through the cacophony of sounds surrounding him, including bawdy ballads, spitting fires and skittish horses.

Fordham couldn't remember the last time he had slept for more than a few hours. He waved his hand in front of his face. Although the swallows and butterflies may have disappeared for the summer, some insects remained. Should any of them bite him and take his blood, then they would spend the evening drunk like him, Fordham fancied. He wished he could just wave his hands and swot away his grief. But maybe not. His grief was all he had left. The soldier's stomach rumbled again. He could have had a suckling pig or manna from heaven in front of him, but he wouldn't have been able to fill the emptiness inside him.

Tonight, at least, he would honour the memory of his friend Owen Morgan and forget about Marie. She would understand. The wine would help wash away any tears, but he would wake to Marie in the morning, her absence lying next to him. He would remember her virtues, like a penitent fingering a rosary and saying his prayers.

Fordham had recently caught Badby praying. A solemn devotion had shaped the features of the kind-hearted fletcher. Badby's faith inspired his good character. Religion was sacred, nourishing. The fletcher always had a few coins to spare for beggars. He was devoid of resentment and greed.

Perhaps Badby's lack of skill as an archer was an act, and he deliberately missed the enemy with his arrows, Fordham thought.

But how can I have faith in you, God, even if you exist? How am I supposed to love you, when you took Marie away from me? Are you punishing me for past sins? I cannot forgive my enemy, turn the other cheek. I will kill him. It's just another death, no more significant than another wave lapping against the shore. Enough people worship your name. You don't need me lighting a candle for you too. Both sides in this war will claim you for their own, but you are willing to see both armies bleed, perhaps to punish them for their sins. Or more likely a battle will just prove to be a spectacle for you — a source of amusement. Everyone knows the lie of God, but still everyone believes it. It's a joke. Or miracle.

John Walworth filled the man-at-arm's cup and proposed a toast for their fallen friend, the first of many in the Welshman's honour. Whilst Cooper got up to fuel the fire with a couple of logs Walworth spoke:

"I remember when I first met Morgan. He had just joined the company — Chaucer having recruited him after the Battle of Shrewsbury. I was suspicious of him. As far as I was concerned he was still the enemy. He was also annoyingly good-humoured and friendly, especially since he had just been on the losing side in a fight. We were sent out on patrol together, to the arse end of nowhere on the Welsh border. The thought crossed my mind that he might try to do me in and head back home, and, sure enough, as night was falling and the mist descended, I turned around to see Morgan with an arrow on his bow, pointing in my direction. I didn't even get a chance to curse him before he loosened the shaft. The arrow whistled past me and I heard it thud into the enemy soldier behind me.

"I thanked Morgan by buying him a pitcher of mead that evening. We drank it together with a pair of trollops sitting on our laps. I said to him, after getting through our third or fourth cup, how I had thought that he was about to kill me. He grinned and replied that his honour was worth more to him than a sense of patriotism. I used to think that the Welsh shouldn't be proud of anything, until I met Morgan. At least they can be proud of him." Walworth's low, rough voice broke a little with fondness and emotion.

"I first met Morgan in earnest when he took part in an archery contest," Cooper enjoined, staring into the fire. "He had a carefree manner, but I could also tell he was a fierce competitor and an accomplished bowman. What with him being Welsh and new to the company quite a few other men mocked him or tried to put him off. He still hit his mark though, and made it into the final with myself. When someone asked why he was shooting so well Morgan replied that he was picturing English faces on the target. The contest was close, but I was able to beat him. I congratulated him on coming second, but he said he had something even better to be pleased about. When I asked him what that was he laughed and explained that he had just won a large sum of money, having placed a bet on me to win."

Cooper raised his cup in the air and toasted his friend. A short pause ensued, before Fordham spoke.

"I visited my mother last year, back on my family's estate in Norfolk, and Morgan accompanied me. To make the stay more interesting, I proposed that he should pretend to be a Welsh nobleman. I arranged some suitably fine clothes for him, and gave him a couple of pieces of jewellery that a mistress had recently bought for me, for services rendered. I remember how my mother showed Morgan around the house. We went into my father's library and my mother asked if he, back on his estate in Wales, had a similar library and which books had he read recently. At first he looked somewhat stumped and I was going to step in and answer for him, for fear of him giving the game away. But he recovered and politely replied, 'I am not one for reading books, save for the Bible. He who increaseth knowledge increaseth sorrow.' My mother, known to be God-fearing rather than scholarly herself, nodded in sympathy. Whilst Owen stayed at the house he was as courteous as any lord, but treated the servants like they were equals. His jokes, for once, were as clean as his new clothes. My mother said that I could learn a lot from his example. He was, as much as any man I've known, a fine gentleman."

Again the soldiers raised their cups to the deceased bowman. The sour wine seemed to strip a layer of skin away from their throats, but they re-filled their cups enthusiastically. The group stared at Jack Mercer. The thief-turned-archer had not taken Morgan's death well. He had remained sullen and bitter on the journey back to the camp. He simmered — and almost came to the boil — when thinking how Cooper was responsible for his friend's fate. Cooper had been the one to volunteer everyone for the mission, in order to kiss the arse of the King. He had also ordered Morgan to attend to the prisoner by himself.

Mercer glared into his cup. The dregs of his red wine prompted a memory of Morgan's blood-stained body. His could feel his friend's dagger weigh heavy on his belt. He would carry the weapon like a cross, until he caught up with the Frenchman. And killed him. Tears began to form in the corner of his eyes, but his anger refused to let them fall down his cheeks.

"I hope you can forgive me, but before our rescue of you, Edward, at Nouvel's estate, I said to Morgan that we should return back to camp and abandon you and Chaucer to your fate. But Owen rightly argued that you wouldn't leave *us* to *our* fate if you had the chance to return the favour. The truth is, I partnered Morgan in rescuing you because I knew he would have tried to free you on his own, should I have insisted on going back to camp. He was the best of men, murdered by the worst of men.

"I want to wash all this mud off me and I want to wash all these bad thoughts away. We shouldn't have come here. Henry will write his name in the history books, for all the wrong reasons. When I was a thief there were some jobs which, we had the good sense to realise, were always too big for us. You can't spend any gold when you're dead. Henry should have admitted to himself — and his country — that he could not steal in and out of France and take the French crown. We'll soon be joining Morgan. And the French will then sail across the channel and lay waste to the country like a new Black Death. A plague be on Henry and his pack of fine gentlemen," Mercer said, before spitting on the ground. His face was contorted in malice. A gust of wind sprang up and disturbed the leaves on the ground, creating a shushing sound.

Grief swirled around the air like the cinders spiralling upwards from the crackling fire. The soldiers were bound to each other — for better or for worse. The ghosts of fallen comrades were sitting in their circle too: the fresh-faced Stephen Hall, the fearsome George Clifford and the amiable Owen Morgan. War, like the plague, feasted upon death. They all shared the same thought, but at different times, during the wine-fuelled night — that not all of them would survive and make it back to England.

Their campaign was nearly at an end.

7

The camp was a hive of activity as it prepared to head northwards. Foraging parties scattered off in all directions. The sound of trees being felled could be heard in the background as archers started to manufacture their large wooden stakes.

Although the two men were still somewhat worse for wear from the previous evening, Fordham still gave Cooper one last lesson in swordsmanship before leaving for Troyes. They had found a quiet corner of a field. The grass was wet with dew. Cooper's swordsmanship was coming on apace. His profession had made his hands and arms strong, and he was surprisingly agile for his size. He also knew that, in the heat and confusion of battle, the veteran soldier would be able to keep his head over that of a young French knight.

"Just remember, the point will always beat the edge," Fordham breathlessly advised, at the end of the session. "Even the finest and thickest armour has its weak points. And an armoured opponent is as good as dead if you can knock him on his arse. You never know, you might be posted away from the action, on a distant hilltop, and you'll only have cause to draw your blade to cut the strings of purses, fastened around French necks."

If anyone deserved to make it back home it was his close friend, Fordham considered. Few men had served king and country as well over the years. Cooper had a wife and future waiting for him in England. Cooper had turned him into a better man, over the course of their friendship. Fordham admired his courage, honesty and loyalty. He had not minded taking orders from the low-born archer, as opposed to vainglorious knights, who were often more concerned with saving love tokens than they were with saving the lives of the men under their command. For a moment Fordham was tempted to offer up a prayer to God, that his friend would survive any encounter with the French. But God was as likely to listen to him as he would to God. And the Almighty worked in malicious, rather than mysterious, ways.

"I'll take my mission over yours. I have only got to kill a Frenchman or two. It seems that you are going to have to impersonate one," Cooper said, having been informed of the plan for Fordham and Chaucer to travel through enemy territory.

"I have been practising my act. I've been sucking on garlic and not washing myself for days. I've trained my horse to run away from battle. I am also now well versed in cursing the English, whilst admiring their lower tax rates and freedoms."

Cooper smiled, and Fordham even forced a small smile too.

"Well, don't immerse yourself in your part too much. You promised me that you would come back to England and visit my farm. You'll be a guest of honour at the wedding. Grace is keen to cook a meal for you. I'll get in some fine Kentish ale and we can drink through the night. We will probably end up talking about the past and various old war stories, but we will both have cause to look to the future. Sooner or later we'll find some peace in this world."

Cooper joined Fordham in forcing a smile, but the rest of his face remained cold. Both men knew that the only thing that Fordham looked forward to was killing Reynard de Troyes.

*

Cooper looked at the line of downcast soldiers as they marched along the muddy road behind Thomas Chaucer. They would look back upon the gruelling siege of Harfleur with fondness — a golden era of the campaign — compared to their fate now.

Chaucer finally turned to the bowman. "No rest for the wicked, eh?" he wryly remarked, dabbing the sweat from his brow with a handkerchief. "I just have one last order to give to you, Robert." He passed a sealed scroll of parchment to the archer. "I am passing over command of the remnants of my company to you. I understand that Sir William Talbot has also offered you the command of his archers. He probably has his eye on poaching you from me at the end of all this, but Grace will have more success in poaching you than Sir William, I warrant."

Cooper nodded in reply. He couldn't quite commit himself to formally declaring his intent to retire.

"I know you will probably disobey this last instruction, Robert, but try to restrain any heroic impulses you might have, when engaging the French. The enemy will come to you soon enough. And whilst I would advise you against surrendering, as that may be tantamount to a death sentence, there will be no dishonour in retreating. You have given everything but your life to the cause. Keep it that way."

The agent looked the bowman in the eyes. Chaucer wanted to praise him further, but the words — and emotion — stuck in his throat. Also, if he confessed what he wanted to, he would be acknowledging that it might be the last time they would see each other. The spy was unused to telling people how he really felt.

"You should devote more time to worrying about yourself than me. Reynard may prove more formidable than the French army. The snake has a habit of slithering his way out of the tightest of corners. His house will be well guarded, and getting close to him could prove as difficult as unlocking a chastity belt."

"Well, thankfully I have someone with me who has unlocked more than one chastity belt in his time," Chaucer replied, glancing towards Fordham, who had just mounted his horse in front of them. "He is keen to depart it seems. As am I. I am not one for long goodbyes, Robert, or vulgar displays of public affection. Our Mediterranean cousins can hug one another. I can but offer you a hearty handshake and say that I will see you again soon."

In this world or the next.

8

The mizzle soaked its way through ragged clothing and dampened spirits. The vanguard of the army cut up the earth so that those following waded ankle deep in mud. Thankfully, a large number of soldiers travelled on horseback. A surplus of horses had been created due to the casualties from Harfleur. Some of the men still clutched their bellies, or relieved themselves by the side of the road. The bloody flux still plagued the army, like a tick which had bored down too deeply to remove.

Cooper rode alongside Sir William Talbot. The infamous knight took a swig of ale and screwed up his face in disgruntlement as he surveyed the grey clouds stretching over the horizon.

"I'm not sure if I've ever travelled for this long through France and not visited a brothel," the veteran mercenary mused. "Calais will welcome us with open arms — and open legs — when we get there."

The bowman was tempted to answer "*if* we get there", but merely nodded his head in reply.

"I sense you may be a little distracted, Robert. I saw Chaucer and Fordham ride off earlier. All will be well on that front. Thomas always has a plan. He will be two moves ahead of his opponent. I sometimes think that he considers life to be a game of chess. Your friend, Fordham, has the look of a devil in his eye too. Even Caesar was toppled. I am sure that this French twat, Reynard, will make a mistake and get what's coming to him."

Before Cooper could respond, however, Talbot dug his heels into his horse and galloped towards a crowd of soldiers up ahead. A circle of men had formed around two opposing figures. One was a slender youth with a wisp of beard and a lazy eye. It was his first campaign. He had signed up to a company after the French had raided his fishing village and murdered his uncle. The other was a grey-haired veteran with a hook nose and bushy eyebrows, that curled upwards like horns. Both held knives in their hands. The old soldier had mocked the youth for days now, to test and belittle him. The adolescent had finally snapped over an insult to his mother. He had drawn his dagger and threatened the cantankerous veteran. But the sight of the blade — and the upstart's challenge — only enraged the old man.

Talbot arrived just as the two men were closing in on each other. His thunderous expression instilled his audience with fear. The line of soldiers parted to allow the brutal-looking knight into the circle. The young man felt a wave of warm air hit his face as Talbot's horse snorted in front of him.

"What the fuck are you two stupid bastards doing? Sheathe those blades, before I end up drawing mine," Talbot barked. "What happened here?" he asked, turning to the pale-faced youth.

"He called my mother a whore," the young soldier replied, timidly, and then hung his head in fear before the armoured knight.

"Your mother is too ugly to be a whore, boy. And you're so decrepit, old timer, it'd be like tupping a corpse. Our grievance is against the French, not each other. Once the campaign is over you can fight — or fuck — each other all the livelong day for all I care. You can prove your manhood, and you can prove that you're not too old, on the battlefield. Not on this shit-filled road at the arse-end of the French countryside. And all you gawping turds can move along too. Calais won't come to you."

The entertainment was over. The clump of soldiers formed itself into a line again and marched along the churned-up road. Cooper rode alongside Talbot again. The knight rolled his eyes and offered up a gentle smile and slight shake of the head. He had broken up — and started — many a fight between soldiers before.

"Can't have us doing the work of the French. An army without discipline is like a church without corruption. It can't survive. I remember a story someone once told me, about John

Hawkwood. He knew what it took to bring a company together and also how to solve disputes between men. He once commanded two knights, who had fallen in love with the same woman. They arranged to fight one another to win her hand. They had cocks for brains, it seems. Anyway, Hawkwood could ill afford to lose either of the knights, or tolerate such clownish behaviour. So what do you think his solution to the problem was? He killed the woman. Ha! Hawkwood was either a bastard or genius. God knows how true the story is though. I might have to adapt the scenario and have Latimer write it into my own biography."

The rain grew heavier and spat against the knight's costly armour. Robert Cooper pursed his lips, knowing the softer ground would slow the army even more. The archer wanted to feel English rain on his face again — and feel Grace's kiss on his lips.

"When I was back on my estate I thought I was getting too old and fat, and yearned to be in the saddle, on campaign, once more. But now I dream of being back in my great hall, with a roaring fire in the background and my hounds curled up by my feet. Instead of admonishing two squabbling soldiers I should be choosing between which serving girl I should bed. Which one will be lucky enough to spend the night with me? Or should I say unlucky? No doubt I've got one or two bastards running about out there," Talbot remarked.

"How do you spend your days, when you are on your estate?"

"When I'm not in my bedchamber or wine cellar I ride and train my horses, and teach others to do so too. Horses are noble creatures. They don't lie, thieve or constantly talk about themselves. Unlike men. Perhaps I should marry and start a family when I return, though. I should make an honest woman out of one of the ladies from the county. God forbid that she makes an honest man out of me in return though," the sanguine knight remarked, slapping his thigh and laughing at his own joke.

9

With every step they rode further and further away from the army and home, Chaucer mused, as they travelled towards Troyes. The agent consoled himself with the thought that they were making good time. Their horses were well-conditioned. The roads were quiet.

Watery sunlight poured through the gaps in the iron-grey clouds. The landscape was a tapestry of undulating tawny fields and autumnal woods. Birds darted across the sky, aiming to reach their nests before nightfall. Wildflowers freckled the scene with colour. As tranquil as the landscape was though, he was not wholly at peace. Demons held sway over the angels in his soul.

"If memory serves there is a village and inn up ahead. We should reach there before dark. The stew will be as thin as soup, and the wine and vinegar will come out the same jar, but we have stayed overnight in worse places over the years, I warrant," Chaucer asserted, as he shifted uncomfortably in his saddle, yearning to rest his aching — and ageing — bones.

Fordham nodded his head in agreement, but his attention was focused on the scene unfolding further on up the track, at a crossroads. His horse's trot turned into a canter, and then a full-bloodied gallop.

A trio of men stood around a young girl, no older than fifteen. The girl's dress had been torn at the front, and she pressed her right arm against her chest to keep herself covered up. Her bright green eyes were wide with shock and terror, as her gaze flitted between her three attackers and the two men who had just approached on horseback. A fresh bruise stained her cheek. Strands of auburn hair stuck to her cheek from the sweat and tears glazing her face. A rivulet of blood ran down her chin from a split lip.

The girl, the daughter of a local farmer, had been raped by the three men.

"Move along. There's nothing to see here," the eldest of the trio remarked. "This is official business," he added, pointing to the badge on his jerkin which signified his position as a tax collector for the crown.

The French tax collector, Vienne, sneered after speaking. A flinty, spiteful face sat beneath a domed forehead. Vienne had considered himself "a man of God", having studied in a seminary, before becoming "a servant of the crown". His damascene moment dawned on him when he realised that he could earn more money as a petty official than as a lowly member of the clergy. Vienne was slight and sinewy. His face was narrow, his blood-shot eyes close-set. Thin lips framed a twisted smile. His clothes were finer than those of his two colleagues, and a short, ornate sword hung down from his belt. The official's mood had been lifted when war was declared between England and France. Taxes would be increased, and so would his ability to skim more off the revenues.

"I think it's time you moved along," Chaucer said firmly, in French. He glanced at his companion. Fordham's expression was as hard and unyielding as a gun-stone. Chaucer knew his friend was weighing up whether to kill the Frenchmen or not.

The two enforcers flanking their employer drew their swords and moved so that they stood between Fordham and Vienne. Both men were used to defending the tax collector and extorting money, through intimidation or brute force. Both men were used to killing. The Frenchman to Fordham's left, Legrand, grinned, revealing a chipped front tooth and fat tongue stained with wine. The stolidly built ex-soldier drew his sword, seemingly relishing the rasping sound of the blade scraping against its scabbard. The man next to him, Binet, owned a nose so flat that it resembled a snout. Binet was round-faced, round-shouldered and round-bellied. He grunted at the stranger who had dared to interfere in their sport, believing him to be some kind of merchant, and believing that he would fight like a merchant too.

Chaucer gestured to the girl, with a subtle movement of his eyes, to circle around the party and conceal herself alongside Fordham's horse. If the worse came to the worst she could still hopefully fashion an escape, he judged. As she positioned herself behind his horse the agent fished out a blanket from his saddlebag so she could cover herself with it.

"Do you really want to sacrifice your life over some dim-witted peasant girl?" Vienne asked, with contempt and confusion lacing his tone. "She's probably already been ridden more times than your horse. If you draw your sword against me, it will be considered an act of drawing your sword against the crown."

Vienne's words increased the Englishman's ire. Fordham calmly drew his sword. Too many crimes were legitimised "in the name of the state". Too many sins went unpunished "for the good of the church".

The official was now wary of the look in Fordham's eye. It was increasingly likely that blood would be spilled. His men might suffer an injury, or fatality, and he would prefer to avoid the inconvenience and cost of replacing them. The good Samaritans were finely attired too. No one would care about a peasant girl being abused, but questions might have to be answered should the deaths of one or two well-connected merchants be on his hands.

"Friends, we should not be drawing our swords against each other. We should be looking to fight the English, who have invaded our lands," Vienne argued, with more conciliation than contempt in his voice.

"Be careful what you wish for," Fordham remarked, in his native tongue.

The shock of realising that an Englishman was standing before them opened up a window of opportunity. Fordham sprang forward, like a hound let loose, towards the stunned Binet. The Frenchman just about managed to raise his sword against his opponent, but Fordham swotted it away and then thrust the point of his weapon through his enemy's mail-lined jacket and into his sternum. Blood gurgled in the dying man's throat, creating a series of desperate, drowning screams.

The man-at-arms raised his leg and kicked Binet backwards, freeing up his blade. Just in time to block Legrand's sword. Curses and spittle poured out of the ex-soldier's mouth in equal measure as he swung his sword, like a club, at the Englishman. Rage, at seeing his friend murdered, fuelled the speed and power of his attack. Fordham was forced on the back foot and was forced to defend himself.

Reality quickly cut through the fog of disbelief and shock that Vienne had experienced. He gripped his short sword in his hand and focused on the sight of the Englishman's back, looming large before him. He crept forward, believing that once he stabbed his enemy then his mounted companion would either retreat, or be bested by himself and Legrand. The fork-bearded Englishman may even be of value as a prisoner. Legrand, realising his master's intention, broke off his attack to lessen the chance of him missing his target. Fordham was unaware of the enemy just behind him.

Vienne drew back his blade, his mouth crooked in a snarl, ready to plunge it into his opponent's spine. He would do so mid-way up, so the point skewered his heart. Death would be inevitable. Like taxes.

But, although Fordham was blind to the threat the official posed, Chaucer had spied the danger. He dug his heels into the flanks of his mare and moved to position his horse in between his friend and his enemy. Vienne let out a womanish yelp and stumbled backwards onto the ground. The sword fell from his hands and he raised his arms in surrender.

Legrand let out another roar and commenced to engage Fordham again, frustrated that Vienne had been unable to bring his opponent down. But the ex-soldier became a little more breathless. His blows lacked the same speed and force as before, and the Englishman knew it. Fordham stepped on his front foot and delivered his own flurry of strokes. His merchant's garb meant that he was not weighed down with armour or restricted in his movements. Legrand's face was now contorted in fear, rather than ire. Finally, Fordham went to thrust his sword downwards at the Frenchman's midriff but, at the last moment, with a sudden swiftness, he brought the blade upwards and then buried the edge of weapon into his adversary's collar bone, letting the blade remain in the body, like a butcher leaving his cleaver in a piece of meat.

Fordham caught his breath for a moment, before removing his sword from the dead Frenchman. Blood, as well as wine, now stained Legrand's tongue. The man-at-arms briefly turned towards the French girl. Her eyes were still puffy from crying.

She had wrapped Chaucer's blanket around her, but still shivered, as much from trauma as from the autumn chill. He then walked over to join the agent, who was standing over the prostrate tax collector.

"Please, have mercy," Vienne pleaded, as he knelt before the Englishmen. His domed forehead was wrinkled, like an old scrap of parchment, in supplication. "I have money. Take it, please. Or give it to the girl's family, as compensation. I was only obeying orders."

Fordham wrinkled in his nose in disgust. The Frenchman's shrill, desperate tone of voice reminded him of Guiche. He would not make the same mistake, as he had with the dishonourable knight, and allow the odious official to live. Fordham wasn't quite sure which circle he would be sentenced to, he just knew that Vienne would be going to hell. Hell was far more real — justified — than heaven.

Jean Vienne gazed up at the stone-faced Englishman. He was about to implore him to spare his life, but Fordham had already sentenced him to death. The man-at-arms kicked the kneeling Frenchman over and then brutally plunged the point of his broadsword into his enemy, as if he were planting a flagpole.

Chaucer winced slightly at the cracking and sluicing sound of steel breaking through bone. But he was in no mood to mourn the ignoble official.

The only good tax collector is a dead tax collector.

10

Morning. There was no sun to speak of. The sharp October wind continued to cut through cloth and chill armour. The English pressed on, like a storm-battered ship sailing home into a headwind. Wet and dry mud clung limpet-like to every soul. Foraging parties were sent out, but the little food they returned with only seemed to feed general grievances. The provisions Henry had negotiated from various French towns in return for his army not laying siege to the areas had also been used up.

"Mouths are grumbling and stomachs are rumbling," John Walworth remarked, believing that Geoffrey Chaucer himself might have been pleased with coming up with such a line. He rode alongside Robert Cooper and Sir William Talbot. Talbot had attached himself to the Duke of York's force, which marched at the vanguard of the army and set the pace. The prize for stoically marching on empty stomachs would be to reach the bridge over the Ternoise first. Should the French control the crossing then they could continue to starve the English or, if brought to battle prematurely, Henry would have no proper line of retreat.

"The French will be aware of the advantage of reaching the river first as well. We're like two dogs, racing towards the same piece of meat," Talbot had commented to his sovereign the night before.

Walworth rubbed tallow into his new honey-coloured bow. The King had rewarded the bowman for his valour at Harfleur and, with part of his bounty, Walworth had purchased a new stave. Percy Badby had recently attached polished pieces of horn at the tips of the weapon. As keen as the archer was in having the English army reach Calais safely by avoiding the

French, he was also eager to test his new bow against the enemy.

He wouldn't have to wait long.

*

After their encounter with Vienne the day before, Chaucer and Fordham escorted the girl back to her family's farm. They then re-joined the main highway leading to Troyes. The two men shared few words. Chaucer silently harboured doubts about his companion's fitness for the mission at hand. His bloodlust could compromise them both, he considered, especially as the agent's plan called for a certain degree of patience and trust. Where Chaucer had once believed Fordham to be an asset, he now judged him to be a potential liability.

When the two men reached the nearest inn they sat in the corner and kept their voices low. The air was pungent with sour wine, stale cheese and the body odour of unwashed Frenchmen. Thankfully the inn garnered lots of passing trade and every time a patron left or entered a gust of fresh air helped ventilate the stuffy room.

The two companions kept themselves to themselves, but Fordham drew a number of looks from the gaggle of prostitutes and serving girls who worked at the less-than-reputable establishment. Despite, or because of, his melancholy features, the well-dressed merchant was approached on more than one occasion by a hopeful whore. Fordham was tempted to discourage any attention by saying that he was married, but thought better of the idea when he realised that would only increase their advances. Married men craved sex — and love — more than anyone, he half-jokingly mused.

They finished their meals and, after buying a jug of the inn's most tolerable wine, they retreated upstairs to their room. The low-roofed chamber was as unwashed as the people populating the inn.

"We have been on many a mission together over the years, Thomas, diplomatic or otherwise," Fordham declared, as he sat down on a creaking chair, next to an uneven table. "I like to think that I have served you well. I am grateful to you for having given me a second chance. You paid off my debts and I signed a contract to join your company, but I believe that I have paid any debt I owe to you. I now owe a debt to someone else. Do not expect me to follow your instructions if I think that they countermand my aim. I do not set my life at a pin's fee. Killing him is all that matters," the brooding man-at-arms asserted, his dark eyes hooded beneath his furrowed brow.

"No matter what happens, Edward, I want you to live to tell the tale. Who else can I sit with at dinner and have the staff serve as attentively?" Chaucer replied, attempting to lighten his friend's woebegone mood. Fordham forced an unconvincing smile.

That night Chaucer dreamed he was back home, on his estate in Oxfordshire. A buttery light was spread across a lush landscape, teeming with greenery and good-hearted people. Pride and contentment mingled in his breast. He would not have traded his modest estate in Ewelme even for a palace in Florence. His wife was tending to her herb garden. His precocious and ambitious daughter, Alice, sat on the quilted lawn, reading a book. Yet when he woke, with the welcome scene still branded in his inner eye, Chaucer knew he would have preferred a nightmare, for the dream was a torturous promise of what might be again, and a reminder of what he could soon lose.

*

A couple of scouts breathlessly reported back to Edward of Norwich, the Duke of York, that an advanced force of French men-at-arms had reached the bridge at Ternoise. The nobleman had won his place at the vanguard of the army through merit rather than social rank. The Duke was a loyal and capable soldier, and knew that he needed to engage the French now rather than wait for reinforcements. A soft, almost sponge-like beard, covered his round jaw and chin. Although Henry had recently executed his younger brother, the Earl of Cambridge, for his part in a plot to usurp the King, Edward bore no animus towards his sovereign and had made good on his word to support the campaign.

William Talbot had been riding alongside the Duke when the scouts delivered their report. Talbot and the Duke had fought — and hunted — together over the years.

"Shall we go on one last hunt, for old time's sake?" Edward asked. Though his voice remained calm and amiable, his innards were addled with anxiety. He did not want to let down Henry, nor the men under his command.

"Aye. Our prey may be making it easy for us by remaining grouped together in one place," the knight grinningly replied. "Let's bowl the bastards over like skittles and knock them off that bridge of ours."

The Duke lacked his friend's confidence, but he was consoled by the veteran soldier's presence. He couldn't recall a battle or skirmish that he and Talbot had both participated in that had ended in defeat, but no candle can burn forever and everyman's store of good luck — and courage — must run out. Edward had promised himself that this would be his last campaign. He had now bloodied his sword under three monarchs. He wanted to retire to his estates. He had enjoyed translating and writing additional chapters to a book on hunting, *The Master of the Game*, and looked forward to composing a chronicle of his own life.

"The pen is mightier than the sword," Edward had remarked to Thomas Chaucer, before sailing for France, after sharing his ambitions to become a writer with the son of the great poet.

"That may well be all good and true, my friend, but concentrate on sharpening the latter, as opposed to the former, over the coming months," the ever dry-witted and pragmatic agent had replied. "And know that you will earn more from doing nothing as a nobleman in one day than you will as a writer from slaving away over a masterwork for ten years."

It wasn't just the Duke of York who was grateful for the presence of William Talbot's sword arm. The men-at-arms and bowmen were also reassured by the knight's authority and humour. The mercenary wheeled his large black courser around to face the column of soldiers. His booming voice carried itself along the highway and through the woodlands which flanked the road.

"It's time we bloodied our blades again. A small force of French are occupying a bridge up ahead. They must have shit for brains if they think they can prevent us from crossing. Once we knock the bastards into the river we'll be another step closer to Calais and home, where the ale is finer and the welcome warmer. I know Henry, St George and God are on our side, but I warrant we are capable of defeating a few

French turds by ourselves. They'll have war wounds, in the form of blisters on their feet from running away, by the day's end."

A chorus of laughter and cheers greeted the worldly soldier's words. After giving his speech and offering three cheers to the King, Talbot gave Cooper and Walworth a subtle and serious nod, instructing them to go about their business. The three men had discussed the scenario they were about to encounter beforehand. They knew that within the next hour the army could be one step closer to home — or ruin.

11

The French forces positioned themselves compactly, phalanx-like, on the bridge. Armour glinted in the weak afternoon sunlight. The wind rustled through the trees on the southern side of the crossing. The rain-swelled river slapped against the bank and stanchions of the wooden structure.

The English appeared from out of the woods. They formed up in a line to match the width of the soldiers occupying the bridge. They were outnumbered, three to one.

Grim, fatigued, and nervous faces peered out of visors on both sides.

The French gripped their shields and weapons more tightly and shuffled their feet a little, causing the timbers beneath them to creak. Each man in the front rank carried a pavisse — a large shield which English arrows, drawn from even the most powerful of bows, would be unable to penetrate.

Philippe Fretin, the commander of the French, clenched his jaw in determination. Blonde curls hung down his forehead framing a young, unblemished face and sculptured cheekbones. Fretin stood in the third rank, ready to urge his forward lines on or prevent them from retreating. His heart was brimming with pride and anticipation. The aristocrat had taken part in tournaments before, but never a battle. As a boy he had devoured history books about Caesar and Charlemagne. He had read every military treatise that his father could purchase for him. Philippe was a happy and faithful husband and regularly attended church, but his spirit yearned to fight for his beloved homeland. His father had battled and killed Englishmen. It was time for him to earn spoils and honour too.

"Not one step back. We will remain here, like a stone wall," Fretin had ordered earlier, when briefing his men. "If we hold this bridge, then we save our nation," the nobleman added, with patriotic fervour pouring out of him like sweat.

A few of the veterans rolled their eyes at Frctin's comments, but they would fight for the young pup all the same. More so, they would fight for the veteran man-at-arms, Henri Moreau, who stood alongside the nobleman. His mail shirt was stretched across his broad chest and brawny arms. A scowl, which widened upon seeing the English, filled his craggy, scar-lined face. Lank strands of black and grey hair fell down across his muscular shoulders. Moreau inspired fear and respect, in equal measure, in the troops around him. The battle-hardened soldier had fought in Italy, the East and had led numerous raiding parties on the southern coast of England.

Moreau thought to himself that his men would be fresher than the English standing before them. The enemy had been marching for over a week. Tiredness and starvation would be gnawing at their bones. Some would be diseased — riddled with the pox or the bloody flux.

Fretin gave the order to close ranks even more. Moreau's growling voice reiterated the command to make sure the young man's instructions were followed. Not even a mouse had space to get through them now, the nobleman thought.

Spears protruded through the line of shields on the bridge to prevent any mounted English troops from charging the French. Fretin dared not blink as he watched a fine-armoured knight take his place at the front of the line. The remainder of the mounted English soldiers were positioned behind and to the sides of the slowly advancing force.

Sir William Talbot held his sword aloft.

Fretin licked his dry lips. The English would attack, as soon as the veteran knight lowered his weapon. Finally he could call himself a real soldier. He felt God and Charlemagne by his side. Fretin drew a frantic breath, intending to offer up a few stirring words to bolster the resolve of his men.

The knight lowered his weapon, but rather than letting out a roar and galloping forward he merely raised the corner of his mouth in a knowing smile. The line of English soldiers refrained from attacking too.

Philippe Fretin died before he knew it. A bodkin-tipped arrow pierced the side of his recently-scoured helmet and buried itself into his temple.

The French had been too focused on the enemy in front of them to notice the two groups of archers stalking through the treeline and flanking their position on both sides. The sodden ground softened their footsteps. Their brown cloaks and russet shirts helped them to blend into the background.

The twang and whistle of arrows being released eclipsed the sound of the wind shimmying through the trees.

"Nock. Pull. Loose," Cooper calmly, firmly and rhythmically commanded. John Walworth offered up the same order, not too far away. The three words were tantamount to a death sentence for any opponent. Dozens of men released — and killed — in unison. A lifetime's worth of practise came to fruition — again. Cooper brought his own bow to bear too, not wishing to diminish the impact of the first volley of missiles in any way.

The arrows flowed as fast and relentlessly as the eddy-filled river. Some of the English archers shot at a flat trajectory whilst others arced them over into the centre of the mass of men, who were too cramped together to raise and angle their shields. No matter how thick or curved the armour, it couldn't deflect the missiles raining down upon them. They were sitting targets. Doomed. Screams sliced through the ears. French curses were directed at the perfidious bowmen and their own inept commander.

The stone wall crumbled.

In order to escape another wave of deadly missiles a number of the French broke rank and sought to attack the force of English in front of them, but the mounted troops flanking the men-at-arms charged forward and swiftly hacked them down.

A smattering of French men-at-arms did reach the English line, through luck or endeavour. A veteran made a beeline for the Duke of York, who stood out in his fine armour. The Frenchman was agile, even in heavy mail, and went about his business with a sense of skill and savagery. His eyes bulged and his face was full of malice. The Duke of York had dismounted. The ageing nobleman did not shirk the challenge of the advancing enemy. He would engage him, rather than order the men serving under him to do so. His tired bones were suddenly awash with vigour and bloodlust. Partly due to his brother's recent treachery, and partly due to the clouds which hung over him in relation to his service to Richard II and his successor, the nobleman wanted to prove something to himself and Henry to show his loyalty to the country and crown.

Broadsword struck broadsword with a dull clang. The French man-at-arms launched the point of his sword forward, like a wild cat, in one sudden movement. The knight turned aside in time, although his enemy's weapon glanced his armour. The Duke reacted quickly, however. He took one hand off his broadsword and punched his opponent in the side of the head. The blow disoriented the Frenchman, granting the Englishman the opportunity to thrust his weapon into his enemy's throat, killing him instantly.

Moreau bared his black, crooked teeth and snarled. The Frenchman took in the sight of the two lead Englishmen: Talbot and the Duke of York. He branded their images in his memory, vowing to kill them should he somehow encounter the men again. He worked his way back through the dying and panicking throng, in order to live to fight another day.

The French mounted troops also surrendered to an impulse of self-preservation and retreated. A few bowmen targeted the fleeing enemy. Arrows briefly pursued them like a swarm of wasps whose nest had been disturbed. The surviving French from the bridge followed them, with shafts sticking out of some soldiers like pin cushions.

The English soon stripped the French casualties of their weapons, armour and valuables. They then duly tossed the dead — and wounded — over the bridge and into the river. A few of the English bowmen spat upon their enemies, as if the poor dead wretches were personally responsible for the hunger and privation they had endured over the past weeks.

"Well, that was a piece of piss. I've known Welsh serving girls to put up more resistance," John Walworth cheerily remarked as he unstrung his bow cord and approached Sir William Talbot and Robert Cooper. "God willing it'll be the last time that we have to fire an arrow in anger. The road to

Calais is now open to us, is it not? I can almost smell the fish stew and harlots' perfumes coming out of the taverns."

"I wouldn't reserve your table quite yet, John," Talbot replied. "I'll warrant that the main French army are still nearby, and intent on blocking the route to Calais. There's many a slip 'tween a cup and a lip. This recent skirmish was just an aperitif. The main course is yet to be served. We are about to engage in a battle to end all battles. But of course there will always be battles. The world wouldn't be the world without them."

The veteran soldier's voice was imbued with a sense of worry and wistfulness. William Talbot wasn't bred for fear, and he vowed that he would not show his back to the French, but he knew that should Henry's army face the full force of France then they would get swept away by the enemy's sheer overwhelming numbers, as surely as the river below him was washing away a procession of corpses.

12

A light rain slanted into Henry's impassioned face. His demeanour was as stoical as a Roman statue's. Even the rain slid smoothly down his freshly shaven skin, as if it were made of marble.

Henry sat upon his equally calm horse on the crest of a hill, which looked down upon a valley and the French army.

His scout had been visibly shaken when he galloped back to deliver his report. The young man-at-arms consciously tightened his hands around his reins to prevent them from trembling. Henry and his forces had just crossed the bridge over the Ternoise. Some men even dared to hope that the road to Calais might be clear. The scout took a deep breath before speaking, though it did little to temper his anxiety.

"A great countless multitude is approaching. Be prepared quickly for battle, for you are about to fight such a huge host that it cannot be numbered."

Shortly afterwards, Sir William Talbot returned from a reconnaissance of their forward position. When asked to put a number to the size of the French army amassing over the ridge the knight laconically replied: "Sire, there are enough to kill, enough to capture, and enough to run away."

The King instructed a party of his closest advisers and most senior soldiers to accompany him and survey the enemy. They too gazed across the valley and watched as the French advanced.

Sir John Holland's mouth was agape. He couldn't recall ever seeing so many men congregate in one place before, and every man carried a blade and wished to kill him. The Duke of York's eyes bulged. The French horde was like a plague of locusts; willing and able to devour anything which stood in its path. Humphrey, the Duke of Gloucester, Henry's youngest brother, hoped that his commander was in possession of a plan for a retreat, rather than attack. The French force, which was still spilling into the valley and yet to form up and reveal its true extent, already appeared to be three times the size of their own army. Sir Walter Hungerford attempted to count the enemy's banners and wished for more men. The Duke of York furrowed his brow and scratched his beard, knowing that even if all of the English bowmen hit their mark with their shafts the French would still have sufficient troops to overwhelm them.

Smoke-grey clouds hung low, but the colourful banners of the French — a tapestry of golds, yellows and blue — vaunted upwards. When the breeze settled down on the brow of the hill, Henry and his knights could hear the faint clink of armour and feel the rumble of the ground shaking from the approaching grand army. Harfleur had stoked a fire inside the breast of every Frenchman, to the point where the warring factions of the Burgundians and Armagnacs were now marching alongside one another, in common cause against the English.

The knights all looked to Henry to issue an order. Some hoped that he would see reason and retreat back across the Ternoise; others believed that their sovereign would negotiate and seek terms from the French. In return for financial recompense, and for the King to relinquish his claims to the French crown, his enemies might grant the English safe passage back to Calais. Some also believed that Henry's self-love would not eclipse his desire for self-preservation; if a pitched battle took place their commander would either die or be captured. If the latter then the ransom would cripple the country, to the point where the young monarch might wish himself dead.

Henry wryly smiled as he pictured himself as a boy placing painted wooden soldiers on a square of green cloth. He used to form up his troops and recreate the battles of Crécy and Poitiers. The few would defeat the many then. *The greater the enemy, the greater the glory.* But this was not a game. Flesh and blood were about to fall, rather than pieces of ornately carved wood. Yet Henry was not overawed. He had faith in his men, and God. Had Caesar and Hannibal experienced the same steadfast sense of self-belief when outnumbered at Pharsalus and Cannae? During the past eight days Henry's thoughts had veered between wishing to encounter and avoid the French. A pitched battle could deliver or damn his campaign. How would he ever prove his mettle like Edward III or his son, the famous and infamous Black Prince, if he was not truly tested in battle? But was there a third choice, between delivery and destruction: would the French not be tempted to seek terms? He could achieve peace with honour, in the eyes of some men. But not his own. The King was not so blinded by martial glory that he couldn't appreciate the merit of returning home and living to fight another day, but such a strategy would allow the French a reprieve too, to continue their raids on England's coastline. They would continue to sew discord in Scotland and Wales. If England could not, or would not, stand up to the tyranny of France then no one would. *Better to die on one's feet than live on one's knees.* Henry was aware that some of his nobles might disagree with his decision, but they would not defy him.

"What are your orders, Sire?" Sir John Holland finally asked. "Should we give word to consolidate our position and march back across the river? Or should we send a delegation to the French to negotiate terms?"

"No retreat. No surrender."

Henry's voice was as sturdy as English oak as he made his reply, whilst still continuing to stare down at his opponents massing together — into the valley of death.

"St George slayed his dragon. It is time, gentlemen, to slay ours. March the infantry forward and have them form up into battles. Have the archers positioned on the wings. We must be prepared, should the French dare to attack us before nightfall. Perhaps by readying ourselves they will be dissuaded from advancing, until they have all of their companies accounted for. Let them bring every man capable of wielding a weapon, 'Tis no matter. We will win at the odds," the King remarked, his breast swelling beneath his cuirass, his neck as taut as a bird of prey's.

Cooper fancied that the steel in his commander's voice was worth a thousand men. Henry's faith and confidence was contagious, though some of his knights were still quietly immune to hope. They knew that they needed even more than an extra thousand men.

"O that we had here but one ten thousand of the men in England who do no work today," Sir William Hungerford opined, to the two knights who resided next to him.

Henry's hawk-like ears heard the comment and he addressed the nobleman.

"What's he that wishes so? The fewer the men, the greater share of honour. God's will! I pray thee, wish not one man more. I am not covetous for gold, nor care I who doth feed upon my cost; it yearns me not if men my garments wear; such outward things dwell not in my desires. But if it be a sin to covet honour I am the most offending soul alive. Wish not another man from England. I would not lose so great an honour as one man more methinks would share from me for the best hope I have. O, do not wish one more! Rather proclaim it — Hungerford — that he which hath no stomach to this fight, let him depart; his passport shall be made, and crowns for convoy put into his purse; we would not die in that man's company that fears his fellowship to die with us."

Something intangible, but real, stirred in the archer's soul. His back straightened with pride, as he sat on his horse. Cooper fancied that the light, glinting off Henry's golden spurs, shone brighter than the sun.

Sir William Talbot nodded his head with approval too. There were times when the mercenary fought for something — and some people — who were worth more than money. The experienced soldier also nodded his head in agreement with the King's orders: *Fail to prepare, prepare to fail*. Better to be safe, than sorry, and form a defensive position now. Just in case the French experienced a rush of blood and advanced on the English immediately. But Talbot believed that the enemy would wait until every soldier it had mustered had joined the battlefield. They could also afford to wait, unlike their starving, careworn opponents. The mass of French troops now occupied the valley, to the point they dwarfed the woods on either side. They were a forest of men.

But forests can be chopped down.

13

Night descended, as did the rain. It pinged upon armour and splattered across the recently ploughed fields. The cold numbed bow fingers. The rain and mud penetrated anything — and everything. Though some attempted to find shelter beneath the trees, they were still exposed to the unforgiving elements, like a broken bone protruding out of the skin. Campfires sprouted up across the soon-to-be battlefield, but did little to warm the skin — or hearts — of troops. Fletchers made sure their arrows were kept dry, squires made sure the weapons under their charge were protected from rust, but laughter and song were absent.

The French had refrained from advancing. D'Albret and Boucicaut decided to wait for the remaining noblemen — and their companies — to swell their ranks even further, but a sizeable part of the French army was ordered to block the road to Calais. Otherwise, the two forces resided across the valley together.

After his speech, in reply to Hungerford, Henry became a whirlwind of activity and encouragement. He charged his noblemen to put fire into the bellies of the soldiers.

"Talk of rewards, of ransoms and getting back home. Talk of the contents of French saddlebags, of food, jewellery and wine. Have your standard bearers raise their colours high when marching. Tell them not to fear their opponents, but pity them, for they are up against God, St George and the finest bowmen in Christendom. Do not pity them much, however, for they would not spare us. The French are as unfamiliar with mercy as they are with bathing."

Henry ordered his army forward, into the valley, so that he could use the woods on both sides to protect his flank. When he could do no more for the night he took shelter in the nearby village of Maisoncelles. He listened to various reports from senior knights before discussing the overall strategy for the imminent engagement. He then dined with the Duke of York to finalise his thoughts and plans. As long a day as it had been — and as much as Henry's bones ached from fatigue — he remained restless. As was his habit, on the night before any engagement, the King decided to don a cloak and hood and move, anonymously, among his troops.

"The men will not be at their best," Edward of Norwich warned, fearing that his friend may lose heart witnessing the downward spiralling morale and physical condition of his army.

"All the more reason to gauge their mood and, if possible, lift their spirits," Henry replied, as he smeared dirt across the silver clasp which held his cloak in place and then walked out into the drear, sodden night.

*

"We can't hear them, but the garlic-munching sards are probably bleating like sheep. They're shivering from fear, not the cold. Hopefully they're also sharing the stories of their forebears at Crécy and Poitiers," John Walworth remarked and then winced, as he took a swig of water instead of wine.

The bowman sat around a dwindling fire along with Jack Mercer and a sleeping Percy Badby, who was curled up like a child, clutching the wooden cross around his neck.

Jack Mercer offered up a grunt in reply. He wore a cloak over his head in a vain attempt to keep his face dry, and wore a scowl on his face. His bitter heart was as heavy as the rain. Whilst Percy Badby had prayed to God a short while ago, Mercer had silently, sullenly, cursed his name. The archer just wanted to return home. To live. But not before killing some more French. He wanted to feel his chest tighten and arm bulge. He imagined the hemp bowstring cutting into his fingers, just before releasing his weapon. But even if he killed a hundred opponents, even if every one of his arrows hit its mark, it would not bring his friend back.

"Evening. Do you mind if I share your fire for a while?" A voice sounded above the hissing rain as a stranger came into their midst. Although the hooded figure lacked the build of an archer he carried a stave in his hands and an arrow bag was slung around his shoulders.

"Aye, that's fine. I'm afraid that the fire is all we have to share, though. The name's John Walworth. What's yours?" the bowman said amiably.

"Harry La Roy. From Kennington. You're part of Thomas Chaucer's company, are you not? What's he like?" Henry asked, curious to find out what his men thought of his friend and agent.

"He's far too quick to have us do the King's bidding, if you ask me," Jack Mercer said, sniffing from disgruntlement. "I'd think more of him if he squared us up with our back pay."

"We could do a lot worse than Chaucer, as the head of a company. Too many noblemen care more for the quality of their armour than the wellbeing of their men," Walworth argued. "So whose company are you attached to? No offense friend, but you're not the biggest archer I've ever seen. We'll have to put you up in the front ranks, I warrant, so your shafts will reach the enemy."

"We may all be in the front rank by the end of tomorrow. We will need our sword arms, as well as our bow arms, once we run out of arrows. The men-at-arms will need us to fight their close-quarters battle as well," Henry said, believing that the battle could hinge on how well the archers acted as a reserve force to support his men-at-arms and knights.

"Do you think that we'll get double-pay if we do the job of the infantry as well?" Jack Mercer sardonically pointed out. "You seem quite young, stranger. Have you ever taken part in a major battle before?"

"I was at Shrewsbury. I even have the scars to prove it."

Henry smiled to himself, as he wiped the rain from his face and felt his fingers brush over the mark, next to his nose, from the near-fatal wound he had received during the engagement. "At the beginning of the day I was a boy, but after the victory I considered myself a young man. A prince among men. What do you think will happen tomorrow? Can we defeat the French?" Henry asked, desirous to hear an honest answer.

John Walworth paused and creased his forehead in thought before replying. "Everything will need to go wrong for the bastard French for them to lose. And everything will need to go right for us. Yet we can win. We'll have to. It's a choice between death or victory."

"Aye, even if the French have God on their side, not even the Almighty and all of his angels and saints can stop a bodkin-tipped arrow cutting through even the finest plate armour," Jack Mercer added, as he imagined the sight of volley after volley of English shafts decimating the grand army of the French.

"Robert Cooper is in your company, is he not? I've heard he's a fine shot," the King remarked, as he began to warm to the archers and their fire. He moved closer to the flames, whilst still trying to keep far enough away so as not to show his face beneath his hood.

"And he's a finer friend," Walworth asserted. "If we had another hundred men of his ilk then Henry would already be sitting on the French throne with the fat bastard of the Dauphin bowed down before him, doubling-up as a footstool."

The King let out a burst of laughter which chimed across the camp. "You are a fine fellow too, John Walworth, it seems, and that's a fine bow you're carrying."

"This was a gift from the King, in a way," Walworth said proudly, as he held up the smooth, honey-coloured stave for the stranger to see clearer. "I was given a reward for my service, the night we burned down the barbican at Harfleur, and so I bought this with the money."

"What do you think of the King?"

"Unlike too many other noblemen he wouldn't ask anyone to do anything that he wouldn't do himself. On the night we took the barbican at Harfleur he could have remained in his tent, pouring wine down his throat and tupping any woman he wanted, but instead he put himself in harm's way, to save others from harm. He's a soldier first and monarch second when he's standing by your side in a fight, ankle deep in blood and shit, with a sword in his hand. I'd be willing to sit around a campfire and share a cup of ale with the man."

"I am sure he would be willing too," Henry said, touched by the archer's loyalty and admiration for him.

"The King turns one eye to God and keeps the other eye on his coffers in his treasury," Jack Mercer argued, slightly less enamoured with his sovereign. "He can't afford to go home empty-handed, which is why we're stuck in the mud, a few hundred paces away from thousands of vengeful Frenchman who want to slaughter us. Percy Badby there, that holy fool asleep by the fire, said earlier that the endless rain was perhaps a sign that God was weeping for us. I'm more inclined to think that it's a sign of God pissing on us. But I'd sit around a campfire with Henry too — if he brought the ale. We're supposed to owe him our duty, but he owes us some spoils. So what do you think of him?" The archer's voice was rough with bitterness and phlegm. Jack Mercer was not in a mood to forgive anyone. The King, the French, Cooper or himself.

Henry peered up into the sky. Splinters of rain prickled his skin. Faith and sorrow swirled and swelled in his chest. He could argue that he was both God's representative on earth and a pride-filled warmonger.

"I think the King is but a man, as I am. Every subject's duty is to the King, but his soul is his own," Henry remarked, with an air of melancholy.

And my soul sometimes seems as if it's blacker than pitch. Yet thankfully I can still see it. Feel it. It's real.

*

The draught blew through the gap in the warped wooden door to his room and caused the flames on the candles to wriggle. Yet they did not extinguish. Henry bowed before the bible and cross, which stood in between the worn down candles.

A half-eaten plate of food sat on the table. At first Henry couldn't eat. He felt too nauseous and nervous. He also felt guilty at having so much, having just witnessed his soldiers suffering from starvation, but then he forced some of the victuals down, believing that he would feel guiltier if the food went to waste. Henry needed to keep his strength up, for himself and for others.

I have nothing left to give them. Except victory, or my life.

The rain continued to fall. Henry fancied that it sounded like a thousand birds of prey pecking at the roof.

The King bowed his head and prayed.

God, make me an instrument of your will. I do not want to merely exercise my will, and claim I am doing so in your name. Too many monarchs before me have been guilty of that sin. There will be more than one French nobleman at the other end of the valley this evening offering up a prayer, asking for your favour. Whose candle will burn brightest and longest? I confess my sin that I yearn for glory. But I yearn for peace more. I buried Prince Hal when I was crowned. You called to me. England called to me. I was no longer a slave to carnal vices. No longer drowning in drink. Please do not let it be fate that Henry V will be buried tomorrow, but rather baptize me in the blood of my enemies, who would look to subjugate my person and my countrymen. Bring me peace tomorrow. And bring me peace tonight. Let me sleep.

The King took to his bed. The night had been a long one. The coming day could prove even longer. Thousands of people — archers, pages, smiths, noblemen, surgeons, esquires, clergy — surrounded him, but Henry had seldom felt lonelier. He willed himself to picture the portrait he carried of Catherine Valois. The daughter of his enemy, and his intended bride. Sometimes Henry felt that the beautiful face in the picture looked at him reprovingly, but at other times there was love and grace in her regal expression. He hoped that she could forgive him for his actions. For if she could then so could her countrymen, he believed. Their marriage would signify a union of two hearts and two nations, but to win the peace, Henry would have to win the war.

It was late. Past midnight. October 25th. St Crispin's Day.

14

Chaucer and Fordham reached the city of Troyes just before dusk. They entered through the Tannery Gate. Despite the late hour the city was still a hive of activity. Ladies, wearing wimples and brightly coloured embroidered dresses, trimmed with furs, headed home, accompanied by attendants, burdened with their mistresses' shopping. Obese clergymen, in their finest weeds, dripping with self-importance and gold, strutted along the main thoroughfares, expecting the populace to respect and envy them. Chaucer noticed more than one priest eye up young women — and young men — with a lascivious leer. He overheard more than one snippet of conversation about the war. The people understandably condemned the English invaders and labelled Henry a heretic, yet they also cursed the French soldiers, and confirmed a number of reports Chaucer had received, that the army were confiscating valuables and destroying or taking crops in the name of the war effort.

The city reminded Fordham of London: one's nostrils could be assailed by cheap perfume at one moment and dung the next. In Troyes, tanneries, butcheries, fishmongers and bakeries were scattered amongst houses, churches and municipal buildings. Fordham was struck by how prosperous the city was: a burgeoning merchant class had built attractive houses with spacious gardens. Goldsmiths, silversmiths, theatres, inns of good repute and shops selling luxury goods lined the streets.

Although the vaunting spire of Troyes Cathedral dominated the skyline, the man-at-arms looked past it, into the distance, at the home of his enemy. The fortified chateaux, which had originally been built by a Templar commander, sat on a hillside, half-concealed by the surrounding woods, a mile or so from the city. Fordham vowed that either he, or the French agent, would meet his fate on the morrow.

"We will ride out at first light," Chaucer remarked to his companion, when they were safely ensconced in their room at the inn. "Reynard will doubtless still be in possession of his small band of mercenaries. The main gate will be guarded. Unfortunately, I will not be able to arrange for someone at such short notice to infiltrate the household. I am loath to attempt to bribe someone, for fear of them betraying us."

"So how will we enter the chateaux?"

"By knocking on the door, in a manner of speaking. Let us hope that Reynard is still home. I received intelligence reports that, due to his failure in Scotland, the French court has turned against him, as have the King and Dauphin. Once the campaign against us ends, I believe that a number of French noblemen will look to confiscate Reynard's lands and valuables. He has made too many enemies. This means, of course, the agent may be planning to disappear, if he has not already absconded, but he will have the ability to come back and haunt us. I do not wish to spend the rest of my days looking over my shoulder, fearing for the safety of my family. Time will not temper the fire inside of him to exact his revenge. I would have preferred it if Henry would have allowed Robert to join us in our mission. We could have just then waited for the snake to stick his head out of the window, and the devil would have received an arrow through his gullet, but unfortunately Henry would have rather parted with his piece of the True Cross than lose Robert from his ranks."

"I wonder how Robert and the rest of the army are getting on?" Fordham asked. They could have fought and won — or lost — a battle by now.

"God knows."

But does God care?

15

Morning. The trees were shedding their leaves. Distant, mournful birdsong weaved its way out of the woods that framed the battlefield. Pools of surface water, from the rains the night before, glistened in the autumnal light across the valley. Robins darted down from their nests and hopped around on the ground in between the two forces, in the hope of digging out a worm or two.

Henry had formed his army. Two wings of archers were positioned either side of a line of men-at-arms, four soldiers deep (the woods prevented any flanking manoeuvres). Companies of archers also intersected the rows of the armoured infantry. Henry would command the centre, the Duke of York the left and Thomas de Camoys the right. Aside from certain senior knights and messengers, the army had dismounted. The horses, along with the baggage, pages, clergy and other non-combatants, remained at the rear.

The King trotted towards a group of bowmen, containing Cooper, situated at the mid-point of the line. Henry was seated on a handsome grey courser, which he would soon dismount from to stand with his troops. His armour had been scoured and polished. Cuirass, greaves, ailettes and gauntlets all appeared spotless, as if he were a god among men. Henry's bascinet was topped with a golden crown, studded with pearls and gemstones. Sir William Talbot had warned the King that his armour would make him a target. French soldiers would swarm towards him, like moths to a flame, hoping to kill or capture the enemy commander. "Let them come," Henry had replied, stoically.

The archers removed their caps and kneeled before their sovereign. Bearded, haggard faces peered up at the youthful monarch. Some wore mail, rusting helms and brigidines, whilst others went shoeless and wore threadbare, padded leather jackets and (sometimes soiled) breeches. Axes and mallets were slung over shoulders, short swords hung down from horse-hide sheaths, ready for when the fighting would become hand-to-hand. Each man carried forty-eight arrows. Some placed a few of the shafts next to their feet, in the ground. Each archer stood next to a wooden stake, hammered into the soft soil, which poked out at an angle, ready to stop French horses from charging through their formation.

The French had no intention of charging the English, however. At least not yet. D'Albret and Boucicaut knew that they had time — and provisions — on their side. They could let their enemy starve, or be decimated by disease or fatigue. A couple of hours had now passed since the opposing armies had formed up and faced off one another. Each commander had read their Pizan and knew that if the mass of the French attacked first it would be to their detriment, *"for the larger army cannot easily move forward, but rather so many men will get in the way of each other, and in battle formation they lunge forward so hastily that they mingle needlessly with the enemy, and are exterminated."*

The King couldn't help but note the apprehension and raw fear in the hollowed-out expressions before him. Chins dug into chests as heads were lowered. Food was scarce, but words could nourish their souls and stiffen courage, Henry believed. Their lines could hold, their arrows find their mark, their sword-arms not waver, if they believed, as he did, that they could win the day. The King broke the eerie, funereal, silence.

"This day is called the feast of Crispin. He that outlives this day, and comes safe home, will stand on tip-toe when this day is named, and rouse him at the name of Crispin. He that shall live this day and see old age, will yearly on the vigil feast his neighbours, and say 'Tomorrow is St Crispin'. Then will he strip his sleeves and show his scars, and say 'These wounds I had on Crispin's Day'. Old men forget; yet all shall be forgot, but he'll remember, with advantages, what feats he did that day. Then shall our names, familiar in his mouth as household words — Harry the King, Bedford and Exeter, Warwick and Talbot, Salisbury and Gloucester — be in their flowing cups freshly remembered. This story shall the good man teach his son; and Crispin shall ne'er go by, from this day to the ending of the world, but in it we shall be remembered — we few, we happy few, we band of brothers; for he today that sheds his blood with me shall be my brother; be he ne'er so vile, this day shall gentle his condition; and gentlemen in England now a-bed shall think themselves accursed they were not here, and hold their manhoods cheap whiles any speaks that fought with us upon St Crispin's Day."

Heads began to nod in agreement. Hums and grunts of assent turned to declarations of assent. Chests swelled, chins jutted out and jaws were clenched together in grim determination. They had come so far, together, and they would not fall at the final hurdle. They would forfeit neither their lives nor bow fingers to an enemy they rightly held in contempt. Their King had faith in them, and they had faith in their King. Their contracts may have been sealed with wax or signed in ink, but they were all bound together by blood.

Robert Cooper felt a wave of new-found optimism and defiance rise up around him. The troops around him stirred, cheering the King and jeering their opponents. Some stuck their two bow fingers up at their enemy, taunting them. Others did not want to tempt fate, however, having heard rumours that the French intended to cut off their bow fingers should they capture any archers.

Cooper gazed out across the battlefield again, surveying the French. Lines of knights, mounted on powerful warhorses, were positioned in the front rank. The nobility, devoted to chivalry, demanded the honour of defeating the English first. They dreamed of bloodying their swords for France, and capturing the English King. A multitude of garish banners, awash with heraldic images, fluttered in the wind, often ruining the sight-lines of the men at the rear. Behind the finely turned-out knights stood a mass of armoured infantry, thirty men deep, ready to finish off the job that the cavalry would commence. Visors covered faces, ready to attack. Lances had been shortened, due to how closely the infantry were packed together. Artillery pieces and companies of low-born crossbowmen were stationed at the rear. Cooper briefly thought of the promise he had made to his intended — that he would survive the campaign and come back to England and purchase a small farm. Retire. The archer also recalled the promise he had made to his King, that he would give his all. Cooper bleakly wondered if it was possible to honour both of his vows, but still he had faith, and offered up a final prayer: *Dear God, let me return home to Grace.*

The King's resonant voice soon brought the soldier back to the battlefield and the task at hand.

"Know my friends that I will not abandon you, for without you I would be nothing. I would rather die than be captured, and then force you and your countrymen to pay my ransom. It is time for all of us to make history, as our forebears did at Crécy. When you fight today, know that you are not only fighting for your life and the lives of the men standing shoulder to shoulder with you, but you are also fighting for your kinsfolk back home. Should we let our enemy break us then the way lies open to your houses, farms and taverns in England. So hold the line. Plant your feet, as firmly as you have hammered those sharpened stakes into the ground. If your aim is equal to your honour and courage then we shall be victorious this day."

Henry rode out so as to be in front of his entire army, to a chorus of cheers for Harry and St George. He also hoped that his opponents might spy the prize of the King of England and be spurred on to break formation and attack. "We need to provoke, rather than be provoked," Henry had remarked to the Duke of York the previous evening, when the two men had formulated their strategy.

The sun was rising over the ridge behind the English army and began to shine directly into the eyes of the French. It was time.

"Banners advance," Henry ordered, his voice as sturdy as oak. The thousand paces which existed between the two forces would soon be shortened to less than four hundred.

"It's about fucking time," John Walworth muttered under his breath, eager to get the day over with, one way or another. Although the hulking bowman had declined the chaplain's offer to confess his sins that morning, the soldier still offered up a few private prayers. He asked God to keep his family safe and prosperous, and that, should he die, his friends might be spared.

Henry cantered back to where Robert Cooper and the companies of bowmen under his charge stood. They had been briefed beforehand and were aware of their role — as bait.

"Let's go," the King remarked, with the confident air of a man about to head off on a hunt.

The archers heaved their wooden stakes out of the soft ground and carried them towards the French. More than one man spat out a curse as he suffered a splinter. The rest of the army followed their lead.

Sir Thomas Erpingham, a veteran knight, who had served under the Black Prince when just eleven years old, led the bowmen forwards on his horse. The old soldier brought a sense of composure and confidence to the archers.

Cooper, Walworth and Mercer stood in the front rank of the company. They were now just three hundred paces from the enemy. They could hear the clink of French armour and the whinnying of restless horses. Although somewhat isolated and vulnerable they dauntlessly turned their backs on their opponent and placed their stakes in the ground again.

Hearts began to beat faster in the French army. A band of enemy archers were now in range. The tide had come in. But no one rode out in front of the troops to deliver an inspiring speech. Too many noblemen would neither give nor take an order. The Duke of Orléans believed he held the highest military rank due to the authority of his social rank, and others concurred. Although nominally at peace with one another, in the name of a greater cause, the Burgundian and Armagnac knights remained more rivals than allies. They watched as the English bowmen strung their weapons. They would soon unleash their deadly missiles. Honour and rank dictated that the knights should advance, and so they did. They were taking the bait.

16

Clouds smeared themselves across the sky, bleaching out the light. A chilling mizzle hung in the air.

Chaucer and Fordham spent the morning reconnoitring the chateau. They kept their distance, but surveyed the fortified house from all sides. Aside from the main gate, there only appeared to be one other entrance to the property; a drawbridge over a moat, situated on the east wall, which was currently raised. Soldiers patrolled the balustrades, which rounded the entire chateau, and there seemed no reason to believe, given the number of torches and lamps they observed, that Reynard's soldiers were not vigilant at night also.

As they circled the extensive property, Chaucer was distracted. He would often stop and peer out away from the chateau as if expecting someone.

"What is it?" Fordham remarked, on more than one occasion.

"Nothing, unfortunately," Chaucer gently replied.

Fordham remembered back to when he had infiltrated a similarly fortified house some years ago, when he had accompanied the agent to Normandy. Chaucer had instructed the charismatic soldier to seduce the wife of a silk merchant, who was also employed by France to act as an envoy and spy. Fordham would not carry out such a mission again. He did not want to be unfaithful to Marie.

"I know you loved her, Edward, but Marie would have wanted you to live your life, rather than have Reynard take it from you," Chaucer remarked, after a period of silence between the two men, as they made their way through a dense wood which bordered the chateau. Chaucer was worried that Fordham might prove too reckless in his desire to confront their enemy – he had suggested that they deliberately be captured; at least they could then enter the house.

Fordham winced in pain on hearing his friend mention her name. It was like a lightning bolt cutting into his heart. The wound was still tender.

"I sometimes feel that I only truly lived my life during my short time with her. It sounds comical, I know, especially coming from me, but before Marie, I just spent my days playing out various roles — of poet, lover and soldier. In some ways we are all our own Canterbury Tales. Our life is populated by idealised and real versions of ourselves. We are all — or have the potential to be — the Knight, Pardoner, Friar, Miller or Wife of Bath, and do we not all sit around and tell tales, to others and ourselves?"

Silence ensued again. The two men eventually exited the bramble-filled wood and came out to a junction on the highway. They stood at the crossroads. Chaucer heard a rustle of leaves, and looked around him once more, but this time they weren't alone. Thirty or so men, some armed with blades, some with crossbows, scrambled out of the opposite treeline and formed a horseshoe around the two Englishmen.

"It seems that we meet again, Thomas."

17

"Nock. Draw. Loose."

The collective twang of thousands of greased hemp bowstrings sang in the air.

The front rank of French horsemen had only advanced fifty paces before the first volley of arrows arced across the sky and decimated the enemy. Such was the density of the attack that the air blackened; the sun was blocked out by countless ash shafts, goose feather flights and steel arrow heads.

Trumpets and drums sounded. The thrum of horse hooves beat in time to human hearts. Broadheaded arrows tore through horse flesh, shattering bone. Often their legs gave way and the mighty war horses threw off their riders or veered into one another. Screeching cries from terrified mares sounded through the air. Mud — and blood — began to mark the banners of the French standard-bearers as they rode forward.

Bodkin-tipped arrows bested the armour of the enemy's finest soldiers. Riders were abruptly knocked back off their mounts, or slowly slid from their saddles into earth. The living and the dead would be trampled upon alike.

Yet still they rode on. French knights held onto their reins as tightly as they held onto the conviction that they would not be defeated by the lowliest peasant soldiers on the battlefield. From a sense of chivalric honour and glory they wanted to be the first to break through the English lines, but still they had not closed in on the bowmen. Mud turned to sludge and their horses, fetlock-deep in the glutinous ground, were unable to advance at full speed.

Another torrent of arrows fell upon the French, but the cacophony of thudding shafts, thundering horses and trill screams could not drown out the sound of the piercing French trumpets, ordering the mass of armoured infantry to commence an advance.

Nock. Draw. Loose.

The ground shook as hundreds of snorting warhorses continued to close in, but Cooper and his brethren had no thought of retreat. The archer momentarily looked to his left, expecting to see Owen Morgan next to him. The thought of his loss made the bowman pull back his string an inch further and, rather than arcing his missile into the massed target, Cooper deliberately picked out a French nobleman, imagining that it was Guiche, and shot his shaft at a flat trajectory. The broadheaded arrow whistled through the air and, although it did not penetrate the enemy's cuirass, the force of the blow knocked him from his mount and the fall broke his spine.

To Cooper's right John Walworth, half-hidden behind the wooden stake which separated them, rhythmically and relentlessly worked his way through his quota of arrows, and bellowed for more, in between cursing the French as he released each missile.

Henry remained flint-faced at the scene. The devastation. Shock and awe. The flowers of French nobility were being scythed down, like weeds. It was God's will, he told himself. His enemy had brought the punishment on themselves. That morning the pious and patriotic King had kneeled and prayed to Edward the Confessor, but the soldier in Henry knew that thanks had to be given to Edward III and his military reforms. Henry watched as a storm of arrows darkened the sky again and rained down on his opponents. An arrow glanced off a helmet and struck a horse riding behind him. Henry observed one French knight lean over to save a comrade next to him from falling from his mount, but the act of saving another damned himself, as a missile struck him in the throat.

The wave of horsemen in the front ranks who had advanced on the enemy thinned into a trickle. The fewer the men, the lesser the glory. Destriers slowed, reared up and threw their riders, rather than impale themselves on the line of sharpened wooden stakes. Jack Mercer wasn't alone, among the archers, to dart out from behind his stake to finish off the fallen knights. Groaning noblemen, unable to get to their feet, borne down by their heavy armour in the mud, were doomed. Visors were lifted and blades were jabbed into the slits in dented faceguards. After a quick search for a purse or valuables the archers would then retreat back to their lines.

Many riderless horses bolted into the safety of the treeline, or ran back across the battlefield, sometimes colliding into the lines of French men-at-arms who marched slowly, but determinedly, towards their foes.

Sir William Talbot offered up a sigh of relief. Horses and men littered the field. Bloody. Contorted. Sinking in the churned up earth. The French cavalry had been bested. The battle was half won. But a battle half won can still be lost, the veteran soldier mused. The archers had all but exhausted their supply of arrows, and the English were still hopelessly outnumbered, devoid of any reserves. The French infantry could trample over them, just as easily as the French warhorses had just buried men in the mud.

Henry clasped his sword that little bit tighter. It seemed that his whole life had been leading up to this moment. *For England and St George.* Would his father have been proud of him, or have envied his success?

"Sire, would it not be wise to provide the enemy with a number of decoys, to lessen the chance of harm coming to your person?" Sir John Holland asked, having already briefed a number of men-at-arms on taking part in such a ruse.

"John, I consider you my friend and the finest of soldiers, but there can only be one King, else what's this campaign been about?" Henry replied, in good humour.

Sir John Holland had tried to advise his sovereign in the morning to carry a lance or poleaxe as his principle weapon, but the sword was the weapon of a king. Henry had instructed one of his armourers to engrave two words along the blade: *I serve*. The same motto could be read upon the sword of Edward of Woodstock. Yet, more than the words of the Black Prince, Henry remembered the conversation he had with the archer, John Walworth, around the campfire, and he was happy to echo the honest man's sentiments, and share his fellow Englishman's fate.

Death or victory.

18

Philippe de Meulan was meeting Thomas Chaucer for the second time. Their first meeting had only been a week or so ago, when the Englishman had turned up at the ageing aristocrat's estate near Abbeville. Chaucer had sent a letter in advance to Meulan, stating that he was in possession of information concerning the death of his younger brother, Louis.

The haughty Meulan was no friend of the English, and he treated his surprise guest with suspicion, but a sense of curiosity meant that Chaucer had been granted an audience.

"Thank you for seeing me," the Englishman, in French, had politely remarked. "Our two countries may be at war, but I believe that we have a mutual enemy, which will compel us to form a temporary alliance." Chaucer had gone on to report that he was an agent to Henry V, and that he had recently been a prisoner of Reynard de Troyes. During his imprisonment, Reynard had confessed to the killing of Louis, by poison, when they had both studied at the seminary as young men.

"I know where Reynard is currently located, but he might soon flee the region and country. It will be now or never, in terms of punishing him for his crimes."

"You are a brave man for coming here. I could well earn a handsome reward for delivering you up to the Marshal Boucicaut," Meulan had remarked, after Chaucer had finished speaking.

"I like to think of myself as a desperate man," Chaucer had wryly replied.

"Why should I trust you?"

"I am unsure of how I can instil trust in you at this time, so let us put the issue of trust aside for one moment. At best, should you join me in executing Reynard, you will be killing the man who murdered your younger brother. I suspect that time has not healed the wound, or the injustice. At worst, you will be murdering a man who the King and French court has turned its back on. Charles, or the Dauphin, may even reward you for the act. And if, as I understand, you have loyalties towards John the Fearless, he will be grateful too. Reynard has been no friend to the Burgundian cause during recent times. If John the Fearless comes to power he will feel no inclination to clasp the snake to his bosom. No one will weep if Reynard de Troyes suffers a bloody end."

"We can agree upon that point, but that does not make us allies. I will think upon what you have said. You will understand if I reserve judgement and do not commit to helping you straightaway. I need to verify your story, as best I can, and find out if you are a man of honour. I do not wish to clasp you to my breast, just to discover you are as sly a serpent as Reynard. However, should you and your story prove to be true, the enemy of my enemy will become my friend, and I will help you consign the vile caitiff to hell," Meulan had remarked, with undisguised anger and hatred.

Now, anger and hatred seeped out of the silver-haired aristocrat again as he rode alongside the two Englishmen, towards Reynard's chateau. The Frenchman had a hard, unforgiving face and, thankfully for Chaucer, an unforgiving heart. Rheumy green eyes, as cold as jade, were deep-set within his liver-spotted face. His hands were bony, arthritic, claw-like. An ornate gold clasp, decorated with his family's crest, held a fine woollen cloak in place. His rasping voice was peppered with bitterness and bile. Meulan was ruthless in business, unfaithful to his wife, vicious towards his servants, but unstintingly loyal to his blood family. "Family is family, everything else means nothing," the Frenchman had, on more than one occasion, remarked to Chaucer. "One must even give the benefit of the doubt to those family members who you know are as worthless as a bucket with a hole in the bottom. Louis was far from an angel. He was spiteful, selfish and preened himself more than a peacock, or over-priced harlot. But he was my brother. And he didn't deserve to die."

Philippe de Meulan had been suspicious of foul play at the time of his brother's death. The feeling that there was more to the tragedy than met the eye was an itch that would not go away, but the victim's older brother was never able to prove anything. Until now.

"Our aim should be to capture the villain alive," the Frenchman asserted to Chaucer as they trotted along the winding track which led up towards the main entrance to Reynard's estate. "As per our agreement I will have the first crack of the whip in torturing our enemy. France will not mourn the canker. His machinations have done more harm than good. My men are experienced soldiers and loyal to me. Reynard's mercenaries will not get the better of them. Boucicaut wrote me a letter himself, asking me to deploy my prized company in service of the state, to defeat Henry, but he has more than enough troops already to best your army, which I understand is now a mere shadow of its former self." The Anglophobe snickered in an attempt to make the Englishman bristle.

"And how do you propose that we best the main gate?" Fordham asked, refusing to rise to Meulan's bait. The man-at-arms already had enough enemies in France to contend with, without making a new one.

"By knocking on the door — with a gun-stone launched from that," Meulan remarked, his aspect shining with glee and cruelty, as he pointed to a cannon up ahead, being carried forward towards the house on a reinforced wagon.

19

The archers had relieved themselves of their bows and now brandished all manner of weapons: short swords, mallets, hand-axes, maces and knives. The bowmen stood, unkempt and undaunted, at either end of the line of men-at-arms, and were also interspersed with the infantry. Unlike the French, the English noblemen had no issue with fighting alongside those lower in social rank.

The enemy moved cumbrously forward. Some of the men stumbled and pages and squires rushed forward to try to get their paymasters back on their feet. A low sucking sound reverberated in the air with each torturously slow step. Not a blade of grass could now be seen across the field. The French infantry passed by fallen men and horses, bending around them as a stream would a rock. Their thighs burned and their helmets felt like ovens, as sweat stung their eyes and their vision was impaired by flecks of mud flicking up and covering their visors. To begin with, the leading French men-at-arms funnelled themselves towards the centre of the English line, keen to secure the glory of engaging and defeating the English king. The mud sapped their strength, but bloodlust, as well as a thirst for glory, fed their spirits. They craved vengeance for Harfleur, and for their recently fallen comrades. A lust for gold also gilded their ire, as some began to spend prospective ransom money in their imaginations.

Henri Moreau surged forward, towards the front ranks. Beneath his breath he cursed the vainglorious noblemen for their suicidal advance. He also cursed d'Albret and Boucicaut for posting the army's artillery and crossbowmen at the rear, rendering them useless. He spat out the names of prominent Burgundians and Armagnacs, for failing to work together, but most of all Moreau cursed the English, for invading his country and killing the young Fretin. The veteran soldier had never been on the losing side in a battle, until the defeat on the bridge, but he would now claim his revenge: make the English pay, in blood and gold. The French could — would — still win the day. They need only break the thin line of men-at-arms, cleave them apart, and then the bastards would surrender or rout. As dangerous as the archers were with their war bows, they would not be able to repel the trained, armoured French infantry. *They will scatter like roaches.* Without their bows they were merely a bunch of farmhands, poachers, peasants and drunkards. Moreau's nostrils widened as he spotted, through the slit in his visor, one of the English lords who had commanded the troops on the bridge. He vowed to kill the elderly knight and anyone who stood in his way.

The rattle and clink of French armour and mail grew louder. Ominous. Menacing. The traditional French war cry of "Montjoie" was spewed out and swirled around in the fetid air.

Robert Cooper offered up a prayer to St Crispin that his boots wouldn't fall apart and he wouldn't lose his footing in the ensuing fight. He was scared. Of losing his life. Of losing Grace. Of breaking her heart.

"The drinks will be on me, John, should we get through this."

"No. The drinks will be on the French. Once I slit their throats, I'll slit open their purses."

A little way along the line, Jack Mercer licked his lips, in anticipation of satisfying his bloodlust. He eyed up prospective figures who he could wound, take prisoner and get a cut of any ransom money.

"Thank God half our army is still suffering from the remnants of the bloody flux, else we'd all be shitting ourselves right now," Mercer joked to Percy Badby, and others standing by him, in order to help ease the tense moments. There was a sense that some of the men were still hoping for a trumpet to sound and negotiations to start, but most just wanted to start the battle and get it over with.

Percy Badby barely heard his friend's remarks over the increasing din. The archer adjusted his kettle helmet and mouthed one last prayer.

The French grew ever nearer. The sea of bobbing French infantry seemed to stretch back for forever. The clang of armour reverberated like a death knell.

"We'll soon be able to smell the garlic on their breath," Sir William Talbot stated. "Don't be tempted to charge the bastards, no matter how much you want to silence their cries of 'Montjoie'. I know I usually say 'not one step back', but when the bastards charge and thrust their weapons forward let them stab the air and fall over themselves. And then counter attack."

God help us.

20

"Can we trust him?" Fordham asked Chaucer, discreetly, whilst glancing over at their ally. Meulan was watching his team of Dutch gunners as they checked over the fearsome weapon one last time. A number of other soldiers, surrounding them, commenced cranking their crossbows and strapping on pieces of armour. They were conscious of overburdening themselves with anything which might slow them down during the assault. Speed would be of the essence. If they could secure the main entrance before it could be reinforced, then they could secure the entire house without suffering too many casualties, they believed.

"We can trust his hatred and desire for revenge. Meulan wants to end Reynard's life as much as we do."

Fordham nodded in reply, but he wasn't confident. A steely sullenness chiselled itself into his features. It had now become the soldier's default expression. Meulan had just instructed the Englishmen that his troops alone would enter the chateau during the attack. Meulan also reasserted, as per his original agreement with Chaucer, that he would have first refusal on any spoils and valuables they discovered in the house. Another of Meulan's mantras was that "Money is money, everything else means nothing."

Chaucer replied that he would still honour their contract, and that he and his man-at-arms would post themselves in the treeline outside of the east gate, along with the small force of Meulan's men positioned there.

"We will not allow Reynard to escape past us," the Englishman had said, displaying a due sense of determination and deference towards the French nobleman.

"Are we really going to just sit idle at the eastern gate?" Fordham asked, his tone awash with disbelief and anger.

"Though it may prove wise not to be at the vanguard of the attack, else our allies might be tempted to bury their blades in our backs, Meulan and his men aren't even familiar with what Reynard looks like. I've not come this far, only to be prevented from finishing the job. Reynard has slipped through the net too many times before."

"Trust me, and trust my desire for revenge. No, we will not be sitting idly by at the eastern gate. I haven't been altogether forthcoming with our erstwhile ally. Today is just another day, like any other, for secrets and lies, Edward."

The English agent smiled confidently, knowingly, to his friend, though in reality he had no idea whether his gamble would pay off.

21

Henry planted his feet and swotted away the first thrust from an enemy lance. The French man-at-arms in front of him roared in exertion and then in agony as the point of Sir John Holland's poleaxe forced itself through the man's aventail and into his neck.

The melee had begun.

The Duke of York bellowed out that no man should retreat a foot behind his standard as he deflected blows and then hacked away at the wall of armour in front him, but his voice could barely be heard over the pandemonium of the battle.

A French knight swung his mace at the ignoble archer in front of him. The lowly bowman would be his first victim before he engaged an enemy of suitable rank. But Cooper swiftly lifted up his left forearm, with a thick piece of plate armour strapped beneath his padded jacket, and blocked the blow. Long-limbed and fleet of foot, the bowman then lifted his leg and kicked his opponent to the ground. Cooper quickly bent down, lifted up the Frenchman's visor and punched the point of his short sword into his terrified face to end the contest.

The numerous individual clashes of armour and weaponry joined together to produce one long ear-splitting and ear-ringing clang. Whimpering voices called out for their mothers or God in the background. Blood and mud splattered across finely woven surcoats, jupons and threadbare jerkins alike.

John Walworth cursed and jabbed away with his mighty poleaxe.

"That's for Hall, that's for George and that's for Owen... Bastard... Cock-sucker... Pox ridden twat..."

Although the point couldn't always penetrate enemy mail or armour, the force of the colossal archer's attacks often knocked opponents backwards. A nimble archer might then dart forward and stick a blade into his armpit, where the armoured soldier was vulnerable. Chivalry was dead. Butchery was alive and flourishing on the battlefield.

Jack Mercer pulled a wounded Frenchman out from underneath a corpse and instructed Percy Badby to take him back to the rear of the battlefield, where the English baggage train was positioned. Other prisoners were also being led there and tied up with spare bowstrings. Not only was Mercer keen to capture one or two French noblemen worth ransoming, but he feared that Badby neither owned the temperament or skill to survive fighting in the frontline. The Christian archer, though, had asked a page to deal with the prisoner. Badby felt a duty to remain with his companion and fight by his side.

Sir William Talbot punched his opponent on the side of his bascinet. He grabbed his faceguard and violently pulled the French man-at-arms to the ground. After stamping on his enemy's head twice, he plunged the spike on top of his poleaxe into his neck. Talbot spat out a curse, drew breath and took a moment or two to survey the progress of the battle. He dared to hope. The front rank of French infantry had failed to breach the English line. The arduous slog across the muddy field had drained the enemy's momentum and vigour. Their heavy mail coats and thick plate armour were proving to be a weakness, not a strength. The English were avoiding their often lumbering attacks, and then striking back with swiftness and precision. The men-at-arms were felling the enemy and the archers were finishing them off, with the dead were forming a defensive barrier between the two forces. Such were the numbers of densely-packed French troops that they were unable to manoeuvre properly. The rear ranks pushed them forward — onto English steel. The French were beginning to trample on their own comrades in their eagerness to join the fray, and the armoured soldiers, unable to get to their feet, were suffocating in the mud.

Henry, his scoured armour streaked with grime and gore, called out one more time for his army to hold the line. In a moment of respite he took a breath and wryly smiled to himself for sending his archers forward to goad his enemy and act as bait. Now his opponents were literally falling over themselves to surge towards him and capture — or kill — a king.

I'm the bait now. But let them come... Dear God, let fortune favour this sword.

The wry smile abruptly fell from his face as, out the corner of his eye, Henry witnessed his younger brother, Humphrey, the Duke of Gloucester, being knocked down and then hauled back towards the French line by a brace of men-at-arms. Humphrey had proved himself more of a scholar than soldier growing up, but he had still loyally followed Henry on campaign. His knowledge of siege craft, gleaned from classical texts rather than from first-hand experience, had also been of use at Harfleur. Henry was immensely fond of his youngest brother, perhaps partly because Humphrey reminded the King of himself, when he was his age. The young nobleman was intelligent, amiable and thoroughly dissolute. He knew his way around a tavern, as well as a library, and Humphrey had long forgotten all of the names of the women he had bedded. Yet Humphrey's sore head had now been caused by a blow from a poleaxe rather than too much ale, as he lay in the mud. One of his French captors opened his victim's visor and demanded to know who he was. Humphrey was tempted to come up with a false name, but his mind went blank.

"Kill him," the second French knight said, lusting for blood more than gold.

With little regard for his own safety, the king barged his way through his own men and launched himself forward, towards where his brother was about to be executed. Henry shoulder-charged the first French knight out of the way and then quickly positioned himself to thrust the point of his sword into the second man's groin.

The gap in the French line was quickly filled, and Henry was cut off from his own troops. His fine armour — and crown — quickly drew the attention of the surrounding French troops. After recovering from the surprise at seeing the English king in their midst they turned their weapons towards him. Henry stood astride of his brother, fending off attacks, as fierce and dominant as a lion, but there were too many jackals approaching from all sides. A French knight poked the tip of his poleaxe forward and struck the King's crown, knocking out one of the gemstones. The blow caused Henry to momentarily lose his balance. A sly esquire was just about to thrust his sword into the base of his enemy's spine, after spying a gap in the plates of his armour, when the Frenchman was felled by a lead-headed mallet striking him square on the chest.

"Cunt!" John Walworth exclaimed, as he charged forward to protect the King.

At the same time Sir John Holland and William Talbot had cut through a swathe of men, as though they were woodsman hacking their way through a forest, to reach their friend and commander.

The ox-like bowman carried the disorientated Duke back to the English line, whilst the King, valiantly supported by others, fought on.

But were they fighting in vain? The centre of the English line was holding, but thinning. The multitude of French infantry were still moving forward and now fanning themselves out across the field. They would soon fully engage the archers on the wings. If the bowmen could not hold their position, then the French could outflank — or even encircle — the remainder of the English army. And slaughter it.

It won't be a contest, it'll be a bloody massacre, William Talbot thought to himself, as he imagined the prospective scenario of a would-be triumph turning into a tragedy. And so the old soldier breathlessly raised his weapon and entered the melee once more.

22

The crash of the gun-stone smashing through the thick oak timbers of the main door could be heard — and felt — throughout the chateau.

Reynard was sitting in his study at the rear of the house. His desk, which he had purchased from the widow of an envoy whose reputation he had ruined by providing fraudulent evidence of treason against him, was filled with various papers and a copy of Plato's *The Republic*. The agent put down his quill, which had been gifted to him by a late Pope, and walked out of the door. He was met by his whey-faced secretary and the distant sounds of confused and irate soldiers. A couple of mercenaries raced past the spindly secretary, nearly toppling him over, as they strapped on pieces of armour and weaponry.

Reynard remained calm and purposeful. Rather than be distracted by thoughts of who his enemy might be, he methodically put into action the plan he had formed for such a scenario. Firstly, he ordered his secretary to call for his personal bodyguard, consisting of three mercenaries. The rest of the soldiers could die in defence of the house, for all Reynard cared; it would save the agent the cost of paying their wages. His secretary was then to gather his private papers, coinage and other portable valuables which he kept in a special locked box, concealed behind the fireplace in his bedchamber.

While his secretary disappeared down the corridor, the captain of Reynard's small force of mercenaries, Chastel, appeared. A small army of French soldiers, armed with crossbows and artillery, had secured the main courtyard at the front of the house, he reported.

"We will not be able to defeat the enemy, but we can perhaps still retreat through the east gate," Chastel said, breathless from fear and from running around the house, in order to locate his paymaster.

"I promise that you will survive this day," the agent stated boldly and determinedly. "Have your men reposition themselves at the east gate and lower the drawbridge. I will join you there in five minutes, and we will escape as one. Together. Hold off the enemy until I arrive. Kill as many of them as you can."

Chastel nodded in reply, bolstered by his employer's faith and loyalty, and sped off to carry out his orders.

Reynard retreated back into his study. He unlocked a trunk and, swiftly yet calmly, tossed various incriminating documents and correspondence onto the fire in the corner of the room. He then removed a false bottom out of a draw in his desk and retrieved a small purse, filled with rubies and sapphires. After carefully attaching the purse to his belt, which he wore around his tailored black cassock, Reynard went to rendezvous with his bodyguards and secretary.

All was still going to plan, the agent considered, as he ventured down the back staircase.

Realising that he was out of favour at court, and that his enemies had the ear of the King and Dauphin, Reynard had already taken steps to leave France. Once the business of defeating Henry's vagabond army was over with, the likes of Charles d'Albret and the Duke of Brabant would turn their attention to prosecuting the diplomat and confiscating his lands and capital. *Nobility has a responsibility, to itself.* And so Reynard had recently sold his chateau to a local merchant at, unfortunately, a fair price. Whether the crown would now take the house away from the merchant was of little concern to him.

With France no longer safe for him, Reynard had arranged to flee to Rome. The church was willing to provide him with sanctuary and forgive his sins, for a price.

But I will still be able to strike at France and my enemies from Rome. No matter how comprehensively the Burgundians and Armagnacs defeat the English, their alliance will prove fleeting. There is too much blood under the bridge between them. I need only prise open the rift between John the Fearless and the Dauphin, rather than create it. Flames need fanning, not sparking. How easy will it be to poison Louis? He's forever clasping his flabby paw around a goblet or bowl of food — when he's not groping the breasts or arse of one of his mistresses. The King will wish himself mad again when, in moments of sanity, he realises how much France is ridden with blood feuds and economic strife. As for those who have trespassed against me, I will brand your names into my skin if I have to, lest I forget. Renaud de Savoisy. You will soon receive an anonymous letter, informing you that your younger brother is tupping your wife. Roland de Landes. Your opponent's sword can be baited during one of your vainglorious fencing sessions. And as for my dear old friend, Guy de Artois, your main creditor is in my debt. I am sure I can encourage him to call in the repayment of loans he has made to you. If anyone can ruin a man's life — or indeed an entire kingdom — without shedding a tear it's a self-serving banker. I will light a candle every day when in Rome and pray for France's damnation, but what fool would rely on an inconstant — or absent — God to fulfil his wishes or to do his dirty work? I will be the author of my fate — and theirs. They have all committed the crime of hubris — being proud in the face of me. Thinking themselves superior to me...

As Reynard descended the spiral staircase towards the wine cellar at the back of the property, he remembered a number of the taunts and insults he had suffered throughout his life. They reverberated in his blackened mind, like an echo in a cathedral. The illegitimate son of the Bishop of Troyes had always felt isolated, shunned. Courtesans had looked down their aquiline noses at him. They had labelled him "the Bastard" and "the Poisoner" when he first entered court and served as an agent to the crown.

It is time that I earned those soubriquets once more.

The agent greeted his bodyguards with a nod, and with a further nod he instructed them to shift a large chest in the middle of the cellar, which revealed a trapdoor. Geoffroi de Torcy, the Templar knight who had first built the chateau, had specially designed the residence so that it contained a concealed passageway, expecting that one day his enemies in the church or, worse, a tax collector would come knocking on his door. The passageway led to a concealed exit at the rear of the grounds, near the river which ran along one side of his estate. A boat was waiting for him there. Once he was across the river he would be safe from his enemies. Although his enemies would not then be safe from him, Reynard solemnly vowed.

23

Moreau let out a roar of triumph and called for his fellow men-at-arms to press home their advantage. The Duke of York lay dead at his feet, his bascinet and skull staved in from a blow by the hammer on the Frenchman's poleaxe.

The Duke and his company had been a rallying point and keystone in the English lines. Moreau had recognised that the strongest section of the line could become the weakest, if he could just defeat the commander. The English ranks were beginning to thin, but they were still holding their ground. The French were taking a greater number of casualties, but still attempting to advance. The second wave of infantry moved forward, crushing or trampling upon the first. The corpses were piling up, and sinking into the earth at the same time. Still the two sides pounded against each other. France could afford the attrition rate, but the English couldn't. If Moreau broke through and divided the English battle then the melee could quickly descend into a massacre.

The tide was turning.

Through a throng of steel, billowing banners and churned-up mud, William Talbot had foreseen the danger, both towards his friend and the English position. By the time he stood opposite Moreau, the Duke of York was slain. Talbot raised his poleaxe and pointed it towards the French man-at-arms. Henri Moreau was now helmetless. He grinned through blackened teeth and swollen gums. He recognised his opponent's armour from the bridge across the Ternoise. God had placed his enemies in front of him — serving them up like two courses of a meal — so he could kill them.

Moreau jabbed his weapon forward, but Talbot parried the thrust. Yet before the Englishman could counterattack, the

Frenchman swiftly swung his poleaxe around and landed a glancing blow on the side of his opponent's head.

The Frenchman's grin grew wider, smugger. He was quicker and stronger than the Englishman.

I have the beating of him.

Talbot let out a curse, directed as much in self-censure as it was towards his enemy. His arms and shoulders ached so much he felt like he had been turned on a rack. He felt more than a trickle of blood run down his neck. His breathing was laboured. His chest and thighs burned. His legs felt like they would buckle at any point. The din of battle now seemed more distant.

Every dog has its day. You always knew that some bastard would put you out of your misery eventually.

At least he would have a friend to keep him company, in heaven or hell, the ailing soldier thought blurrily as he gazed down at the Duke of York.

I don't much care where I cross over to, as long as there's women and wine there. And nothing to fight for. I have seen enough of the world to not want to see any more of it. I have feasted at enough banquets, fucked enough whores and pissed out enough wine for ten men. I've killed enough men to know that you can never kill enough of them to feel at peace...

"You lose," Henri Moreau triumphantly remarked, in English, before finishing the old knight off.

Talbot felt weak, cold, as if his body was shrivelling up inside his armour. It was likely he would indeed lose, die, if he did not retreat from the fight. The Frenchman was a quick and skilful brute, but although the grizzled soldier was resigned to his own fate he wanted to see Henry and his country win. Endure. Prosper. *Perhaps I'm not such a selfish bastard after all.* He wanted the likes of Cooper and Walworth return home, with money in their pockets and stories to tell throughout all the alehouses of England.

Not that you owe this old, unrepentant sinner anything, God, but give me one last throw of the dice.

With that plea Talbot mustered what reserves of strength he had left and threw his helmet at his opponent. The improvised missile struck Moreau on his chest. He kept his footing and managed to keep his weapon aloft, but it was still too late. The

Englishman had charged forward, committed to the kill (or dying in the attempt). The tip of his poleaxe split the bridge of the Frenchman's nose in two and then cleaved his brain apart.

Shouts of "Montjoie" no longer reverberated in the air.

*

Henry watched, with a sense of dread and faith, as the might of the French infantry lined up and attacked the ranks of archers of the wings of his army. While a moment ago he had been gasping for air, he now held his breath. Military theory dictated that they would be cut down or routed. Armoured infantry should defeat archers, as surely as Goliath should defeat David, but the cloying mud tempered the speed and impact of the infantry's charge. Their slow, funereal march across the ploughed, sodden field defeated them as much as the mallets, axes and swords which came out at them, fast and furiously. The archers swarmed against their enemy like rats. The strength of the powerfully-built bowmen joined them. Blades punched through steel, or found weak spots, and bit into French flesh. Standards were toppled. French war cries soon turned into blood curdling wails and death rattles. The English were braver, quicker or more desperate. A quotation from Pizan seemed to light up like a lamp in Henry's mind, as he watched the bowmen fight like a pride of lions: "*It has often been noted that a small number of desperate men can conquer a large and powerful army, because they would rather die fighting than fall into the cruel hands of the enemy.*"

Henry believed he was witnessing a miracle unfold as the archers not only held the line, but began to counter-attack. The dead French formed a wall between the two sides, but the archers, fuelled by bloodlust and a scent of victory, climbed over the fallen men-at-arms and took the fight to their opponents. Hacking. Screaming. Brawling. Killing. Mallet heads were matted with hair and blood. Axes cut through metal, and then bone. Knives were slick with sinew and gore as they slid between face guards, and any and all gaps in French armour. Ordinary Englishmen — and Welshmen — were performing acts of extraordinary courage, and brutality. Henry breathed once more, in a sigh of relief and thankfulness, grateful for God's favour, and the thousands of bowmen he had brought with him on the campaign.

The tide was turning again. The front rank of French men-at-arms had fallen or were turning back into their oncoming comrades. The crush was chaotic, and deadly. Noblemen were trampled underfoot. Lords and knights died, drowned, as they fell face down in the watery mud. The knight who had been given command of France's second battle of infantrymen had long abandoned his post to join the front rank of other glory-hunting noblemen. He was now just another contorted corpse, half buried in the ground.

The centre of the French line, seeing or sensing the reverse, also began to withdraw, like waves retreating from the shore.

One Englishman chased ten Frenchmen, and ten Englishman could be seen pursuing a hundred of the enemy. The bearded, bedraggled archers hunted in packs and ran down those wearing the finest armour. They first grounded their quarry in the mud, and then slit their throats and robbed them of any valuables, or used their bow cords to tie them up and take them prisoner.

The first and second ranks of the French infantry waded again through the mud, back to the remainder of their army. Corpses littered the field. Arrows littered the corpses. There were few noblemen left with sufficient experience or authority to issue orders through their trumpeters. There were few trumpeters left. Yet the reserve force of French infantry still possessed the might to engage and best the enemy, as much as they were loath to walk in their countrymen's footsteps and feed failure with failure. The English could not cheer and celebrate yet.

"Sire, I have just come from Maisoncelles. We've received reports that the French have sent a small mounted force around the wood to attack the baggage train from behind. The pages and esquires will need support to counter them," the messenger remarked, before stroking the neck of his horse and whispering in its ear in an attempt to calm the skittish animal.

Henry creased his brow in concern. He worried little for any baubles contained in the baggage train, but the field next to Maisoncelles contained French prisoners, a small army of them, including several noblemen willing and able to take command. Should the cavalry force liberate their comrades then the English would be in danger of being caught between two armies. The third wave of French men-at-arms might be inspired to advance. Henry's exhausted army would be trapped. It could barely now survive fighting on one front, let alone two.

Henry lowered his head in sorrow. His heart sank and he momentarily questioned whether God was testing him or punishing him. He knew what needed to be done. To be both a soldier and Christian is beyond the scope of man. It was beyond the scope of a king. Henry remembered the sage, but sorrowful, words of his father once more: *Uneasy lies the head that wears the crown.* The words stuck in his throat at first, but he knew there was no other way. He would soon be sending the prisoners to their graves, and the executioners might someday be sent to hell.

"We must execute the prisoners, although I will provide you with a list of prominent noblemen that you must first escort to safety. Before I am compelled to order someone to carry out the task, I am willing to ask for volunteers," Henry decreed. His voice was pained, yet purposeful.

An eerie, understandable silence ensued. Perhaps chivalry wasn't altogether dead. The knights and men-at-arms surrounding the King peered at the ground, not wishing to look Henry in the eye for fear of attracting his attention and being instructed to carry out the task. The sin.

"I'll do it," Jack Mercer asserted, his guttural accent brimming with ire and bitterness. The archer was standing over the body of Percy Badby. His once placid face was now an open wound. Bloody and disfigured. A French man-at-arms had bludgeoned the bowman to death with a rusty mace.

24

Reynard, his secretary and three bodyguards had come out of the escape tunnel. They approached the tree-laden river bank where a small boat, tethered to a crooked pier, gently bobbed up and down.

The agent glanced back at the chateau. There was sufficient distance between himself and his enemies. His one regret was that he hadn't had the time to prepare a trap for his uninvited guests. He possessed the necessary gunpowder — and will — to use it. Reynard consoled himself with the thought that, once he had identified his enemies, he would make them suffer. As ever the scales of justice needed to be balanced, in his favour.

The Frenchman was suddenly distracted from his machinations by the sound of rustling leaves and several twigs snapping. His enemies were closer than he had initially thought.

Fordham quickened his steps as he crept up behind the first bodyguard and stabbed him in the back with the freshly sharpened point of his sword. The man-at-arms swiftly yanked his weapon out of the French soldier and he fell to the ground, dropping his loaded crossbow as he did so.

Chaucer attacked his man almost simultaneously, although he only managed to wound the mercenary in the shoulder. The Frenchman let out a yell and took a step backwards. He cried in pain as he went to draw his sword, but Chaucer closed in and ran him through properly.

A clang of swords sounded over the noise of the gulping, dimpled river as Fordham engaged the remaining bodyguard. The Englishman forced his opponent backwards. The bodyguard caught his foot on a tree root protruding out of the ground, and fell awkwardly. The scar-faced mercenary dropped his blade and held his hands up in surrender. Fordham was not in a forgiving mood. He stabbed the wide-eyed, terrified Frenchman twice in the throat.

The sound of rustling leaves Reynard now heard came from his secretary, fleeing down the riverbank. The agent assessed the situation quickly and rushed to pick up the nearby crossbow. Reynard held the weapon up confidently and comfortably, moving it threateningly between the two Englishmen, who were standing several paces away from him. The last time he had shot a crossbow he had killed Marie Nouvel, the harlot, who had betrayed France. She deserved to die.

For all of the rancour Reynard felt, burning like sulphur in his stomach and throat, he thinly smiled before speaking.

"I must confess that I am somewhat surprised to see you here, Thomas. Have you just lost your way whilst trying to get back to England? Given the state of diplomatic relations between our two kingdoms I am impressed that you have been able to recruit a band of my countrymen to your cause, though I really should have learned by now not to underestimate you."

Chaucer glanced at his friend briefly before replying. Fordham appeared remarkably calm, perhaps dangerously so.

"I have you to thank for my new allies. Your sins have come back to haunt you, Reynard. Do you remember how you told me the story of the first time you killed a man? You confessed with an air of a boast, more than with a sense of contrition. The man who knocked on your door earlier was none other than Philippe de Meulan, your first victim's brother."

The Frenchman's smile turned into a sneer.

"I had not foreseen such a move. I should congratulate you for outfoxing me, Thomas, but may I ask how you came to find me here?"

"Divine inspiration. Or a fortunate guess. You always provide yourself with a way out, or back door. It was just a case of judging where that backdoor might be. But there is no way out now."

"There is always a way out. I have come to realise there are no certainties in life. The firmest of stances can be altered. Negotiations should never cease. We are, after all, diplomats, Thomas. We should at least attempt a dialogue before acting too rashly. It is not our vocation to get our own hands dirty, or bloody them. I will tell you what is going to happen now. You will refrain from killing me, else one of you will risk losing his life in the attempt. You have witnessed first-hand how willing and able I am to use one of these weapons. I am going to climb into this boat and reach the other side of the river. But before I do so I would like to call a truce, Thomas. Allow me my freedom now, and I promise that this will be the last you see of me. I will not interfere in your affairs if you would return the courtesy of not interfering in mine. I have no desire for a rematch between us. You are too wily an opponent."

Reynard edged towards the pier as he spoke. Once ensconced in Rome he would dedicate his time to the ruination of the Englishmen. He would arrange to have Chaucer's family tortured and murdered in front of him, as surely as night follows day.

"Let me tell you what is actually going to happen," Fordham remarked, measuredly. "I will shortly walk towards you, with the intention of killing you. In order to defend yourself, you will shoot that quarrel into me. But I will die a happy man, knowing that you will soon be dead too, as my friend here will be free to cut you down with his sword without fear of injury. Please pass on my apologies to Robert. Say that I was sorry I couldn't make the wedding. But say too that I finally found some peace."

Before Chaucer could reply, the man-at-arms started walking towards Reynard. Fordham's expression and will seemed forged from iron. At first the agent believed he might be bluffing, but then he believed he might be mad. For once the diplomat was lost for words. The French agent unleashed the weapon. The quarrel sprang out and embedded itself in the Englishman's stomach. At first Fordham remained on his feet, and even stoically took another couple of steps forward, but then the soldier fell to the ground. His features were corrugated in agony, his skin grew paler every second. He clawed the ground and, mustering what strength and focus he could manage, Fordham turned to Chaucer and then to their enemy, as a prompt for his companion to complete their mission.

Chaucer gripped his sword tightly and slowly strode towards his French counterpart.

"You do not have to do this, Thomas," Reynard babbled, desperately. He edged backwards once more, but there was nowhere left to go. "Our passions should not dictate to our reason. We are cut from the same cloth. You have schemed like me, tortured like me, killed like me. If you condemn me, then you are condemning yourself. I have money. Everyone serves Mammon over God, do they not, in the end? I am also of greater value to you alive. Think of me as a prize, that you can take back to Henry. I have in my possession certain secrets and documents that England can use against France."

Thomas Chaucer was barely listening to the French agent as the distance closed between them. With every step, the Englishman pictured one of Reynard's victims. Stephen Hall. Hugh Kempton. Charles and Marie Nouvel. Edward Fordham.

When Reynard realised that his appeals for mercy were failing he spat out his final words in a spirit of defiance and contempt.

"Do you think that by ridding the world of me you will be somehow curing the world of all evil?"

Chaucer plunged his sword into the Frenchman's sternum. Reynard howled in pain like a jackal. And Chaucer twisted the blade slightly, briefly revelling in the suffering which spilled out from his dark, bestial eyes.

"No. But it's a start."

Reynard de Troyes was dead. Chaucer concerned himself now with Fordham, who was dying, but there was nothing he could do for his friend.

His breathing was shallow. His pulse was weak.

"Reynard was wrong," the soldier asserted. "There is at least one certainty in life. Death."

The agony on his face had been replaced not with ecstasy, but with a serene contentment. Satisfaction. He just wanted to see her again. Fordham closed his eyes for the last time and uttered his last word, as sweetly and dreamily as if it were his first kiss.

"Marie."

25

Another terrified, piteous look was followed by another slit of a throat as Jack Mercer executed another French prisoner. A line of blood ran across the pallid nobleman's neck like a crimson silk ribbon.

Mercer had rounded up a force of archers, with some more willing than others, to carry out Henry's orders.

Some killed because their blood was up. Others killed because they were only following orders. Others, like Henry, appreciated the dangers of the prisoners being liberated and rejoining the battle. They were not willing to trade their own lives for those of their enemies.

And so the English slaughtered the French like cattle in a frenzy of butchery. Maisoncelles became the village of the damned. The metallic tang of blood hung in the air and, like a stain on one's conscience, couldn't be scrubbed clean. Sometimes the blood gushed. Sometimes it oozed. Despite most of the bowmen putting their hands over the mouths of their victims, a barrage of screams still plagued the ears and soul. Pleas and curses rang out, like a refrain to a dirge. In the background was the constant sluicing sound of steel entering and exiting human flesh and the thud and crack of a soldier clubbing a Frenchman to death.

A few of the unfettered French prisoners attempted to flee or fight back, but in vain. A barn, containing dozens of French soldiers, was set alight. The English surgeons, tending to their own wounded and those on the other side, averted their eyes from the atrocities and shook their heads in abject sorrow and shame.

*

Whilst Jack Mercer recruited a sufficient number of men to execute the prisoners Robert Cooper was charged with mobilising a group of bowmen to engage the French raiding party and prevent them from freeing their countrymen. The archers initially scrambled around the battlefield and collected what arrows they could find, whether they had to be prised from the ground or from corpses.

The sleeve of Cooper's jacket was damp with blood where a sword thrust had glanced his right bicep. Hunger gnawed at his belly and barked like a dog. The tightening pain in his shoulder seemed to be spreading across the rest of his body like a cancer. His boots squelched when he walked from the burst blisters inside of them. Mud caked his clothes and countenance. He looked no better than a savage, he imagined, but it was not surprising given that he had just fought like one. Exhaustion — and sin — weighed him down. He hoped that Grace would still recognise him. Love him. But somehow Cooper knew he wouldn't quite be the same again, for better or worse, after this campaign. He didn't know whether he felt half-dead or half-alive as he looked to confront the enemy one more — or possibly one last — time.

When the baggage train came into view, it was clear that Cooper was too late to stop the raid. Pages and esquires lay dead on the ground, like uprooted saplings. Wagons had been ransacked. The only consolation was that most of the French troops had no intention of riding on and liberating the prisoners. Indeed a fair number of them were riding in the opposite direction to Maisoncelles, back towards their own lines on the other side of the woods. Even from a distance the keen-eyed Cooper noticed how saddle-bags were bulging with loot.

Yet a contingent of horsemen, witnessing the archers line up across the field, dared to trot towards the enemy and form its own battle line.

"Form into two ranks, spread yourself out," Cooper ordered, in the hope of creating the impression that their numbers were greater than they really were. The bowmen didn't need to kill the enemy, they just needed to prevent them from advancing to where the prisoners were being held. "Nock."

"Are we not too far away to make our shots count? And are we not all too low on arrows?" a young, anxious archer asked Cooper.

"Aye, we are too far away. We're exposed as well. And we don't have enough arrows. But they don't know that, lad," Cooper replied, his steely gaze focused on the figure of a helmetless enemy horseman.

*

Pierre Guiche was tempted to order his men to advance up the sloping field and attack the English bowmen. He needed to regain his honour. His days and nights were still plagued by the visceral memories of his capture. The indignity of the episode could perhaps only be expunged by killing an archer on the field of battle, or, better still, more than one. Guiche had hoped to be lauded as a hero after escaping from the English, but instead he felt shunned and shamed. He had been bested by a small group of bedraggled bowmen. Men had died needlessly under his command. Marshal Boucicault had silently looked askance at him during his briefing, as if he were no better than a peasant. Guiche gave his word of honour to his commander, d'Albert, that he hadn't compromised the French army in any way during his interrogation. The aristocrat swore on his mother's grave and his son's life. However, at best, only d'Albert half-believed the nobleman.

"Let's go, Pierre. We have done well," the pox-scarred man-at-arms, Gouges, said to his friend, mounted on his piebald mare next to Guiche. The soldier duly patted his saddle bag, clinking with loot, as he spoke.

"The archers may be reinforced at any moment," Vaurus, another soldier in the nobleman's retinue, enjoined.

Guiche was still tempted to valiantly ride forward, but prudence proved sovereign over his desire for vengeance and glory.

*

Any temptation Robert Cooper felt to avenge Owen Morgan's death was tempered by his will to survive and return home to Grace. The battle was almost won. He did not want to tempt fate. He spared a fleeting thought for Chaucer and Fordham, and hoped that they too were venturing home, having successfully completed their mission.

We should all retire, after this campaign.

"It's him. Guiche. What are we waiting for?" Jack Mercer exclaimed to Cooper, pointing, baring his teeth in a snarl, as he joined the line of bowmen at the top of the slope. The archer was covered in more blood than a butcher's apron. He clenched his war bow and snorted heavily. Owen Morgan's knife hung from his belt, bloody and blunted through recent use, but it was still sharp enough to slit one last throat, the Englishman determined.

After executing more than his fair share of prisoners Mercer had decided to head over towards the north of the village. He judged that his fellow bowmen might be in need of his help, and he wasn't alone in thinking that there were potential spoils to be gained from defending the English baggage train. *Once a thief, always a thief.*

"Let it go, Jack. He's not worth it. The battle's over," Cooper advised.

But Mercer curled his lip up and shook his head in reply. Ruled by his desire for vengeance he set off running down the slope towards his enemy, his arrow bag slapping against his thigh. The rogue wanted to commit at least one noble act, in the name of his fallen friend, during his lifetime.

A few of the French mounted troops looked on in amusement as the lone archer ran towards his enemies, pointing his weapon towards the helmetless figure at the centre of the formation, calling him out. Military doctrine dictated that cavalry should charge archers, not the other way around. Many wondered what was possessing the soldier to break ranks in such a way.

But Pierre Guiche knew the reason. He recognised the figure as one of his captors. The Englishman had ambushed his companions and caused him humiliation.

Cooper was haunted by Mercer's reproving look and, in another life, he might have joined his friend in rushing headlong towards the enemy, but he thought of Grace. She had no wish to marry a dead man, and Cooper could not order the rest of his fellow archers to sacrifice all of their lives in the name of him keeping a promise to a deceased brother-in-arms.

Pierre Guiche would not shirk the challenge and insult offered up by a lowly, feral archer. He ordered the two men-at-arms by his side, Gouges and Vaurus, to follow him forward. A trot turned into canter and a canter soon turned into a gallop.

Rage drove the archer on, putting the wind into his sails. The two aggrieved men, racing towards each other, were like two wild boars, about to ram and gore one another with their tusks. Once his enemy was in range Mercer stopped, retrieved the four arrows he had left out of his bag and stuck them in the soft turf. He knew he wasn't as accomplished a shot as Cooper or Walworth – or his late best friend, Morgan – but he would now need to be.

Nock. Draw. Loose.

The first arrow went woefully off target as his fingers, slick with blood, slipped off the bowstring prematurely. Mercer cursed, whilst quickly and vigorously wiping his bloody hands on his sinew-stained breeches.

The ground began to throb beneath his feet. The wind chilled the film of sweat forming across his grimy, crimson-tinged face.

Nock. Draw. Loose.

The arrow tore through the air, sliced the piebald mare's ear and struck Gouges' left breast. If the rapacious soldier hadn't been dead before he hit the ground, he was shortly afterwards.

Drool spilled from Vaurus' mouth, as he spat out a curse. The Frenchmen urged their horses on to close the gap between themselves and the suicidal bowman. Or were they now the suicidal ones?

Mercer's hand began to tremble from fear and exhaustion. He told himself to breath properly, rather than pant.

Nock. Draw. Loose.

The archer aimed the shaft at Guiche, but, feeling his arm begin to wobble from fatigue, he snatched at the shot and missed him. Yet the arrow veered off and found its way into Vaurus' thigh. The soldier spat out another curse, after he roared and seethed in pain, before peeling away from the direction of the Englishman and retreating back towards his lines. Guiche could finish what he started, the man-at-arms bitterly judged.

The ground shook even more. Quaking. Mercer's heart was galloping in time to the horse's hooves. He winced a little as he heard the unmistakable sound of a sword scraping out of its scabbard.

A single arrow remained.

That's all I'll need.

But Jack Mercer's fate was sealed when, as he pulled the shaft from the turf, the arrow-head broke off.

Pierre Guiche grinned and held his razor-sharp sword aloft.

Mercer knew he would die. It wouldn't be worth running. There was nowhere to go.

Steel cut through Guiche's throat — steel from Robert Cooper's arrowhead. The Frenchman fell from his mount, steering it out of the way of the English archer as he did so.

Honour was more than just a word to the veteran bowman. As much as Cooper wanted to see Grace again, the soldier needed to be able to look himself in the eye. He had instructed his men to continue to hold the line, ere he raced down the slope to keep his friend safe and keep the promise he had made to himself — to kill Pierre Guiche. Cooper had been further away than he would have liked when he paused to take his shot. His target had been moving, but thankfully moving towards him. When his arm had straightened and bulged the wound opened up again on his bicep. The tendons in his shoulder had burned, as if someone had inserted hot coals beneath his skin. Cooper had had but a second or two, to aim whilst maintaining the strength to pull the yew bow back further than it had ever been drawn. Guiche had been too focused on his target to realise he was being targeted. The arrow had sung through the air and climaxed with the familiar crescendo of a dull thud.

The mounted French troops lined up behind the dead knight had little desire to avenge their commander's death, especially after seeing the rows of archers slowly advance towards them and place arrows upon their staves. They would not mourn Guiche, although they would miss the spoils contained in his saddle bags. There was nothing to be done. The French wheeled their horses around and retreated.

As Cooper approached Mercer, the two soldiers merely nodded to one another in silence, but in their expressions could be found a solemn sense of contrition and gratitude.

Epilogue

The third wave of French infantry had declined to advance. Instead, a solitary, forlorn herald had made his way across the corpse-strewn field to inform the English king that the day was his.

The battle was over (and as such Henry immediately rescinded the order to continue the execution of the prisoners), but feelings of grief, as much as triumphalism, chequered the mood of the victors. Many had been too tired to raise their arms and cheer. The priority had been to tend to the wounded. Unfortunately this meant putting many of the wounded out of their misery.

Before the French herald had returned to his own lines, Henry asked the man to name the large castle, which loomed over them, behind the woods on their left, before proclaiming: "Then, as all battles shall bear the name of the fortress nearest to the field on which they are fought, this shall forever be called the Battle of Agincourt."

Henry had walked along the lines and clasped the palms of lowly archers and landed lords alike in thanks, but he often found himself forcing a smile, when in the background all he could see was a charnel house. Melancholy and mournfulness shaped his expression, as well as guilt and relief.

Henry had sought out his injured brother. Humphrey suggested that they humiliate the remaining aristocratic prisoners, including the Duke of Orléans and Marshal Boucicaut, by having them serve their English counterparts at dinner that evening, but Henry ordered that their guests should be treated with respect and courtesy, and be served with food and wine.

Shortly afterwards the king had stood over the corpse of the Duke of York and, after saying a prayer for his old friend, bent down, kissed his forehead and closed his eyes.

"I am grateful to you, Sir William. You fought with skill and honour today," the King had remarked to Talbot, who was one of the first to liberate a vintage or two from the baggage train of their defeated foes.

"It is I who should be grateful to you. You've furnished me with the perfect chapter to end my book on, although I might be at pains to explain to my biographer just how we managed to win the day. How did we do it?"

"God knows," Henry replied.

He ordered more than one attendant to discover the fate of Robert Cooper.

"Is he a nobleman, Sire?" one page responded.

"No, an archer, but there are few men nobler."

When the bowman finally appeared before his eyes Henry, for the first time that day, smiled fulsomely.

The sunlight was weak, like the colour of unploughed wheat. The clouds were off-white, like old bones.

End note

Band of Brothers: Agincourt is a work of fiction. The events and chronology of the story do not wholly align with the real history of the battle. However, I hope I have at least conveyed the courage of the soldiers who fought under the flag of St George, and also the leadership and personal bravery of Henry throughout the engagement.

Should you wish to read more about the campaign and battle I can recommend the following books: *1415*, by Ian Mortimer; *Cursed Kings*, by Jonathan Sumption; *Agincourt*, by Juliet Barker; *24 Hours at Agincourt*, by Michael Jones. I'm also not sure if I ever would have embarked upon this project without having first read Bernard Cornwell's *Azincourt* or Shakespeare's *Henry V*.

I am always keen to hear from readers. Should you have enjoyed *Band of Brothers* (or indeed *Sword of Rome*, *Warsaw*, *Raffles* or any of my other books) please do get in touch. I can be reached via @rforemanauthor on Twitter or you can email me via richard@endeavourpress.com

Richard Foreman

If you enjoyed *Band of Brothers: The Complete Campaigns* check out Endeavour Press's other books here: Endeavour Press - the UK's leading independent publisher of digital books.

For weekly updates on our free and discounted eBooks sign up to our newsletter.

Follow us on Twitter **and** Goodreads.

Printed in Great Britain
by Amazon